'I don't  **u permiss** **mine said.**

Instead of ...gers down to the bones of her wrists and encircled them like a pair of gentle handcuffs.

Jasmine tested his hold, but all that did was take him with her to the door frame, which was just an inch or so behind her. She pressed her back against it for stability—because right then her legs weren't doing such a great job of holding her upright. He was now so close she could see the individual pinpricks of stubble along his jaw and around his nose and mouth. She could feel their breath intermingling. His muscle-packed thighs were within a hair's breadth of hers, his booted feet toe to toe with her bare ones.

'Wh-what are you doing?' she said, in a voice she barely recognised as her own.

His eyes went to her mouth, lingering there for endless heart-stopping seconds. 'Ever wondered what would happen if we kissed?'

Like just about every day for the last seven years.

'You'd get your face slapped, that's what.'

A smile hitched up one side of his mouth. 'Yeah, that's what I thought.'

ENGAGED TO HER RAVENSDALE ENEMY

BY

MELANIE MILBURNE

MILLS & BOON

First published in Great Britain 2016
By Mills & Boon, an imprint of HarperCollins*Publishers*
1 London Bridge Street, London, SE1 9GF

© 2016 Melanie Milburne

ISBN: 978-0-263-92109-0

Our policy is to use papers that are natural, renewable and recyclable
products and made from wood grown in sustainable forests. The logging
and manufacturing processes conform to the legal environmental
regulations of the country of origin.

Printed and bound in Spain
by CPI, Barcelona

An avid romance reader, **Melanie Milburne** loves writing the books that gave her so much joy as she was busy getting married to her own hero and raising a family. Now a *USA TODAY* bestselling author, she has won several awards—including the Australian Readers' Association most popular category/series romance in 2008 and the prestigious Romance Writers of Australia R*BY award in 2011.

She loves to hear from readers!

MelanieMilburne.com.au
Facebook.com/Melanie.Milburne
Twitter @MelanieMilburn1

Visit the Author Profile page at
millsandboon.co.uk for more titles.

To Monique Scott. You left an indelible mark on our family, enriching our lives in so many fabulous ways. You are the daughter I never had. You are the most amazing young woman, a gorgeous mother, and a wonderful friend. Love always. xxxx

CHAPTER ONE

IT WASN'T GIVING back the engagement ring Jasmine Connolly was most worried about. She had two more sitting in her jewellery box in her flat in Mayfair above her bridal-wear shop. It was the feeling of being rejected. *Again.* What was wrong with her? Why wasn't she good enough? She hadn't been good enough for her mother. Why did the people she cared about always leave her?

But that wasn't all that had her stomach knotting in panic. It was attending the winter wedding expo next weekend in the Cotswolds as a singleton. How could she front up *sans* fiancé? She might as well turn up at the plush hotel she'd booked months and months ago with 'loser' written on her forehead. She had so looked forward to that expo. After a lot of arm-twisting she had secured a slot in the fashion parade. It was her first catwalk show and it had the potential to lead to bigger and more important ones.

But it wasn't just about designing wedding gowns. She loved everything to do with weddings. The commitment to have someone love you for the rest of your life, not just while it was convenient or while it suited them. Love was supposed to be for ever. Every time she designed a gown she stitched her own hopes into it. What if she never got to wear one of her own gowns? What sort of cruel irony would that be?

She glanced at her empty ring finger where it was gripping the steering wheel. She wished she'd thought to shove on one of her spares just so she didn't have to explain to everyone that she was—to quote Myles— 'taking a break'.

It didn't matter how he termed it, it all meant the same thing as far as Jaz was concerned. She was dumped. Jilted. Cast off. Single.

Forget about three times a bridesmaid, she thought sourly. What did it mean if you were three times a dumped fiancée?

It meant you sucked at relationships. Really sucked.

Jaz parked the car in her usual spot at Ravensdene, the family pile of the theatre-royalty family where she had grown up as the gardener's daughter and surrogate sister to Miranda Ravensdale and her older twin brothers, Julius and Jake.

Miranda had just got herself engaged. Damn. It.

Jaz was thrilled for her best mate. Of course she was. Miranda and Leandro Allegretti were perfect for each other. No one deserved a happy ending more than those two.

But why couldn't she have hers?

Jaz put her head down against the steering wheel and banged it three times. *Argh!*

There was a sound of a car growling as it came up

the long driveway. Jaz straightened and quickly got out of her car and watched as the Italian sports car ate up the gravel with its spinning tyres, spitting out what it didn't want in spraying arcs of flying stones. It felt like a fistful of those stones were clenched between her back molars as the car came to a dusty standstill next to hers.

Jacques, otherwise known as Jake, Ravensdale unfolded his tall, athletic frame from behind the wheel with animal grace. Jaz knew it was Jake and not his identical twin brother Julius because she had always been able to tell them apart. Not everyone could, but she could. She felt the difference in her body. Her body got all tingly and feverish, restless and antsy, whenever Jake was around. It was as if her body picked up a signal from his and it completely scrambled her motherboard.

His black hair was sexily tousled and wind-blown. Another reason to hate him, because she knew if she had just driven with the top down in that chilly October breeze her hair would have looked like a tangled fishing net. He was dressed casually because everything about Jake was casual, including his relationships—if you could call hook-ups and one-night stands relationships.

His dark-blue gaze was hidden behind designer aviator lenses but she could see a deep frown grooved into his forehead. At least it was a change from his stock-standard mocking smile. 'What the hell are you doing here?' he said.

Jaz felt another millimetre go down on her molars.

'Nice to see you too, Jake,' she said with a sugar-sweet smile. 'How's things? Had that personality transplant yet?'

He took off his sunglasses and continued to frown at her. 'You're supposed to be in London.'

Jaz gave him a wide-eyed, innocent look. 'Am I?'

'I checked with Miranda,' he said, clicking shut the driver's door with his foot. 'She said you were going to a party with Tim at his parents' house.'

'It's Myles,' she said. 'Tim was my…erm…other one.'

The corner of his mouth lifted. 'Number one or number two?'

It was extremely annoying how he made her ex-fiancés sound like bodily waste products, Jaz thought. Not that she didn't think of them that way too these days, but still. 'Number two,' she said. 'Lincoln was my first.'

Jake turned to pop open the boot of the car with his remote device. 'So where's lover-boy Myles?' he said. 'Is he planning on joining you?'

Jaz knew she shouldn't be looking at the way Jake's dark-blue denim jeans clung to his taut behind as he bent forward to get his overnight bag but what was a girl to do? He was built like an Olympic athlete. Lean and tanned with muscles in all the right places and in places where her exes didn't have them and never would. He was fantasy fodder. Ever since her hormones had been old enough to take notice, that was exactly what they had done. Which was damned inconvenient, since she absolutely, unreservedly loathed him. 'No…erm…he's staying in town to do some work,' she said. 'After the party, I mean.'

Jake turned back to look at her with a glinting smile. 'You've broken up.'

Jaz hated it that he didn't pose it as a question but as if it were a given. *Another Jasmine Connolly engagement bites the dust.* Not that she was going to admit it to him of all people. 'Don't be ridiculous,' she said. 'What on earth makes you think that? Just because I chose to spend the weekend down here while I work on Holly's dress instead of partying in town doesn't mean I'm—'

'Where's that flashy rock you've been brandishing about?'

Jaz used her left hand to flick her hair back over her shoulder in what she hoped was a casual manner. 'It's in London. I don't like wearing it when I'm working.' Which at least wasn't a complete lie. The ring was in London, safely in Myles' family jewellery vault. It miffed her Myles hadn't let her keep it. Not even for a few days till she got used to the idea of 'taking a break'. So what if it was a family heirloom? He had plenty of money. He could buy any number of rings. But no, he had to have it back, which meant she was walking around with a naked ring finger because she'd been too upset, angry and hurt to grab one of her other rings on her way out of the flat.

How galling if Jake were the first person to find out she had jinxed another relationship. How could she bear it? He wouldn't be sympathetic and consoling. He would roll about the floor laughing, saying, *I told you so.*

Jake hooked his finger through the loop on the collar of his Italian leather jacket and slung it over his shoulder. 'You'd better make yourself scarce if you're not in the mood for a party. I have guests arriving in an hour.'

Jaz's stomach dropped like a lift with snapped cables. 'Guests?'

His shoes crunched over the gravel as he strode towards the grand old Elizabethan mansion's entrance. 'Yep, the ones that eat and drink and don't sleep.'

She followed him into the house feeling like a teacup Chihuahua trying to keep up with an alpha wolf. 'What the hell? How many guests? Are they all female?'

He flashed her a white-toothed smile. 'You know me so well.'

Jaz could feel herself lighting up with lava-hot heat. Most of it burned in her cheeks at the thought of having to listen to him rocking on with a harem of his Hollywood wannabes. Unlike his identical twin brother Julius and his younger sister Miranda, who did everything they could to distance themselves from their parents' fame, Jake cashed in on it. Big-time. He was shameless in how he exploited it for all it was worth—which wasn't much, in Jaz's opinion. She had been the victim of his exploitative tactics when she'd been sixteen on the night of one of his parents' legendary New Year's Eve parties. He had led her on to believe he was serious about...

But she never thought about that night in his bedroom. *Never.*

'You can't have a party,' Jaz said as she followed him into the house. 'Mrs Eggleston's away. She's visiting her sister in Bath.'

'Which is why I've chosen this weekend,' he said. 'Don't worry. I've organised the catering.'

Jaz folded her arms and glowered at him. 'And I bet I know what's on the menu.' *Him.* Being licked and ego-stroked by a bevy of bimbo airheads who drank champagne like it was water and ate nothing in case they put on an ounce. She only hoped they were all of age.

'You want to join us?'

Jaz jerked her chin back against her neck and made a scoffing noise. 'Are you out of your mind? I couldn't think of anything worse than watching a bunch of wannabe starlets get taken in by your particular version of charm. I'd rather chew razor blades.'

He shrugged one of his broad shoulders as if he didn't care either way. 'No skin off my nose.'

Jaz thought she would like to scratch every bit of skin off that arrogant nose. She hadn't been alone with him in years. There had always been other members of his family around whenever they'd come to Ravensdene. Why hadn't Eggles told her he would be here? Mrs Eggleston, the long-time housekeeper, knew how much Jaz hated Jake.

Everyone knew it. The feud between them had gone on for seven years. The air crackled with static electricity when they were in the same room even if there were crowds of other people around. The antagonism she felt towards Jake had grown exponentially every year. He had a habit of looking at her a certain way, as if he was thinking back to that night in his room when she had made the biggest fool of herself. His dark-blue eyes would take on a mocking gleam as if he could remember every inch of her body where it had been lying waiting for him in his bed in nothing but her underwear.

She gave a mental cringe. Yes, her underwear. What had she been thinking? Why had she fallen for it? Why hadn't she realised he'd been playing her for a fool? The humiliation he had subjected her to, the shame, the embarrassment of being hauled out of his bed in front of his… *Grrhh!* She would *not* think about it.

She. Would. Not.

Jaz's father wasn't even here to referee. He was away on a cruise of the Greek Islands with his new wife. Her father didn't belong to Jaz any more—not that he ever had. His work had always been more important than her. How could a garden, even one as big as the one at Ravensdene, be more important than his only child? But no, now he belonged to Angela.

Going back to London was out of the question. Jaz wasn't ready to announce the pause on her engagement. Not yet. Not until she knew for sure it was over. Not even to Miranda. Not while there was a slither of hope. All she had to do was make Myles see what he was missing out on. She was his soul mate. Of course she was. Everybody said so. Well, maybe not everybody, but she didn't need everyone's approval. Not even his parents' approval, which was a good thing, considering they didn't like her. But then, they were horrid toffee-nosed snobs and she didn't like them either.

Jaz did everything for Myles. She cooked, she cleaned, she organised his social calendar. She turned her timetable upside down and inside out so she could be available for him. She even had sex with him when she didn't feel like it. Which was more often than not, for some strange reason. Was that why Myles wanted a break? Because she wasn't sexually assertive enough? Not raunchy enough? She could do raunchy. She could wear dress-up costumes and play games. She would hate it but if it won him back she would do it. Other men found her attractive. Sure they did.

She was fighting off men all the time. She wasn't vain but she knew she had the package: the looks, the figure, the face and the hair. And she was whip-smart. She had her own bridal design company and she was not quite twenty-four.

Sure, she'd had a bit of help from Jake's parents, Richard and Elisabetta Ravensdale, in setting up. In fact, if it hadn't been for them, she wouldn't have had the brilliant education she'd had. They had stepped in when her mother had left her at Ravensdene on an access visit when she was eight and had never returned.

Not that it bothered Jaz that her mother hadn't come back for her. Not really. She was mightily relieved she hadn't had to go back to that cramped and mouldy, rat-infested flat in Brixton where the neighbours fought harder than the feral cats living near the garbage collection point. It was the principle of the thing that was the issue. Being left like a package on a doorstep wasn't exactly how one expected to be treated as a young child. But still, living at the Elizabethan mansion Ravensdene in Buckinghamshire had been much preferable. It was like being at a country spa resort with acres of verdant fields, dark, shady woods and a river meandering through the property like a silver ribbon.

This was home and the Ravensdales were family.

Well, apart from Jake, of course.

Jake tossed the bag on his bed and let out a filthy curse. What the hell was Jasmine Connolly doing here? He had made sure the place was empty for the weekend. He had a plan and Jasmine wasn't part of it. He did everything he could to avoid her. But when he couldn't he did everything he could to annoy her. He got a kick out of seeing her clench her teeth and flash those grey-blue eyes at him like tongues of flame. She was a pain in the backside but he wasn't going to let her dictate what he could and couldn't do. This was his family home, not hers. She might have benefited from being raised with his kid sister Miranda but she was still the gardener's daughter.

Jaz had been intent on marrying up since she'd been a kid. At sixteen she'd had her sights on him. *On him!* What a joke. He was ten years older than her; marriage hadn't been on his radar then and it wasn't on it now. It wasn't even in his vocabulary.

Jaz did nothing but think about marriage. Her whole life revolved around it. She was a good designer, he had to give her that, but it surely wasn't healthy to be so obsessed with the idea of marriage? Forty per cent of marriages ended in divorce—his parents' being a case in point. After his father's love-child scandal broke a month ago, it had looked like they were going to have a second one. The couple had remarried after their first divorce, and if another was on the way he only hoped it wouldn't be as acrimonious and publicly cringe-worthy as their last.

His phone beeped with an incoming message and he swore again when he checked his screen. Twenty-seven text messages and fourteen missed calls from Emma Madden. He had blocked her number but she must have borrowed someone else's phone. He knew if he checked his spam folder there would be just as many emails with photos of the girl's assets. Didn't that silly little teenager go to school? Where were her parents? Why weren't they monitoring her phone and online activity?

He was sick to the back teeth with teenaged girls with crushes. Jasmine had started it with her outrageous little stunt seven years ago. He'd had the last word on that. But this was a new era and Emma Madden wasn't the least put off by his efforts to shake her off. He'd tried being patient. He'd tried being polite. What was he supposed to do? The fifteen-year-old was like a leech, clinging on for all she was worth. He was being stalked. By a teenager! Sending him presents at work. Turning up at his favourite haunts, at the gym, at a business lunch, which was damned embarrassing. He'd had his work cut out trying to get his client to believe he wasn't doing a teenager. He might be a playboy but he had some standards and keeping away from underage girls was one of them.

Jake turned his phone to silent and tossed it next to his bag on the bed. He walked over to the window to look at the fields surrounding the country estate. Autumn was one of his favourite times at Ravensdene. The leaves on the deciduous trees in the garden were in their final stages of turning and the air was sharp and fresh with the promise of winter around the corner. As soon as his guests arrived he would light the fire in the sitting room, put on some music, pour the champagne, party on and post heaps of photos on social media so Emma Madden got the message.

Finally.

CHAPTER TWO

THE CARS STARTED arriving just as Jaz got comfortable in the smaller sitting room where she had set up her workstation. She had to hand-sew the French lace on Julius's fiancée Holly's dress, which would take hours. But she was happiest when she was working on one of her designs. She outsourced some of the basic cutting and sewing of fabric but when it came to the details she did it all by hand. It gave her designs that signature Jasmine Connolly touch. Every stitch or every crystal, pearl or bead she sewed on to a gown made her feel proud of what she had achieved. As a child she had sat on the floor in this very sitting room surrounded by butcher's paper or tissue wrap and Miranda as a willing, if not long-suffering, model. Jaz had dreamed of success. Success that would transport her far away from her status as the unwanted daughter of a barmaid who turned tricks to feed her drug and alcohol habit.

The sound of car doors slamming, giggling women and high heels tottering on gravel made Jaz's teeth grind together like tectonic plates. At this rate she was going to be down to her gums. But no way was she going back to town until the weekend was over. Jake could party all he liked. She was not being told what to do. Besides, she knew it would annoy him to have her here. He might have acted all cool and casual about it but she knew him well enough to know he would be spitting chips about it privately.

Jaz put down her sewing and carefully covered it with the satin wrapping sheet she had brought with her. This she had to see. What sort of women had he got to come? He had a thing for busty blondes. Such a cliché but that was Jake. He was shallow. He lived life in the fast lane and didn't stay in one place long enough to put down roots. He surrounded himself with showgirls and starlets who used him as much as he used them.

It was nauseating.

Jake was standing in the great hall surrounded by ten or so young women—all blonde—who were dressed in skimpy cocktail wear and vertiginous heels. Jaz leaned against the doorjamb with her arms folded, watching as each girl kissed him in greeting. One even ruffled his hair and another rubbed her breasts—which Jaz could tell were fake—against his upper arm.

He caught Jaz's eye and his mouth slanted in a mocking smile. 'Ah, here's the fun police. Ladies, this is the gardener's daughter, Jasmine.'

Jaz gave him an 'I'll get you for that later' look before she addressed the young women. 'Do your parents know where you all are?' she said.

Jake's brows shot together in a brooding scowl. 'Knock it off, Jasmine.'

Jaz smiled at him with saccharine sweetness. 'Just checking you haven't sneaked in a minor or two.'

Twin streaks of dull colour rode high along his aristocratic cheekbones and his mouth flattened until it was a bloodless line of white. A frisson of excitement coursed through her to have riled him enough to show a crack in his 'too cool for school' façade. Jaz was the only person who could do that to him. He sailed through life with that easy smile and that 'anything goes' attitude but pitted against her he rippled with latent anger. She wondered how far she could push him. Would he touch her? He hadn't come anywhere near her for seven years. When the family got together for Christmas or birthdays, or whatever, he never greeted her. He never hugged or kissed her on the cheek as he did to Miranda or his mother. He avoided Jaz like she was carrying some deadly disease, which was fine by her. She didn't want to touch him either.

But, instead of responding, Jake moved past her as if she was invisible and directed the women to the formal sitting room. 'In here, ladies,' he said. 'The party's about to begin.'

Jaz wanted to puke as the women followed him as though he were the Pied Piper. Couldn't they see how they were being used to feed his ego? He would ply them with expensive champagne or mix them exotic cocktails and tell them amusing anecdotes about his famous parents and their Hollywood and London theatre friends. Those he wouldn't bother sleeping with he would toss out by two or three in the morning. The one—or two or three, according to the tabloids—he slept with would be sent home once the deed was done. They would never get a follow-up call from him. It was a rare woman who got two nights with Jake Ravensdale. Jaz couldn't remember the last one.

The doorbell sounded behind her. She let out a weary sigh and turned to open it.

'I'll get that,' Jake said, striding back into the great hall from the sitting room.

Jaz stood to one side and curled her lip at him. 'Ten women not enough for you, Jake?'

He gave her a dismissive look and opened the door. But the smile of greeting dropped from his face as if he had been slapped. 'Emma…' His throat moved up and down. 'What? Why? How did you find me?' The words came spilling out in a way Jaz had never seen before. He looked agitated. *Seriously* agitated.

'I had to see you,' the girl said with big, lost waif, shimmering eyes and a trembling bottom lip. 'I just *had* to.'

And she was indeed a girl, Jaz noted. Not yet out of her teens. At that awkward age when one foot was in girlhood and the other in adulthood, a precarious position, and one when lots of silly mistakes that could last a lifetime could be made. Jaz knew it all too well. Hadn't she tried to straddle that great big divide, with devastating consequences?

'How'd you get here?' Jake's voice had switched from shocked to curt.

'I caught a cab.'

His brows locked together. 'All the way from London?'

'No,' Emma said. 'From the station in the village.'

Poor little kid, Jaz thought. She remembered looking at Jake exactly like that, as if he was some demigod and she'd been sent to this earth solely to worship him. It was cruel to watch knowing all the thoughts that were going through that young head. Teenage love could be so intense, so consuming and incredibly irrational. The poor kid was in the throes of a heady infatuation, travelling all this way in the hope of a little bit of attention from a man who clearly didn't want to give her the time of day. Jake was here partying with a bunch of women and Emma thought she could be one of them. What a little innocent.

Jaz couldn't stand by and watch history repeat itself. What if Emma was so upset she did something she would always regret, like *she* had done? There had to be a way to let the kid down in such a way that would ease the hurt of rejection. But brandishing a bunch of party girls in Emma's face was not the way to do it.

'Why don't you come in and I'll—?' Jaz began.

'Stay out of it, Jasmine,' Jake snapped. 'I'll deal with this.' He turned back to the girl. 'You have to leave. Now. I'll call you a cab but you have to go home. Understand?'

Emma's eyes watered some more. 'But I can't go home. My mother thinks I'm staying with a friend. I'll get in heaps of trouble. I'll be grounded for the rest of my life.'

'And so you damn well should be,' Jake growled.

'Maybe I could help,' Jaz said and held out her hand to the girl. 'I'm Jaz. I'm Jake's fiancée.'

There was a stunned silence.

Jake went statue-still beside Jaz. Emma looked at her with a blank stare. But then her cheeks pooled with crimson colour. 'Oh… I—I didn't realise,' she stammered. 'I thought Jake was still single otherwise I would never have—'

'It's fine, sweetie,' Jaz said. 'I totally understand and I'm not the least bit offended. We've been keeping our relationship a secret, haven't we, darling?' She gave Jake a bright smile while surreptitiously jabbing him in the ribs.

He opened and closed his mouth like a fish that had suddenly found itself flapping on the carpet instead of swimming safely in its fishbowl. But then he seemed to come back into himself and stretched his lips into one of his charming smiles. 'Yeah,' he said. 'That's right. A secret. I only just asked her a couple of minutes ago. That's why we're…er…celebrating.'

'Are you coming, Jakey?' A clearly tipsy blonde came tottering out into the hall carrying a bottle of champagne in one hand and a glass in the other.

Jaz took Emma by the arm and led her away to the kitchen, jerking her head towards Jake in a non-verbal signal to get control of his guest. 'That's one of the bridesmaids,' she said. 'Can't handle her drink. I'm seriously thinking of dumping her for someone else. I don't want her to spoil the wedding photos. Can you imagine?'

Emma chewed at her bottom lip. 'I guess it kind of makes sense...'

'What does?'

'You and Jake.'

Jaz pulled out a kitchen stool and patted it. 'Here,' she said. 'Have a seat while I make you a hot chocolate—or would you prefer tea or coffee?'

'Um...hot chocolate would be lovely.'

Jaz got the feeling Emma had been about to ask for coffee in order to appear more sophisticated. It reminded her of all the times when she'd drunk vile-tasting cocktails in order to fit in. She made the frothiest hot chocolate she could and handed it to the young girl. 'Here you go.'

Emma cupped her hands around the mug like a child. 'Are you sure you're not angry at me turning up like this? I had no idea Jake was serious about anyone. There's been nothing in the press or anything.'

'No, of course not,' Jaz said. 'You weren't to know.' *I didn't know myself until five minutes ago.* 'We haven't officially announced it yet. We wanted to have some time to ourselves before the media circus begins.' And it would once the news got out. Whoopee doo! If this didn't get Myles' attention, nothing would.

'You're the gardener's daughter,' Emma said. 'I read about you in one of the magazines at the hairdresser's. There was an article about Jake's father's love-child Katherine Winwood and there were pictures of you. You've known Jake all your life.'

'Yes, since I was eight,' Jaz said. 'I've been in love with him since I was sixteen.' *It didn't hurt to tell her one more little white lie, did it?* It was all in a good cause. 'How old are you?'

'Fifteen and a half,' Emma said.

'Tough age.'

Emma's big brown eyes lowered to study the contents of her mug. 'I met Jake at a function a couple of months ago,' she said. 'It was at my stepfather's restaurant. He sometimes lets me work for him as a waitress. Jake was the only person who was nice to me that night. He even gave me a tip.'

'Understandable you'd fancy yourself in love with him,' Jaz said. 'He breaks hearts just by breathing.'

Emma's mouth lifted at the corners in a vestige of a smile. 'I should hate you but I don't. You're too nice. Kind of natural and normal, you know? But then, I guess I would hate you if I didn't think you were perfect for him.'

Jaz smiled over clenched teeth. 'How about we give your mum a call and let her know where you are? Then I'll drive you to the station and wait with you until you get on the train, okay? Have you got a mobile?'

Silly question. What teenager didn't? It was probably a better model than hers.

When Jaz got back from sending Emma on her way home, Jake was in the main sitting room clearing away the detritus of his short-lived party. Apparently he had sent his guests on their merry way as well. 'Need some help with that?' she said.

He sent her a black look. 'I think you've done more than enough for one night.'

'I thought it was a stroke of genius, actually,' Jaz said, calmly inspecting her nails.

'Engaged?' he said. '*Us?* Don't make me laugh.'

He didn't look anywhere near laughing, Jaz thought. His jaw was locked like a stiff hinge. His mouth was flat. His eyes were blazing with fury. 'What else was I supposed to do?' she said. 'That poor kid was so love-struck nothing short of an engagement would've convinced her to leave.'

'I had it under control,' he said through tight lips.

Jaz rolled her eyes. 'How? By having a big bimbo bash? Like that was ever going to work. You're going about this all wrong, Jake—or should I call you Jakey?'

His eyes flashed another round of sparks at her. 'That silly little kid has been stalking me for weeks. She gate-crashed an important business lunch last week. I lost a valuable client because of her.'

'She's young and fancies herself in love,' Jaz said. 'You were probably the first man to ever speak to her as if she was a real person instead of a geeky kid. But throwing a wild party with heaps of women isn't going to convince her you're not interested in her. The only way was to convince her you're off the market. Permanently.'

He snatched up a half-empty bottle of champagne and stabbed the neck of it in her direction. 'You're the last woman on this planet I would ever ask to marry me.'

Jaz smiled. 'I know. Isn't it ironic?'

His jaw audibly ground together. 'What's your fiancé going to say about this?'

Here's the payoff. She would have to tell Jake about the break-up. But it would be worth it if it achieved the desired end. 'Myles and I are having a little break for a month,' she said.

'You conniving little cow,' he said. 'You're using me to make him jealous.'

'We're using each other,' Jaz corrected. 'It's a win-win. We'll only have to pretend for a week or two. Once the hue and cry is over we can go back to being frenemies.'

His frown was so deep it closed the gap between his eyes. 'You're thinking of making an...*an announcement*?'

Jaz held up her phone. 'Already done. Twitter is running hot with it. Any minute now I expect your family to start calling.' As if on cue, both of their phones starting ringing.

'Don't answer that.' He quickly muted his phone. 'We need to think this through. We need a plan.'

Jaz switched her phone to silent but not before she saw Myles' number come up. Good. All going swimmingly so far. 'We can let your family in on the secret if you think they'll play ball.'

'It's too risky.' Jake scraped a hand through his hair. 'If anyone lets slip we're not the real deal, it could blow up in our faces. You know what the press are like. Do you think Emma bought it? Really?'

'Yes, but she'll know something's up if you don't follow through.'

He frowned again. 'Follow through how? You're not expecting me to marry you, are you?'

Jaz gave him a look that would have withered a plastic flower. 'I'm marrying Myles, remember?'

'If he takes you back after this.'

She heightened her chin. 'He will.'

One side of his mouth lifted in a cynical arc. 'What's Miranda going to say? You think she'll accept you're in love with me?'

Miranda was going to be a hard sell, but Jaz knew she didn't like Myles, so perhaps it would work. For a time. 'I don't like lying to Miranda, but she's never been...'

'You should've thought of that when you cooked up this stupid farce,' Jake said. 'No. We'll run with it.'

'What did you tell your party girls?' Jaz said. 'I hope I didn't make things too awkward for you.' Ha ha. She *loved* making things awkward for him. The more awkward, the better. What a hoot it was to see him squirm under the shackles of a commitment.

'I'm not in the habit of explaining myself to anyone,' he said. 'But no doubt they'll hear the news like everyone else.'

Jaz glanced at her bare ring finger. Who would take their engagement seriously unless she had evidence? 'I haven't got a ring.'

His dark eyes gleamed with malice. 'No spares hanging around at home?'

She sent him a beady look. 'Do you really want me to wear some other man's ring?'

His mouth flattened again. 'Right. I'll get you a ring.'

'No fake diamonds,' she said. 'I want the real thing. The sort of clients I attract can tell the difference, you know.'

'This is what this is all about, isn't it?' he said. 'You don't want your clients to think you can't hold a man long enough to get him to marry you.'

Jaz could feel her anger building like a catastrophic storm inside her. This wasn't about what her clients thought. It was about what *she* felt. No one in their right mind wanted to be rejected. Abandoned. To be told they weren't loved in the way she desperately dreamed of being loved. Not after she had invested so much in her relationship with Myles.

What did Jake know of investing in a relationship? He moved from one woman to the next without a thought of staying long enough to get to know someone beyond what they liked to do in bed. Only Jake could make her this angry—angry enough to throw something. It infuriated her that he alone could reduce her to such a state. 'I can hold a man,' she said. 'I can hold him just fine. Myles has cold feet, that's all. It's perfectly normal for the groom to get a little stressed before the big day.'

'If he loved you he wouldn't ask for a break,' Jake said. 'He wouldn't risk you finding someone else.'

That thought had occurred to Jaz but she didn't want to think about it. She was good at not thinking about things she didn't want to think about. 'Listen to you,' she said with a scornful snort. 'Jake Ravensdale, playboy extraordinaire, talking like a world expert on love.'

'Where did you take Emma?'

'I put her on the train once I'd talked to her mother and made sure everything was cool,' Jaz said. 'I didn't want her to get into trouble or do anything she might regret.' *Like I did.* She pushed the thought aside. She wouldn't think about the rest of that night after she had left Jake's bedroom.

Jake picked up a glass, filled it with champagne and knocked it back in one gulp. He shook his head like a dog coming out of water and then poured another glass. With his features cast in such serious lines, he looked more like his twin Julius than ever.

'We need a photo,' Jaz said. 'Hand me a glass.'

He looked at her as if she had just asked him to poke a knitting needle in his eye. 'A photo?' he said. 'What for?'

She helped herself to a glass of champagne and came to stand beside him but he backed away as if she was carrying dynamite. Or knitting needles. 'Get away from me,' he said.

'We have to do this, Jake,' she said. 'Who's going to believe it if we don't do an engagement photo?'

'You don't have a ring,' he said. 'Yet.' The way he said 'yet' made it sound as though he considered the task on the same level as having root canal therapy.

'Doesn't matter,' Jaz said. 'Just a shot with us with a glass of champers and grinning like Cheshire cats will be enough.'

'You're a sadist,' he said, shooting her a hooded

look as she came to stand beside him with her camera phone poised. 'You know that, don't you? A totally sick sadist.'

It was impossible for Jaz not to notice how hard and warm his arm was against hers as she leaned in to get the shot. Impossible not to think of those strongly muscled arms gathering her even closer. Was he as aware of her as she was of him? Was that why he was standing so still? He hadn't been this close to her in years. When family photographs had been taken—even though strictly speaking she wasn't family—she had always been up the other end of the shot close to Miranda or one of Jake's parents. She had never stood right next to Jake. Not so close she could practically feel the blood pumping through his veins. She checked the photo and groaned. 'Oh, come on,' she said. 'Surely you can do better than that. You look like someone's got a broomstick up your—'

'Okay, we'll try again.' He put an arm around her shoulders and leaned his head against hers. She could feel the strands of his tousled hair tickling her skin. Her senses were going haywire when his stubbly jaw grazed her face. He smelt amazing—lime and lemongrass with a hint of ginger or some other spice. 'Go on,' he said. 'Take the goddamn shot.'

'Oh…right,' Jaz said and clicked the button. She checked the photo but this time it looked like she was the one being tortured. Plus it was blurred. 'Not my best angle.' She deleted it and held up the phone. 'One more take. Say cheese.'

'That's enough,' he said, stepping away from her

once she'd taken the shot. 'You have to promise me you'll delete that when this is all over, okay?'

Jaz criss-crossed her chest with her hand. 'Cross my heart and hope to die.'

He grunted as if her demise was something he was dearly praying for.

She sent the tweet and then quickly sent a text to Miranda:

I know you never liked Myles. You approve of fiancé # 4?

Miranda's text came back within seconds.

OMG! Definitely!!! Congrats. Always knew you were hot for each other. J Will call later xxxxx

'Who are you texting?' Jake asked.

'Miranda,' Jaz said, putting her phone down. 'She's thrilled for us. We'll finally be sisters. Yay.'

He muttered a curse and prowled around the room like a shark in a fishbowl. 'Julius is never going to fall for this. Not for a moment.'

'He'll have to if you want Emma to go away,' Jaz said. 'If you don't play along I'll tell her the truth.'

He threw her a filthy look. 'You're enjoying this, aren't you?'

She smiled a victor's smile. 'What's that saying about revenge is a dish best eaten cold?'

He glowered at her. 'Isn't it a little childish to be harking on about that night all these years later? I did you a favour back then. I could've done you that night but how would that have worked out? Ever thought about that? No. You want to paint me as the big, bad guy who made you feel a little embarrassed about that schoolgirl crush. But, believe me, I could have done a whole lot worse.'

Jaz stepped out of his way as he stormed past her to leave the room. *You did do a whole lot worse*, she wanted to throw after him. But instead she clamped her lips together and turned back to look at the discarded bottles and glasses.

Typical. Jake had a habit of leaving his mess for other people to clean up.

CHAPTER THREE

JAKE WAS SO mad he could see red spots in front of his eyes. Or maybe he was having a brain aneurysm from anger build-up. Seven years of it. He paced the floor of his room, raking his hair, grinding his teeth, swearing like a Brooklyn rapper at what Jasmine had done to him. Engaged! What a freaking farce. No one would believe it. Not him. Not the playboy prince of the pick-ups.

His stomach turned at the thought. Committed. Tied down. Trapped. He was the last person who would ever tie himself down to one woman and certainly not someone like Jasmine Connolly. She was a manipulative little witch. She was using him. Using him to lure back her third fiancé. Who on earth got engaged three times? Someone who was obsessed with getting married, that was who. Jasmine didn't seem to care who she got engaged to as long as they had money and status.

But through the red mist of anger he could see her solution had some merit. Emma Madden had taken the news of their 'engagement' rather well. He had been poleaxed to see that kid standing on the doorstep. He could count on half a hand how many times he'd been caught off guard but seeing that kid there was right up there. If anyone had seen her—anyone being the press, that was—he would have been toast. He didn't want to be cruel to the girl but how else could he get rid of her? Jasmine's solution seemed to have worked. So far. But how long would he have to stay 'engaged'?

Then there was his family to deal with. He could probably pull off the lie with his parents and Miranda but not his twin. Julius knew him too well. Julius knew how much he hated the thought of being confined in a relationship. Jake was more like his father in that way. His father wasn't good at marriage. Richard and Elisabetta fought as passionately as they made up. It was a war zone one minute and a love fest the next. As a child Jake had found it deeply unsettling—not that he'd ever showed it. His role in the family was the court jester. It was his way of coping with the turbulent emotions that flew around like missiles. He'd never known what he was coming home to.

Then eventually it had happened. The divorce had been bitter and public and the intrusion of the press terrifying to a child of eight. He and Julius had been packed off to boarding school but, while Julius had relished the routine, structure and discipline, Jake had not. Julius had excelled academically while Jake had scraped through, not because he wasn't intellectually capable but because in an immature and mostly subconscious way he hadn't wanted his parents to think their divorce had had a positive effect on him.

But he had more than made up for it in his business analysis company. He was successful and wealthy and had the sort of life most people envied. The fly-in, fly-out nature of his work suited his personality. He didn't hang around long. He just got in there, sorted out the problems and left. Which was how he liked to conduct his relationships.

Being tied to Jasmine, even if it was only a game of charades, was nothing less than torture. He had spent the last seven years avoiding her. Distancing himself from all physical contact. He had even failed to show up for some family functions in an effort to avoid the tension of being in the same room as her. He'd had plenty of lectures from Julius and Miranda about fixing things with Jasmine but why should *he* apologise? He hadn't done anything wrong. He had done the opposite. He had solved the problem, not made it worse. It was her that was still in a snit over something she should have got over years ago.

She had been a cute little kid but once she'd hit her teens she'd changed into a flirty little vamp. It had driven him nuts. She had followed him around like a loyal puppy, trying to sneak time with him, touching him 'by accident' and batting those impossibly long eyelashes at him. He had gone along with it for a while, flirting back in a playful manner, but in the end that had backfired, as she'd seemed to think he was serious about her. He wasn't serious about anyone. But on the night of his parents New Year's Eve party, when she'd been sixteen and he twenty-six, he had drawn the line. He'd activated a plan to give her the message loud and clear: He was a player, not the soppy, romantic happy-ever-after beau she imagined him to be.

That night she had dressed in a revealing outfit that was far too old for her and had worn make-up far too heavy. To Jake she had looked like a kid who had rummaged around in her mother's wardrobe. In the dark. He had gone along with her flirtation all evening, agreeing to meet with her in his room just after midnight. But instead of turning up alone as she'd expected he'd brought a couple of girls with him, intending to shock Jasmine into thinking he was expecting an orgy. It had certainly done the trick. She had left him alone ever since. He couldn't remember the last time she had spoken to him other than to make some cutting remark and the only time she looked at him was to spear him with a death-adder glare. Which had suited him just fine.

Until now.

Now he had to work out a way of hanging around with her without wanting to... Well, he didn't want to admit to what he wanted to do with her. But he was only human and a full-blooded male, after all. She was the stuff of male fantasies. He would never admit it to anyone but over the years he'd enjoyed a few fantasies of her in his morning shower. She was sultry and sulky, yet she had a razor-sharp wit and intelligence to match. She had done well for herself, building her business up from scratch, although he thought she was heading for a burnout by trying to do everything herself. Not that she would ever ask his advice. She was too proud. She would rather go bankrupt than admit she might have made a mistake.

Jake dragged a hand down his face. This was going to be the longest week or two of his life. What did Jasmine expect of him? How far did she want this act to go? She surely wouldn't want to sleep with him if she was still hankering after her ex? Not that she showed any sign of being attracted to him, although she did have a habit of looking at his mouth now and again. But everyone knew how much she hated him. Not that a bit of hate got in the way of good sex.

Sheesh. He had to stop thinking about sex and Jasmine in the same sentence. He had never seen her as a sister, even though she had been brought up as one at Ravensdene. Or at least not since she'd hit her teens. She'd grown from being a gangly, awkward teenager into an unusual but no less stunning beauty. Her features were not what one could describe as classically beautiful, but there was some indefinable element to the prominence of her brows and the ice-blue and storm-grey of her eyes that made her unforgettable. She had a model-slim figure and lustrous, wavy honey-brown hair that fell midway down her back. Her skin was creamy and smooth and looked fabulous with or without make-up, although she used make-up superbly these days.

Her mouth… How could he describe it? It was perfect. Simply perfect. He had never seen a more beautiful mouth. The lower lip was full and shapely, the top one a perfect arc above it. The vermillion borders of her lips were so neatly aligned it was as if a master had drawn them. She had a way of slightly elevating her chin, giving her a haughty air that belied her humble beginnings. Her nose, too, had the look of an aristocrat about it with its ski-slope contour. When she smiled—which she rarely did when he was around—it lit up the room. He had seen grown men buckle at the knees at that smile.

Jake's phone vibrated where he'd left it on the bedside table. He glanced at the screen and saw it was Julius. His twin had called six times now. *Better get it over with*, he thought, and answered.

'Is this some kind of prank?' Julius said without preamble.

'No, it's—'

'Jaz and you?' Julius cut him off. 'Come on, man. You hate her guts. You can't stand being in the same room as her. What happened?'

'It was time to bury the hatchet,' Jake said.

'You think I came down in the last shower?' Julius said. 'I know wedding fever has hit with Holly and me, and now Miranda and Leandro, but you and Jaz? I don't buy it for a New York picosecond. What's she got on you? Is she holding a AK-47 to your head?'

Jake let out a rough-edged sigh. He could lie to anyone else but not his identical twin. All that time in the womb had given them a connection beyond what normal siblings felt. They even felt each other's pain. When Julius had had his appendix out when he was fifteen Jake had felt like someone was ripping his guts out. 'I've been having a little problem with a girl,' he said. 'A teenager.'

'I'm not sure I want to hear this.'

'It's not what you think,' Jake said and explained the situation before adding, 'Jasmine intercepted Emma at the door and told her we were engaged.'

'How did this girl Emma take it?'

'Surprisingly well,' Jake said.

'What about Jaz's fiancé?'

'I have no idea,' Jake said. 'He's either relieved she's off his hands or he's going to turn up at my place and shoot out my kneecaps.'

'Always a possibility.'

'Don't remind me.'

There was a beat of silence.

'You're not going to sleep with her, are you?' Julius said.

'God, no,' Jake said. 'I wouldn't touch her with a barge pole.'

'Yes, well, I suggest you keep your barge pole zipped in your pants,' Julius said dryly. 'What actually happened with you guys that night at the party? I know she came to your room but you've never said what went on other than you didn't touch her.'

'I didn't do anything except send her on her way,' Jake said. 'You know what she was like, always following me about, giving me sheep's eyes. I taught her a lesson by offering her a foursome but she declined.'

'A novel approach.'

'It worked.'

'Maybe, but don't you think her anger is a little out of proportion?' Julius said.

'That's just Jasmine,' Jake said. 'She's always had a rotten temper.'

'I don't know... I sometimes wonder if something else happened that night.'

'Like what?'

'She'd been drinking and was obviously upset after leaving your room,' Julius said. 'Not a good combination in a teenage girl.'

Jake hung up a short time later once they'd switched topics but he couldn't get rid of the seed of unease Julius had planted in his mind. Had something happened that night after Jasmine had left his room? Was that why she had been so protective of young Emma, making sure she got home safely with an adult at the other end to meet her? The rest of that night was a bit of blur for him. Most of his parents' parties ended up that way. Even some of his parties were a little full-on too. There was always a lot of alcohol, loud music blaring and people coming and going. He had been feeling too pleased with himself for solving the Jasmine problem to give much thought to where she'd gone after leaving his room. At twenty-six what he had done had seemed the perfect solution. The only solution.

Now, at thirty-three, he wasn't quite so sure.

Jaz was making herself a nightcap in the kitchen when Jake strolled in. 'Finding it hard to sleep without a playgirl bunny or three in your bed to keep you warm?'

'What happened after you left my room that night?'

Jaz lowered her gaze to her chocolate drink rather

than meet his piercing blue eyes. The chocolate swirled as she stirred it with the teaspoon, creating a whirlpool not unlike the one she could feel in the pit of her stomach. She never thought about that night. That night had happened to another person. It had happened to a foolish, gauche kid who'd had too much to drink and had been too emotionally unstable to know what she was doing or what she was getting into.

'Jasmine. Answer me.'

Jaz lifted her gaze to his and frowned. 'Why do you always call me Jasmine instead of Jaz? You're the only one in your family who insists on doing that. Why?'

'It's your name.'

'So? Yours is Jacques but you don't like being called that,' Jaz pointed out. 'Maybe I'll start to.'

'Julius knows.'

Her heart gave a little stumble. 'Knows what?'

'About us,' he said. 'About this not being real.'

Jaz took a moment to get her head sorted. She'd thought he meant Julius knew about *that night*... But how could he? He would have said something if he did. He was the sort of man who would have got her to press charges. He wouldn't have stood by and let someone get away with it. 'Oh...right; well, I guess he's your twin and all.'

'He won't tell anyone apart from Holly.'

'Good,' Jaz said. 'The less people who know, the better.'

Jake pulled out a kitchen stool and sat opposite her at the island bench. 'You want to make me one of those?'

She lifted her chin. 'Make it yourself.'

A slow smile came to his mouth. 'I guess I'd better in case you put cyanide in it.'

Jaz forced her gaze away from the tempting curve of his mouth. It wasn't fair that one man had so much darn sex appeal. It came off him in waves. She felt it brush against her skin, making her body tingle at the thought of him touching her for real. Ever since his arm had brushed against hers, ever since he'd slung his arm around her shoulders and leaned in against her, she had longed for him to do it again. It was like every nerve under her skin was sitting bolt upright and wide awake, waiting with bated breath for him to touch her again.

She was aware of him in other parts of her body. The secret parts. Her breasts and inner core tingled from the moment he'd stepped into the same room. It was like he could turn a switch in her body simply by being present. She watched covertly as he moved about the kitchen, fetching a cup and the tin of chocolate powder and stirring it into the milk before he turned to put it in the microwave.

She couldn't tear her eyes away from his back and shoulders. He was wearing a cotton T-shirt that showcased every sculpted muscle on his frame. How would it feel to slide her hands down his tautly muscled back? To slip one of her hands past the waistband of his jeans and cup his trim buttocks, or what was on the other side of his testosterone-rich groin?

Jaz gave herself a mental shake. She was on a mission to win back Myles. Getting involved with Jake was out of the question. Not that he would ever want *her*. He loathed her just as much as she loathed him. But men could separate their emotions from sex. She of all people knew that. Maybe he would want to make the most of their situation—a little fling to pass the time until he could get back to his simpering starlets and Hollywood hopefuls. Her mind started to drift... What would it feel like to have Jake make love to her? To have his hands stroke every inch of her flesh, to have his mouth plunder hers?

Jake turned from the microwave. 'Is something wrong?'

Jaz blinked to reset her vision. 'That was weird. I thought I saw you actually lift a finger in the kitchen. I must be hallucinating.'

He laughed and pulled out one of the stools opposite hers at the kitchen bench. 'I can find my way around a kitchen when I need to.'

Jaz's top lip lifted in a cynical arc. 'Like when no slavishly devoted woman is there to cater to your every whim?'

His eyes held hers in a penetrating lock. She felt the power of it go through her like a current of electricity. 'How much did you have to drink that night?' he asked.

She pushed her untouched chocolate away and slipped off the stool. 'Clean up your mess when you're done in here. Eggles won't be back till Sunday night.'

Jaz almost got to the door, but then Jake's hand came out of nowhere and turned her to face him. His warm, strong fingers curling around her arm sent a

shockwave through her body, making her feel as if
someone inside her stomach had shuffled a deck of
cards. Quickly. Vegas-quick. She moistened her lips
with her tongue as she brought her gaze to his dark-
blue one. His ink-black lashes were at half-mast, giving him a sexily hooded look. She looked at his mouth
and felt that shuffle in her heart valves this time. She
could look at his twin's mouth any time without this
crazy reaction. What was it about Jake's mouth that
turned her into a quivering mess of female hormones?
Was it because, try as she might, she couldn't stop
thinking about how it would feel pressed to hers? 'I
don't remember giving you permission to touch me,'
she said.

Instead of releasing her he slid his fingers down
to the bones of her wrist and encircled it like a pair
of gentle handcuffs. 'Talk to me,' he said in a deep,
gravel-rough voice that made the entire length of her
spine soften like candle wax in a steam room.

Jaz tested his hold but all it did was take him with
her to the doorframe, which was just an inch or so
behind her. She pressed her back against it for stability because right then her legs weren't doing such a
great job of holding her upright. He was now so close
she could see the individual pinpricks of stubble along
his jaw and around his nose and mouth. She could
feel their breath intermingling. His muscle-packed
thighs were within a hair's breadth of hers, his booted
feet toe-to-toe with her bare ones. 'Wh-what are you
doing?' she said in a voice she barely recognised as
her own.

His eyes went to her mouth, lingering there for endless, heart-stopping seconds. 'Ever wondered what would happen if we kissed?'

Like just about every day for the last seven years. 'You'd get your face slapped, that's what.'

A smile hitched up one side of his mouth. 'Yeah, that's what I thought.'

Jaz felt like her heart rate was trying to get into the *Guinness Book of Records*. She could smell those lime and lemongrass notes of his aftershave and something else that was one part musk and three parts male. 'But you're not going to do it, right?'

He moved around her mouth like a metal detector just above the ground where something valuable was hidden. He didn't touch down but he might as well have because she felt the tingling in her lips as if he was transmitting raw sexual energy from his body to hers. 'You think about it, don't you? About us getting down to business.'

Oh, dear God in heaven, where is my willpower? Jaz thought as her senses went haywire. She had never wanted to be kissed more in her life than right then. She had never wanted to feel a man's arms go around her and pull her into his hard body. Desire moved through her like a prowling, hungry beast looking for satiation. She felt it in her blood, the tick of arousal. She felt it in her breasts, the prickly sensation of them shifting against the lace of her bra as if they couldn't wait for him to get his hands or mouth on them. She felt it in her core, the pulse and contraction of her inner muscles in anticipatory excitement. 'No, I don't. I never think about it.'

He gave a soft chuckle as he stepped back from her. 'No, nor do I.'

Jaz stood in numb silence as he went back to the island bench to pick up his hot chocolate. She watched as he lifted the mug to his lips and took a sip. He put the mug down and cocked a brow at her. 'Something wrong?'

She pushed herself away from the doorframe, tucking her hair back over one shoulder with a hand that wasn't as steady as she would have liked. 'We haven't discussed the rules about our engagement.'

'Rules?'

Jaz gave him a look. 'Yes, rules. Not your favourite word, is it?'

His eyes glinted. 'Far as I'm concerned, they're only there to be broken.'

She steeled her spine. 'Not this time.'

'Is that a dare?'

Jaz could feel every cell in her body being pulled and tugged by the animal attraction he evoked in her. She couldn't understand why someone she hated so much could have such a monumental effect on her. She wanted to throw herself at him, tear at his clothes and crawl all over his body. She wanted to lock her mouth on his and tangle her tongue with his in an erotic salsa. She wanted him *inside* her body. She could feel the hollow vault of her womanhood pulsating with need. She could even feel the dew of her intimate moisture gathering. She wanted him like a drug she knew she shouldn't have. He was contraband. Dangerous. 'Is the thought of being celibate for a week or two really that difficult for you?'

He gave a lip shrug. 'Never done it before, so I wouldn't know.'

Jaz mentally rolled her eyes. 'Do you have shares in a condom manufacturer or something?'

His dark eyes gleamed with amusement. 'Now there's an idea.'

She picked up her mug of chocolate, not to drink, but to give her hands something to do in case they took it upon themselves to touch him. 'I find your shallow approach to relationships deeply offensive. It's like you only see women as objects you can use to satisfy a bodily need. You don't see them as real people who have feelings.'

'I have the greatest respect for women. That's why I'm always honest with them about what I want from them.'

Jaz eyeballed him. 'I think it's because you're scared of commitment. You can't handle the thought of someone leaving you so you don't let yourself bond with them in the first place.'

He gave a mocking laugh. 'You got a printout of that psychology degree you bought online?'

'That's another thing you do,' Jaz said. 'You joke your way through life because being serious about stuff terrifies you.'

His mouth was smiling but his eyes were not. They had become as hard as flint. 'Ever wondered why your three fiancés have dumped you before you could march them up the aisle?'

Jaz ground her teeth together until her jaw ached. 'Myles hasn't dumped me. We're on a break. It's not the same as being…breaking up.'

'You're a ballbreaker. You don't want a man. You want a puppet. Someone you can wind around your little finger to do what you want when you want. No man worth his testosterone will stand for that.'

Jaz could feel her anger straining at the leash of her control like a feral dog tied up with a piece of cotton. Her fingers around the mug of chocolate twitched. How she would love to spray it over Jake's arrogant face. 'You enjoy humiliating me, don't you? It gives you such a big, fat hard-on, doesn't it?'

His jaw worked as if her words had hit a raw nerve. 'While we're playing Ten Things I Hate About You, here's another one for my list. You need to get over yourself. You've held onto this ridiculous grudge for far too long.'

Jaz saw the hot chocolate fly through the air before she fully registered she'd thrown it. It splashed over the front of his T-shirt like brown paint thrown at a wall.

Jake barely moved a muscle. He was as still as a statue on a plinth. Too still.

The silence was breathing, heaving with menace.

But then he calmly reached over the back of his head, hauled the T-shirt off, bunched it up into a rough ball and handed it to her. 'Wash it.'

Jaz swallowed as she looked at the T-shirt. She had

lost control. A thing she had sworn she would never do. Crazy people like her mother lost control. They shouted and screamed and threw things. Not her. She never let anyone do that to her. A tight knot of self-disgust began to choke her. Tears welled up behind her eyes, escaping from a place she had thought she had locked and bolted for good. Tears she hadn't cried since that night when she had finally made it back to her bedroom with shame clinging to her like filth. No amount of showering had removed it. If she thought about that night she would feel it clogging every pore of her skin like engine grease. She took the T-shirt from him with an unsteady hand. 'I'm sorry...'

'Forget about it.'

I only wish I could, Jaz thought. But when she finally worked up the courage to look up he had already turned on his heel and gone.

CHAPTER FOUR

JAKE WAS VAINLY trying to sleep when he heard the
sound of the plumbing going in the other wing of
the house where Jasmine's room was situated next to
Miranda's. He lay there for a while, listening as the
pipes pumped water. Had Jasmine left on a tap? He
glanced at the bedside clock. It was late to be having
a shower, although he had to admit for him a cold one
wouldn't have gone astray. He rarely lost his temper.
He preferred to laugh his way out of trouble but something about Jasmine's mood had got to him tonight.
He was sick of dragging their history around like a
dead carcass. It was time to put it behind them. He
didn't want Julius and Holly's or Miranda and Leandro's wedding ruined by a ridiculous feud that had
gone on way too long.

He shoved off the bed covers and reached for a
bathrobe. He seemed to remember Jasmine had a ten-
dency for long showers but he still thought he'd better
check to make sure nothing was amiss. He made his
way to the bathroom closest to her room and rapped
his knuckles on the door. 'You okay in there?' he said.

No answer. He tapped again, louder this time, and called out but the water continued. He tried the door but it was locked. He frowned. Why did she think she had to lock the door? They were alone in the house. Didn't she trust him? The thought sat uncomfortably on him. He might be casual about sex but not *that* casual. He always ensured he had consent first.

Not that he was going to sleep with Jasmine. That would be crazy. Crazy but tempting. Way too tempting, if he was honest with himself. He had spent many an erotic daydream with her body pinned under his or over his, or with her mouth on him, sucking him until he blew like a bomb. She had that effect on men. She didn't do it on purpose; her natural sensuality made men fall over like ninepins. Her beauty, her regal manner, her haughty 'I'm too good for the likes of you' air made men go weak at the knees, himself included. Just thinking about her naked body under that spray of water in the shower was enough to make him rock-hard.

He waited outside her door until the water finally stopped. 'Jasmine?'

It was a while before she opened the door. She was wearing a bathrobe and her hair was wrapped turban-like with a towel. Her skin was rosy from the hot water and completely make-up free, giving her a youthful appearance that took him back a decade. 'What?' She frowned at him irritably. 'Is something wrong with your bathroom?'

He frowned when he saw her red-rimmed eyes and pink nose. 'Have you been crying?'

Her hand clutching the front of her bathrobe clenched a little tighter but her tone was full of derision. 'Why would I be crying? Oh, yes, I remember now. My fiancé wanted a month's break. Pardon me for being a little upset.'

Jake felt a stab of remorse for not having factored in her feelings. He had such an easy come, easy go attitude to his relationships he sometimes forgot other people invested much more emotionally. But did she really love the guy or was she in love with the idea of love and marriage? Three engagements in three years. That must be some sort of record, surely? Had she been in love each time? 'You want to talk about it?'

Her eyes narrowed in scorn. 'What—with *you*?'

'Why not?'

She pushed past him and he got a whiff of honeysuckle body wash. 'I'm going to bed. Good night.'

'Jasmine, wait,' Jake said, capturing her arm on the way past. His fingers sank into the soft velour of her bathrobe as he turned her to face him. He could feel the slenderness of her arm in spite of the pillowy softness of the thick fabric, reminding him of how feminine she was. A hot coil of lust burned in his groin, winding tighter and tighter. 'I might've been a little rough on you downstairs earlier.'

Her brows lifted and she pulled out of his light hold. 'Might've been?'

He let out a whooshing breath. 'Okay, I *was* rough on you. I didn't think about how you'd be feeling about the break-up.'

'It's not a break-up. It's a *break*.'

Jake wasn't following the semantics. 'You don't think it's permanent?'

Her chin came up. 'No. Myles just needs a bit of space.'

He frowned. 'But what about us? Don't you think he's going to get a little pissed you found someone else so soon?'

She looked at him as if he were wearing a dunce's cap. 'Yes, but that's the whole point. Sometimes people don't know what they've got until it's gone.'

'Has he called you since the news of our—' Jake couldn't help grimacing over the word '—engagement was announced?'

'Heaps of times but I'm not answering,' Jaz said. 'I'm letting him stew for a bit.'

'Do you think he believes it's true?'

'Why wouldn't he? Everyone else bought it. Apart from Julius, of course.'

'I'm surprised Miranda fell for it, to tell you the truth,' Jake said.

Jaz frowned. 'Why do you say that? Have you spoken to her?'

'She sent me a congratulatory text but I haven't spoken to her. I've been dodging her calls. But you're her closest friend. She'll suss something's amiss once she sees us together.'

Her lips compressed for a moment. 'I don't think it will be a problem. Anyway, she's busy with her own engagement and wedding plans.'

Jake studied her for a beat. 'Are you in love with this Myles guy?'

Her brow wrinkled. 'What sort of question is that? Of course I am.'

'Were you in love with Tim and Linton?'

'*Lincoln*,' she said with a scowl. 'Yes, I was.'

'You're pretty free and easy with your affection, aren't you?'

Jaz gave him a gelid look. 'That's rich coming from the man who changes partners faster than tyres are changed in a Formula One pit lane.'

Jake couldn't help smiling. 'You flatter me. I'm fast but not that fast.'

'Have you heard from Emma?'

'No.'

'So my plan is working.'

'So far.' He didn't like to admit it but there was no denying it. From being bombarded with texts, emails and calls there had been zilch from Emma since Jasmine had delivered her bombshell announcement. Another thing he didn't like to acknowledge was how he'd had nothing but congratulations from all his friends and colleagues. Even his parents had stopped slinging insults at each other via the press long enough to congratulate him. He had even had an email from a client he'd thought he'd lost, promising not just his business but that of several high-profile contacts.

This little charade was turning out to be much more of a win-win than Jake had expected.

'What we need is to be seen out in public,' Jaz said. 'That will make it even more believable.'

'In public?'

'Yes, like on a date or dinner or something.'

'You reckon we could get through a whole meal together without you throwing something at me?'

Her gaze moved out of reach of his. 'I'll do my best.'

Jaz woke the next morning to a call from Miranda. 'I know it's early but I can't get Jake on his phone to congratulate him,' Miranda said. 'I figured he'd be in bed with you. Can you hand me to him? That is, if it's not inconvenient?' The way she said 'inconvenient' was playful and teasing.

Jaz swallowed back a gulp. 'Erm…he's having a shower right now. I'll get him to call you, okay?'

'Okay,' Miranda said. 'So how's it going? Does it seem real? I mean, for all this time you've been at each other's throats. Is it good to be making love instead of war?'

Jaz got out of bed but on her way to the window caught sight of her reflection in the mirror. How could she lie to her best friend? Lying by text was one thing. Lying in conversation was another. It didn't seem right. Not when they had been friends for so long. 'Miranda, listen, things aren't quite what they seem… I'm not really engaged to Jake. We're pretending.'

'*Pretending?*' Miranda sounded bitterly disappointed. 'But why?'

'I'm trying to win Myles back,' Jaz said. 'He wanted to take a break and I thought I'd try and make him jealous.'

'But why did Jake agree to it?' Miranda said.

'I didn't give him a choice.' Jaz explained the situation about Emma briefly.

'Gosh,' Miranda said. 'I was so excited for you. Now I feel like someone's punched me in the belly.'

'I'm sorry for lying but—'

'Are you sure about Myles?' Miranda said. 'I mean, *absolutely* sure he's the one?'

'Of course I'm sure. Why else would I be going to so much trouble to win him back?'

'Pride?'

Jaz pressed her lips together. 'It's not a matter of pride. It's a matter of love.'

'But you fall in and out of love all the time,' Miranda said. 'How do you know he's the right one for you when you could just as easily fall in love with someone else tomorrow?'

'I'm not going to fall in love with anyone else,' Jaz said. 'How can I when I'm in love with Myles?'

'What do you love about him?'

'We've had this conversation before and I—'

'Let's have it again,' Miranda said. 'Refresh my memory. List three things you love about him.'

'He's…'

'See?' Miranda said. 'You're hesitating!'

'Look, I know you don't like him, so it wouldn't matter what I said about him; you'd find some reason to discount it.'

'It's not that he's not nice and polite, handsome and well-educated and all that,' Miranda said. 'But I worry you only like him because you can control him. You've got a strong personality, Jaz. You need someone who'll stand up to you. Someone who'll be your equal, not your puppet.'

Jaz swung back from the window and paced the carpet. 'I don't like controlling men. I hate them. I always have and I always will. I could never fall in love with someone like that.'

'We'll see.'

She frowned. 'What do you mean, "we'll see"? I hope you're not thinking what I think you're thinking because it's not going to happen. No way.'

'Come on, Jaz,' Miranda said. 'You've had a thing for Jake since you were sixteen.'

'I was a kid back then!' Jaz said. 'It was just a stupid crush. I got over it, okay?'

'If you got over it then why have you avoided him like the black plague ever since?'

Jaz was close to Miranda but not close enough to tell her what had happened that night after she'd left Jake's room. She wasn't close enough to anyone to tell them that. Sharing that shame with someone else wouldn't make it go away. The only way she could make it go away was not to think about it. If she told anyone about it they would look at her differently. They might judge her. Blame her. She didn't want to take the risk. Her tough-girl façade was exactly that—a façade.

Underneath all the bravado she was still that terrified sixteen-year-old who had got herself sexually assaulted by a drunken guest at the party. It hadn't been rape but it had come scarily close to it. The irony was the person who did it had been so drunk they hadn't remembered a thing about it the following morning. The only way Jaz could deal with it was to pretend it hadn't happened. There was no other way. 'Look, I'm not avoiding Jake now, so you should be happy,' she said. 'Who knows? We might even end up friends after this charade is over.'

'I certainly hope so because I don't want Julius and Holly's wedding, or mine and Leandro's, spoilt by you two looking daggers at each other,' Miranda said. 'It's bad enough with Mum and Dad carrying on World War Three.'

'That reminds me. Have you met Kat Winwood yet?' Jaz asked.

'No.' Miranda gave a sigh. 'She won't have anything to do with any of us. I guess if I were in her shoes I might feel the same. What Dad did to her mother was pretty unforgiveable.'

'Yes, well, paying someone to have an abortion isn't exactly how to win friends and influence people, I'll grant you that,' Jaz said.

'What about you?' Miranda said. 'You mentioned a couple of weeks back you were thinking about meeting her. Any luck?'

'Nope,' Jaz said. 'I might not be a Ravensdale but I'm considered close enough to your family to be on the black list as well.'

'Maybe Flynn can get her to change her mind,' Miranda said, referring to the family lawyer, Flynn Carlyon, who had been a year ahead of Jake and Julius at school. 'If anyone can do it he can. He's unlikely to give up until he gets what he wants.'

'But I thought the whole idea was to get her to go away,' Jaz said. 'Wasn't that what Flynn was supposed to do? Pay her to keep from speaking to the press?'

'Yes, but she wouldn't take a penny off him. She hasn't said a word to the media anyway and it's been over a month,' Miranda said. 'Dad's agent called him last night about putting on a party to celebrate his sixty years in showbiz in January. Dad wants Kat there. He says he won't go ahead with it unless she comes.'

'Sixty years?' Jaz said. 'Gosh. What age did he start?'

'Five. He had a walk-on part in some musical way back. Hasn't he shown you the photos?'

'Nope,' Jaz said. 'I must've missed that bragging session.'

'Ha ha,' Miranda said. 'But what are we going to do about Kat? She has to come to Dad's party otherwise he'll be devastated.'

'Well, at least Flynn will have a few weeks to change her mind.'

'I can't work her out,' Miranda said. 'She's a struggling actor who's only had bit parts till now. You'd think she'd be jumping at the chance to cash in on her biological father's fame.'

'Maybe she needs time to get her head around who her father is,' Jaz said. 'It must've come as a huge shock finding out like that just before her mother died.'

'Yes, I guess so.' Miranda sighed again and then added, 'Are you sure you know what you're doing,

Jaz—I mean with Jake? I can't help worrying this could backfire.'

'I know exactly what I'm doing,' Jaz said. 'I'm using Jake and he's using me.'

There was a telling little silence.

'You're not going to sleep with him, are you?' Miranda said.

Jaz laughed. 'I know he's your brother and all that but there are some women on this planet who can actually resist him, you know.'

And I had better keep on doing it.

Jake was coming back in from a morning run around the property when he saw Jaz coming down the stairs, presumably for breakfast. She was wearing light-grey yoga pants and a baby-girl pink slouch top that revealed the cap of a creamy shoulder and the thin black strap of her bra. Her slender feet were bare apart from liquorice-black toenail polish and her hair was in a messy knot on the top of her head that somehow managed to look casual and elegant at the same time. She wasn't wearing a skerrick of make-up but if anything it made her look all the more breath-snatchingly beautiful. But then, since when had her stunning grey-blue eyes with their thick, spider-leg long lashes and prominent eyebrows needed any enhancement?

He caught a whiff of her bergamot-and-geranium essential oil as she came to stand on the last step, making her almost eye-to-eye with him. The urge to touch her lissom young body was overpowering. He had to curl his hands into fists to prevent himself from running a hand down the creamy silk of her cheek or tracing that gorgeous mouth with his finger.

Her eyes met his and a punch of lust slammed him in the groin. The fire and ice in that stormy sea of grey and blue had a potent impact on him. It happened every time their eyes collided. It was like a bolt of electricity zapping him, making everything that was male in him stand to attention. 'I told Miranda the truth about us,' she said with a touch of defiance.

Jake decided to wind her up a bit. 'That we have the hots for each other and are about to indulge in a passionate fling that's been seven years in the making?'

She folded her arms like a schoolmistress who was dealing with a particularly cheeky pupil, but he noticed her cheeks had gone a faint shade of pink. 'No,' she said as tartly as if she had just bitten into a lemon. 'I told her we aren't engaged and we still hate each other.'

He picked up a stray strand of hair that had escaped her makeshift knot and tucked it safely back behind the neat shell of her ear. He felt her give a tiny shiver as his fingers brushed the skin behind her ear and her mouth opened and closed as if she was trying to disguise her little involuntary gasp. 'You don't hate me, sweetheart. You *want* me.'

The twin pools of colour in her cheeks darkened another shade and her eyes flashed with livid blue-tipped flames. 'Do you get charged extra on flights for carrying your ego on board?'

Jake smiled crookedly as he trailed his fingertip from the crimson tide on her cheekbone to the neat hinge of her jaw. 'I see it every time you look at me. I feel it when I'm near you. You feel it too, don't you?'

The point of her tongue sneaked out over her lips in a darting movement. 'All I feel when I'm near you is the uncontrollable urge to scratch my nails down your face.'

He unpeeled one of her hands from where it was tucked in around her middle and laid it flat against his jaw. 'Go on,' he said, challenging her with his gaze. 'I won't stop you.'

Her hand was like cool silk against his skin. A shiver scooted down his spine as he felt the slight scrape of her nails against his morning stubble but then, instead of scoring his face, she began to stroke it. The sound of her soft skin moving over his raspy jaw had an unmistakably erotic element to it. Her touch sent a rocket blast through his pelvis and he put a hand at the base of her spine to draw her closer to his restless, urgent heat. The contact of her body so intimately against his was like fireworks exploding. His mouth came down in search of hers but he didn't have to go far as she met him more than halfway. Her soft lips were parted in anticipation, her vanilla-milkshake breath mingling with his for a spine-tingling microsecond before her mouth fused with his.

She gave a low moan of approval as he moved his mouth against hers, seeking her moist warmth with the stroke and glide of his tongue. She melted against him, her arms winding around his neck, her fingers delving through his hair, holding his head in place as if she was terrified he would pull back from her.

Jake had no intention of pulling back. He was enjoying the taste of her too much, the heat and unbridled passion that blossomed with every stroke and flicker of his tongue against hers. She pressed herself against him, her supple body fitting along his harder contours as if she had been fashioned just for him. He cupped her neat behind, holding her against the throbbing urgency of his arousal as his mouth fed hungrily off the sweet and drugging temptation of hers.

He lifted his mouth only far enough to change position but she grabbed at him, clamping her lips to his, her tongue darting into his mouth to mate wantonly with his. His blood pounded with excitement. His heart rate sped. His thighs fizzed with the need to take charge, to possess the hot, tight, wet vault of her body until this clawing, desperate need was finally satisfied.

Hadn't he always known she would be dynamite in his arms? Hadn't he always wanted to do this? Even that night when she'd been too young to know what she was doing. He had ached and burned to possess her then and he ached and burned now. One kiss wasn't going to be enough. It wasn't enough to satisfy the raging lust rippling through his body. He wanted to feel her convulsing around him as he took her to heaven and back. He knew they would be good together. He had always known it on some level. He felt it whenever their eyes met—the electric jolt of awareness that triggered something primitive in him.

Nothing would please him more than to see her gasping out his name as she came. Nothing would give him more pleasure than to have her admit she wanted him as much as he wanted her. To prove to her it wasn't her 'taking a break' fiancé she was hankering after but *him* she wanted. The man she had wanted since she was a teenager. The man she said she hated but lusted after like a forbidden drug. *That* was what he saw in her eyes—the desire she didn't want to feel but was there, simmering and smouldering with latent heat.

Jake slipped a hand under her loose top in search of the tempting globe of her breast. She hummed her pleasure against his lips as he moved her bra aside to make skin-on-skin contact. For years he had wanted to touch her like this—to feel her soft, creamy skin against his palm and hear her throatily express her need. He passed his thumb over her tightly budded nipple and then circled it before he bent his head and took it into his mouth. She gave another primal moan as he suckled on her breast, using the gentle scrape of his teeth and the sweep and salve of his tongue to tantalise her.

He slipped a hand down between their hard-pressed bodies, cupping her mound, his own body so worked up he wondered if he was going to jump the gun for the first time since he'd been a clumsy teenager.

But suddenly Jaz pulled back, pushing against his chest with the heels of her hands. 'Stop,' she said in a breathless-sounding voice. 'Please...stop.'

Jake held his hands up to show he was cool with her calling a halt. 'Your call, sweetheart.'

She pressed her lips together as she straightened

her top, her hands fumbling and uncoordinated. 'You had no right to do that,' she said, shooting him a hard look.

He gave a lazy smile. 'Well, look who's talking. I wonder what lover boy would say if he'd been a fly on the wall just now? His devoted little "having a break" fiancée getting all hot and bothered with just a friendly kiss.'

Her eyes went to hairpin-thin slits. 'There was nothing friendly about it. You don't even like me. You just wanted to prove a point.'

'What point would that be?'

She tossed her head in an uppity manner as she turned to go back upstairs. 'I'm not having this conversation. You had no right to touch me and that's the end of it. Don't do it again.'

Jake waited until she was almost to the top of the stairs before he said, 'What about when we're out in public? Am I allowed to touch you then?'

A circle of ice rimmed her flattened mouth as she turned to glare at him. 'Only if it's absolutely necessary.'

He smiled a devilish smile. 'I'll look forward to it.'

CHAPTER FIVE

JAZ STORMED INTO her room and shut the door. She would have slammed it except she had already shown Jake how much he had rattled her. She didn't want to give his over-blown ego any more of a boost. She was furious with him for kissing her. How dared he take such liberties? A little voice reminded her that she hadn't exactly resisted but, on the contrary, had given him every indication she was enjoying every pulse-racing second of it.

Which she had been. Damn it.

His kiss had made her face what she didn't want to face. What she hadn't wanted to face for seven years. She wanted him. It was like it was programmed into her genes or something. He triggered something in her that no other man ever had. Her body sizzled when he was around. His touch created an earthquake of longing. How could a kiss make her feel so…so alive? It was crazy. Madness. Lunacy.

It was just like him to make a big joke about everything. This was nothing but a game to him. He enjoyed baiting her. Goading her. *Tempting* her. Why had she allowed him to get that close to her? She should have stepped back while she'd had the chance. Or maybe she hadn't had the chance because her body had other ideas. Wicked ideas that involved him touching her and pleasuring her in a way she had never quite felt before. Why had *his* touch made her flesh tingle and quake with delight? Why had *his* kiss made her heart race and her pulse thrum with longing?

It was just a kiss. It wasn't as if she hadn't been kissed before. She'd had plenty of kisses. Heaps. Dozens. Maybe hundreds… Well, maybe things had been a bit light on that just lately. She couldn't quite recall the last time Myles had kissed her. Not properly. Not passionately, as if he couldn't get enough of her taste and touch. Over the last few weeks their kisses had turned into a rather perfunctory peck on the cheek at hello and goodbye. And as to touching her breasts, well, Myles wasn't good at breasts. He didn't seem to understand she didn't like being pinched or squeezed, like he was someone checking a piece of fruit for ripeness.

Jaz let out a frustrated breath. Why did Jake have to be the expert on kissing her and handling her breasts? It wasn't fair. She didn't want him to have such sensual power over her. He could turn her on by just looking at her with that glinting dark gaze.

Of course it would be *so* much worse now. Now he had actually kissed her and touched her breasts and her lady land. God, she'd almost come on the spot when he'd cupped her down there. How could one man's touch have such an effect on her? She didn't even like him. She loathed him. He was her arch-enemy. He wasn't just a thorn in her side. He was the whole damn rose bush. Unpruned. He was everything she avoided in a partner.

But he sure could kiss. Jaz had to give him that. His lips had done things to hers no man had ever done before. His tongue had lit a blazing fire in her core and it hadn't gone out. The hot coals were smouldering there even now. Her body felt restless. Feverish. Hungry. Starving for more of his electrifying caresses. What would it feel like to have him deep inside her? Moving in her body in that hectic rush for release?

Sex had always been a complicated issue for her. She put it down to the fact her first experience of it had been so twisted and tangled up with shame. She had taken a drink from a young man at the party, more to get back at Jake for rejecting her. She had flirted with the man, hoping Jake would see that not all men found her repulsive. But she hadn't factored in the amount of alcohol she had already consumed or her overwrought emotional state. She couldn't quite remember how she had ended up in one of the downstairs bathrooms with the man, sweaty and smelling of wine as he tore at her clothes and groped and slobbered all over her until she'd finally got away. All she could remember was the shame—the sickening shame of not being in control.

Now whenever she had sex that same shame lurked at the back of her mind. Although she enjoyed some aspects of making love—the touching and being needed—she hadn't always been able to relax enough to orgasm. Not that any of her partners had seemed to notice. She might not be a proper Ravensdale but she sure could act when she needed to. Pretending to orgasm every time hadn't been her intention. But once had turned into twice and then it had been far easier than explaining.

How could she explain her behaviour that night? The rational part of her knew the man at the party had some responsibility to acquire proper consent before he touched her, but how did she know if she'd given it or not? It would be his word against hers, that was, if he'd actually remembered. She'd seen him the next morning as the overnight guests were leaving but he had looked right through her as if he had never seen her before. Had she agreed to kiss him in the bathroom or had he come in on her and seized the opportunity to assault her? She didn't know and it was the not knowing that was the most shameful thing for her.

Jaz wasn't into victim blaming but when it came to herself she struggled to forgive herself for allowing something like that to happen. She had buried her shame behind a 'don't mess with me' façade and a sharp tongue but deep inside she was still that shocked and terrified girl.

And she had a scary feeling if she spent too much time alone with Jake Ravensdale he would begin to see it.

Jaz was doing some work on Holly's dress in her room and when her phone rang she picked it up without thinking. 'Jasmine Connolly.'

'Jaz. Finally you answered,' Myles said. 'Why on earth haven't you returned my calls?'

'Oh, hi, Myles,' she said breezily. 'How are you?'

He released a whooshing breath. 'How do you think I am? I turn my back for a moment and my fiancée is suddenly engaged to someone else.'

Jaz smiled as she put her needle and thread down. It was working. It was actually working. Myles was insanely jealous. She had never heard him speak so possessively before. 'You were the one who suggested we take a break.'

'Yes, but dating other people is not the same as getting engaged to them. We'd only been apart twenty-four hours and you hooked up with him. No one falls in love that quickly. No one, and especially not Jake bloody Ravensdale.'

Jaz hadn't really taken in that bit. The bit where Myles had said they were free to date other people. She'd thought he was just having some breathing space. Her 'engagement' to Jake wouldn't have the same power if Myles was seeing someone else. What if he fell in love? What if *he* got engaged to someone else? 'Are you seeing other people?'

There was a short silence.

'I had a drink with an old friend but I haven't got myself bloody engaged to them,' he said in a sulky tone.

Jaz twirled a tendril of her hair around her finger as she walked about the room with the phone pressed to her ear. How cool was this, hearing Myles sound all wounded and affronted by her moving on so quickly?

Didn't that prove he still loved her? The irony was he'd been the first to say those three magical little words. But he hadn't said it for weeks. Months, even. But a couple more weeks of having Jake Ravensdale brandished in his face would do the trick. Myles would soon be begging her to take him back. 'I have to go,' she said. 'Jake is taking me out to dinner.'

'I give it a week,' Myles said. 'Two at the most. He won't stick around any longer than that. You mark my words.'

Two is all I need. The winter wedding expo in the Cotswolds was the coming weekend. It was her stepping stone to the big time. She hoped to expand her business and what better way than to attend with a heart-stopping, handsome fiancé in tow? There was no way she wanted to go alone. She would look tragic if she went without a fiancé. She couldn't bear to be considered a fraud, making 'happy ever after' dresses but failing to find love herself. But if she took Jake Ravensdale as her fiancé —the poster boy for pick-ups—it would give her serious street cred. Besides, it would be the perfect payback to him for humiliating her. It would be unmitigated torture for commitment-phobe Jake to be dragged around a ballroom full of wedding finery.

She smiled a secret smile. Yes, staying 'engaged' to Jake suited her just fine.

Jake was scrolling through his emails in the library— thankfully none were from Emma Madden—when Jaz came sashaying in, bringing with her the scent of flowers and temptation. His body sprang to attention when she approached the desk where he was sitting. She had changed out of her yoga pants and top and was now wearing skin-tight jeans, knee-length leather boots and a baby-blue cashmere sweater with a patterned scarf artfully gathered around her slim neck. Her honey-brown hair was loose about her shoulders and her beautiful mouth was glistening with lip-gloss, drawing his gaze like a magnet. He could still taste her. Could still feel the way her tongue had danced with his in sensual heat. He saw her gaze drift to his mouth as if she were recalling that erotic interlude. 'Forgiven me yet?' he said.

She tossed her hair back over her shoulders in a haughty manner, giving him an ice-cool glare. 'For?'

'You know exactly what for.'

She shifted her gaze, picked a pen off the desk and turned it over in her slender hands as if it was something of enormous interest to her. 'I was wondering what you're up to next weekend.'

He leaned back in the leather chair and balanced one ankle over his thigh. 'My calendar is pretty heavily booked. What did you have in mind?'

Her grey-blue eyes came back to his. 'I have a function I need to attend in Gloucester. I was hoping you'd come with me—you know, to keep up appearances.'

'What sort of function?'

'Just a drinks thing.'

Jake steepled his fingers against his nose and mouth. The little minx was up to something but he would play along. He might even get another kiss or two out of her. 'Sure, why not?'

She put the pen down. 'I'm going to head back to London now.'

He felt a swooping sensation of disappointment in his gut. It would be deadly boring staying here without her to spar with. They hadn't had any time together without anyone else around for years. He hadn't realised how much he was enjoying it until the prospect of it ending now loomed. But there would be other opportunities as long as this charade continued. And he was going to make the most of them. 'You're not staying till morning?'

'No, I have stuff to do at the boutique first thing and I don't want to get caught up in traffic.'

Jake suspected she was wary of spending any more time with him in case she betrayed her desire for him. He wasn't being overly smug about it. He could see it as plain as day. It mirrored his raging lust for her. Not that he was going to act on it but it sure was a heap of fun making her think he was. 'Are you going to see Myles?'

Her gaze slipped out of reach of his. 'Not yet. We agreed on a month's break.'

'A lot can happen in a month.'

Her lips tightened as if she was trying to remove the sensation of his on them. 'I know what I'm doing.'

'Do you?'

Her eyes clashed with his. 'I know you think relationships are a complete waste of time but commitment is important to me.'

'He's not the right man for you,' Jake said.

Her hands went to her slim hips in a combative

pose. 'And I suppose you think you're an expert on who exactly would be?'

He pushed back his chair to come around to her side of the desk. She took half a step backwards but the antique globe was in the way. Her eyes drifted to his mouth and her darting tongue took a layer of lip-gloss off her lips. 'If Myles was the right man for you he'd be down here right now with his hands at my throat.'

Her eyes glittered with enmity. 'Not all men resort to Neanderthal tactics to claim a partner.'

He took a fistful of her silky hair and gently anchored her. 'If I was in love with you I would do whatever it took to get you back.'

Her eyelids went to half-mast as her gaze zeroed in on his mouth for a moment. 'Men like you don't know the meaning of the word love. Lust is the only currency you deal in.'

Jake glided his hand down from her hair to cup her cheek, his thumb moving over the creamy perfection of her skin like the slow arm of a metronome. He watched as her pupils enlarged like widening pools of black ink, her mouth parting, her soft, milky breath coming out in a soundless gasp. 'There's nothing wrong with a bit of lust. It's the litmus test of a good relationship.'

'You don't have relationships,' she said, still looking at his mouth. 'You have encounters that don't last longer than it takes to change a light bulb.'

He gave a slanted smile. 'Who needs a light bulb when we've got this sort of electricity going on?'

She pursed her lips. 'Don't even think about it.'

He brushed his thumb across her bunched up lips. 'I think about it all the time. How it would feel to have you scraping your nails down my back as I make you come.'

She gave a tiny shudder. Blinked. Swallowed. 'I'd much rather scrape them down your arrogant face.'

Jake smiled. 'Liar. You're thinking about it now, aren't you? You're thinking about how hot I make you feel. How turned on. I bet if I slipped my fingers into you now you'd be dripping wet for me.'

Twin pools of pink flagged her cheekbones. 'It's not going to happen, Jake,' she said through tight lips. 'I'm engaged to another man.'

'Maybe you'll feel different once you're wearing my ring. I'll pick you up at lunchtime tomorrow at the boutique. Be ready at two p.m.'

Her eyes flashed with venom. 'I have an appointment with a client.'

'Cancel it.'

She looked as if she was going to argue the point but then she blew out a hiss of a breath and stormed out of the room, slamming the door behind her for good measure.

Barely a minute later he heard her car start with a roar and then the scream of her tyres as she flew down the driveway.

He smiled and turned back to his laptop. *Yep. A heap of fun.*

CHAPTER SIX

JAZ HAD JUST finished with a customer who had purchased one of her hand-embroidered veils for her daughter when Jake came into the boutique. The woman smiled up at him as he politely held the door open for her. 'Thank you,' she said. 'I hear congratulations are in order. You've got yourself a keeper there.' She nodded towards Jaz. 'She'll make a gorgeous bride. When's the big day?'

Jake smiled one of his laidback smiles. 'We haven't set a date yet, have we, sweetheart?'

'No, not yet,' Jaz said.

'I can't wait to see the ring,' the woman said. 'I bet you'll give her a big one.'

Jake's dark-blue eyes glinted as they glanced at Jaz. 'You bet I will.'

Jaz felt a tremor go through her private parts at his innuendo. Did the man have no shame? She was trying to act as cool and professional as she could and one look at her from those glittering midnight-blue eyes and she felt like she was going to melt into a sizzling pool at his feet. She wouldn't have mentioned anything about their 'engagement' to the customer but it seemed there wasn't a person in the whole of London who hadn't heard fast-living playboy Jake Ravensdale was getting himself hitched.

The woman left with a little wave, and the door with its tinkling bell closed. Jake came towards the counter where Jaz had barricaded herself. 'So this is your stamping ground,' he said, glancing around at the dresses hanging on the free-standing rack. 'How much of a profit are you turning over?'

She gave him a flinty look. 'I don't need you to pull apart my business.'

His one-shoulder shrug was nonchalant. 'Just asking.'

'You're not just asking,' Jaz said. 'You're looking for an opportunity to tell me I'm rubbish at running my business, just like you keep pointing out how rubbish I am at running my personal life.'

'You have to admit three engagements—four, if you count ours—is a lot of bad decisions.'

She gripped the edge of the counter. 'And I suppose you've never made a bad decision in the whole of your charmed life, have you?'

'I've made a few.'

'Such as?'

He looked at her for a long moment, his customary smile fading and a slight frown taking its place. 'It was crass of me to bring those girls to my room that night. There were other ways I could've handled the situation.'

Jaz refused to be taken in by an admission of regret seven years too late. 'Did you sleep with them?'

'No.'

There was a pregnant pause.

'Where did you go after that?' he said. 'I didn't see you for the rest of the night.'

Jaz looked down at the glass-topped counter where all the garters were arranged. 'I went back to my room.'

He reached across the counter to take one of her hands in his. 'Look at me, Jasmine.'

She slowly brought her gaze up to his, affecting the expression of a bored teenager preparing for a stern lecture from a parent. 'What?'

His eyes moved between each of hers as if he was searching for something hidden behind the cool screen of her gaze. She could feel the warm press of his hand against hers, his long, strong, masculine fingers entwining with hers, making her insides slip and shift. She could smell the sharp citrus of his aftershave. She could see the dark shadow of his regrowth peppered along his jaw. She could see every fine line on his mouth, the way his lips were set in a serious line— such a change from his usual teasing slant. He began to move the pad of his thumb in a stroking fashion over the back of her hand, the movements drugging her senses.

'It wasn't that I wasn't attracted to you,' he said. 'I just didn't want to make things awkward with you being such a part of the family. That and the fact you were too young to know what you were doing.'

Jaz pulled her hand away. 'Then why lead me on as if you were serious about me? That was just plain cruel.'

He let out a deep sigh. 'Yeah, I guess it was.'

She studied his features for a moment, wondering if this too was an act. How could she believe he was sorry for how he'd made her think he was falling in love with her? He had been so charming towards her, telling her how beautiful she was and how he couldn't wait to get her alone. She had fallen for every lie, waiting in his room, undressing down to her underwear for him in her haste to do anything she could to please him. She had been too emotionally immature to realise he had been winding her up. She had been too enamoured with him to see his charm offensive for what it was. He had pulled her strings like a puppet master. Hating him was dead easy when he wasn't sorry for how he'd treated her. For the last seven years she had stoked that hatred with every look or cynical lip curl he aimed her way. But if this apology were genuine she would have to let her anger and hatred go.

That was scary.

Her anger was a barrier. A big, fat barricade around her heart because falling in love with Jake would be nothing less than an exercise in self-annihilation. She only fell in love with men she knew for certain would love her back. Her ex-fiancés were alike in that they had each been comfortable with commitment. They'd wanted the same things she wanted…or so they had said.

Jake glanced at his watch. 'We'd better get a move

on. I made an appointment with the jeweller for two-fifteen. Have you got an assistant to hold the fort for you till you get back?'

'No, my last girl was rude to the clients,' Jaz said. 'I had to let her go. I haven't got around to replacing her. I'll just put a "back in ten minutes" sign on the door.'

He frowned. 'You mean you run this show all by yourself?'

She picked up her purse and jacket from underneath the counter. 'I outsource some of the cutting and sewing but I do most of everything else because that's what my customers expect.'

'But none of the top designers do all the hack work,' Jake said as they walked out of the boutique into the chilly autumn air. 'You'll burn yourself out trying to do everything yourself.'

'Yes, well, I'm not quite pulling in the same profit as some of those houses,' Jaz said. 'But watch this space. I have a career plan.'

'What about a business plan? I could have a look at your company structure and—'

'No thanks,' Jaz said and closed and locked the boutique door.

'If you're worried about my fee, I could do mate's rates.'

She gave him a sideways look. 'I can afford you, Jake. I just choose not to use your…erm…services.'

He shrugged one of his broad shoulders. 'Your loss.'

The jeweller was a private designer who had a studio above an interior design shop. Jaz was acutely conscious of Jake's arm at her elbow as he led her into the viewing area. After brief introductions were made a variety of designs was brought forward for her to peruse. But there was one ring that was a stand out. It was a mosaic collection of diamonds in an art deco design that was both simple yet elegant. She slipped it on her finger and was pleased to find it was a perfect fit. 'This one,' she said, holding it up to see the way the light bounced off the diamonds.

'Good choice,' the designer said. 'It suits your hand.'

Jaz didn't see the price. It wasn't the sort of jeweller where price tags were on show. But she didn't care if it was expensive or not. Jake could afford it. She did wonder, however, if he would want her to give it back when their 'engagement' was over.

Jake took her hand as they left the studio. 'Fancy a quick coffee?'

Jaz would have said no except she hadn't had lunch and her stomach was gurgling like a drain. 'Sure, why not?'

He took her to a café a couple of blocks from her boutique but they had barely sat down before someone from a neighbouring table took a photo of them with a camera phone. Then a murmur went around the café and other people started aiming their phones at them. Jaz tried to keep her smile natural but her jaw was aching from the effort. Jake seemed to take it all in his stride, however.

One customer came over with a napkin and a pen. 'Can I have your autograph, Jake?'

Jake slashed his signature across the napkin and handed back the pen with an easy smile. 'There you go.'

'Is it true you and Miss Connolly are engaged?' the customer asked.

Jaz held up her ring hand. 'Yes. We just picked up the ring.'

More cameras went off and the Twitter whistle sounded so often it was as if a flock of small birds had been let loose in the café.

'Nice work,' Jake said when the fuss had finally died down a little.

'You were the one who suggested a coffee,' Jaz said, shooting him a look from beneath her lashes.

'I heard your stomach rumbling at the jeweller's. Don't you make time for lunch?'

She stirred her latte with a teaspoon rather than lose herself in his sapphire-blue gaze. 'I've got a lot on just now.'

He reached across the table and took her left hand in his, running his fingertip over the crest of the mosaic ring. 'You can keep it after this is over.'

Jaz brought her gaze back to his. 'You don't want to recycle it for when you eventually settle down?'

He released her hand and sat back as he gave a light laugh. 'Can you see me doing the school run?'

'You don't ever want kids?'

'Nope,' he said, reaching for the sugar and tipping two teaspoons in. 'I don't want the responsibility. If I'm going to screw anyone's life up, it'll be my own. *That* I can live with.'

'Why do you think you'd screw up your children's lives?' Jaz said.

He stirred his coffee before he answered. 'I'm too much like my father.'

'I don't think you're anything like your father,' she said. 'Maybe in looks but not in temperament. Your father is weak. Sorry if I'm speaking out of turn but he is. The way he handled his affair with Kat Winwood's mother is proof of it. I can't see you paying someone to have an abortion if you got a girl pregnant.'

He shifted his lips from side to side. 'I wouldn't offer to marry her, though.'

'Maybe not, but you'd support her and your child,' Jaz said. 'And you'd be involved in your child's life.'

He gave her one of his slow smiles that did so much damage to her resolve to keep him at a distance. 'I didn't realise you had such a high opinion of me.'

She pursed her lips. 'Don't get too excited. I still think you'd make a terrible husband.'

'In general or for you?'

Jaz looked at him for a beat or two of silence. She had a sudden vision of him at the end of the aisle waiting for her with that twinkling smile on his handsome face. Of his tall and toned body dressed in a sharply tailored suit instead of the casual clothes he preferred. Of his dark-blue eyes focused on her, as if she were the only woman he ever wanted to gaze at, with complete love and adoration.

She blinked and refocused. 'Good Lord, not for me,' she said with a laugh. 'We'd be at each other's throats before we left the church.'

Something moved at the back of his gaze as it held hers, a flicker like a faulty light bulb. But then he picked up his coffee cup and drained it before putting it down on the table with a decisive clunk. 'Ready?'

Jake walked Jaz back to the boutique holding her hand for the sake of appearances. Or so he told himself. The truth was he loved the feel of her small, neat hand encased in his. He couldn't stop himself from thinking about those soft, clever little fingers on other parts of his body. Stroking him, teasing him with her touch. Why shouldn't he make the most of their situation? He had a business deal to secure and being engaged to Jasmine Connolly was going to win him some serious brownie points with his conservative client Bruce Parnell. It wasn't as if it was for ever. A week or two and it would be over. Life would go back to normal.

'I have a work function on Wednesday night,' he said when Jaz had unlocked the door of the boutique. 'Dinner with a client. Would you like to come?'

She looked at him with a slight frown. 'Why?'

He tugged a tendril of her hair in a teasing manner. 'Because we're madly in love and we can't bear to be apart for a second.'

Her frown deepened and a flash of irritation arced in her gaze. 'What's the dress code?'

'Lounge suit and cocktail.'

'I'll have to check my calendar.'

Jake put his hand beneath her chin and tipped up her face so her eyes couldn't escape his. 'I'm giving you the weekend for the wedding expo. The least you could do is give me one week night.'

Her cheeks swarmed with sheepish colour. 'How did you know it was a wedding expo?'

He gave her a teasing grin. 'I knew there had to be a catch. Why else would you want me for a whole weekend?'

Her mouth took on that disapproving schoolmarm, pursed look that made him want to kiss it back into pliable softness. 'I don't want *you*, Jake. You'll only be there for show.'

He bent down and pressed a brief kiss to her mouth. 'I'll pick you up from here at seven.'

Jaz was still doing her hair when the doorbell sounded on Wednesday evening. She had run late with a client who had taken hours to choose a design for a gown. She gave her hair one last blast with the dryer and shook her head to let the waves fall loosely about her shoulders. She smoothed her hands down her hips, turning to one side to check her appearance in the full-length mirror. The black cocktail dress had double shoestring straps that criss-crossed over her shoulders, the silky fabric skimming her figure in all the right places. She was wearing her highest heels because she hadn't been able to wear them when going out with Myles, as he was only an inch taller than her. A quick spray of perfume and a smear of lip-gloss and she was ready.

Why she was going to so much trouble for Jake was not something she wanted to examine too closely. But when she opened the door and she saw the way his eyes ran over her appreciatively she was pleased she had chosen to go with the wow factor.

But then, so had he. He was dressed in a beautifully tailored suit that made his shoulders seem all the broader and, while he wasn't wearing a tie, the white open-necked shirt combined with the dark blue of his suit intensified the navy-blue of his eyes.

Jaz opened the door a little wider. 'I'll just get my wrap.'

Jake stepped into her flat and closed the door. She turned to face him as she draped her wrap over her shoulders, a little shiver coursing over her flesh as she saw the way his gaze went to her mouth as if pulled there by a powerful magnet.

The air quickened the way it always did when they were alone.

'Is something wrong?' she said.

He closed the small distance between their bodies so that they were almost touching. 'I have something for you,' he said, reaching into the inside pocket of his jacket.

Jaz swallowed as he took out a narrow velvet jewellery case the same colour as his eyes. She took it from him and opened it with fingers that were suddenly as useless as a glove without a hand. Jake took it from her and deftly opened it to reveal a stunning diamond pendant on a white-gold chain that was as fine as a gossamer thread.

Jaz glanced up at him but his face was unreadable. She looked back at the diamond. She had jewellery. Lots of it. Most of it she had bought herself because jewellery was so personal, a bit like perfume and make-up. She hadn't had a partner yet who had ever got her taste in jewellery right. But this was... perfect. She would have chosen it herself if she could have afforded it. She knew it was expensive. Hideously so. Why had Jake spent so much money on her when he didn't even like her? 'I'll give it back once we're done,' she said. 'And the ring.'

'I chose it specifically for you,' he said, taking it out of the box. 'Turn around. Move your hair out of the way.'

Jaz did as he commanded and tried not to shudder in pleasure as his long strong fingers moved against the sensitive skin on the back of her neck as he secured the pendant in place. She could feel the tall, hard frame of his body against her shoulder blades, his strongly muscled thighs against her trembling ones. She knew if she leaned back even half an inch she could come into contact with the hot, hard heat of him. She felt his hands come down on the tops of her shoulders, his fingers giving her a light squeeze as he turned her to face him. She looked into the midnight blue of his inscrutable gaze and wondered if her teenage crush was dead and buried after all. It felt like it was coming to life under the warm press of his hands on her body.

He trailed a lazy fingertip from beneath her ear to her mouth, circling it without touching it. But it felt like he had. Her lips buzzed, fizzed and ached for the pressure of his. 'You look beautiful.'

'Amazing what a flashy bit of jewellery can do.'

He frowned as if her flippant comment annoyed him. 'You don't suit flashy jewellery and I wouldn't insult you by insisting on you wearing it.'

'All the same, I don't expect you to spend so much money on me. I don't feel comfortable about it, given our relationship.'

His eyes went to her mouth for a moment before meshing with hers. 'Why do you hate me so much?'

Jaz couldn't hold his gaze and looked at the open neck of his shirt instead. But that just made it worse because she could see the long, strong, tanned column of his throat and smell the light but intoxicating lemony scent of his aftershave. She didn't know if it was the diamond olive branch he had offered her, his physical closeness or both that made her decide to tell him the truth about that night. Or maybe it was because she was tired of the negative emotion weighing her down. 'That night after I left your room... I... Something happened...'

Jaz felt rather than saw his frown. She was still looking at his neck but she noticed the way he had swallowed thickly. 'What?' he said.

'I accepted a drink off one of the guests. I'm not sure who it was. One of the casual seasonal theatre staff, I think. I hadn't seen him before or since. I was upset after leaving you. I didn't care if I got drunk. But then... I, well, you've probably heard it dozens of times before. Girls who get drunk and then end up regretting what happened next.'

'What happened next?' Jake's voice sounded raw,

as if something had been scraped across his vocal chords.

Jaz still couldn't meet his gaze. She couldn't bear to see his judgement, his criticism of her reckless behaviour. 'I had a non-consensual encounter. Or at least I think it was non-consensual.'

'You were...*raped*?'

She looked at him then. 'No, but it was close to it. Somehow I managed to fight him off, but I was too ashamed to tell anyone what happened. I didn't even tell Miranda. I haven't told anyone before now.'

Jake's expression was full of outrage, shock and horror. 'The man should've been charged. Do you think you'd recognise him if you saw him again? We could arrange a police line-up. We could check the guest list of that night. Track down everyone who attended...'

Jaz pulled out from under his hold and crossed her arms over her body. 'No. I don't want to even think about that night. I don't even know if I gave the guy the okay to mess around. I was the one who started flirting with him in the first place. But then things got a little hazy. It would be his word against mine and you know what the defence lawyers would make of that. I was too drunk to know what I was doing.'

'But he might've spiked your drink or something,' Jake said. 'He committed a crime. A crime for which he should be punished.'

'That only happens in the movies,' Jaz said. 'I've moved on. It would make things so much harder for me if I had to revisit that night in a courtroom.'

His frown made a road map of lines on his forehead. 'I can see why you hate me so much. I'm as guilty as that lowlife.'

'No,' she said. 'That's not true.'

'Isn't it?'

Jaz bit her lip. 'I know it looks like I've blamed you all this time but that's just the projection of negative emotion. I guess I used you as a punching bag because I felt so ashamed.'

Jake came over to her and took her hands from where they were wrapped around her body, holding them gently in his. 'You have no need to be ashamed, Jaz. You were just a kid. I was the adult and I acted appallingly. I shouldn't have given you any encouragement. Leading you on like that only to throw those girls in your face was wrong. I should've been straight with you right from the get-go.'

Jaz gave him a wobbly smile. 'You just called me Jaz. You haven't done that in years.'

His hands gave hers a gentle squeeze. 'We'd better get a move on. My client isn't the most patient of men. That is if you're still okay with going? I can always tell him you had something on and go by myself.'

'I'm fine,' she said. And she was surprised to find it was true. Having Jake of all people being so understanding, caring and protective made something hard and tight inside her chest loosen like a knotted rope suddenly being released.

He gently grazed her cheek with the backs of his knuckles. 'Thank you for telling me.'

'I'd rather you didn't tell anyone else,' Jaz said. 'I don't want people to look at me differently.'

'Not even Miranda?'

She pulled at her lip with her teeth. 'Miranda would be hurt if I told her now. She'd blame herself for not watching out for me. You know what a little mother hen she is.'

Jake's frown was back. 'But surely—?'

'No,' Jaz said, sending him a determined look. 'Don't make me regret telling you. Promise me you won't betray my trust.'

He let out a frustrated sigh. 'I promise. But I swear to God, if I find out who hurt you I'll tear him apart with my bare hands.'

CHAPTER SEVEN

LATER, IN THE car going back to Jaz's place, Jake wondered how on earth he'd swung the deal with his client. His mind hadn't been on the game the whole way through dinner. All he'd been able to think about was what Jaz had told him about that wretched night after she had left his room. He was so churned up with a toxic cocktail of anger, guilt and an unnerving desire for revenge that he'd given his client, Bruce Parnell, the impression he was a distracted, lovesick fool rather than a savvy businessman. But that didn't seem to matter because at the end of the dinner his client had signed on the dotted line and wished Jake and Jaz all the best for their future.

Their future.

What *was* their future?

Jake was so used to bickering with her that he wasn't sure how he was going to navigate being friends with her instead. While it had been pistols and pissy looks at dawn, he'd been able to keep his distance. But now she'd shared her painful secret with him he couldn't carry on as if nothing had changed.

Everything had changed. The whole dynamic of their relationship was different. He wanted to protect her. To fix it for her. To give her back her innocence so she didn't have to carry around the shame she felt. A shame she had no need to feel because the jerk who had assaulted her was the one who should be ashamed.

But Jake too felt shame. Deep, gut-clawing shame. Shame that he hadn't handled her infatuation with him more sensitively. His actions had propelled her into danger—danger that could have been avoided if he had been a little more understanding. He could see now why Jaz had stepped in with the engagement charade when Emma Madden had turned up at the door. She had been sensitive to the girl's need for dignity, offering her a safe way home with someone at the other end to make sure she was all right.

What had *he* done? He had sent Jaz from his room in an acute state of public humiliation only to fall into the hands of some creep who'd plied her with drink and drugs and God knew what else. Had that been her first experience of sex—being groped and manhandled by a drunken idiot? He couldn't remember if she'd had a boyfriend back then. Miranda had been going out with Mark Redbank from a young age but Jaz had never seemed all that interested in boys. Not until she'd developed that crush on him.

He couldn't bear the thought of her being touched in such a despicable way. Was that why she only ever dated men she could control? None of her ex-fiancés were what one would even loosely consider as alpha men. Was that deliberate or unconscious on her part?

Jake glanced at her sitting quietly in the passenger seat beside him. She was looking out at the rain-lashed street, her hands absently fiddling with the clasp on her evening bag. 'You okay?' he said.

She turned her head to look at him, a vacant smile on her face. 'Sorry. I think I used up all my scintillating conversation at dinner.'

'You did a great job,' Jake said. 'Bruce Parnell was quite taken with you. He was being cagey about signing up with me but you had him at hello.'

'Did you know he fell in love with his late wife the very first time they met? And they married three months later and never spent more than two nights apart for the whole of their marriage? He would fly back by private jet if he had to just to be with her.'

He glanced at her again between gear changes. 'He told you all that?'

'And he's still grieving her loss even though it's been ten years. It reminded me of Miranda after Mark died.'

'Luckily Leandro got her to change her mind,' Jake said. 'I was sure she was going to end up a spinster living with a hundred cats.'

Jaz gave a tinkling laugh. 'I was worried too, but they're perfect for each other. I've known it for ages. It was the way Leandro looked at her. He got this really soft look in his eyes.'

Jake grunted. 'Another one bites the dust.'

'What have you got against marriage? It doesn't always end badly. Look at Mr Parnell.'

'That sort of marriage is the exception,' Jake said.

'Look at my parents. They're heading for another show-stopping divorce as far as I can tell. It was bad enough the first time.'

'Clearly Julius doesn't hold the same view as you,' she said. 'And yet he went through the same experience of your parents' divorce.'

'It was different for Julius,' Jake said. 'He found solace in studying and working hard. I found it hard to adjust to boarding school. I pushed against the boundaries. Rubbed the teachers up the wrong way. Wasted their time and my own.'

'But you've done so well for yourself. Aren't you happy with your achievements?'

Was he happy? Up until a few days ago he had been perfectly happy. But now there was a niggling doubt chewing at the edge of his conscience. He moved around so much it was hard to know where was home. He had a base in London but most of the time he lived out of hotel rooms. He never cooked at home. He ate out. He didn't spend the night with anyone because he hated morning-after scenes. He didn't do reruns. One night was enough to scratch the itch. But how long could he keep on moving? The fast lane was a lonely place at times. Not that he was going to admit that to Jaz—or to anyone, when it came to that.

But this recent drama with Emma Madden had got him thinking. Everyone saw him as shallow and self-serving. He hadn't given a toss for anyone's opinion before now but now it sat uncomfortably on him like an ill-fitting jacket. What if people thought he was like the man who had groped Jaz? That he was taking advantage of young women who were a little star-struck. It had never concerned him before. He had always enjoyed exploiting his parents' fame. He had used it to open doors in business and in pleasure. But how long could he go on doing it? He was turning into a cliché. The busty blondes he attracted only wanted him because he was good looking and had famous parents. They didn't know him as a person.

Jake pulled up outside Jaz's flat above her boutique. 'How long have you been living above the shop?' he asked as he walked her to the door.

She gave him a wary look. 'Is this another "how to run your business" lecture?'

'It's a nice place but pretty small. And the whole living and working in the same place can be a drag after a while.'

'Yes, well, I was planning to move in with Myles but he put the brakes on that,' she said, scowling. 'His parents don't like me. They think I'm too pushy and controlling. I think that's the main reason he wanted a break.'

What's not to like? What parents wouldn't be proud to have her as their daughter-in-law? She was smart and funny, and sweet when she let her guard down. His parents were delighted with their 'engagement'. He hadn't figured out yet how he was going to tell them when it was over. They would probably never speak to him again. 'Do you really want to take Myles back?'

Her chin came up. 'Of course.'

'What if he doesn't want to come back?'

She averted her gaze. 'I deal with that *if* it happens.'

Jake looked at her for a long beat. 'You're not in love with him.'

Her eyes flashed back to his. 'And you know this how?'

'Because you're more concerned about what other people think of you than what he does. That's what this thing between us is all about. You're trying to save face, not your relationship.'

She flattened her lips so much they disappeared inside her mouth. 'I know what I'm doing. I know Myles better than anyone.'

'If you know him so well why haven't you told him about that night?'

She flinched as if he had struck her. But then she pulled herself upright as if her spinal column were filling with concrete. 'Thank you for dinner,' she said. 'Good night.'

'Jaz, wait—'

But the only response he got was the door being slammed in his face.

Jaz was at the boutique the next morning when Miranda came in carrying coffee and muffins. 'I thought I'd drop in to start the ball rolling on my wed—' Miranda said, but stopped short when her gaze went to Jaz's ring hand. 'Oh, my God. Did Jake buy that for you?'

'Yes, but it's just for show.'

Miranda snatched up Jaz's hand and turned it every which way to see how the light danced off the diamonds. 'Wow. I didn't realise he had such good taste in rings *and* in women.'

Jaz gave her a speaking look. 'You do realise none of this is for real?'

Miranda's eyes twinkled. 'So you both say, but I was just at Jake's office and he's like a bear with a sore paw. Did you guys have a tiff?'

'That's nothing out of the normal,' Jaz said, taking her coffee out of the cardboard holder.

Miranda cocked her head like an inquisitive bird. 'What's wrong?'

'Nothing. We just argued…about stuff.'

'All couples argue,' Miranda said. 'It's normal and healthy.'

'We're *not* a couple,' Jaz said. 'We're an act.'

Miranda frowned. 'You're not seriously still thinking of going back to Myles?'

Jaz pushed back from her work table. 'That's the plan.'

'It's a dumb plan,' Miranda said. 'A stupid plan that's totally wrong for you and for Myles. Can't you see that? You're not in love with him. You're in love with Jake.'

Jaz laughed. 'No, I'm not. I'm not that much of a fool.'

'I think he's in love with you.'

Jaz frowned. 'What makes you think that?'

'He bought you that ring for one thing,' Miranda said. 'Look at it. It's the most beautiful ring I've ever seen—apart from my own, of course.'

'It's just a prop.'

'A jolly expensive one.' Miranda leaned over the counter and lifted the scarf Jaz had tied around her neck. 'Aha! I knew it. More diamonds. That brother of mine has got it *so* bad.'

'It's a goodwill gesture,' Jaz said. 'I helped him nail an important business deal last night.'

Miranda stood back with a grin. 'Has he sent you flowers?'

Just then the bell at the back of the door pinged and in came a deliveryman with an armful of long-stemmed snow-white roses tied with a black satin ribbon. 'Delivery for Miss Jasmine Connolly.'

'I'll take that as a yes,' Miranda said once the deliveryman had left.

'They might be from Myles,' Jaz said. Not that Myles had ever bought flowers in the past. He thought they were a waste of money—ironic, given he had more money than most people ever dreamed of having.

'Read the card.'

Jaz gave her a brooding look as she unpinned the velum envelope from the arrangement. She took out the card and read the message: *I'm sorry. Jake.*

'They're from Jake, aren't they?' Miranda said.

'Yes, but—'

Miranda snatched the card out of Jaz's hand. 'Oh, how sweet! He's saying sorry. Gosh, only a man in love does that.'

'Or a man in the wrong.'

Miranda's smooth brow furrowed in a frown. 'What did he do?'

Jaz shifted her lips from side to side. Why was everything suddenly so darn complicated? 'Haven't you got heaps of dusty old paintings to restore?' she said.

Miranda chewed at her lower lip. 'Is it about that night? I know that's always been a sore point between you two. Is that what he was apologising for?'

Jaz let out a long breath. 'In a way.'

'But he didn't do anything. He didn't sleep with you. He's always flatly denied it. He would never have done anything like that. He thought you were just a kid.' Miranda swallowed. 'He didn't sleep with you… did he?'

'No, but someone else tried to,' Jaz said.

Miranda's eyes went wide in horror. 'What do you mean?'

'I stupidly flirted with this guy at the party after I left Jake's room,' Jaz explained. 'I only did it as a payback to Jake. I don't know how it happened but I suddenly found myself fighting off this drunken guy in one of the downstairs bathrooms. I thought he was going to rape me. I was so shocked and frightened but somehow I managed to get away.'

Miranda's hands were clasped against her mouth in shock. 'Oh, my God! That's awful! Why didn't you tell me?'

'I wanted to tell you,' Jaz said. 'Many times. But I just couldn't bring myself to do it. You were dealing with Mark's cancer and I didn't want to add to your misery. I felt so ashamed and dirty.'

'Oh, you poor darling,' Miranda said, flinging her arms around Jaz and hugging her. 'I wish I'd known so I could have done something to help you. I feel like I've let you down.'

'You didn't,' Jaz said. 'You've always been there for me.'

Miranda pulled back to look at her. 'So that's why you only ever dated vanilla men, isn't it?'

She scrunched up her nose. 'What do you mean?'

'You know exactly what I mean,' Miranda said. 'Bland men. Men you can control. You've never gone for the alpha type.'

Jaz gave a little lip shrug. 'Maybe…'

Miranda was still looking at her thoughtfully. 'So Jake was the first person you've ever told?'

Jaz nodded. 'Weird, huh?'

'Not so weird,' Miranda said. 'You respect him. You always have. That's why he annoys you so much. He sees the you no one else sees.'

Jaz fingered the velvet-soft petals of the roses once Miranda had left. Why had Jake sent her white roses? They were a symbol of purity, virtue and innocence. Was that how he saw her?

Miranda was full of romantic notions because she was madly in love herself. Of course she would like to think her brother was in love with her best friend. But Jake wasn't the type to fall in love. He was too much of a free agent.

Not that Jaz had any right to be thinking along those lines. She was on a mission to win back Myles. Myles was the man she planned to settle down with. Not a man like Jake who would pull against the re-

straints of commitment like a wild stallion on a leading rein.

Myles was safe and predictable.

Jake was danger personified.

But that didn't mean she couldn't flirt with danger
just a wee bit longer.

Jake had never been so fed up with work. He couldn't
get his mind to focus on the spreadsheets he was supposed to be analysing. All he wanted to do was go to
Jaz's boutique and see if she was still speaking to him.
She hadn't called or texted since they had parted last
night. The absence of communication would have delighted him a week ago. Now it was like a dragging
ache inside his chest. She was a stubborn little thing.
She would get on her high horse and not come down
even if it collapsed beneath her. That was why she was
still hung up on Myles. She wasn't in love with her
ex. It was her pride that had taken a hit. She hadn't
even told the guy the most devastating thing that had
happened to her.

Jake couldn't think about that night without feeling sick. He blamed himself. He had brought that on
her by being so insensitive. Why hadn't he gone and
checked on her later? He could at least have made an
effort to see she was okay. But no, he had partied on
as if nothing was wrong, leaving her open to exploita-
tion at the hands of some lowlife creep who had tried
to take advantage of her in the worst way imaginable.

Jake's phone buzzed with an incoming message.
He picked it up to read it:

Thanks for the roses. Jaz.

He smiled and texted back:

Free for dinner tonight?

Her message came back:

Busy.

He frowned, his gut tensing when he thought of whom she might be busy with. Was it Myles? Was she meeting her ex to try and convince him to come back to her? He waited a minute or two before texting back:

We still on for the w/end?

She texted back.

If u r free?

Jake grimaced as he thought of wandering around a wedding expo all weekend but he figured a man had to do what a man had to do.

He texted back.

I'm all yours.

CHAPTER EIGHT

JAZ WAS READY and waiting for Jake to come to her flat on Friday after work to pick her up. They had only communicated via text messages since yesterday. He had called a couple of times but she hadn't answered or returned the calls. Not that he had left a voice mail message. She hadn't realised how much she had been looking forward to hearing his voice until she checked her voice mail and found it annoyingly silent. Myles, on the other hand, had left several messages asking to meet with her to talk. They were each a variation on his earlier call where he'd told her Jake would never stick around long enough to cast a shadow.

The funny thing was Jake had cast a very long shadow. It was cast all over her life. She could barely recall a time when he hadn't been in it. Ever since she was eight years old she had been a part of his life and he of hers. Even once their charade was over he would still be a part of her life. There would be no avoiding him, not with Julius and Holly's wedding coming up, not to mention Miranda and Leandro's a few months after. Jaz was going to be a bridesmaid at both. There would be other family gatherings to navigate: Christmas, Easter and birthdays. His mother Elisabetta was turning sixty next month in late November and there was no way either Jake or Jaz could ever do a no-show without causing hurt and the sort of drama everyone could do without.

The doorbell sounded and her heart gave a little flutter. Jake was fifteen minutes early. Did that mean he was looking forward to the weekend? Looking forward to being with her? She opened the door to find Myles standing there with a sheepish look on his face. 'Myles...' Jaz faltered. 'Erm... I'm kind of busy right now.'

'I have to talk to you,' he said. 'It's important you hear it from me before you hear it from someone else.'

'Hear what?'

'I'm seeing someone else. It's...serious.'

Jaz blinked. 'How serious?'

'I know it seems sudden but I've known her for ages. We were childhood friends. Do you remember me telling you about Sally Coombes?'

'Yes, but—'

'I wasn't unfaithful to you, if that's what you're thinking,' Myles said. 'Not while we were officially together.'

Jaz hadn't been thinking it, which was kind of weird, as she knew she probably should have been. All she could think was that she had to get rid of Myles before Jake got here, as she didn't want Jake to end their 'engagement' before she attended the wedding expo. She couldn't bear to go to it alone.

Everyone would be taking photos and posting messages about her being so unlucky in love. Not a good look for a wedding designer. What would that do to her credibility? To her pride? People would find out eventually. She couldn't hope to keep Jake acting as her fiancé indefinitely. But one weekend—maybe another couple of weeks—was surely not too much to ask? 'But you've been calling and leaving all those messages,' she said. 'Why didn't you say something then?'

'I wanted to tell you in person,' Myles said. 'I'm sorry if I've hurt you, Jaz. But I've had my doubts about us for a while now. I guess that's why I instigated the break. It was only when I caught up with Sally I realised why I was baulking. As soon as we started talking, I realised she was the one. We dated when we were younger. She was my first girlfriend and I was her first boyfriend. It's like it's meant to be. I hope you can understand and find it in yourself to forgive me for messing you around.'

'I don't know what to say...' Jaz said. 'Congratulations?'

Myles looked a little pained. 'I want you to be happy. I really do. You're a great girl. I care about you. That's why I'm so concerned about your involvement with Jake Ravensdale. I don't want him to break your heart.'

Jaz stretched her lips into a rictus smile. 'I'm a big girl. I can handle Jake.'

Myles looked doubtful. 'Sally and I aren't making a formal announcement for a week or two. We thought it would be more appropriate to wait for a bit. I just wanted you to be one of the first to know.'

'Thanks for dropping by,' Jaz said. 'I appreciate it. Now, I'm sure you have heaps to do. I won't keep you. Say hi to Sally for me. Tell her if she wants a good deal on a wedding dress I'm the person she needs to see.'

'No hard feelings?' Myles said.

'No hard feelings,' Jaz said, and was surprised and more than a little shocked to find it was true.

Myles had not long disappeared around the corner when Jake's sports car prowled to the kerb. Jaz watched as he unfolded himself from behind the wheel with athletic grace. He was wearing dark-blue jeans and a round-neck white T-shirt with a charcoal-grey cashmere sweater over the top. His hair was still damp from a recent shower as she could see the deep grooves where either his fingers or a wide-toothed comb had been. His jaw was freshly shaven and as he came up to where she was standing on the doorstep she could smell the clean, sharp citrus tang of his aftershave.

Funny, but she hadn't even noticed what Myles had been wearing, the scent of his aftershave or even if he had been wearing any.

'Am I late?' Jake asked with the hint of a frown between his brows.

'No,' Jaz said. 'Perfect timing.'

He leaned down to press a light-as-air kiss to her mouth. 'That's for the neighbours.' Then he put his arms around her and pulled her close. 'And this one's for me.'

Jaz closed her eyes as his lips met hers in a drugging kiss that made her toes curl in her shoes. His tongue mated with hers in a sexy tangle that mimicked the driving need rushing through her body, and his, if the hard ridge of his erection was any indication.

Her hands went around his waist and her pelvis jammed against the temptation of his, her heart skipping all over the place as he made a deep, growly sound of male pleasure as she gave herself up to the kiss. His hands pressed against her bottom to pull her closer, his touch so intimate, so possessive, she could feel her body preparing itself for him. The ache of need pulsed between her legs, her thighs tingling with nerves activated by the anticipation of pleasure.

Only the fact they were on a busy public street was enough to break the spell as a car went past tooting its horn.

Jake released her with a teasing smile. 'Nice to know you've missed me.'

Jaz gave a dismissive shrug. 'You're a good kisser. But then, you've had plenty of practice.'

'Ah, but there are kisses and there are kisses. And yours, baby girl, are right up there.'

Don't fall for his charm. Don't fall for him, she thought as she followed him to the car.

The drive to Gloucester took just over two hours but the time passed easily with Jake's superb driving and easy conversation. He told her about Bruce Parnell, who was so impressed with Jake's choice of fiancée he had recommended several other big-name clients. 'It's the sort of windfall I'd been hanging out for,' he said. 'Word travels fast in the corporate sector.'

'What are you going to say to him when we're no longer a couple?'

He didn't answer for a moment and when he flashed her a quick smile she noticed it didn't quite make the distance to his eyes. 'I'll think of something.'

It was only as Jaz entered the hotel where the wedding expo was being held that she remembered she had only booked one room. It would look suspicious if she asked for another room or even a twin. She and Jake were supposed to be engaged. Everyone would automatically assume they would share a suite. People had already taken out their camera phones and taken snapshots as they came in. She would look a fool if she asked for separate rooms. What woman in her right mind would pass on the chance to spend the night with Jake Ravensdale? Herself included.

Hadn't she always wanted him? It had been there ever since she'd been old enough to understand sexual attraction. It had gone from a teenage crush to a full-blown adult attraction. It simmered in the air when they were together. How long could she ignore it or pretend it wasn't there? Hadn't she already betrayed herself by responding so enthusiastically to his kiss? Had her overlooking of the hotel reservation been her subconscious telling her what she didn't want to face?

As if Jake sensed her dilemma he leaned down close to her ear and whispered, 'I'll sleep on the sofa.'

Jaz was so distracted by the sensation of his warm breath tickling the sensitive skin around her ear she didn't hear the attendant call her to the counter. Jake put a gentle hand at her back and pressed her forward. She painted a smile on her face and said, 'I have a booking for Connolly.'

'Welcome, Miss Connolly,' the attendant said. 'We have your king deluxe suite all ready for you.'

King deluxe. At least there would be enough room in the bed to put a bank of pillows up as a barricade, Jaz thought as she took the swipe key.

The hotel was going to town on the wedding theme. The suite, on the thirteenth floor, was decked out like a honeymoon suite. French champagne was sitting chilled and frosted in a silver ice bucket with a white satin ribbon tied in a big bow around it. There were two crystal champagne flutes and a cheese-and-fruit plate with chocolate-dipped strawberries on the table. The bed was covered in fresh rose petals and there were heart-shaped chocolates placed on the pillows.

'Hmm,' Jake said, rubbing thoughtfully at his chin. 'No sofa.'

Something in Jaz's belly slipped like a Bentley on black ice. There were two gorgeous wing chairs in the bay window, and a plush velvet-covered love seat, but no sofa. 'Right; well, then, we'll have to use pillows,' she said.

'Pillows?'

'As a barricade.'

He gave a soft laugh. 'Your virtue is safe, sweetheart. I won't touch you.'

Jaz rolled her lips together. Shifted her weight from foot to foot. Knotted her hands in front of her body where they were clutching her tote bag straps. Of course she didn't want to sleep with him. He was her enemy. She didn't even like him… Well, maybe a little. More like a lot. Why the heck didn't he want to sleep with her? She hadn't cracked any mirrors lately. She might not be his usual type but she was female and breathing, wasn't she? Why was he being so fussy all of a sudden? He'd kissed her and she'd felt his reaction to her. He wanted her. She knew it as surely as she knew he was standing there. 'What?' she said. 'You don't find me attractive?'

He frowned. 'Listen, a kiss or two or three is fine, but doing the deed? Not going to happen. Not us.'

'Why not us?'

'You're not my type.'

Jaz bristled. 'I was your type when you kissed me outside my flat. Half of flipping Mayfair was witness to it.'

His frown carved a little deeper. 'You're not serious about taking this to that extreme, are you? This is supposed to be an act. When actors do a love scene they don't actually have sex, you know.'

She moved to the other side of the room to stand in front of the window, folding her arms across her body. 'Fine. I get the message. I'd better tape up all the mirrors. The last thing I need is another seven years of bad luck.'

Jake came up behind her, placed his hands on the tops of her shoulders and gently turned her to face him. He searched her face for endless seconds. 'What about Myles?'

Jaz pressed her lips together and lowered her gaze. 'He's engaged to someone else.'

'God, that was quick.'

'He's known her since childhood. I'm happy for him. I really am. It's just I can't bear the thought of everyone knowing I've been dumped,' she said. 'Especially this weekend.'

His fingers massaged her shoulders. 'What's so important about this weekend?'

Jaz rolled her eyes. 'Duh! Look around you, Jake. This is a winter wedding expo. One of my designs is in the fashion parade tomorrow. Next year I want ten. This is my chance to expand my business. To network and get my name out there.'

'But your personal life should have nothing to do with your talent as a designer.'

'Yes, but you told me on the way down how Mr Parnell looks at you differently now you're—' she put her fingers up in air-quotation marks '—"engaged". It's the same for me. I design wedding gowns for everyone else but I'm totally rubbish at relationships. What sort of advertising for my brand is that?'

He drew in a breath and dropped his hands from her shoulders, using one hand to push through his hair. 'So...what do you want me to do?'

'Just play along a little longer,' she said. 'I know it's probably killing you but please can you do this one thing for me? Just pretend to be my fiancé until... well, a few more days.'

His brow was furrowed as deep as a trench. 'How many days?'

Jaz blew out an exasperated breath. 'Is it such torture to be tied to me for a week or two? *Is* it? Am I so hideous you can't bear the thought of people thinking you've sunk so low as to do it with—?'

Jake's hands came back to hold her by the upper arms. 'Stop it. Stop berating yourself like that.'

She looked into his midnight-blue gaze, trying to control her spiralling emotions that were like a twisted knot inside her stomach. 'Do you know what it's like to be the one no one wants?' she said. 'No, of course you don't, because everyone wants you. Even my mother didn't want me. She made that perfectly clear by dumping me on my dad. Not that he wanted me either.'

'Your dad loves you,' Jake said.

Jaz gave him a jaded look. 'Then why did he let me move into the big house instead of staying with him at the gardener's cottage? He was relieved when your parents offered to take me in and pay for my education. He didn't know what to do with an eight-year-old kid. I was an inconvenience he couldn't wait to pass off.'

Jake's expression was clenched so tightly in a frown his eyebrows met over his eyes. 'Did he actually say that to you?'

'He didn't need to,' she said on an expelled breath. 'I'm the one no one wants. It should be tattooed across my forehead—*Unwanted.*'

Jake's hands tightened on her arms. 'That's not true. I want you. I've wanted you for years.'

Jaz moistened her tombstone-dry lips. 'You do? You're not just saying that to make me feel better?'

He brought her close against his body. 'Do you think I could fake that?'

She felt the thickened ridge of him swelling against her body. 'Oh…'

'I've always kept my distance because I don't want the same things you want,' he said. 'I'm not interested in marriage—it's not my gig at all. But a fling is something else. I don't even do those normally. My longest relationship was four days when I was nineteen.'

She pulled at her lower lip with her teeth. 'So you'd agree to a fling with me? Just for a week or two?'

He brushed his thumb over her savaged lip. 'As long as you're absolutely clear on the terms. I'm not going to be that guy waiting at the altar of a church aisle for the bride to show up. I'm the guy working his way through the bridesmaids.'

'I happen to be one of the bridesmaids,' Jaz said. 'At two weddings.'

He gave her a sinful smile as his mouth came down to hers. 'Perfect.'

It was a smouldering kiss with an erotic promise that made Jaz's body quake and shudder with want. Every time his tongue touched hers a dart of lust speared her between the legs. Her body wanted him with a desperation she had never felt with such intensity before. It moved through her flesh in tingling waves, making her aware of her erogenous zones as if it was the first time they had been activated. Her breasts were pressed up against his chest, her nipples already puckered from the friction of his hard body. Her hands fisted in his sweater, holding him in case he changed his mind and pulled back.

His mouth continued its passionate exploration of hers, his tongue making love with hers until she was making whimpering sounds of encouragement and delight.

His light stubble grazed her face as he changed position, his hands splaying through her hair as he held her in an achingly tender embrace. He lifted his mouth off hers, resting his forehead against hers. 'Let's not rush this,' he said.

'I thought you lived in the fast lane?' Jaz said, tracing his top lip with her fingertip.

His expression was gravely serious as he caught her hand and held it in the warmth of his against his chest. 'You deserve more than a quick tumble, Jaz. Way more.'

She looked into the sapphire density of his gaze and felt a fracture form in the carapace around her heart like a fissure running through a glacier. 'Are you worried about what happened in the past? Then don't be. I'm fine with sex. I've had it heaps of times.'

'But do you enjoy it?'

'Of course I do,' she said then added when he gave her a probing look, 'Well, mostly.'

He threaded his fingers through her hair like a parent finger-combing a child's hair. 'Are you sure you want to go through with this? It's fine if you've changed your mind. No man's ever died from having an erection, you know.'

Jaz couldn't help smiling. 'Perhaps not, but I think I might if you don't finish what you started.'

He brought his mouth back down to hers, giving her a lingering kiss that was hot, sexy, sweet and tender at the same time. His hands gently moved over her, skimming her breasts at first before coming back to explore them in exquisite detail. He peeled away her top but left her bra in place, allowing her time to get used to being naked with him. He kissed his way down the slope of her breast, drawing on her nipple through the lace of her bra, which added a whole new dimension of feeling. Then, when he had removed his sweater and shirt, he unhooked her bra and gently cradled her breasts in his hands.

Jaz wasn't generously endowed but the way he held her made her feel as if she could be on a high street billboard advertising lingerie. His thumbs brushed over each of her nipples and the sensitive area surrounding them. He lowered his mouth to her puckered flesh and subjected her to the most delicious assault on her senses. The nerves beneath her skin went into a frenzy of excitement, her blood thrumming with the escalation of her desire.

She ran her hands over his muscled chest, delighting in the lean, hard contours of his body. He hadn't followed the trend of being completely hairless. The masculine roughness of his light chest hair tickled her fingers and then her satin-smooth breasts as he drew her closer. It made her feel more feminine than she had ever felt before.

His hands settled on her hips, holding her against his erection, letting her get the feel of him; not rushing her, not pressuring her. Just holding her. But Jaz's body had urgent needs it wanted assuaged and she moved against him in a silent plea for satiation. She had rarely taken the initiative with a partner before. But with Jake she wanted to express her desire for him, to let him know her body ached to be joined to his.

Jaz went for the waistband of his jeans, unsnapping the metal stud and then sliding down his zip. He sucked in air but let her take control. She traced her fingertips over the tented fabric of his underwear, her belly doing a cartwheel when she thought of how potent he was, of how gorgeously turned on he was for her, yet controlling it to make her feel safe. She peeled back his underwear, stroking him skin to skin, flicking her gaze up to his to see how he was reacting to her touch. 'You like that?'

'This is getting a little one sided,' he said, pushing her hand away. 'Ladies come first according to my rules.'

'I think I like your rules,' Jaz said as he carried her to the bed as if she weighed no more than one of the feather pillows.

He placed her down amongst the scented rose petals and then, shucking off his jeans but leaving his underwear in place, he joined her. He helped her out of her trousers but left her knickers on. Not that they hid much from his view. Had that been another sub-conscious thing on her part, to wear her sexiest underwear?

He traced the seam of her body through the gossamer-sheer lace. 'Do you have any idea of how long I've wanted to do this?'

Jaz shivered as his touch triggered her most secret nerves into a leaping dance of expectation. 'Me too,' she said but it was more a gasp of sound as he brought his mouth to her and pressed a kiss to her abdomen just above the line of her knickers.

He slowly peeled the lace down to reveal her womanhood. For once she didn't feel that twinge of shame at being naked and exposed in front of a man. It was like he was worshiping her body, treating it with the utmost respect with every stroke and glide of his hands.

He put his mouth to her, separating her folds so he could pleasure the most sensitive part of all. She had never been entirely comfortable with being pleasured this way. Occasionally she had been tipsy enough to get through it. But this time she didn't need the buffer of alcohol. Nor did she need to pretend. The sensations took her by surprise, every nerve pulling tight before exploding in a cascade of sparks that rippled through her body in pulsating waves.

When it was over she let out a breath of pure bliss. 'Wow. I think that might've measured on the Richter scale.'

He stroked a hand down the flank of her thigh in a smooth-as-silk caress. 'Want to try for a ten?'

Jaz reached for him, surrounding his taut thickness with her fingers. 'I'd like to see you have some fun first, in the interests of being fair and all.'

He smiled a glinting smile. 'I can't argue with that.'

He reached across her to where he'd left his wallet when he'd removed his jeans and took out a condom, dealing with the business of applying it before he came back to her. He moved over her so she was settled in the cradle of his thighs, one of his legs hitched over her hip so she wasn't taking his whole weight. 'Not too heavy for you?' he said. 'Or would you like to go on top?'

Jaz welcomed the press of his body against hers, the sexy tangle of their limbs sending a frisson of anticipation through her female flesh. 'No, I like it like this. I don't like feeling like I'm riding a horse.'

He gave a deep chuckle. 'I wouldn't throw you off.'

No, but you'll cast me off when you're ready to move on. Jaz pushed the thought aside and ran her hands up his body from his pelvis to his chest and back again. This was for now. A fling she'd wanted since she was a teenager. This was her chance to have what she had always wanted from him: his sole attention, his searing touch, his mind-blowing caresses, and his gorgeously hot body. She knew and understood the rules. There were no promises being made. There was no hope of 'happy ever after'. It was a mutual lust fest to settle the ache of longing that had started so long ago and had never been sated. It was a way—she rationalised it—to rewrite that night seven years ago. This was what she had wanted from

Jake way back then—not to be pawed over by some drunk but to be treated with respect, to be pleasured as well as give it. This was the healing she needed to move on with her life, to reclaim her self-respect and her sexual confidence. 'I want you,' she said. 'I don't think I've ever wanted to have sex more than right now.'

He brushed a wayward strand of hair off her face, his dark gaze lustrous with desire. 'I'm pretty turned on myself.'

She stroked him again, watching as his breathing rate increased with every glide of her hand. 'So I can tell.'

He moved her hand so he could access her body, taking his time to caress her until she was swollen and wet. Her need for him was a consuming ache that intensified with every movement of his fingers. She writhed beneath him, restless to feel the ultimate fulfilment, wanting him to possess her so they both experienced the rapture of physical union.

Finally he entered her, but only a short distance, holding back, allowing her to get used to him. His tenderness made her feel strangely emotional. She couldn't imagine him being so tender with his other lovers. She knew it didn't necessarily mean he was falling in love with her. She wasn't that naïve. But it made her feel special all the same. Wasn't this how her teenaged self had imagined it would be? Jake being so tender and thoughtful as he made beautiful, magical love to her?

He thrust a little deeper, his low, deep groan of

pleasure making her skin come up in a spray of goose bumps. He began to move, setting a slow rhythm that sent her senses reeling with delight. Each movement of his body within hers caused a delicious friction that triggered all her nerve endings, making them tingle with feeling. She lifted her hips to meet each downward thrust, aching for the release that was just out of reach. Her body was searching for it, every muscle contracting, straining, swelling and quivering with the need to fly free.

He slipped his hand down between their rocking bodies, giving her that little bit of extra coaxing that sent her flying into blessed oblivion. Her body shook with the power of it as each ripple turned into an earthquake. It was like her body had split into thousands of tiny pieces, each one spinning off into the stratosphere. She lost all sense of thought. Her mind had switched off and allowed her body free rein.

He didn't take his own pleasure until hers was over. She held him to her as his whole body tensed before he finally let go, but he did so without any increase in pace, without sound. Had he done that for her sake? Held back? Restrained his response so she hadn't felt overwhelmed or threatened? He hadn't rushed to the end. He hadn't breathed heavily or gripped her too hard, as if he had forgotten she was there.

He didn't roll away but continued to hold her as if he was reluctant to break the intimate union of their bodies.

Or was she deluding herself?

Had he been disappointed? Had she not measured

up to his other lovers? She was hardly in the same league. She might have had multiple partners but still nowhere near the number he'd had. Compared to him, she was practically a novice.

One of his hands glided up and down the length of her forearm in a soft caress that made her skin tingle as if champagne bubbles were moving through her blood. 'You were amazing,' he said.

Jaz couldn't ignore the doubts that were winding their way through her mind like a rampant vine. Hadn't she been exciting enough for him? Hadn't her body delighted his the way his had delighted hers? Was that why his response had been so toned down? Maybe he hadn't toned it down. Maybe she hadn't quite 'done it' for him. The chemistry he had talked about hadn't delivered on its promise.

It was *her* fault. Of course it was. Wasn't that why she had been engaged three times and summarily dumped?

She was rubbish at sex.

Jaz eased out of his embrace, reached for one of the hotel bathrobes and slipped it on, tying the waist ties securely. 'You don't have to lie to me, Jake,' she said. 'I know I'm not crash-hot in bed. There's no point pretending I am.'

He frowned as if she was speaking Swahili instead of English. 'Why on earth do you think that?'

She folded her arms, shooting him a flinty look. 'It's probably my fault for talking you into it. If you didn't want to do it then you should've said.'

He swung his legs over the edge of the bed and

came over to stand in front of her. He was still completely naked while Jaz was wrapped as tightly as an Egyptian mummy. He put one of his hands on her shoulder and used the other to edge up her chin so her eyes meshed with his. 'You didn't talk me into anything, Jaz,' he said. 'I just didn't want you to feel uncomfortable. Not our first time together.'

She rolled her lips together before releasing a little puff of air. 'Oh...'

He gently brushed back her hair, his eyes searching hers for a moment or two. 'Was that night at the party your first experience of kissing and touching?' he finally asked.

Jaz chewed one corner of her mouth. 'I wanted it to be you. That was my stupid teenage fantasy—that you would be the first person to make love to me.'

He gave her a pained look, his eyes dark and sombre with regret. 'I'm sorry.'

She twisted her lips in self-deprecating manner. 'I guess that's why sex has always been a bit awkward for me. I never felt comfortable unless I was in a committed relationship. But even then I often felt I wasn't up to the mark.'

'You have no need to feel inadequate,' he said. 'No need at all.'

She rested her hands on the wall of his naked chest, her lower body gravitating towards his arousal as if of its own volition. 'You said "our first time together". Does that mean there's going to be a second or a third?'

He put a hand in the small of her back and drew

her flush against him, his eyes kindling with sensual promise. 'Start counting,' he said and lowered his mouth to hers.

CHAPTER NINE

JAKE HAD NEVER made love with such care and concern for a partner. Not that he'd been unduly rough or selfish with any of his past lovers, but being with Jaz made him realise what he had been missing in his other encounters. The level of intimacy was different, more focused, more concentrated. The slow burn of desire intensified and prolonged the pleasure. Each stroke of her soft hands made his blood pound until he could feel it in every cell of his body. Her lips flowered open beneath his, her tongue tangling with his in an erotic duel that sent a current of electricity through his pelvis. He held her to his hardness, delighting in the feel of her lithe body moulded against his.

He slipped a hand through the V-neck of her bathrobe to cup her small but perfect breasts; her skin was as smooth as satin, her nipples pert with arousal. He lowered his mouth to her right breast, teasing her areola with his tongue, skating over her tightly budded nipple, before drawing it into his mouth as she gave a breathless moan of approval. He moved to her left breast, taking his time to explore and caress it with the same attention to detail.

He worked his way up from her breasts to linger over the delicate framework of her collarbone, dipping his tongue into the shallow dish below her neck. Her skin was perfumed with grace notes of honeysuckle and lilac with a base note of vanilla. He spread his fingers through her hair, cradling her head as he kissed her deeply. Her soft little sounds of longing made his heart race and his blood run at fever pitch. Her tongue danced with his in flicks, darts and sweeps that made him draw her even closer to his body.

He eased her bathrobe off her shoulders, letting it fall in a puddle at her feet. He slid his hands down her body to grasp her by the hips, letting her feel the fullness of his erection against her mound. She moved against him, silently urging him on. He left her only long enough to get another condom, quickly applying it before he led her back to the bed. She held her arms out to him as he joined her on the mattress, wrapping them around his neck as he brought his mouth back down to hers.

When he entered her tight, wet heat he felt every ripple of her body welcoming him, massaging him, thrilling him. He began to move in slow thrusts, each one going deeper than the first, letting her catch his rhythm. She whimpered against his mouth, soft little cries of need that made the hairs on his scalp tingle. He continued to rock against her, with her, each movement of their bodies building to a crescendo. He could feel the build-up of tension in her body, the way she strained, gasped and urged him on by gripping his shoulders, as if anchoring herself.

He reached down to touch her intimately, stroking her slick wetness, feeling her swell and bud under his touch, the musky scent of her arousal intermingled with his, intoxicating his senses like the shot of an illicit drug. Her orgasm was so powerful he could feel it contracting against his length, triggering his own release until he was flying as high and free as she.

This time he didn't hold back. He couldn't. He gave a deep groan and pumped and spilled. The rush of pleasure swept through him, spinning him away from everything but what was happening in his body.

Jake had never been big on pillow talk or cuddling in the afterglow. He'd never been good at closeness and contact once the deed had been done.

But with Jaz it was different.

He felt different.

He wasn't sure why. Maybe it was because she wasn't just another girl he had picked up hardly long enough to catch her name. She was someone he knew. Had known for years. She was someone who mattered to him. She was a part of his life—always had been and probably always would be.

He felt protective of her, especially knowing his role in what had happened to her. He wanted her to feel safe and respected. To be an equal partner in sex, not a vessel to be used and cast aside.

But isn't that what you usually do? Use them and lose them?

The thought came from the back of his conscience like a lone heckler pushing through a crowd.

He used women, yes, but they used him back. They knew the rules and played by them. If he thought a woman wasn't going to stick to the programme, he wouldn't allow things to progress past a drink and a flirty chat. He was a dab hand at picking the picket-fence-and-puppies type. But the women that pursued him were mostly out for a good time, not a long time, which suited him perfectly.

He didn't want the responsibility of a relationship. He found the notion of a committed relationship suffocating. Having to answer to someone, having to take care of their emotional needs, being blamed when things didn't work out, seemed to him to nothing short of torture. He didn't need that sort of drama. He had seen enough during his childhood. Watching his parents fight and tear each other down only to make up as if nothing was wrong had deeply unsettled him. He never knew what was real, what was dependable and what wasn't. Life with his parents had been so unpredictable and tempestuous he had decided the only way he could tolerate a connection with someone would be to keep it focused solely on the physical. Emotion had no place in his flings with women.

But for some reason it felt right to hold Jaz in his arms: to idly stroke his fingers up and down her silky skin, her slender back, her neat bottom, her slim thighs. He liked the feel of her lying up against him, her legs still entangled with his. He liked the soft waft of her breath tickling the skin against his neck where her head was buried against him.

He liked the thought that she trusted him enough to share her body with him without fear or shame.

Or maybe it was a pathetic attempt on his part to right the wrongs of the past. To absolve himself from the yoke of guilt about what had happened to her.

As if that's ever going to happen.

Jaz lifted her head out from against his neck and shoulder to look at him. 'Thank you,' she said softly.

Jake tucked a strand of her hair back behind her ear. 'For what? Giving you a ten on the Richter scale?'

'It was a twelve,' she said with a crooked little smile, then added, 'But no. For being so…considerate.'

He picked up one of her hands and kissed the ends of her fingers. 'I'm not sure anyone I know would ever describe me as considerate.'

'You like people to think you're selfish and shallow but deep down I know you're not. You're actually really sensitive. The rest is all an act. A ruse. A defence mechanism.'

He released her hand as he moved away to get off the bed. He shrugged on the other fluffy bathrobe, watching as her teeth started pulling at her lower lip as if she sensed what was coming. *Good*, he thought. *Because I'm not going to pull any punches.* There was no way he was going to play at happy families. No way. Sure, the sex was good. Better than good, when it came to that. But that was all it was: sex. If she was starting to envisage him dressed in a tux standing at the end of the aisle then she had better think again.

Freaking hell. Next she would be talking about kids and kindergarten bookings.

'Here's what a selfish bastard I am, Jasmine,' he said. 'If you don't stop doing that doe-eyed thing to me, I'm going to head back to London and leave you to face that bunch of wedding-obsessed wackos downstairs all on your own.'

She sat up and pulled the sheet up, hugging her knees close to her chest, her misty eyes entreating. 'Please don't leave... This weekend is important to me. I have everything riding on it. I don't want anything to go wrong.'

He wanted to leave. Bolting when things got serious was his way of dealing with things. But there was young Emma Madden to consider. If Jaz took it upon herself to let that particular cat out of the bag as payback if he left then he could say goodbye to his business deal. Bruce Parnell would withdraw from the contract for sure. That sort of mud had a habit of sticking and making a hell of a mess while it did. Jake's reputation would be shot. He wouldn't be seen in the public eye as just a fun-loving playboy. He would be seen as a lecherous cradle snatcher with all its ghastly connotations.

'I signed up for two weeks.' He held up two fingers for emphasis. 'That's all. After that, we go our separate ways. Those are the rules.'

'Fine,' she said. 'Two weeks is all I want from you.'

He sent her a narrow look. 'Is it?'

Her expression was cool and composed but he noticed how her teeth kept pulling at her lip. 'I'm not falling in love with you, Jake. I was merely making an observation about your character. Your prickliness proves my point. You don't like people seeing your softer, more sensitive side.'

What softer side? She had romantic goggles on. A couple of good orgasms and she was seeing him as some sort of white knight. 'Don't confuse good physical chemistry with anything else, okay? I'm not interested in anything else. And nor should you be until you've sorted out why you keep attracting the sort of guys who won't stick around long enough to put a ring on your finger and keep it there.'

She gave him a pert look. 'Maybe you could tell me what I'm doing wrong, since you're the big relationships expert.'

Jake watched as she took her sweet ass time getting off the bed to slip on a bathrobe. She didn't bother doing up the waist ties but left the sides hanging open, leaving her beautiful body partially on show. For some reason it was more titillating than if she had been standing there stark naked. His blood headed south until he was painfully erect.

Everything about her turned him on. The way she moved like a sleek and graceful cat. The way she tossed her hair back behind her shoulders like some haughty aristocrat. The way she looked at him with artic eyes while her body radiated such sensual heat. It was good to see her act more confident sexually but he couldn't help feeling she was driving home a point. But he was beyond fighting her over it. He wanted her and he only had two weeks to make the most of it. 'What time do you have to be downstairs?' he asked.

She pushed back her left sleeve to check the watch on her slender wrist. It was one his parents had bought for her for her twenty-first birthday. Another reminder of how entwined with his life she was and always would be. 'An hour,' she said. 'I have to check my dress is properly steamed and pressed for the fashion parade tomorrow.'

He held out his hand. 'Have a shower with me.'

She looked at his hand. Returned her gaze to his with a little flicker of defiance in hers. 'Won't you be quicker on your own?'

'Yeah, but it won't be half as much fun.'

CHAPTER TEN

Jaz's body was still tingling when she went down-stairs with Jake for the welcome-to-the-expo drinks party. He kept giving her smouldering glances as they mingled amongst the other designers and expo staff. She wondered if people knew what they had been up to in the shower only minutes earlier. She had hardly had time to get her hair dry and put on some make-up after he had pleasured every inch of her body.

Of course people knew. He was Jake Ravensdale. What he didn't know about sex wasn't worth knowing. Wasn't her thrumming body proof of that? He only had to look at her with that dark-as-midnight gaze and her inner core would leap in excitement. She saw the effect he had on every woman in the room. Hers wasn't the only pulse racing, the only breath catching in her throat, the only mind conjuring up what she would like to do with him when she got him alone.

Congratulations came thick and fast from the people Jaz knew, as well as many she didn't. It made her feel a little less conflicted about continuing the charade. It was only for two weeks. Two weeks to enjoy the sensual magnificence of a man she had hated for years.

Just shows how easy it is to separate emotion from sex.

One of the models came over with a glass of champagne in one hand. 'Hi, Jake, remember me? We met at a company party last year.'

Jake gave one of his charming smiles. 'Sure I do. How are you?'

The young woman gave a little pout. 'I was fine until I heard you got yourself engaged. No one saw *that* coming.'

Jaz was getting a little tired of being ignored like she was a piece of furniture. 'Hi,' she said holding out her hand to the model. 'I'm Jake's fiancée, Jasmine Connolly. And you are...?'

'Saskiaa with two "a"s,' the girl said with a smile that lasted only as long as her handshake. 'When's the big day?'

'December,' Jaz said. 'Boxing Day, actually.' Why shouldn't she make Jake squirm a bit while she had the chance? 'We're hoping for a white wedding in every sense of the word.'

Jake waited until the model had moved on before he leaned down close to Jaz's ear. 'Boxing Day?'

Jaz looked up at him with a winsome smile. 'I quite fancy the idea of a Christmas wedding. The family will already be gathered so it would be awfully convenient for everyone, don't you think?'

He smiled but it got only as far as his mouth, and that was probably only for the benefit of others who were looking at them. 'Don't overplay it,' he said in an undertone only she could hear.

Jaz kept her smile in place. 'You didn't remember that girl, did you?'

A frown pulled at his brow. 'Why's that an issue for you?'

'It's not,' she said. 'I don't expect you even ask their name before you sleep with them.'

'I ask their permission, which is far more important in my opinion.'

Jaz held his look for as long as she dared. 'I know it comes as naturally to you as breathing, but I would greatly appreciate it if you wouldn't flirt with any of the women, in particular the models. Half of them look as if they should still be in school.'

His mouth curved upward in a sardonic smile. 'My parents would be enormously proud of you. You're doing a perfect jealous fiancée impersonation.'

She snatched a glass of champagne off a passing waiter for something to do with her hands. 'Don't screw this up for me, Jake,' she said through tight lips in case anyone nearby could lip-read. 'I need to secure the booking for next year's expo. Once that's in the bag, you can go back to your "single and loving it" life.'

He trailed a lazy fingertip down her arm from the top of her bare shoulder to her wrist. 'Just wait until I get you alone.'

Jaz shivered as his eyes challenged hers in a sexy duel. His touch was like a match to her tinderbox senses. Every nerve was screaming for more. 'Now who's overplaying it?'

He slipped a hand to the nape of her neck and drew her closer, bending down to press a lingering kiss on her lips. Even though Jaz's eyes were closed in bliss she could see the bright flashes of cameras going off around them. After a moment he eased back and winked at her devilishly. 'Did I tell you how gorgeous you look tonight?'

Jaz knew he was probably only saying it for the benefit of others but a part of her wanted to believe it was true. She placed a hand on the lapel of his suit jacket, smoothing away an imaginary fleck of lint. 'You've scrubbed up pretty well yourself,' she said. 'Even without a tie.'

He screwed up his face. 'I hate the things. They always feel like they're choking me.'

Typical Jake. Hating anything that confined or restrained him. 'I suppose that's why you got all those detentions for breaking the uniform code at that posh school you went to?'

He grinned. 'I still hold the record for the most detentions in one term. Apparently I'm considered a bit of a legend.'

Jaz shook her head at him, following it up with a roll of her eyes. 'Come on.' She looped her arm through his. 'I want to have a look at the displays.'

Oh, joy, Jake thought as Jaz led him to where the wedding finery was displayed in one of the staterooms. The sight of all those meringue-like wedding gowns and voluminous veils was enough to make him break out in hives. Or maybe it was the flowers. There were arrangements of every size and shape: centrepieces, towers of flowers, bouquets, bunches and buttonholes. There were displays of food, wine and French champagne, a honeymoon destination stand and a bespoke jeweller in situ. There were a few men there partnering their fiancées or girlfriends but they were pretty thin on the ground. Jake understood Jaz wanted to secure her signing for next year but he couldn't help feeling she had insisted he accompany her as a punishment.

But that was one of the things he secretly admired in her. She was feisty and stood her ground with him. She was the only woman he knew who didn't simper at him or adapt to suit him. He felt the electric buzz of her will tussling with his every time she locked gazes with him. For years they had done their little stand-off thing. What would they do once they parted company? Would they go back to their old ways or find a new way of relating? With two family weddings coming up, it would be tasteless to be at loggerheads. There was enough of that going around with his parents' carry-on. The dignified thing would be to be mature and civil about it and be friends.

But would he ever be able to look at her as a friend without thinking of how she came apart in his arms? How it felt when he held her close? How her mouth tasted of heat, passion and sweetness mixed in a combustible cocktail that made his senses whirl out of control? Would he ever be able to stand beside her and not want to pull her into his arms?

He'd slept with a lot of women but none of them had had that effect on him. He barely gave his lovers another thought once he moved on to the next. Was it because Jaz was someone who had always been on the periphery of his life? Sometimes even at the centre, at the very heart, of his family?

Had that familiarity added something to their love-making?

It wasn't just physical sex with her. There were feelings there…feelings he couldn't describe. He cared about her. But then everyone in his family cared about her.

Every time he looked at her he felt the stirring in his groin. He couldn't look at her mouth without thinking of how it felt fused to his own. How her tongue felt as it played with his, how her body felt as she pushed herself, as if she wanted to crawl into his skin and never leave. Even now with her arm looped through his he could feel the brush of her beautiful body against his side. He couldn't wait to get her back to their suite and get her naked.

They walked past a photographer's stand but then Jaz suddenly swivelled and, pulling Jake by the hand, led him back to where the photographer had set up a romantic set with love-hearts, red roses and a velvet-covered sofa in the shape of a pair of lips. 'Can you take our picture?' she asked the photographer.

'Sure,' the photographer said. 'Just sit together on the sofa there for a sec while I frame the shot.'

Jake looked down at Jaz sitting snuggled up by his side as if butter wouldn't melt in her hot little mouth.

'I'm keeping a score,' he said in an undertone. 'Just thought I'd put that out there.'

She gave him a sly smile. 'So am I.'

Jaz thought she might have overdone it with the champagne, or maybe it was being with Jake all evening. Being with him made her tipsy, giddy with excitement. He never left her side; his arm was either around her waist or he held hands with her as she worked the room. It was a torturously slow form of foreplay. Every look, every touch, every brush of his body against hers was a prelude to what was to come. She could see the intention in his dark-blue gaze. It was blatantly, spine-tinglingy sexual. It made every inch of her flesh shiver behind the shield of her clothes, every cell of her body contracting in feverish anticipation.

'Time for bed?' Jake said, his fingers warm and firm around hers.

Jaz felt something in her belly slip sideways. When he touched her like that she couldn't stop thinking of where else he was going to touch her when he got her alone. Her entire body tingled in anticipation. Even the hairs on the nape of her neck shivered at the roots. 'I wonder if we'll win the "most loved-up couple" photo competition?' she said. 'Or the all-expenses-paid wedding and honeymoon package? That would be awesome.'

His eyes sent her a teasing warning. 'Don't push it, baby girl.'

She laughed as he led her to the lift. 'I can't remember a time when I've enjoyed myself more. You should have seen your face when that florist threw you that bouquet. You looked like you'd caught a detonated bomb.'

The lift doors sprang open and Jake pulled her in, barely waiting long enough for the doors to close to bring his mouth down to hers in a scorching kiss. Jaz linked her arms around his neck, pressing as close to him as she could to feel the hardened length of him against her tingling pelvis. He put a hand on one of her thighs and hooked it over his hip, bringing her into closer contact with the heat and potency of him. She could see out of the corner of her eye their reflection in the mirrored walls. It was shockingly arousing to see the way their bodies strained to be together, the flush on both of their faces as desire rode hard and fast in their blood.

Jake put his hand on the stop button and the lift came to a halt. Jaz looked at the erotic intent in his eyes and a wave of lust coursed through her so forcefully she thought she would come on the spot. He nudged her knickers to one side while she unzipped his trousers with fingers that shook with excitement. How he got a condom on so quickly was a testament to how adept he was at sex, she thought. He entered her with a slick, deep thrust that made her head bang against the wall of the elevator. He checked himself at her gasp, asking, 'Are you okay?'

Jaz was almost beyond speech, her breath coming out in fractured, pleading bursts. 'Yes…oh, yes… Don't stop. *Please* don't stop.'

He started moving again, each thrust making her wild with need. He put one of his hands on the wall beside her head to anchor himself as he drove into her with a frantic urgency that made the blood spin, sizzle and sing in her veins. He brought his hand down between their joined bodies, his fingers expertly caressing her until her senses exploded. She clung to him as the storm broke in her, through her, over her.

He followed close behind, three or four hard pumps; a couple of deep, primal grunts and it was over.

Jaz wriggled her knickers back in place and smoothed her dress down as the lift continued up to their floor. 'I reckon you must hold some sort of record for getting a condom on,' she said into the silence. 'It's like a sleight of hand thing. Amazing.'

He gave her a glinting look as he zipped his trousers. 'Always pays to be prepared.'

A shiver danced its way down her spine as he escorted her out of the lift to their suite, his hand resting in the small of her back. Once they were inside their suite he closed the door and pulled her to him until she was in the circle of his arms. 'Happy with how tonight went?' he said.

Was he talking about her business or their lovemaking? 'I've got a meeting with the expo organisers next week,' Jaz said. 'It's an exciting opportunity. I'm hoping it will lead to bigger events, maybe even internationally.'

He smoothed a wisp of her hair back off her face. 'Why did you choose to design wedding gear? Why not evening, or fashion in general?'

Jaz slipped out of his hold, feeling a lecture coming on. Of course he would think weddings were a waste of time and money. He was a playboy. A wedding was the last thing on earth that would interest him. But to her they signified everything she had dreamed about as a child. Her parents hadn't married. They hadn't even made a formal commitment to each other. They had just hooked up one night and look how that had turned out. She had been passed between them like a parcel no one wanted until finally her mother had dumped her with her dad without even saying good-bye or 'see you later'.

'Jaz?'

She turned to look at him, her mouth set. 'Do you know what it's like to grow up without a sense of family? To have to *borrow* someone else's family in order to feel normal?'

Jake frowned. 'I'm not sure what that has to do with your choice of career but—'

'It has *everything* to do with it,' Jaz said. 'For as long as I can remember, I wanted to be normal. To have normal parents, not one who's off her face most of the time and the other who hadn't wanted a kid in the first place. I didn't have anything from either of my parents that made me feel a part of a unit. I was a mistake, an accident, an inconvenience.' She folded her arms and continued. 'But when a couple marries, it's different. It's a public declaration of love and commitment and mostly—not always, but mostly—one expressing a desire to have children.'

Jaz looked at him as the silence swelled. Had she said too much? Revealed too much? What did it matter? She was tired of him criticising her choices. 'A wedding dress is something most brides keep for the rest of their lives,' she said. 'It can be passed down from a mother to a daughter. General fashion isn't the same. It's seasonal, transient. Some pieces might be passed on but they don't have the emotional resonance a wedding dress has. That's why I design wedding gowns. Every woman deserves to be a princess for a day. I like being able to make that wish come true.' *Even if I can't make it come true for myself.*

Jake gave a slow nod. 'Sounds reasonable.'

'But you think I'm crazy.'

'I didn't say that.'

Jaz went to the drinks fridge and poured a glass of mineral water, taking a sip before she turned to face him again. He was looking at her with a contemplative look on his face, his brows drawn together, his mouth set in a serious line, his gaze centred on hers. 'I'm sorry if tonight's been absolute torture for you but this weekend's really important to me.'

His mouth tilted in a wry smile. 'You're not one bit sorry. You've enjoyed every minute, watching me squirm down there.'

Jaz smiled back. 'It was rather fun, I have to admit. I can't wait to see what press photos show up. I wonder if they got the one of you with the bouquet. Or maybe I should text it or post it online?'

He closed the distance between them and pulled her down to the bed in a tangle of limbs. 'Cheeky minx,' he said, eyes twinkling with amusement.

Jaz stroked the sexy stubble on his face, her belly fluttering with excitement as his hard body pressed against hers. His hooded gaze went to her mouth, his thumb coming up to brush over her lower lip until it tingled, as if teased by electrodes. 'What are you thinking?'

'You mean you can't tell?' he said with a wicked sparkle in his eyes.

She snatched in a breath as his body moved against her, triggering a tide of want that flooded her body, pooling hotly in her core. 'When you hook up with someone, how many times do you have sex with them in one night?'

A frown creased his forehead. 'Why do you want to know?'

Jaz traced the trench of his frown with her finger. 'Just wondering.'

He caught her hand and pinned it on the bed beside her head, searching her gaze for a pulsing moment. 'Wondering what?'

'If you've done it more with me than with any-one else.'

'And if I have?'

She looked at his mouth. 'Is it…different…? With me, I mean?'

He nudged up her chin with a blunt fingertip, lock-ing his gaze with hers. 'Different in what way?'

Jaz wasn't sure why she was fishing so hard for compliments. He had made it clear how long their fling was going to last. Just because he had made love to her several times tonight didn't mean any-thing other than he had a high sex drive. He was, after all, a man in his sexual prime. But their love-making was so different from anything she had experienced with other partners. It was more exciting, more satisfying, more addictive, which was a problem because she couldn't afford to get too used to having him. 'I don't know...more intense?'

He slid his hand along the side of her face to splay his fingers through her hair. It was an achingly tender hold that made Jaz's heart squeeze as if someone had crushed it in a vice. Could it be possible he was coming to care for her? *Really* care for her? Was that why their intimacy was so satisfying? Did their physical connection reflect a much deeper one that had been simmering in the background for years?

But she didn't love him.

Not the slavish way she had as a teenager. She was an adult now. Her feelings for him were mature and sensible. She knew his faults and limitations. She didn't whitewash his personality to make him out to be anything he was not. She was too sensible to hanker after a future with him because he wasn't the future type. He was the 'for now' type.

Falling in love with Jake Ravensdale once had been bad enough. To do it twice would be emotional suicide.

'It is different,' Jake said. 'But that doesn't mean I want it to continue longer than we agreed.'

'I'm not asking for an extension,' Jaz said. 'I can't afford to waste my time having a long-term fling with someone who docsn't want the same things I want. I want to get on with my life and find my soul mate. I want to start a family before I'm thirty.'

His frown hadn't quite gone away but now it was deeper than ever. 'You shouldn't rush into your next relationship. Take your time getting to know them. And what's the big rush on having kids? You're only twenty-three. You've got heaps of time.'

'I don't want to miss out on having kids,' Jaz said. 'I know so many women who've left it too late or circumstances have worked against them. I can't imagine not having a family. It's what I've wanted since I was a little girl.'

He moved away from her and got off the bed, scraping a hand through his hair before dropping it back by his side.

Jaz chewed at her lower lip. 'Did I just kill the mood?'

He turned around with a smile that didn't involve his eyes. 'It's been a long day. I'm going to have a shower and hit the sack. Don't wait up.'

When Jake came out of the bathroom after his shower half an hour later, Jaz wasn't in the bed. In fact, she wasn't in the suite. He frowned as he searched the room, even going so far as to check under the bed. Where the hell was she? He glanced at her bag on the luggage rack. She obviously hadn't checked out of the hotel as her things were still here. Although, come to think of it, he wouldn't put it past her to flounce off, leaving him to pack her things. What was she up to? Their conversation earlier had cut a little close to the bone…for him, that was. Why did she have to carry on about marriage and kids all the time? She was a baby herself. Most twenty-three-year-olds were still out partying and having a good time.

But no, Jaz wanted the white picket fence and a bunch of wailing brats. What would happen to her stellar career as a wedding designer then? She would be doing more juggling than a circus act.

And as to finding her soul mate… Did she really believe such a thing existed? There was no such thing as a perfect partner. She was deluding herself with romantic notions of what her life could be like.

Well, he had news for her. It would be just like everyone else's life—boring and predictable.

Jake called her number but it went straight through to voice mail. He paced about the suite, feeling more and more agitated. The weird thing was he spent hours of his life in hotel rooms, mostly alone. He rarely spent the whole night with anyone. It was less complicated when it came to the 'morning after the night before' routine.

But every time he looked at that bed he thought of how it had felt with Jaz, her arms and legs wrapped around him and her hot little mouth clamped to his. He couldn't stop thinking about the lift either. He probably wouldn't be able to get into one ever again without thinking of taking Jaz up against that mirrored wall. His blood pounded at the memory of it. He had been close to doing it without a condom. He still didn't know how he'd got it on in time. He had been as worked up as a teenager on his first 'sure thing' date.

What was it about Jaz that made him so intensely attracted to her? It wasn't like this with his other flings. Once or twice was usually enough before he was ready for more excitement. But with Jaz he was mad with lust. Crazy with it. Buzzing with it. Making love with her eased it for a heartbeat before he was aching for her again. It had to blow out eventually. It *had* to. He wasn't putting down tent pegs just because the sex was good. Just as well they'd agreed on an end date. Two weeks was pushing it. He didn't take that long for holidays because he always got bored. There was no way this was going to continue indefinitely.

No. Freaking. Way.

Jake threw on some clothes and finger-combed his damp hair on his way to the lift. She had to be in the hotel somewhere. He jabbed at the call button. Why the hell was it so slow? Was some other couple holed up in there, doing it? His gut tightened. Surely Jaz wouldn't pick up someone and…? No. He slammed his foot down on the thought like someone stomping on a noxious spider.

The lift was empty.

So was his stomach as he searched the bar for the glimpse of that gorgeous honey-brown head. He went to the restaurant, and then looked through the foyer, but there was no sign of her anywhere. He hadn't re-alised until then what had fuelled his heart-stopping panic. It hit him like a felling blow right in the middle of his chest. He couldn't draw breath for a moment. His throat closed. He could feel his thudding pulse right down to his fingertips.

He had dismissed her. Rejected her. What if she had been upset and gone downstairs to God knew what? What if some unscrupulous guy had intercepted her? Shoved her into a back room and done the unthinkable?

The stateroom where the displays were set up was closed with a burly security guard posted outside.

The security guard gave Jake the eye as he tried the doorknob. 'Sorry, buddy,' the guard said with a smirk. 'You'll have to wait till morning to try a dress on.'

Jake wanted to punch him.

He retraced his steps; his growing dread making his skin break out in a clammy sweat until his shirt was sticking to his back like cling-film. Where could she have gone? He couldn't get the image of her trapped in some room—*some locked bathroom*—with an opportunist creep mauling her. He would never be able to live with himself if she got hurt under his watch. She was with him. He was supposed to be her partner. Her 'fiancé'. What sort of fiancé would let her wander off alone to be taken advantage of by some stranger? She was gullible with men. Look at the way she'd got engaged three times. He hadn't liked one of them. They were nice enough men but not one of them was worthy of her.

Jake strode past the restrooms. Could she be in there? Locked inside one of the cubicles with someone? He did a quick whip round and checked that no one was watching before he pushed open the outer door. 'Jaz? Are you in there?' There was no answer so he went in through to where the cubicles were.

A middle-aged woman turned from the basins with

her eyes blazing in indignation. 'This is the ladies' room!'

'I—I know,' Jake said, quickly back-pedalling with the woman following him like an army sergeant. 'I'm looking for my...er...fiancée.'

The woman blasted him with a look that was as icy as the wind off the North Sea in winter. 'I've met men like you before. Lurking around female toilets to get your sick thrills. I've a good mind to call security.'

Jake looked at her in open-mouthed shock, which didn't seem to help his cause one little bit, because it looked like he'd been sprung doing exactly what the woman accused him of. 'No, no, no,' he said, trying to placate her as she took out her phone. If she took a snapshot of him in the female restrooms and it went viral he could forget about his reputation and his career. Both would be totally screwed. 'My fiancée is this high...' He put his hand up to demonstrate. 'Really pretty with light-brown hair and grey-blue eyes and—'

'Is there a problem?' The security guard from outside the display room spoke from behind Jake.

Jake rolled his eyes. This was turning into such a freaking farce. And meanwhile Jaz was still missing. He turned to face the guard. 'I'm looking for my fiancée. She's not answering her phone. I thought she might be in the ladies' room.'

The security guard's mouth curled up on one side. 'You seem to have a thing for what belongs to the ladies, don't you, buddy?'

Jake clenched his hands in case he was tempted

to use them to knock that sneer off the guard's face. *Time to play the famous card.* 'Look, I'm Jake Ravensdale,' he said. 'I'm—'

'I don't care if you're Jack the bloody Ripper,' the guard said. 'I want you out of here before I call the cops.'

'You can check with Reception,' Jake said. 'Get them to check the bookings. I'm here with Jasmine Connolly, the bridal designer.' *Dear God, had Jaz put him on the booking information?* he thought in panic as the guard took out his intercom device and called the front desk.

The guard spoke to someone at Reception and then put his device back on his belt, his expression now as nice as pie. 'Nice to meet you, Mr Ravensdale,' he said. 'Enjoy your stay. Oh, and by the way...' He put on a big, cheesy grin. 'Congratulations.'

Jake went back to the suite with his whole body coiled as tight as a spring. He pushed open the door to see Jaz getting ready for bed. 'Where the bloody hell have you been?' he said. 'I've been scouring the hotel from top to bottom for the last hour looking for you.'

'I went down to check on my dress before the room was locked.'

'Did you not think to leave a note or a send me a text?'

A spark of defiance shone in her grey-blue gaze as it collided with his. 'I assumed you were finished with me for the evening. You told me not to wait up.'

Jake smothered a filthy curse under his breath. 'Do you have any idea of how damned worried I was?'

She looked at him blankly. 'Why would you be worried?'

He pushed his hand back through his hair. 'I was worried, that's all.'

She came over to him to lay a hand on his arm. Her soft fingers warmed his flesh, making every one of his taut muscles unwind and others south of the border tighten. 'Are you okay?'

Was he okay? No. He felt like he would never be okay again. *Ever.* His head was pounding with the mother of all headaches. His heart rate felt like someone had given him an overdose of adrenalin. Two overdoses. His legs were shaking. His guts had turned to gravy. 'I'm fine.' Even to his own ears he knew he sounded unnecessarily curt.

'You don't sound it,' Jaz said, frowning at him in concern. 'Are you unwell? Have you caught food poisoning or something? You look so pale and sweaty and—'

'I almost got myself arrested.'

Her eyes rounded. 'What on earth for?'

'Long story.'

'Tell me what happened, Jake,' she said. 'I need to know, since we're here at this expo together, because it could reflect badly on me.'

Should he tell her it all or just a cut-down version? 'I panicked when you weren't in the suite. I didn't know where you'd gone.'

She began to stroke his arm, her eyes as clear, still

and lustrous as a mountain tarn as she looked into his. 'Were you worried I wasn't coming back?'

His hands came down on her shoulders in a grip that was unapologetically possessive. 'I was out of my mind with worry,' he said. 'I tried to check the display room but the security guard gave me a hard time. And then he found me coming out of the ladies' toilets—'

Her brow puckered. 'Why'd you go in there?'

Jake swallowed. 'I was worried someone might have cornered you in there and…' He couldn't even say what he'd thought. It was too sickening to be vo-calised.

Her eyes softened. 'Oh, you big goose,' she said. 'I'm a big girl now. I can fend for myself, but thanks anyway.'

He brought her closer so her hips were against his, watching the way her tongue came out to moisten her lips; it made every one of those muscles in his groin go rock-hard. 'I swear to God I've aged a decade in the last hour.'

'Doesn't feel like it to me.'

He pressed her even closer. 'I want you.'

A little light danced like a sprite in her gaze. 'Again?'

He walked her backwards toward the bed, thigh to thigh, hip to hip, need to need. 'How much sleep do you need?' he said as he nibbled at her mouth, their breaths intermingling.

'Seven hours—five in an emergency—otherwise I get ratty.'

Jake helped her out of her clothes with more haste than finesse. 'I can handle ratty.'

She gave a tinkling laugh. 'Don't say I didn't warn you.'

He put his mouth on her naked breast, drawing her tight nipple into his mouth. It was music to his ears to hear her breathless moan of pleasure. It made his blood pump all the more frantically. He pushed her gently down on the bed, shoving pillows, petals and clothes out of the way as he came down beside her. He wanted to go slow but his earlier panic did something to his self-control. He needed to be inside her. He needed to be fused with her, to have her writhing and shuddering as he took her to paradise. He needed to quell this feverish madness racing in his blood. Her body gripped him like a fist as he surged into her velvet heat. The ripples of her inner core massaged him inexorably closer to a mind-blowing lift-off. He held on only long enough to make sure she was with him all the way. When she came around him he gave a part-growl, part-groan as he lost himself to physical bliss…

CHAPTER ELEVEN

JAZ WAS TRYING not to show how nervous she was the next morning but Jake must have sensed it because he kept looking at her with a watchful gaze. She picked at the breakfast he had had delivered to their suite but barely any made it to her mouth.

'At least have a glass of juice,' he said, pushing a glass of freshly squeezed orange juice towards her.

'I think I'm going to be sick.'

He took her hand from across the table and gave it an encouraging squeeze. 'Sweetheart, you're going to knock them for six down there.'

She bit down on her lip, panic and nerves clawing at her insides like razor blades whirled in a blender. 'Who am I fooling? I'm just a gardener's daughter from the wrong side of the tracks. What am I doing here pretending I'm a high street designer?'

'Imposter syndrome,' Jake said, leisurely pouring a cup of brewed coffee. 'That's what all this fuss is about. You don't believe in yourself. You think you've fluked it, that someone is going to come up behind you and tap you on the shoulder and tell you to get the hell out of here because you're not up to standard.'

That was exactly what Jaz was thinking. She had been thinking it most of her life. Being abandoned by her mother had always made her feel as if she wasn't good enough. She tried so hard to be the best she could be so people wouldn't leave her. But invariably they eventually did. Three times she had got engaged and each time it had ended. Her fiancés had ended it, not her. She was ashamed to admit she might well have married each and every one of them if they hadn't pulled the plug first. She was so terrified of failing, she over-controlled everything: her work, her relationships, her life. Her business was breaking even…just. But she'd had a lot of help. If it hadn't been for Jake's parents, she might never have got to where she was.

How long could she go on doing everything herself? She was constantly juggling. Sometimes she felt like a circus clown on stilts with twenty plates in the air. She couldn't remember the last time she'd taken a holiday. She took her work everywhere. She had Holly's dress with her in case there was a spare minute to work on the embroidery. She hadn't had a chance to draw a single sketch for Miranda. How long could she go on like that? Something had to give. She was going to get an ulcer at this rate. Maybe she already had one.

'You're right,' she said on a sigh. 'Every time I get myself to a certain place, I make myself sick worrying it's going to be ripped out from under me.'

'That's perfectly understandable given what happened with your mother.'

Jaz lowered her gaze as she smoothed out a tiny crease in the tablecloth. 'For years I waited for her to come back. I used to watch from the window whenever a car came up the drive. I would get all excited thinking she was coming back, that she had got herself sorted out and was coming back to take me to the new life she'd always promised me. But it never happened. I haven't heard from her since. I don't even know if she's still alive.'

Jake covered her hand with the warm solidity of his. 'You've made your own new life all by yourself. You didn't need her to come back and screw it up.'

'Not *all* by myself,' Jaz said. 'I'm not sure where I'd be if it hadn't been for your parents.' She waited a beat before adding, 'Do you think you could have a look over my books some time? I'm happy to pay you.'

'Sure, but you don't have to pay me.'

'I insist,' Jaz said. 'Your family has helped me enough. I don't want to be seen as a charity case.'

Jake lightly buttered some toast and handed it to her. 'One mouthful. It'll help to settle your stomach.'

Jaz took the toast and bit, chewed and swallowed but it felt like she was swallowing a cotton ball. 'Do you have it?'

'Have what?'

'Imposter syndrome?'

He smiled crookedly, as if the thought was highly amusing. 'No.'

'I suppose it was a silly question,' she conceded. 'Mr Confidence in all situations and with all people.'

A shadow passed over his features like a hand moving across a beam of light. 'There have been times when I've doubted myself.'

'Like when?'

'At boarding school, especially in my senior year,' he said, frowning slightly as he stirred his coffee. 'I played the class clown card so often I lost sight of who I really was. It wasn't until I left school and went to university that I finally found my feet and became my own person instead of being Julius's badly behaved twin brother.'

Jaz had always seen Jake as a supremely confident person. He seemed to waltz through life with nary a care of what others thought of him. She was the total opposite. Her desperate desire to fit in had made her compromise herself more times than she cared to admit. Weren't her three engagements proof of that? She had wanted to be normal. To belong to someone. To be wanted. 'I guess it must be hard, being an identical twin and all,' she said. 'Everyone is always making comparisons between you and Julius.'

There was a small silence.

'Yeah. We look the same but we're not the same,' Jake said. 'Julius is much more grounded and focused than I am.'

'I don't know about that,' Jaz said. 'You seem pretty grounded to me. You know what you want and go for it without letting anyone get in your way.'

He was frowning again as if a thought was wandering around in his head and he wasn't quite sure where to park it. 'But I don't stick at stuff,' he finally said. 'Not for the long haul.'

'But you're happy living your life that way, aren't you?'

After another moment of silence he gave her an absent smile. 'Yeah, it works for me. Now, have a bit more toast. It'd be embarrassing if you were to faint just when it's your chance to shine.'

Jaz did a last-minute check with the model for the gown she had prepared for the show. It was the first time any of her work would be worn by a profes- sional model on a catwalk. The advertising she had done in the past had been still shots with models from an agency and a photographer who was a friend of a friend.

But this was different. This was her dream coming to life in front of her. Hundreds, possibly thousands or even millions, would see her design if the images went global. It would be the start of the expansion of her business she had planned since she had left de- sign college.

Why then did she still feel like a fraud?

Because she was a fraud.

A fake.

Not because she didn't know how to design and sew a beautiful wedding gown. But because she wasn't in a committed relationship and the ring she was wear- ing on her finger was going to be handed back in two weeks' time. She was like the blank-faced models wearing the wedding gowns. They weren't really brides. They were acting a role.

Like *she* was acting a role.

She was pretending to be engaged to Jake when all she wanted was to be engaged to him for real. How had she not realised it until now? Or had she been shying away from it because it was a truth she hadn't wanted to face?

She was in love with Jake.

Hadn't she always been in love with him? As a child she had looked up to him as a fun older brother. He had been the playful twin, the one she could have a laugh with. Then when her female hormones had switched on she had wanted him as a woman wanted a man. But she hadn't been a woman back then—she had been a child. He had respected that and kept his distance. Wasn't that another reason why she loved him? He hadn't exploited her youthful innocence. Yes, he hadn't handled her crush with the greatest sensitivity, but at least he hadn't taken advantage of her.

Jaz was done with acting. Done with pretending. How could she stretch this out another week or two? Jake wasn't in love with her. Didn't their conversation over breakfast confirm it? He was happy with the way his life was a single man. He would go back to that life as soon as their 'engagement' ended.

Jake said she could keep the ring but why would she do that? It was little more than a consolation prize. A parting gift. Every time she looked at it she would be reminded of what she wanted and couldn't have. It might be enormous fun being with Jake. It might be wonderful to be his lover and feel the thrill of his desire and hers for him.

But what was she *doing*?

She was living a lie. That was what she was doing. Fooling people that she was in a real relationship with real hopes and dreams for the future. What future? Two weeks of fantastic, mind-blowing sex and then what? Jake would pull the plug on their relationship just like her three exes had done. She would be abandoned. Rejected. Left hanging. Alone.

Not this time. Not again.

This time she would take control. Do the right thing by herself and set the boundaries. Two weeks more of this and she would want it to be for ever. Good grief! She wanted it to be for ever now. That was how dangerous their fling had become. One night of amazing sex and she was posting the wedding invitations.

It was ridiculous.

She was ridiculous.

Jake wasn't a 'for ever' type of guy. He wanted her but only for as long as it took to burn out their mutual attraction. How long would it take? He had set the limit at two weeks. Most of his relationships didn't last two days. Why should she think *she* was so special? Sure they knew each other. They had a history of sorts. They would always be in each other's lives in some way or another.

It would be best to end it now.

On *her* terms.

Before things got crazy. Crazier…because what was crazier than falling in love with a man just because you couldn't have him? That was what she had done. It was pathological. She was in love with a man who didn't—*couldn't*—love her.

It was time to rewrite the script of her life. No longer would she fall for the wrong men. No longer would she settle for second best...even though there was no way she would ever describe Jake as second best. He was first best. *The* best. The most fabulous man she had ever known—but he wasn't hers.

He wasn't anyone's.

It would break her heart to end their affair. Weird to think she'd thought her heart had been broken by her three failed engagements; none of them, even all of them put together, had made her feel anywhere near as sad as ending her fling with Jake.

It wasn't just the sex. It was the way he made her feel as a person. He valued her. He understood her. He knew her doubts and insecurities. He had taught her to put the dark shadow of the past behind her. He protected her. He made her feel safe. He had helped her heal. His touch, his kisses, his glorious love-making, had made her fully embrace her femininity.

He had given her the gift of self-acceptance, but with that gift had come realisation. The realisation she could no longer pretend to be something she was not. She had to stop hiding behind social norms in order to feel accepted. If she never found love with a man who loved her equally, unreservedly and for ever, then she would be better off alone. Settling for anything less was settling for second best. It was compromising and self-limiting and would only bring further heartbreak in the end.

But it would be hard to be around Jake as just a friend. She would go back to being the gardener's daughter—the little ring-in who didn't really belong in the big house.

The girl who didn't belong to anyone.

Jake watched from the front row beside Jaz as her design came down the catwalk. She had only just got to her seat in time to see her moment in the spotlight. The dress was amazing. He found his mind picturing her wearing it. It had a hand-sewn beaded bodice and a frothy tulle skirt that was just like a princess's dress. The veil was set back from the model's head and flowed out behind her like a floating cloud.

If anyone had told him a week ago he'd be sitting at a wedding expo oohing and aahing at wedding gowns he would have said they were nuts. The atmosphere was electric. The ballroom was abuzz with expectation. The music was upbeat and stirring, hardly bridal or churchy at all. The applause was thunderous when Jaz's design was announced and continued even after the model had left the catwalk. He clapped as loudly as anyone, probably louder. 'Told you they'd love your work,' he said. 'You'll have orders coming out of your ears after this.'

She looked at him with a tremulous smile. 'You think?'

She still doubted herself. Amazing, he thought. What would it take for her to believe she was as good if not better than any of the other designers here? He tapped her on the end of her retroussé nose. 'Sure of it.'

Jake took her hand while the press did their interviews after the show. He was getting quite used to the role of devoted fiancé. Who said he couldn't act? Maybe some of that Ravensdale talent hadn't skipped a generation after all. Or maybe he was getting used to being part of a couple. There was certainly something to be said about knowing who he was going to sleep with that night—earlier, if he could wangle it. Instead of wondering how the sex would be, he knew for certain it would be fantastic. He had never had a more satisfying lover.

Jaz's body was a constant turn-on as it brushed against his as the crowd jostled them. He drew her closer as a photographer zoomed in on them. Her cheek was against his; the fresh, flowery scent of her made his sinuses tingle. She turned her head and he swooped down and stole a kiss from her soft-as-a-pillow mouth, wishing he could get her alone right here and now.

But instead of continuing the kiss she eased back, giving him a distracted-looking smile. Her hands went back to her lap where she was gripping the programme as if she had plans to shred it.

'You okay?' Jake said.

Her gaze was trained on the next set of models strutting their stuff. 'We need to talk,' she said. 'But not here.'

Here it comes. The talk. The talk where she would say she wanted the whole shebang: the promises of for ever, the kids, the dog and the house. The things he didn't want. Had never wanted. Would never want. Why had he thought she would be any different? He had broken his own rules for what? For a fling that should never have started in the first place.

Might as well get it over with. Once the show was over, he took her by the elbow and led her back to their suite. *Their suite.* How cosy that sounded. Like they were a couple. But they weren't a couple. A couple of idiots, if anything. They had no right to be messing around. *He* had no right. She was a part of his family. By getting involved with her he had jeopardised every single relationship she had with his family. Would everyone treat her differently now they knew she had been his lover? Would they look at her differently? Would he be harangued for the next decade for not doing the right thing by her and leaving her alone?

'I know what you're going to say,' Jake said even before he had closed the door of the suite.

She pressed her lips together for a moment. Turned and put the programme and her bag on the bed, then turned back to him and handed him her engagement ring. 'I think it's best if we end things now,' she said. 'Before we head back to London.'

Jake stared at the ring and then at her. She wanted to end it? *Now?* Before the two weeks were up? That wasn't how 'the talk' usually went. Didn't she want more? Didn't she want them to continue their affair? Wasn't she going to cry, beg and plead with him to fall in love with her and marry her? She looked so composed, so determined, as if she had made up her mind hours ago.

'But I thought you said two weeks?'

'I know but I can't do it any more, Jake,' she said, putting the ring in the top pocket of his jacket and patting it as if for safekeeping. 'It was fun while it lasted but I want to move on with my life.'

'This seems rather…sudden.'

She stepped back and looked up at him with those beautiful storm, sea and mountain-lake eyes. 'Remember when we talked at breakfast?' she said. 'I've been thinking since… I can't pretend to be someone I'm not. It's not right for me or for you. You're not the settling down type and it was wrong of me to shackle you to me in this stupid game of pretend. I should've just accepted Myles's break-up with dignity instead of doing this crazy charade. It will hurt too many people if we let it continue. It has to stop.'

Jake wanted it to stop. Sure he did. But not yet. Not until he was satisfied his attraction to her had burned itself out. It was nowhere near burning out. It had only just started. They'd been lovers two days. *Two freaking days!* That wasn't long enough. He was only just starting to understand her. To know her. How could she want to end it? They were good together. Brilliant. The best. Why end it when they could have two more weeks, maybe even longer, of fantastic sex?

But how *much* longer?

The thought stood up from a sofa in the back of his mind where it had been lounging and stretched. Started walking toward his conscience…

Jake knew she was right. They had to end it some time. It was just he was usually the one to end flings. He was the one in the control seat. It felt a little weird to be on the receiving end of rejection. 'What about Emma Madden?' he said. 'Aren't you worried she might make a comeback when she hears we've broken up?'

'I think Emma is sensible enough to know you're not the right person for her. It will hurt her more if we tell even more lies.'

'What about Bruce Parnell?' *God, how pathetic was he getting? Using his clients as a lever to get her to rethink her decision?*

'Tell him the truth,' she said. 'That you're not in love with me and have no intention of marrying me or anyone.'

The truth always hurt, or so people said. But it didn't look like it hurt Jaz. She didn't seem to be the least bit worried he wasn't in love with her. She hadn't even asked him to declare his feelings, which was just as well, because they were stuffed under the cushions on that sofa in his mind and he wasn't going looking for them any time soon.

'You're right,' he said. 'Best to end it now before my parents start sending out invitations.'

She bit her lip for a moment. 'Will you tell them or will I?'

'I'll tell them I pulled the plug,' Jake said. 'That's what they'll think in any case.'

Her forehead puckered in a frown. 'But I don't want them to be angry with you or anything. I can say I got cold feet.'

'Leave it to me. Do you still want me to have a look over your business?'

'You wouldn't mind?'

'Why would I?' he said with a smile that was harder work than it had any right to be. 'We're friends, aren't we?'

Her smile was a little on the wobbly side but he could see relief in every nuance of her expression. 'Yes. Of course we are.'

It was on the tip of his tongue to ask for one more night but before he could get the words out she had turned and started packing her things. He watched her fold her clothes and pack them neatly into her bag. Every trace of her was being removed from the suite.

'I'm getting a lift back to London with one of the photographers,' she said once she was done. 'I thought it would be easier all round.'

'Is the photographer male?' The question jumped out before Jake could stop it and it had the big, green-eyed monster written all over it.

His question dangled in the silence for a long beat.

'Yes,' she said. 'But I've known him for years.'

Jaz had known *him* for years and look what had happened, Jake thought with a sickening churning in his gut.

She stepped up on tiptoe to kiss his cheek. 'Goodbye, Jake. See you at Julius's wedding.'

Wedding.

Jake clenched his jaw as the door closed on her exit. That word should be damned well banned.

CHAPTER TWELVE

JAZ WAS WORKING on Miranda's dress a few days later when the bell on the back of her shop door tinkled. She looked up and saw Emma Madden coming in, dressed in her school uniform. 'Hi, Emma,' she said, smiling as she put down the bodice she was sewing freshwater pearls on. 'How lovely to see you. How are you?'

Emma savaged her bottom lip with her teeth. 'Is it because of me?'

Jaz frowned. 'Is what because of you?'

'Your break-up with Jake,' she said. 'It's because of me, isn't it? I made such a stupid nuisance of myself and now you've broken up and it's all my fault.'

Jaz came out from behind the work counter and took the young girl's hands in hers. 'Nothing's your fault, sweetie. Jake and I decided we weren't ready to settle down. We've gone back to being friends.'

Emma's big, soulful eyes were misty. 'But you're so perfect for each other. I can't bear the thought of him having anyone else. You bring out the best in him. My stepdad says so too.'

Jaz gave Emma's hands a little squeeze before she

released them. 'It's sweet of you to say so but some things are not meant to be.'

'But aren't you…*devastated*?' Emma asked, scrunching up her face in a frown.

Jaz didn't want to distress the girl unnecessarily. No point telling Emma she cried every night when she got into her cold bed. *On. Her. Own.* No point saying how she couldn't get into a lift without her insides quivering in erotic memory. No point saying how every time she ate a piece of toast or drank orange juice she thought of Jake helping her through her fashion show nerves at the expo. 'I'm fine about it,' she said. 'Really. It's for the best.'

Emma sighed and then started looking at the dresses on display. She touched one reverently. 'Did you really make this from scratch?'

'Yup,' Jaz said. 'What do you think? Not too OTT?'

'No, it's beautiful,' Emma said. 'I would love to be able to design stuff like this.'

'Have you ever done any sewing?'

'I did some cross-stitch at school but I'd love to be able to make my own clothes,' Emma said. 'I sometimes get ideas for stuff… Does that happen to you?'

'All the time,' Jaz said. 'See that dress over there with the hoop skirt? I got the idea from the garden at Ravensdene. There's this gorgeous old weeping birch down there that looks exactly like a ball gown.'

Emma traced the leaf-like pattern of the lace. 'Wow… You're amazing. So talented. So smart and beautiful. So everything.'

So single, Jaz thought with a sharp pang. 'Hey, do

you fancy a part-time job after school or at weekends?
I could do with a little help and I can give you some
tips on pattern-making and stuff.'

Emma's face brightened as if someone had turned
a bright light on inside her. 'Do you mean it? *Really?*'

'Sure,' Jaz said. 'Who wants to work for a fast-food
chain when you can work for one of London's up-and-
coming bridal designers?'

Take that, Imposter Syndrome.

Three weeks later...

'Jake, can I get you another beer?' Flynn Carlyon
asked on his way to the bar at Julius's stag night. 'Hey,
you haven't finished that one—you've barely taken a
mouthful. You not feeling well or something?'

Jake forced a quick smile. 'No, I'm good.'

He wasn't good. He was sick. Not physically but
emotionally. He hadn't eaten a proper meal in days.
He couldn't remember the last time he'd had a decent
sleep. Well, he could, but remembering the last time
he'd made love with Jaz caused him even more emotional distress.

Yes, *emotional* distress.

The dreaded E-word—the word he'd been trying
to escape from for the last few weeks. Maybe he'd
been trying to escape it for the last seven years. He
couldn't stop thinking about Jaz. He couldn't get the
taste of her out of his mouth. He couldn't get the
feel of her out of his body. It had been nothing short of
torture to drop in the business plan for her last week

and not touch her. She had seemed a little distracted, but when she told him she'd employed Emma Madden to help in the shop after school he'd put it down to that—Jaz was worried he would have a problem with it. He didn't. He thought it was a stroke of genius, actually. He wished he'd thought of it himself.

Julius came over with a basket of crisps. 'He's off his food, his drink and his game,' he said to Flynn. 'He hasn't looked twice at any of the waitresses, even the blonde one with the big boobs.'

Flynn grinned. 'No kidding?'

'I reckon it's because he's in love with Jaz,' Julius said. 'But he's too stubborn to admit it.'

Jake glowered at his twin. 'Just because you're getting married tomorrow doesn't mean everyone else wants to do the same.'

'Mum's still not speaking to him,' Julius said to Flynn. 'She quite fancied having Jaz as a daughter-in-law.'

'Pity she isn't so keen on having Kat Winwood as a daughter,' Flynn said wryly.

'So, how's all that going with you and Kat?' Jake said, desperate for a subject change. 'You convinced her to come to Dad's Sixty Years in Showbiz party yet?'

'Not so far but I'm working on it,' Flynn said with an enigmatic smile.

'Better get your skates on, mate,' Julius said. 'You've only got a month and a bit. The party's in January.'

'Leave Kat Winwood to me,' Flynn said. 'I know how to handle a feisty Scotswoman.'

'I bet you've handled a few in your time,' Jake said.

'You can talk,' Flynn said with another grin. 'How come you haven't handled anyone since Jaz?'

Good question. Why hadn't he? Because he couldn't bear to wipe out the memory of her touch with someone else. He didn't want anyone else. But Jaz wanted marriage and kids. He had never seen himself as a dad. He had always found it so...terrifying to be responsible for someone else. He was better off alone. Single and loving it, that was his credo.

Jake put his untouched beer bottle down. 'Excuse me,' he said. 'I'm going to have an early night. See you lot in church.'

'You look amazing, Holly,' Jaz said outside the church just before they were to enter for Julius and Holly's wedding. 'Doesn't she, Miranda?'

Miranda was wiping at her eyes with a tissue. 'Capital A amazing. Gosh, I've got to get control of myself. My make-up is running. If I'm like this as a bridesmaid, what I am going to be like as a bride?'

Holly smiled at both of them. She was a radiant bride, no two ways about that. But happiness did that to you, Jaz thought. There could be no happier couple than Julius and Holly... Well, there was Miranda and Leandro, who were also nauseatingly happy. It was downright painful to be surrounded by so many blissfully happy people.

But Jaz was resolved. She wasn't settling for anything but the real deal. Love without limits. That was what she wanted. Love that would last a lifetime.

Love that was authentic and real, not pretend.

As Jaz led the way down the aisle she saw Jake standing next to Julius. It was surreal to see them both dressed in tuxedos looking exactly the same. No one could tell them apart, except for the way Julius was looking at Holly coming behind Miranda. Had a man ever looked at a woman with such love? *Yes*, Jaz thought when she caught a glimpse of Leandro, who was standing next to Jake looking at Miranda as if she was the most adorable girl in the world. Which she was, but that was beside the point. It was so *hard* not to be jealous.

Why couldn't Jake look at her like that?

Jaz caught his eye. He was looking a little green about the gills. Her own stomach lurched. Her heart contracted. Had he hooked up with someone last night after Julius's stag night? Had he had a one-nighter with someone? Several someones? She hadn't heard anything much in the press about him since they had announced they'd ended their 'engagement'. But then she had been far too busy with getting Holly's dress done on time to be reading gossip columns.

Miranda had let slip that Jake had left the stag night early. Did that mean he had hooked up with some-one? One of the barmaids at the wine bar the boys had gone to? Why else would he leave early? He was the party boy who was usually the last man standing. It didn't bear thinking about. It would only make the knot of jealousy tighten even more in the pit of her stomach. She had to put a brave face on. She couldn't let her feelings about Jake interfere with Julius and Holly's big day.

Jaz smiled at Elisabetta and Richard Ravensdale, who were sitting together and giving every appearance of being a solid couple, but that just showed what excellent actors they both were. Elisabetta had dressed the part, as she always did. She would have outshone the bride but Jaz had made sure Holly's dress was a show-stopper. Holly looked like a fairy-tale princess. Which was how it should be, as she'd had a pretty ghastly life up until she'd met Julius, which kind of made Jaz feel hopeful that dreams did come true... at least sometimes.

The service began and Jaz tried not to look at Jake too much. She didn't want people speculating or commenting on her single status. Or worse—pitying her. Would she ever be seen as anything other than the charity case? The gardener's daughter who'd made good only by the wonderful largesse of the Ravensdales?

Even the business plan Jake had drawn up for her was another example of how much she owed them. He wouldn't take a penny for his time. He hadn't stayed for a coffee or anything once he'd talked her through the plan. He hadn't even kissed her on the cheek or touched her in any way.

But looking at him now brought it all back. How much she missed him. How much she loved him. Why couldn't he love her?

Young Emma was right—they were perfect together. Jake made her feel safe. He watched out for her the way she longed for a partner to do. He stood up *to* her and stood up *for* her. How could she settle for anyone else? She would never be happy with anyone else. It wouldn't matter how many times she got engaged, no one would ever replace Jake. Nor would she want them to.

Jake was her soul mate because only with him could she truly be herself.

The vows were exchanged and for the first time in her life Jaz saw Julius blinking away tears. He was always so strong, steady and in charge of his emotions. He was the dependable twin. The one everyone went to when things were dire. Seeing him so happy made her chest feel tight. She wanted that same happiness for herself. She wanted it so badly it took her breath away to see others experiencing it.

Jake was still looking a little worse for wear. What was *wrong* with him? Didn't he have the decency to pull himself together for his brother's wedding? Or maybe it was the actual wedding that was making him look so white and pinched. He hated commitment. It had been bad enough at the wedding expo, although she had to admit he'd put on a good front. Maybe some of that Ravensdale acting talent had turned up in his genes after all. He could certainly do with some of it now. The very least he could do was look happy for his twin brother. He fumbled over handing Julius the wedding rings. He had to search in his pocket three times. But at least he had remembered to bring them.

Jaz decided to have a word with him while they were out with the bride and groom for the signing of the register. If she could put on a brave front, then so could he. He would spoil the wedding photos if he didn't get his act together. She wasn't going to let anyone ruin Julius and Holly's big day. No way.

Jake couldn't take his eyes off Jaz. She looked amazing in her bridesmaid dress. It was robin's-egg blue and the colour made her eyes pop and her creamy skin glow. How he wanted to touch that skin, to feel it against his own. His fingers ached; his whole body ached to pull her into his arms and kiss her, to show her how much he missed her. Missed what they'd had together.

Seeing his identical twin standing at the altar as his bride came towards him made Jake feel like he was seeing another version of himself. It was like seeing what he might have been. What he could *have* if he were a better man. A more settled man—a man who could be relied on; a man who could love, not just physically, but emotionally. A man who could commit to a woman because he could see no future without her by his side. A man who could be mature enough to raise a family and support them and his wife through everything that life threw at them.

That was the sort of man his twin was.

Why wasn't *he* like that?

Or was he like that in the part of his soul he didn't let anyone see? Apart from Jaz, of course. She had seen it. And commented on it.

Jake gave himself a mental shake. No wonder he hated weddings. They made him antsy. Restless.

Frightened.

For once he didn't shove the thought back where it came from. It wasn't going back in any case. It was front and centre in his brain. He *was* frightened. Frightened he wouldn't be good enough. Frightened he would love and not be loved in return. Frightened of feeling so deeply for someone, allowing someone to have control over him, of making himself vulnerable in case they took it upon themselves to leave.

He loved Jaz.

Hadn't he always loved her? Firstly as a surrogate sister and then, when she'd morphed into the gorgeous teenager with those bedroom eyes, he had been knocked sideways. But she had been too young and he hadn't been ready to admit he needed someone the way he needed her.

But he was an adult now. He'd had a taste of what they could be together—a solid team who complemented each other perfectly. She was his equal. He admired her tenacity, her drive, her passion, her talent. She was everything he wanted in a partner.

Wasn't that why he'd been carrying the engagement ring she had given back to him everywhere he went? It was like a talisman. The ring of truth. He loved Jaz and always would.

How could he have thought he could be happy without her? He had been nothing short of morose since they'd ended their fling. He was the physical embodiment of a wet weekend: gloomy, miserable, boring as hell. He had been dragging himself through each day. He hadn't dated. He hadn't even looked at anyone. He couldn't bear the thought of going through the old

routine of chatting some woman up only so he could
have sex with her. He was tired of no-strings sex. No-
strings sex was boring. He wanted emotional sex, the
sort of sex that spoke to his soul, the kind of sex that
made him feel alive and fulfilled as a man.

He had to talk to Jaz. He had to get her alone. How
long was this wretched service going to take? Oh,
they were going to sign the wedding register. Great.
He might be able to nudge Jaz to one side so he could
tell her the words he had told no one before.

Jaz wasted no time in sidling up to Jake when Julius
and Holly were occupied with signing the register.
'What is *wrong* with you?' she said in an undertone.

'I have to talk to you,' he said, pulling at his bow
tie as if it were choking him.

She rolled her eyes. 'Look, I know this is torture
for you, but can you just allow your brother his big
day without drawing attention to yourself? It's just a
bow tie, for pity's sake.'

He took her by the hand, his eyes looking suspi-
ciously moist. Did he have an allergy? There were certainly a lot of flowers about. But then the service had
been pretty emotional. Maybe it was a twin thing. If
Julius cried, Jake would too, although she had never
seen it before.

'I love you,' he said.

Jaz's eyelashes flickered at him in shock. *'What?'*

His midnight-blue eyes looked so amazingly soft
she had to remind herself it was actually Jake looking at her, not Julius looking at Holly. 'Not just as a

friend,' he said. 'And not just as a lover, but as a life partner. Marry me, Jaz. Please?'

Jaz's heart bumped against her breastbone. 'You can't ask me to marry you in the middle of your brother's wedding!'

He grinned. 'I just did. What do you say?'

She gazed at him, wondering if wedding fever had got to her so bad she was hallucinating. Was he really telling her he loved her and wanted to marry her? Was he really looking at her as if she was the only woman in the world who could ever make him completely happy? 'You're not doing this as some sort of joke, are you?' she asked, narrowing her eyes in suspicion. It would be just like him to want to have a laugh to counter all the emotion, to tone down all the seriousness, responsibility and formality.

He gripped her by the hands, almost crushing her bridesmaid's bouquet in the process. 'It's no joke,' he said. 'I love you and want to spend the rest of my life proving it to you. The last three weeks have been awful without you. You're all I think about. I'm like a lovesick teenager. I can't get you out of my head. As soon as I saw you walking down the aisle, I realised I couldn't let another day—another minute—go by without telling you how I feel. I want to be with you. Only you. Marry me, my darling girl.'

Jaz was still not sure she could believe what she was hearing. And nor, apparently, could the bridal party as they had stalled in the process of signing the register to watch on with beaming faces. 'But what about kids?' she said.

'I love kids. I'm a big kid myself. Remember how great I was with you and Miranda when you were kids? I reckon I'll be a great dad. How many do you want?'

Jaz remembered all too well. He had been fantastic with her and Miranda, making them laugh until their sides had ached. It was her dream coming to life in front of her eyes. Jake wanted to marry her and he wanted to have babies with her. 'Two at least,' she said.

He pulled her closer, smiling at her with twinkling eyes. 'I should warn you that twins run in my family.'

Jaz smiled back. 'I'll take the risk.'

'So you'll marry me?'

Could a heart burst with happiness? Jaz wondered. It certainly felt like hers was going to. But, even better, it looked like Jake was feeling exactly the same way. 'Yes.'

Jake bent his head to kiss her mouth with such heart-warming tenderness it made Jaz's eyes tear up. When he finally lifted his head, she saw similar moisture in his eyes. 'I was making myself sick with worry you might say no,' he said.

She stroked his jaw with a gentle hand, her heart now feeling so full it was making it hard for her to breathe. 'You're not an easy person to say no to.'

He brushed her cheek with his fingers as if to test she was real and not a figment of his imagination. 'How quickly can you whip up a wedding dress?'

She looked at him in delighted surprise. 'You want to get married sooner rather than later?'

He pressed a kiss to her forehead, each of her eyelids, both of her cheeks and the tip of her nose. 'Yes,' he said. 'As soon as it can be arranged. I don't even mind if it's in church or a garden, on the top of Big Ben or twenty leagues under the sea. I won't be happy until I can officially call you my wife.'

'Ahem.' Julius spoke from behind them. 'We're the ones trying to get married here.'

Jake turned to grin at his brother. 'We should've made it a double wedding.'

Julius smiled from ear to ear. 'Congratulations to both of you. Nothing could have made my and Holly's day more special than this.'

Miranda was dabbing at her eyes as she came rushing over to give Jaz a bone- and bouquet-crushing hug. 'I'm so happy for you. We're finally going to be sisters. Yay!'

Jaz blinked back tears as she saw Leandro looking at Miranda just the way Jake was looking at her—with love that knew no bounds. With love that would last a lifetime.

She turned back to Jake. 'Do you still have that engagement ring?'

Jake reached into his inside jacket pocket, his eyes gleaming. 'I almost gave it to Julius instead of the wedding rings.' He took it out and slipped it on her finger. 'There. That's got to stay there now. No taking it off. Ever. Understood?'

Jaz wrapped her arms around his waist and smiled up at him in blissful joy. 'I'm going to keep it on for ever.'

* * * * *

Look out for the dramatic conclusion of
THE RAVENSDALE SCANDALS
THE MOST SCANDALOUS RAVENSDALE
Available May 2016

And if you missed where it all started, check out
RAVENSDALE'S DEFIANT CAPTIVE
AWAKENING THE RAVENSDALE HEIRESS
Available now!

'Why did you want to marry me?'

Marco stared at her for a moment, furious that he felt cornered. Damn it, how dared she ask him—accuse him—when *she* was the one who should be called to account? What did it matter why he'd married her when she'd agreed?

Sierra had moved closer to the fire, and the flames cast dancing shadows across her face. She looked utterly delectable wearing his too-big clothes. The belt she'd cinched at her waist showed off its narrowness and the high, proud curve of her breasts. He remembered the feel of them in his hands when he'd given his desire free rein for a few intensely exquisite moments.

That memory had the power to stir the embers of his desire, and he turned away from her, willing the memories and the emotion back. He didn't want to feel anything for Sierra Rocci now. Not even simple lust.

'Damn it, Sierra, you have some nerve, asking me why I behaved the way I did. You're the one who chose to leave without so much as a note.'

'I know.'

'And you still haven't given me a reason why. Don't you think I deserve an explanation? Your parents are no longer alive to hear why you abandoned them, but I am.' His voice hardened, rose. 'So why don't you just tell me the truth?'

After spending three years as a die-hard New Yorker, **Kate Hewitt** now lives in a small village in the English Lake District with her husband, their five children and a golden retriever. In addition to writing intensely emotional stories, she loves reading, baking and playing chess with her son—she has yet to win against him, but she continues to try. Learn more about Kate at kate-hewitt.com.

INHERITED BY FERRANTI

BY
KATE HEWITT

First Published in Great Britain 2016
By Mills & Boon, an imprint of HarperCollins*Publishers*
1 London Bridge Street, London, SE1 9GF

© 2016 Kate Hewitt

ISBN: 978-0-263-92109-0

Printed and bound in Spain
by CPI, Barcelona

INHERITED
BY FERRANTI

CHAPTER ONE

TOMORROW WAS HER wedding day. Sierra Rocci gazed at the fluffy white meringue of a dress hanging from her wardrobe door and tried to suppress the rush of nerves that seethed in her stomach and fluttered up her throat. She was doing the right thing. She had to be. She had no other choice.

Pressing one hand to her jumpy middle, she turned to look out of the window at the darkened gardens of her father's villa on the Via Marinai Alliata in Palermo. The summer night was still and hot, without even a breath of wind to make the leaves of the plane trees in the garden rattle. The stillness felt expectant, even eerie, and she tried to shake off her nervousness; she'd *chosen* this.

Earlier that night she'd dined with her parents and Marco Ferranti, the man she was going to marry. They'd chatted easily, and Marco's gaze had rested on her like a caress, a promise. She could trust this man, she'd told herself. She had to. In less than twenty-four hours she would promise to love, honour and obey him. Her life would be in his hands.

She knew the hard price of obedience. She prayed Marco truly was a gentle man. He'd been kind to her so far, in the three months of their courtship. Gentle and patient, never punishing or pushing, except perhaps for that one time, when they'd gone for a walk in the gardens and he'd kissed her in the shadow of a plane tree, his mouth hard and insistent and surprisingly exciting on hers.

Another leap in her belly, and this was a whole different kind of fear. She was nineteen years old, and she'd only been kissed by her fiancé a handful of times. She was utterly inexperienced when it came to what happened in the bedroom, but Marco had told her, when he'd stopped his shockingly delicious onslaught under the plane tree, that he would be patient and gentle when it came to their wedding night.

She believed him. She'd chosen to believe him—an act of will, a step towards securing her future, her freedom. And yet... Sierra's unfocused gaze rested on the darkened gardens as nerves leapt and writhed inside her and doubt crept into the dark corners of her heart, sly and insidious as that old serpent. Did she really know Marco Ferranti? When she'd first glimpsed him in the courtyard of her father's *palazzo*, she'd watched as one of the kitchen cats had wound its scrawny body around Marco's legs. He'd bent down and stroked the cat's ears and the animal had purred and rubbed against him. Her father would have kicked the cat away, insist its kittens be drowned. Seeing Marco exhibit a moment of unthinking kindness when he thought no one was looking had lit the spark of hope inside Sierra's heart.

She knew her father approved of the marriage between her and Marco; she was not so naïve not to realise that it was his strong hand that had pushed Marco towards her. But she'd encouraged Marco; she'd made a choice. As much as was possible, she'd controlled her own destiny.

On that first evening he'd introduced himself, and then later he had asked her out to dinner. He'd wooed her gently, always courteous, even tender. She wasn't in love with him; she had no interest in that deceitful, dangerous emotion, but she wanted a way out of her father's house and marriage to Marco Ferranti would provide it...if she could truly trust him. She would find out tomorrow, when the vows were said, when the bedroom door closed...

Heaven help her. Sierra bit her knuckles as a fresh wave of fear broke coldly over her. Could she really do this? How could she not? To back out now would be to incur her father's endless wrath. She was marrying in order to be free, and yet she was not free to cry off. Perhaps she would never be truly free. But what other choice was there for a girl like her, nineteen years old and completely cut off from society, from life? Sheltered and trapped.

From below she heard the low rumble of her father's voice. Although she couldn't make out the words, just the sound of his voice had her tensing, alarm prickling the nape of her neck. And then she heard Marco answer, his voice as low as her father's and yet somehow warm. She'd liked his voice the first time she'd heard it, when he'd been introduced to her. She'd liked his smile, too, the quirking of one corner of his mouth, the slow way it lit up his face. She'd trusted him instinctively, even though he worked for her father. Even though he was a man of great power and charm, just as her father was. She'd convinced herself he was different. But what if she'd been wrong?

Before she could lose her nerve Sierra slipped out of her bedroom and hurried halfway down the front stairs, the white marble cold under her bare feet. She paused on the landing, out of view of the men in the foyer below, and strained to listen.

'I am glad to welcome you into my family as a true son.' Her father was at his best, charming and authoritative, a benevolent *papà*, brimming with good will.

'And I am glad to be so welcomed.'

Sierra heard the sound of her father slapping Marco's back and then his good-humoured chuckle. She knew that sound so well. She knew how false it was.

'*Bene*, Marco. As long as you know how to handle Sierra. A woman needs a firm hand to guide her. Don't be too gentle or they get notions. You can't have that.' The words were abhorrent and yet so terribly familiar, the tone gentle, almost amused, her father as assured as ever and completely in control.

Every muscle in Sierra's body seemed to turn to iron as she waited for Marco's response.

'Don't worry, *signor*,' Marco said. 'I know how to handle her.'

Sierra shrank back against the wall, horror and fear churning inside her. *I know how to handle her.* Did he really think that way, like her father did? That she was some beast to be guided and tamed into subservience?

'Of course you do,' Arturo Rocci said, his voice smug with satisfaction. 'I've groomed you myself, chosen you as my son. This is what I wanted, and I could not be more pleased. I have no doubts about you, Marco.'

'You honour me, *signor*.'

'Papà, Marco. You may call me Papà.'

Sierra peeked around the edge of the landing and saw the two men embracing. Then her father gave Marco one more back slap before disappearing down the corridor, towards his study.

Sierra watched Marco, a faint smile curving that mobile mouth, the sharp angle of his jaw darkened with five o'clock shadow, his silvery-grey eyes hooded and sleepy. He'd loosened his tie and shed his suit jacket, and he looked rumpled and tired and overwhelmingly male. *Sexy.*

But there was nothing sexy about what he'd just said. Nothing romantic or loving or remotely attractive about a man who thought women needed to be *handled*. Her stomach clenched hard with fear and, underneath, anger. Anger at Marco Ferranti, for clearly thinking as her father did, and anger at herself for being so naïve to think she actually knew a man after just three months, a handful of arranged dates, all of them carefully orchestrated evenings where Marco was at his best, guiding her gently towards the inevitable conclusion. She'd thought she'd chosen him, but now she wondered how well she'd been manipulated. *Handled*. Perhaps her fiancé was as false as her father, presenting a front she wanted to see while disguising the true man underneath. Would she ever know? Yes, when it was too late. When she was married to him and had no way to escape.

'Sierra?' Marco's silvery gaze flicked upwards, one eyebrow lifted as he gazed at her peeking around the landing, his faint smile deepening, revealing a dimple in one cheek. When Sierra had first seen that dimple it had made him seem friendlier. Kinder. She'd liked him more because of a *dimple*. She felt like such a child, naïve to the point of stupidity, thinking she'd wrested some control for herself when in fact she'd been the merest puppet.

'What are you doing hiding up there?' he asked, and he stretched one hand towards her.

'I…' Sierra licked dry lips as her mind spun. She could not think of a single thing to say. The only thing she could hear on an endless, awful reel was Marco's assured, indulgent words. *I know how to handle her*.

Marco glanced at his watch. 'It's after midnight, so technically I suppose I shouldn't see you. It's our wedding day, after all.'

Wedding day. In just a few hours she would marry this man. She would promise to love him. To honour and obey him…

I know how to handle her.

'Sierra?' Marco asked, concern sharpening his voice. 'Is something wrong?'

Everything was wrong. Everything had been wrong for ever, and she'd actually thought she'd been fixing it. She'd thought she was finally escaping, that she was choosing her own destiny. The thought seemed laughable now. How could she have fooled herself for so long? 'Sierra?' Impatience edged his voice now, and Sierra heard it. Heard how quickly the façade of concern fell away, revealed the true man underneath. Just as it did with her father.

'I'm only tired,' she whispered. Marco beckoned her towards him and on shaking legs she came down the stairs and stood before him, trying not to tremble. Not to show her fear. It was one small act of defiance she'd nurtured for most of her life, because she knew it infuriated her father. He wanted his women to cower and cringe. And Sierra had done her fair share of both, to her shame, over the years. But when she had the strength to stand tall, to act cool and composed, she did. Cloaking herself in numbness had been a way of coping since she was small. She was glad of it now.

Marco cupped her cheek with one hand. His palm was warm and dry and even now the tender gesture sent sparks shooting through her belly, and her legs shook.

'It's not long now,' he murmured, and his thumb brushed her lips. His expression was tender, but Sierra couldn't trust it any more. 'Are you nervous, little one?'

She was terrified. Wordlessly she shook her head. Marco chuckled, the sound indulgent, perhaps patronising. The assumptions she'd made about this man were proving to be just that: assumptions. She didn't really know who he was, what he was capable of. He'd been kind to her, yes, but what if it had just been an act, just like her father's kindness in public was? Marco smiled down at her, his dimple showing. 'Are you certain about that, *mi amore*?'

Mi amore. My love. But Marco Ferranti didn't love her. He'd never said he did, and she didn't even want him to. Looking back, she could see how expedient their relationship had been. A family dinner that led to a walk in the gardens that led to a proper date that led to a proposal. It had been a systematic procedure orchestrated by this man—and her father. And she hadn't realised, not completely. She'd thought she'd had some say in the proceedings, but now she wondered at how well she'd been manipulated. Used.

'I'm all right, Marco.' Her voice came out in a breathy whisper, and it took all the strength she possessed to step away from him so his hand dropped from her cheek. He frowned, and she wondered if he didn't like her taking even that paltry amount of control. She'd let him dictate everything in the three months of their courtship, she realised now. When and where they went, what they talked about—everything had been decided by him. She'd been so desperate to get away, and she'd convinced herself he was a kind man.

'One last kiss,' Marco murmured and before Sierra could think to step farther away he was pulling her towards him, his hands sliding up to cup her face as his lips came down on hers. Hard and soft. Hot and cold. A thousand sensations shivered through her as her lips parted helplessly. Longing and joy. Fear and desire. All of the emotions tangled up together so she couldn't tell them apart. Her hands fisted in his shirt and she stood on her tiptoes to bring his body closer to hers, unable to keep herself from it, not realising how revealing her response was until Marco chuckled and eased her away from him.

'There will be plenty of time later,' he promised her. 'Tomorrow night.'

When they were wed. Sierra pressed her fingers to her lips and Marco smiled, satisfied by her obvious response.

'Goodnight, Sierra,' he said softly, and Sierra managed to choke out a response.

'Goodnight.' She turned and hurried up the stairs, not daring to look back, knowing Marco was watching her.

In the quiet darkness of the upstairs hallway she pressed a hand to her thundering heart. Hated herself, hated Marco, for they were both to blame. She never should have let this happen. She should have never thought she could escape.

Sierra hurried down the hallway to the far wing of the house, knocking softly on the door of her mother's bedroom.

Violet Rocci opened the door a crack, her eyes wide with apprehension. She relaxed visibly when she saw it was Sierra, and opened the door wider to let her daughter in.

'You shouldn't be here.'

'Papà's downstairs.'

'Even so.' Violet clutched the folds of her silk dressing gown together, her face pale with worry and strain. Twenty years ago she'd been a beautiful young woman, a world-class pianist who played in London's best concert halls, on the cusp of major fame. Then she'd married Arturo Rocci and virtually disappeared from the public, losing herself in the process.

'Mamma…' Sierra stared helplessly at her mother. 'I think I may have made a mistake.'

Violet drew her breath in sharply. 'Marco?' Sierra nodded. 'But you love him…' Even after twenty years of living with Arturo Rocci, cringing under his hand, Violet believed in love. She loved her husband desperately, and it had been her destruction.

'I've never loved him, Mamma.'

'What?' Violet shook her head. 'But Sierra, you said...'

'I trusted him. I thought he was gentle. But the only reason I wanted to marry him was to escape...' Even now she couldn't say it. *Escape Papà.* She knew the words would hurt her mother; Violet hid from the truth as much as she could.

'And now?' Violet asked after a moment, her voice low.

'And now I don't know.' Sierra paced the room, the anxiety inside her like a spring that coiled tighter and tighter. 'I realise I don't know him at all.'

'The wedding is tomorrow, Sierra.' Violet turned away from her, her hand trembling at the throat of her dressing gown. 'What can you do? Everything has been arranged—'

'I know.' Sierra closed her eyes as regret rushed through her in a scalding wave. 'I'm afraid I have been very stupid.' She opened her eyes as she blinked back useless tears and set her jaw. 'I know there's nothing I can do. I have to marry him.' Powerlessness was a familiar feeling. Heavy and leaden, a mantle that had weighed her down for far too long. Yet she'd made her own trap this time. In the end she had no one to blame but herself. She'd agreed to Marco's proposal.

'There might be a way.'

Sierra glanced at her mother in surprise; Violet's face was pale, her eyes glittering with uncharacteristic determination. 'Mamma...'

'If you are certain that you cannot go through with it...'

'Certain?' Sierra shook her head. 'I'm not certain of anything. Maybe he is a good man...' *A man who was marrying her for the sake of Rocci Enterprises? A man who worked hand in glove with her father and insisted he knew how to handle her?*

'But,' Violet said, 'you do not love him.'

Sierra thought of Marco's gentle smile, the press of his lips. Then she thought of her mother's desperate love for her father, despite his cruelty and abuse. She didn't love Marco Ferranti. She didn't want to love anyone. 'No, I don't love him.'

'Then you must not marry him, Sierra. God knows a woman can suffer much for the sake of love, but without it…' She pressed her lips together, shaking her head, and questions burned in Sierra's chest, threatened to bubble up her throat. How could her mother love her father, after everything he'd done? After everything she and her mother had both endured? And yet Sierra knew she did.

'What can I do, Mamma?'

Violet drew a ragged breath. 'Escape. Properly. I would have suggested it earlier, but I thought you loved him. I've only wanted your happiness, darling. I hope you can believe that.'

'I do believe it, Mamma.' Her mother was a weak woman, battered into defeated submission by life's hardships and Arturo Rocci's hand. Yet Sierra had never doubted her mother's love for her.

Violet pressed her lips together, gave one quick nod. 'Then you must go, quickly. Tonight.'

'*Tonight…?*'

'Yes.' Swiftly, her mother went to her bureau and opened a drawer, reached behind the froth of lingerie to an envelope hidden in the back of the drawer. 'It's all I have. I've been saving it over the years, in case…'

'But how?' Numbly, Sierra took the envelope her mother offered her; it was thick with euros.

'Your father gives me housekeeping money every week,' Violet said. Spots of colour had appeared high on each delicate cheekbone, and Sierra felt a stab of pity. She knew her mother was ashamed of how tied she was to her husband, how firmly under his thumb. 'I rarely spend it. And so over the years I've managed to save. Not much…a thousand euros maybe, at most. But enough to get you from here.'

Hope and fear blazed within her, each as strong as the other. 'But where would I go?' She'd never considered such a thing—a proper escape, unencumbered, independent, truly free. The possibility was intoxicating and yet terrifying; she'd spent her childhood in a villa in the country, her adolescent years at a strict convent school. She had no experience of anything, and she knew it.

'Take the ferry to the mainland, and then the train to Rome. From there to England.'

'England…' The land of her mother's birth.

'I have a friend, Mary Bertram,' Violet whispered. 'I have not spoken to her in many years, not since…' Since she'd married Arturo Rocci twenty years ago. Wordlessly, Sierra nodded her understanding. 'She did not want me to marry,' Violet said, her voice so low now Sierra strained to hear it, even when she was standing right next to her mother. 'She didn't trust him. But she told me if anything happened, her door would always be open.'

'You know where she lives?'

'I have her address from twenty years ago. I am afraid that is the best I can do.'

Sierra's insides shook as she considered what she was about to do. She, who did not venture into Palermo without an escort, a guard. Who never handled money, who had never taken so much as a taxi. How could she do this?

How could she not? This was her only chance. Tomorrow she would marry Marco Ferranti, and if he was a man like her father, as his wife she would have no escape. No hope.

'If I leave…' she whispered, her voice thickening. She could not continue, but she didn't need to.

'You will not be able to return,' Violet said flatly. 'Your father would…' She swallowed, shaking her head. 'This will be goodbye.'

'Come with me, Mamma—'

Violet's expression hardened. 'I can't.'

'Because you love him?' The hurt spilled from her like a handful of broken glass, sharp and jagged with pain. 'How can you love him, after everything…?'

'Do not question my choices, Sierra.' Violet's face was pale, her mouth pinched tight. 'But make your own.'

Her own choice. Freedom at last. Overwhelming, frightening freedom, more than she'd ever had before, more than she'd even know what to do with. Instead of shackling herself to a man, even a good man, she would be her own person. Free to choose, to live.

The realisation made her feel sick with fear, dizzy with hope. Sierra closed her eyes. 'I don't know, Mamma…'

'I cannot choose for you, Sierra.' Her mother brushed her cheek lightly with her fingertips. 'Only you can decide your own destiny. But a marriage without love…' Her mother swallowed hard. 'I would not wish that on anyone.'

Not every man is like Arturo Rocci. Not every man is cruel, controlling, hard. Sierra swallowed down the words. Marco Ferranti might not be like her father, but he might very well be. After what she'd heard and realised tonight, she knew she couldn't take the risk.

Her hand clenched on the envelope of euros. Violet nodded, seeing the decision made in Sierra's face. 'God go with you, Sierra.'

Sierra hugged her mother tightly, tears stinging her eyes. 'Quickly now,' Violet said, and Sierra hurried from the room. Down the hall to her own bedroom, the wedding dress hanging from the wardrobe like a ghost. She dressed quickly and then grabbed a bag and stuffed some clothes into it. Her hands shook.

The house was quiet, the night air still and silent. Sierra glanced at the violin case under her bed and hesitated. It would be difficult to bring, and yet…

Music had been her only solace for much of her life. Leaving her violin would be akin to leaving a piece of her soul. She grabbed the case and swung the holdall of clothes over her shoulder. And then she tiptoed downstairs, holding her breath, her heart pounding so hard her chest hurt. The front door was locked for the night, but Sierra slid the bolt from its hinges without so much as a squeak. From the study she heard her father shift in his chair, rustle some papers. For a terrible moment her heart stilled, suspended in her chest as she froze in terror.

Then he let out a sigh and she eased the door open slowly, so slowly, every second seeming to last an hour. She slipped through and closed it carefully behind her before glancing at the dark, empty street. She looked back at the house with its lit windows one last time before hurrying into the night.

CHAPTER TWO

Seven years later

'SHE MIGHT NOT COME.'

Marco Ferranti turned from the window and his indifferent perusal of Palermo's business district with a shrug. 'She might not.' He glanced at the lawyer seated behind the large mahogany desk and then strode from the window, every taut, controlled movement belying the restlessness inside him.

'She didn't come to her mother's funeral,' the lawyer, Roberto di Santis, reminded him cautiously.

Marco's hands curled into fists and he unclenched them deliberately before shoving them into the pockets of his trousers and turning to face the man. 'I know.'

Violet Rocci had died three years ago; cancer had stalked her and killed her in a handful of months. Sierra had not come back for her mother's illness or funeral, despite Arturo's beseeching requests. She had not even sent a letter or card, much to her father's sorrow. The last time Marco had seen her had been the night before their wedding, when he'd kissed her and felt her trembling, passionate response.

The next morning he'd waited at the front of the church of Santa Caterina for his bride to process down the aisle. And waited. And waited. And waited.

Seven years later he was still waiting for Sierra Rocci to show up.

The lawyer shuffled some papers before clearing his throat noisily. He was nervous, impatient, wanting to get the ordeal of Arturo Rocci's will over with. He'd assured Marco it was straightforward if uncomfortable; Marco had seen the document himself, before Arturo had died. He knew what it said. He didn't think Sierra did, though, and he grimly looked forward to acquainting her with its details.

Surely she would come?

Marco had instructed the lawyer to contact her personally. Marco had known where Sierra was for a while; about five years ago, when the first tidal wave of rage had finally receded to a mist, he'd hired a private investigator to discover her whereabouts. He'd never contacted her, never wanted to. But he'd needed to know where she was, what had happened to her. The knowledge that she was living a seemingly quiet, unassuming life in London had not been satisfying in the least. Nothing was.

'She said she would come, didn't she?' he demanded, although he already knew the answer.

When di Santis had called her at her home, she'd agreed to meet here, at the lawyer's office, at ten o'clock on June fifteenth. It was now nearing half past.

'Perhaps we should just begin…?'

'No.' Marco paced the room, back to the window where he gazed out at the snarl of traffic. 'We'll wait.' He wanted to see Sierra's face when the will was read. He wanted to see the expression in her eyes as realisation dawned of how much she'd lost, how much she'd sacrificed simply to get away from him.

'If it pleases you, *signor*,' di Santis murmured and Marco did not bother to answer.

Thirty seconds later the outer door to the building

opened with a telling cautious creak; di Santis's assistant murmured something, and then a knock sounded on the office door.

Every muscle in Marco's body tensed; his nerves felt as if they were scraped raw, every sense on high alert. It had to be her.

'Signor di Santis?' the assistant murmured. 'Signorina Rocci has arrived.'

Marco straightened, forcing himself to relax as Sierra came into the room. She looked exactly the same. The same long, dark blond hair, now pulled back into a sleek chignon, the same wide blue-grey eyes. The same lush mouth, the same tiny, kissable mole at its left corner. The same slender, willowy figure with gentle curves that even now he itched to touch.

Desire flared through him, a single, intense flame that he resolutely quenched.

Her gaze moved to him and then quickly away again, too fast for him to gauge her expression. She stood straight, her shoulders thrown back, her chin tilted at a proud, almost haughty angle. And then Marco realised that she was not the same.

She was seven years older, and he saw it in the faint lines by her eyes and mouth. He saw it in the clothing she wore, a charcoal-grey pencil skirt and a pale pink silk blouse. Sophisticated, elegant clothing for a woman, rather than the girlish dresses she'd worn seven years earlier.

But the inner sense of stillness he'd always admired she still possessed. The sense that no one could touch or affect her. He'd been drawn to that, after the tempest of his own childhood. He'd liked her almost unnatural sense of calm, her cool purpose. Even though she'd only been nineteen she'd seemed older, wiser. *And yet so innocent.*

'Signorina Rocci. I'm so glad you could join us.' Di

Santis moved forward, hands outstretched. Sierra barely brushed her fingertips with his before she moved away, to one of the club chairs. She sat down, her back straight, her ankles crossed, ever the lady. She didn't look at Marco.

He was looking at her, his stare burning. Marco jerked his gaze from Sierra and moved back to the window. Stared blindly out at the traffic that crawled down the Via Libertà.

'Shall we begin?' suggested di Santis, and Marco nodded. Sierra did not speak. 'The will is, in point of fact, quite straightforward.' Di Santis cleared his throat and Marco felt his body tense once more. He knew just how straightforward the will was. 'Signor Rocci, that is, your father, *signorina*—' he gave Sierra an abashed smile that Marco saw from the corner of his eye she did not return '—made his provisions quite clear.' He paused, and Marco knew he was not relishing the task set before him.

Sierra sat with her hands folded in her lap, her chin held high, her gaze direct and yet giving nothing away. Her face looked like a perfect icy mask. 'Could you please tell me what they are, Signor di Santis?' she asked when di Santis seemed disinclined to continue.

The sound of her voice, after seven years' silence, struck Marco like a fist to the gut. Suddenly he was breathless. Low, musical, clear. And yet without the innocent, childish hesitation of seven years ago. She spoke with an assurance she hadn't possessed before, a confidence the years had given her, and somehow this knowledge felt like an insult, a slap in his face. She'd become someone else, someone stronger perhaps, without him.

'Of course, Signorina Rocci.' Di Santis gave another apologetic smile. 'I can go through the particulars, but in essence your father left the bulk of his estate and business to Signor Ferranti.'

Marco swung his gaze to her pale face, waiting for her

reaction. The shock, the regret, the acknowledgement of her own guilt, the realisation of how much she'd chosen to lose. *Something.*

He got nothing.

Sierra merely nodded, her face composed, expressionless. 'The bulk?' she clarified quietly. 'But not all?'

At her question Marco felt a savage stab of rage, a fury he'd thought he'd put behind him years ago. So she was going to be mercenary? After abandoning her family and fiancé, offering no contact for seven long years despite her parents' distress and grief and continued appeals, she still wanted to know how much she'd get.

'No, not all, Signorina Rocci,' di Santis said quietly. He looked embarrassed. 'Your father left you some of your mother's jewellery, some pieces passed down through her family.'

Sierra bowed her head, a strand of dark blond hair falling from her chignon to rest against her cheek. Marco couldn't see her expression, couldn't tell if she was overcome with remorse or rage at being left so little. Trinkets, Arturo had called them. A pearl necklace, a sapphire brooch. Nothing too valuable, but in his generosity Arturo had wanted his daughter to have her mother's things.

Sierra raised her eyes and Marco saw that her eyes glistened with tears. 'Thank you,' she said quietly. 'Do you have them here?'

'I do…' Di Santis fumbled for a velvet pouch on his desk. 'Here they are. Your father left them into my safe-keeping a while ago, when he realised…' He trailed off, and Sierra made no response.

When he realised he was dying, Marco filled in silently. Had the woman no heart at all? She seemed utterly unmoved by the fact that both her parents had died in her absence, both their hearts broken by their daughter's running away. The only thing that had brought her to tears was knowing she'd get nothing more than a handful of baubles.

'They won't be worth much, on the open market,' Marco said. His voice came out loud and terse, each word bitten off. Sierra's gaze moved to him and he felt a deep jolt in his chest at the way she looked at him, her gaze opaque and fathomless. As if she were looking at a complete stranger, and one she was utterly indifferent to.

'Is there anything else I need to know?' Sierra asked. She'd turned back to the lawyer, effectively dismissing Marco.

'I can read the will in its entirety…'

'That won't be necessary.' Her voice was low, soft. 'Thank you for my mother's jewels.' She rose from the chair in one elegantly fluid movement, and Marco realised she was leaving. After seven years of waiting, wondering, wanting a moment where it all finally made sense, he got nothing.

Sierra didn't even look at him as she left the room.

Sierra's breath came out in a shudder as she left the lawyer's office. Her legs trembled and her hands were clenched so tightly around the little velvet pouch that her knuckles ached.

It wasn't until she was out on the street that her breathing started to return to normal, and it took another twenty minutes of driving out of Palermo, navigating the endless snarl of traffic and knowing she'd left Marco Ferranti far behind, before she felt the tension begin to unknot from her shoulders.

The busy city streets gave way to dusty roads that wound up to the hill towns high above Palermo, the Mediterranean glittering blue-green as she drove towards the Nebrodi mountains, and the villa where her mother was buried. When di Santis had rung her, she'd thought about not going to Sicily at all, and then she'd thought about simply going to his office and returning to London on the very same day. She had nothing left in Sicily now.

But then she'd reminded herself that her father couldn't hurt her any longer, that Sicily was a place of ghosts and memories, and not of threats. She'd forgotten about Marco Ferranti.

A trembling laugh escaped her as she shook her head wryly. She hadn't forgotten about Marco; she didn't think she could ever do that. She'd simply underestimated the effect he'd have on her after seven years of thankfully numbing distance.

When she'd first caught sight of him in the office, wearing an expensive silk suit and reeking of power and privilege, looking as devastatingly attractive as he had seven years ago but colder now, so much colder, her whole body had trembled. Fortunately she'd got herself under control before Marco had swung that penetrating iron-grey gaze towards her. She had forced herself not to look at him.

She had no idea how he felt about her seven years on. Hatred or indifference, did it really matter? She'd made the right decision by running away the night before her wedding. She'd never regret it. Watching from afar as Marco Ferranti became more ingrained in Rocci Enterprises, always at her father's side and groomed to be his next-in-line, told her all she needed to know about the man.

The road twisted and turned as it climbed higher into the mountains, the air sharper and colder, scented with pine. The hazy blue sky she'd left in Palermo was now dark with angry-looking clouds, and when Sierra parked the car in front of the villa's locked gates she heard a distant rumble of thunder.

She shivered slightly even though the air was warm; the

wind was picking up, the sirocco that blew from North Africa and promised a storm. The pine trees towered above her, the mountains seeming to crowd her in. She'd spent most of her childhood at this villa, and while she'd loved the beauty and peace of its isolated position high above the nearest hill town, the place held too many hard memories for her to have any real affection for it.

Standing by the window as dread seeped into her stomach when she saw her father's car drive up the winding lane. Fear clenching her stomach hard as she heard his thunderous voice. Cringing as she heard her mother's placating or pleading response. No, she definitely didn't have good memories of here.

But she wouldn't stay long now. She'd see her mother's grave, pay her respects and then return to Palermo, where she'd booked into a budget hotel. By this time tomorrow she'd be back in London, and she'd never come to Sicily again.

Quickly, Sierra walked along the high stone wall that surrounded the estate. She knew the property like her own hand; she and her mother had always stayed here until Arturo called them into service, to play-act at being the perfect family for various engagements or openings of the Rocci hotels that now graced much of the globe. Her mother had lived for her husband's summons; Sierra had dreaded them.

Away from the road she knew the wall had crumbled in places, creating a gap low enough for her to climb over. She doubted her father had seen to repairs in the last seven years; she wondered if he'd come to the villa at all. He'd preferred to live his own life in Palermo except when he needed his wife and daughter to play at happy families for the media.

She stepped into the shelter of a dense thicket of pine

trees, the world falling to darkness as the trees overhead shut out any remnant of sunlight. Thunder rumbled again, and the branches snagged on her silk blouse and narrow skirt, neither a good choice for walking through woods or climbing walls.

After a few moments of walking she came to a crumbled section of wall and with effort, thanks to her pencil skirt, she managed to clamber over it. Sierra let out a breath of relief and started towards the far corner of the estate, where the family cemetery was located.

She skirted the villa, not wanting to attract attention to herself; she had no idea if anyone was in residence. Arturo had installed a housekeeper when she'd lived here with her mother, a beady-eyed old woman who had been her father's henchman and spy. If she was still here, Sierra had no wish to attract her attention.

In the distance the ghostly white marble headstones of the Rocci family plot appeared through the stormy gloom like silent, still ghosts, and Sierra's breath caught in her throat as she approached. She knew where her mother's marker lay, in the far corner; it was the only one that hadn't been there when she'd left.

Violet Rocci, Beloved Wife

She stared at the four words written starkly on the tombstone until they blurred and she blinked back tears. Beloved mother, yes, but *wife*? Had her father loved her mother at all? Sierra knew Violet believed so, but Sierra wanted to believe love was better and bigger than that. Love didn't hurt, didn't punish or belittle. She wanted to believe that, but she didn't know if she could. She certainly had no intention of taking the risk of finding out for herself.

'*Ti amo*, Mamma,' she whispered, and rested her hand on top of the cool marble. She'd missed her mother so much over these past seven years. Although she'd written Violet a few letters over the years, her mother had discouraged contact, fearing for Sierra's safety. The few letters she'd had were precious and all too rare, and had stopped completely well before Violet's illness.

She drew a deep breath and willed the tears away. She wouldn't cry now. There had been enough sadness already. Another deep breath and her composure was restored, as she needed it to be. Cloak herself in coolness, keep the feelings at bay. She turned away from the little cemetery plot and started walking back towards her car. She hoped Violet Rocci was at peace now, safe from her husband's cruelty. It was the smallest comfort, but the only one she could cling to now.

Thunder rumbled and forked lightning split the sky as the first heavy raindrops fell. Sierra ducked her head and started hurrying back to the section of wall she'd climbed over. She didn't want to be caught in a downpour, and neither did she relish the drive back down the steep mountain roads in this weather.

She climbed over the wall and hurried through the stand of pines, the branches snagging on her blouse and hair as the rain fell steadily, soaking her. Within seconds her pink silk blouse was plastered to her skin and her hair fell out of its chignon in wet rat's tails.

She cursed under her breath, thankful to emerge from the trees, only to have her insides freeze as she caught sight of a second car, a dark SUV, parked behind her own. As she came onto the road the door to the car opened, and an all too familiar figure emerged.

Marco Ferranti strode towards her, his white dress shirt soon soaked under the downpour so every well-defined muscle was outlined in glorious detail. Sierra flicked her gaze upwards, but the anger she saw snapping in his eyes, the hard set of his mouth and jaw, made her insides quell and she looked away. The rain was sheeting down now and she stopped a few feet from him, sluicing rainwater from her face.

'So.' Marco's voice was hard, without a shred of warmth. 'What the bloody hell do you think you're doing here?'

CHAPTER THREE

SIERRA DREW A deep breath and pushed the sodden mass of her hair away from her face. 'I was paying my respects.' She tried to move past him to her car but he blocked her way. 'What are *you* doing here?' she challenged, even though inside she felt weak and shaky with fear. Here was the real man Marco had hidden from her before, the angry, menacing man who loomed above her like a dark shadow, fierce and threatening. But, just as with her father, she wouldn't show her fear to this man.

'It's my home,' Marco informed her. 'As of today.'

She recoiled at that, at the triumph she heard in his tone. He was glad he'd got it all, and that she'd got almost nothing. Of course he was. 'I hope you enjoy it then,' she bit out, and his mouth curved in an unpleasant smile.

'I'm sure I will. But you were trespassing on private property, you do realise?'

She shook her head, stunned by the depth of his anger and cruelty. So this was the true face of the man she'd once thought of marrying. 'I'm leaving anyway.'

'Not so fast.' He grabbed her arm, his powerful fingers encircling her wrist, making her go utterly still. The commanding touch was so familiar and instinctively she braced herself for a blow. But it didn't come; Marco simply stared at her, and it took Sierra a moment to realise the fingers around her wrist were actually exerting only a gentle pressure.

'I want to know why you were here.'

'I told you,' she bit out. 'To pay my respects.'

'Did you go inside the villa?'

She stared at him, nonplussed. 'No.'

'How do I know that? You might have stolen something.'

She lct out an incredulous laugh. If she'd had any doubts about whether jilting Marco Ferranti had been the right thing to do, he was dispelling them with dizzying speed.

'What on earth do you think I stole?' She shook his hand off her wrist and spread her arms wide. 'Where would I hide it?' She saw Marco's gaze flick down to her breasts and too late she realised the white lace bra she wore was visible through the soaked, near-transparent silk. Sierra kept her head held high with effort.

'I can't be sure of anything when it comes to you, except that you can't be trusted.'

'Did you follow me all the way from Palermo?'

His jaw tightened. 'I wanted to know where you were going.'

'Well, now you know. And now I'm going back to Palermo.' She started to move away but Marco stilled her with one outflung hand. He nodded towards the steep, curving road that led down the mountain.

'The road will be impassable now with flash flooding. You might as well come into the villa until it is over.'

'And you'll frisk me for any possible stolen goods?' Sierra finished. 'I'll take my chances with the flooding.'

'Don't be stupid.' Marco's voice was harsh, dismissive, reminding her so much of her father. Clearly, he'd decided to emulate his mentor.

'I'm not being stupid,' she snapped. 'I mean every word I say.'

'You'd rather risk serious injury or even death than come into a dry house with me?' Marco's mouth twisted. 'What did I ever do to deserve such disgust?'

'You just accused me of *stealing*.'

'I simply wanted to know why you were here.'

Above them an ear-splitting crack of thunder sounded, making Sierra jump. She was completely soaked and unfortunately she knew Marco spoke the truth. The roads would be truly impassable, most likely for some time.

'Fine,' she said ungraciously and got into her car.

Marco unlocked the gates with the remote control in his car, and they swung silently back, revealing the villa's long, curving drive.

Taking a deep breath, Sierra drove up with Marco following like her jailer. As soon as his car had passed, the gates swung closed again, locking her inside.

She parked in front of the villa and turned off the engine, reluctant to get out and face Marco again. And to face all the unwelcome memories that crowded her brain and heart. Coming back to Sicily had been a very bad idea.

Her door jerked open and Marco stood there, glowering at her. 'Are you going to get out of your car?'

'Yes, of course.' She climbed out, conscious of his nearness, of the animosity rolling off him even though he'd sounded cold and controlled. After seven years, did he still hate her for what she'd done? It seemed so.

'Is anyone living in the villa?' she asked as he pressed the security code into the keypad by the front door.

'No. I've left it empty for the time being, while I've been in Palermo.' He glanced back at her, his expression opaque. 'While your father was in hospital.'

Sierra made no reply. The lawyer, di Santis, had told her

that her father had died of pancreatic cancer. He'd had it for several years but had kept it secret; when the end came it had been swift. After the call she'd tried to dredge up some grief for the man who had sired her; she'd felt nothing but a weary relief that he was finally gone.

Marco opened the front door and ushered her into the huge marble foyer. The air was chilly and stale, the furniture shrouded in dust cloths. Sierra shivered.

'I'll turn the hot water on,' Marco said. 'I believe there are clothes upstairs.'

'My clothes…?'

'No, those were removed some time ago.' His voice was clipped, giving nothing away. 'But some of my clothes are in one of the guest bedrooms. You can borrow something to wear while your own clothes dry.'

She remained shivering in the foyer, dripping rainwater onto the black and white marble tiles, while Marco set about turning on lights and removing dust covers. It felt surreal to be back in this villa, and she couldn't escape the clawing feeling of being trapped, not just by the locked gates and the memories that mocked her, but by the man inhabiting this space, seeming to take up all the air. She felt desperate to leave.

'I'll light a fire in the sitting room,' Marco said. 'I'm afraid there isn't much food.'

'I don't need to eat. I'm going to leave as soon as possible.'

Marco's mouth twisted mockingly as he glanced back at her. 'Oh, I don't think so. The roads will be flooded for a while. I don't think you'll be leaving before tomorrow morning.' His eyes glinted with challenge or perhaps derision as he folded his powerful arms across his chest. Even angry and hostile, he was a beautiful man, every taut muscle radiating strength and power. But she didn't like brute strength. She hated the abuse of power. She looked away from him.

'Why don't you take a bath and change?'

Sierra's stomach clenched at the prospect of spending a night under the same roof as Marco Ferranti. Of taking a bath, changing clothes…everything making her feel vulnerable. He must have seen something in her face for he added silkily, 'Surely you're not worried for your virtue? Trust me, *cara*, I wouldn't touch you with a ten-foot bargepole.'

She flinched at both the deliberate use of the endearment and the contempt she saw in his face. The casual cruelty had been second nature to her father, but it stung coming from Marco Ferranti. He'd been kind to her once.

'Good,' she answered when she trusted her voice. 'Because that's the last thing I'd want.'

His gaze darkened and he took a step towards her. 'Are you sure about that?'

Sierra held her ground. She knew her body had once responded to Marco's, and even with him emanating raw, unadulterated anger she had a terrible feeling it would again. A single caress or kiss and she might start to melt, much to her shame. 'Very sure,' she answered in a clipped voice, and then she turned towards the stairs without another word.

She found Marco's things in one of the guest bedrooms; he hadn't taken the master bedroom for himself and she wondered why. It was all his now, every bit of it. The villa, the *palazzo* in Palermo, the Rocci business empire of hotels and real estate holdings. Her father had given everything to the man he'd seen as a son, and left his daughter with nothing.

Or almost nothing. Carefully she took the velvet pouch out from the pocket of her skirt. The pearl necklace and sapphire brooch that had been her mother's before she married were hers now. She had no idea why her father had allowed her to have them; had it been a moment of kindness on his deathbed, or had he simply been saving face, trying to seem like the kind, grieving father he'd never been?

It didn't matter. She had a keepsake to remind her of her mother, and that was all she'd wanted.

Quickly, Sierra slipped out of her wet clothes and took a short, scaldingly hot shower. She dressed in a soft grey T-shirt and tracksuit bottoms of Marco's; it felt bizarrely intimate to wear his clothes, and they swam on her. She used one of his belts to keep the bottoms from sliding right off her hips, and combed her hair with her fingers, leaving it hanging damply down her back.

Then, hesitantly, she went downstairs. She would have rather hidden upstairs away from Marco until the storm passed but, knowing him, he'd most likely come and find her. Perhaps it would be better to deal with the past, get that initial awful conversation out of the way, and then they could declare a silent truce and ignore each other until she was able to leave.

She found him in the sitting room, crouched in front of the fire he was fanning into crackling flame. He'd changed into jeans and a black T-shirt and the clothes fitted him snugly, emphasising his powerful chest and long legs, every inch of him radiating sexual power and virility.

Sierra stood in the doorway, conscious of a thousand things: how Marco's damp hair had started to curl at the nape of his neck, how the soft cotton of the T-shirt she wore—*his* T-shirt—rubbed against her bare breasts. She felt a tingling flare of what could only be desire and tried to squelch it. He hated her now, and in any case she knew what kind of man he was. How could she possibly desire him?

He glanced back at her as she came into the room, and with a shivery thrill she saw an answering flare of awareness in his own eyes. He straightened, the denim of his jeans stretching across his powerful thighs, and Sierra's gaze was drawn to the movement, to the long, fluid length of his legs, the powerful breadth of his shoulders. Once he would have been hers, a thought that had filled her with apprehension and even fear. Now she felt a flicker of curiosity and even loss for what might have been, and she quickly brushed it aside.

The man was handsome. Sexy. She'd always known that. It didn't change who he was, or why she'd had to leave.

'Come and get warm.' Marco's voice was low, husky. He gestured her forward and Sierra came slowly, reluctant to get any closer to him. Shadows danced across the stone hearth and her bare feet sank into the thick, luxuriously piled carpet.

'Thank you,' she murmured without looking at him. The tension in the room was thick and palpable, a thousand unspoken words and thoughts between them. Sierra stared at the dancing flames, having no idea how to break the silence, or whether she wanted to. Perhaps it would be better to act as if the past had never happened.

'When do you return to London?' Marco asked. His voice was cool, polite, the question that of an acquaintance or stranger.

Sierra released the breath she'd bottled in her lungs without realising. Maybe he would make this easy for her. 'Tomorrow.'

'Did you not think you'd have affairs to manage here?'

She glanced at him, startled, saw how his silvery eyes had narrowed to iron slits, his mouth twisted mockingly. His questions sounded innocuous, but she could see and feel the latent anger underneath the thin veneer of politeness.

'No. I didn't expect my father to leave me anything in his will.'

'You didn't?' Now he sounded nonplussed, and Sierra shrugged.

'Why would he? We've neither spoken nor seen each other in seven years.'

'That was your choice.'

'Yes.'

They were both silent, the only sound the crackling of the fire, the settling of logs in the grate. Sierra had wondered how much Marco guessed of her father's abuse and cruelty. How much he would have sanctioned. The odd slap? The heaping of insults and emotional abuse? Did it even matter?

She'd realised, that night she'd left, that she could not risk it. She'd been foolish to think she could, that she could entrust herself to any man. Leaving Marco had been as much about her as about him.

'Why did you come back here, to this villa?' Marco asked abruptly, and Sierra looked up from her contemplation of the fire.

'I told you—'

'To pay your respects. To what? To whom?'

'To my mother. Her grave is in the family plot on the estate.'

He cocked his head, his silvery gaze sweeping coldly over her. 'And yet you didn't return when your mother was ill. You didn't even send a letter.'

Because she hadn't known. But would she have come back, even if she had known? Could she have risked her father's wrath, being under his hand once more? Sierra swallowed and looked away.

'No answer?' Marco jibed softly.

'You know the answer. And anyway, it wasn't a question.'

He shook his head slowly. 'You are certainly living up—or should I say down—to my expectations.'

'What does that mean?'

'For seven years I've wondered just how cold a bitch I almost married. Now I know.'

The words felt like a slap, sending her reeling. She blinked past the pain, told herself it didn't matter. 'You can think what you like.'

'Of course I can. It's not as if you've ever given me any answers, have you? Any possible justification for what you did, not just in leaving me, but in deserting your family?'

She didn't reply. She didn't want to argue with Marco, and in any case he hadn't really been asking her a question. He'd been stating a fact, making a judgement. He'd made his mind up about her years ago, and nothing she could say would change it now, not even the truth. Besides, he'd been her father's right-hand man for over a decade. Either he knew how her father had treated his family, or he'd chosen not to know.

'You have nothing to say, Sierra?'

It was the first time he'd called her by her first name and it sent a shiver of apprehensive awareness rippling through her. He sounded so *cold.* For one brief blazing second she remembered the feel of his lips on hers when he'd kissed her in the garden. His hands on her body, sliding so knowingly up to cup her breasts; the electric tingle of excitement low in her belly, kindling a spark she hadn't even known existed, because no man had ever touched her that way. No man had ever made her feel so desired.

Mentally, Sierra shrugged away the memory. So the man could kiss. Marco Ferranti no doubt had unimaginable sexual prowess. He'd probably been with dozens— hundreds—of women. It didn't change facts.

'No,' she told him flatly. 'I have nothing to say.'

* * *

Marco stared at Sierra, at the cool hauteur on her lovely face, and felt another blaze of anger go off like a firework in his gut. How could she be so cold?

'You know, I admired how cool you were, all those years ago,' he told her. Thankfully, his voice sounded as flat as hers, almost disinterested. He'd given away too much already, too much anger, too much emotion. He'd had seven years to get over Sierra. In any case, it wasn't as if he'd ever loved her.

'Cool?' Sierra repeated. She looked startled, wary.

'Yes, you were so self-possessed, so calm. I liked that about you.' She didn't reply, just watched him guardedly. 'I didn't realise,' Marco continued, his tone clipped as he bit off each word precisely, 'that it was because you had no heart. You were all ice underneath.' Except she hadn't been ice in his arms.

Still she said nothing, and Marco could feel the anger boiling inside him, threatening to spill out. 'Damn it, Sierra, didn't you ever think that I deserved an explanation?'

Her gaze flicked away from his and her tongue darted out to touch her lips. Just that tiny gesture set lust ricocheting through him. He felt dizzy from the excess of emotion, anger and desire twined together. He didn't want to feel so much. After seven years of cutting himself off from such feelings, the force of their return was overwhelming and unwelcome.

'Well?' Marco demanded. Now that he'd asked the question, he realised he wanted an answer.

'I thought it was explanation enough that I left,' Sierra said coolly.

Marco stared at her, his jaw dropping before he had the presence of mind to snap it shut, the bones aching. 'How on earth could you think that?'

Her gaze moved to his and then away again. 'Because it was obvious I'd changed my mind.'

'Yes, I do realise. But I've never understood why, and your father didn't, either. He was devastated when you left, you know. Utterly bereft.' He still remembered how Arturo had wept and embraced him when he'd told him, outside the church, that Sierra was gone. Marco had been numb, disbelieving; he'd wanted to send search parties until the truth of what Arturo was saying slammed home. She wasn't missing. She'd *left*. She'd left him, and for a second he wasn't even surprised. His marriage to Sierra, his acceptance into the Rocci family, it had all been too good—too wonderful—to be true.

Now Sierra's mouth firmed and she folded her arms, her blue-grey eyes turning as cold as the Atlantic on a winter's day. 'Why did you want to marry me, Marco, if we're going to rake through the past? I never quite understood that.' She paused, her cool gaze trained on him now, unflinching and direct, offering an unspoken challenge. 'It's not because you loved me.'

'No.' He could admit that much. He hadn't known her well enough to love her, and in any case he'd never been interested in love. Love meant opening yourself up to emotional risk, spreading your arms wide and inviting someone to take a shot. In his mother's case, she'd sustained a direct hit. Not something he'd ever be so foolish or desperate to do.

'So?' Sierra arched an eyebrow, and it disconcerted him how quickly and neatly she'd flipped the conversation. He was no longer the one on the attack. How dare she put him on the defensive—she, who'd walked away without a word?

'I could ask the same of you,' he said. 'Why did you agree to marry me?' *And then change your mind?*

Sierra's mouth firmed. 'I'd convinced myself I could be happy with you. I was wrong.'

'And what made you decide that?' Marco demanded.

She sighed, shrugging her slim shoulders. 'Do we really want to go through all this?' she asked. 'Do you think it will help? So much has happened. Seven years, Marco. Maybe we should just agree to—'

'Disagree? We're not talking about a little spat we had, Sierra. Some petty argument.' His voice came out harshly—too harsh, ragged and revealing with the force of his emotion. Even so, he couldn't keep himself from continuing. 'We're talking about *marriage*. We were a few hours away from pledging our lives to one another.'

'I know.' Her lips formed the words but he could barely hear her whisper. Her face had gone pale, her eyes huge and dark. Still she stood tall, chin held high. She had strength—more strength than he'd ever realised—but right now it only made him angry.

'Then why...?'

'You still didn't answer my question, Marco.' Her chin tilted up another notch. 'Why did you want to marry me?'

He stared at her for a moment, furious that he felt cornered. 'I need a drink,' he said abruptly, and stalked into the kitchen. She didn't follow him.

He yanked a bottle of whisky from the cupboard and poured a healthy measure that he downed in one swallow. Then he poured another.

Damn it, how dare she ask him, accuse *him*, when she was the one who should be called to account? What did it matter why he'd wanted to marry her, when she'd agreed?

He drained his second glass and then went back to the sitting room. Sierra had moved closer to the fire and the flames cast dancing shadows across her face. Her hair was starting to dry, the ends curling. She looked utterly delectable wearing his too-big clothes. The T-shirt had slipped off one shoulder, so he could see how golden and smooth her skin was. The belt she'd cinched at her waist showed off its narrowness and the high, proud curve of her breasts. He remembered the feel of them in his hands, when he'd given his desire free rein for a few intensely exquisite moments. He'd felt her arch into him, heard her breathy gasp of pleasure.

The memory now had the power to stir the embers of his desire and he turned away from her, willing the memories, the emotion, back. He didn't want to feel anything, not even simple lust, for Sierra Rocci now.

'Damn it, Sierra, you have some nerve asking me why I behaved the way I did. You're the one who chose to leave without so much as a note.'

'I know.'

'And you still haven't given me a reason why. You changed your mind. Fine. I accept that. It was patently obvious at the time.' His voice came out sharp with bitterness and he strove to moderate it. 'But you still haven't said why. Don't you think I deserve an explanation? Your parents are no longer alive to hear why you abandoned them, but I am.' His voice hardened, rose. 'So why don't you just tell me the truth?'

CHAPTER FOUR

A LOG SETTLED in the grate and popped, sparks scattering across the hearth before turning to cold ash. The silence stretched on and Sierra let it. What could she say? What would Marco believe or be willing to hear?

It was obvious he'd manufactured his own version of events, no doubt been fed lies by her father, who would have pretended to grieve for her. Marco wouldn't believe the truth now, even if she fed it to him with a spoon.

'Well?' His voice rang out, harsh and demanding. 'No reply?'

She shrugged, not meeting his gaze. 'What do you want me to say?'

'I told you—the truth. Why did you leave, Sierra? The night before our wedding?'

Sierra took a deep breath and forced herself to meet his hard gaze; looking into his eyes felt like slamming into a wall. 'Fine. The truth is I had second thoughts. Cold feet. I realised I was putting my life in the hands of a virtual stranger, and that it was a mistake. I couldn't do it.'

He stared at her, his gaze like concrete, a muscle flickering in his jaw. 'You realised all this the night before our wedding? It didn't occur to you at any point during the month of our engagement?'

'I'd thought I was making the right decision. That night I realised I wasn't.'

He shook his head derisively. 'You make it sound so simple.'

'In some ways it was, Marco.' Another deep breath. 'We didn't love or even know each other, not really. We'd had a handful of dates, everything stage-managed by my father. Our marriage would have been a disaster.'

'You can be so sure?'

'Yes.' She looked away, wanting to hide the truth she feared would be reflected in her eyes. She *wasn't* sure. Not completely. Maybe their marriage would have worked. Maybe Marco really was a good and gentle man. Although the fact that he'd remained at her father's right hand since then made her wonder. Doubt. How much of her father's shallow charm and ruthless ways had rubbed off on her ex-fiancé? Judging from the cold anger she'd seen from him today, she feared far too much. No, she'd made the right choice. She had to believe that.

'Fine.' Marco exhaled in one long, low rush of breath. 'You changed your mind. Why didn't you tell me, then? Talk to me and tell me what you were thinking? Did I not deserve that much courtesy? A note, at the very least? Maybe I could have convinced you...'

'Exactly. You would have convinced me.' He stared at her, nonplussed, and she continued, 'I was nineteen, Marco. You were a man of nearly thirty, sophisticated and worldly, especially compared to me. I had no life experience at all, and I was afraid to stand up to you, afraid that you'd sweep my arguments aside and then I'd marry you out of fear.'

'Did I ever give you any reason to be afraid of me?' he demanded. 'What a thing to accuse me of, Sierra, and with no proof.' His voice vibrated with anger and she fought not to flinch.

Now was the time to say it. To admit what she'd overheard, how it had made her feel. Why shouldn't she? What did she have to lose? She'd lost it all already. She'd gained a new life—a small, quiet life that was safe and was *hers*. She had nothing she either needed or wanted from this man. 'I heard you,' she said quietly.

His gaze widened and his mouth parted soundlessly before he finally spoke. 'You *heard* me? Am I supposed to know what that means?'

'The night before our wedding, I heard you talking to my father.'

He shook his head slowly, not understanding. Not wanting to understand. 'I'm still in the dark, Sierra.'

A deep breath, and she let it buoy her lungs, her courage. 'You said, "I know how to handle her", Marco.' Even after all the years the memory burned. 'When my father told you how women get notions. You spoke about me as if I were a dog, a beast to be bridled. Someone to be managed rather than respected.'

A full minute passed where Marco simply stared at her. Sierra held his gaze even though she ached to look away. To hide. The fire crackled and a spark popped, the loud sound breaking the stillness and finally allowing her to look somewhere else.

'And for this, this one statement I can't even remember,' Marco said in a low voice, 'you condemned me? Damned me?'

'It was enough.'

He swore, a hiss under his breath. Sierra flinched, tried not to cringe. A man's anger still had the power to strike fear into her soul. Make her body tense as she waited to ward off the blow.

'How could you—' He broke off, shaking his head. 'I don't even want to know. I'm not interested in your excuses.' He stalked into the kitchen. After a moment Sierra followed him. She'd rather creep back upstairs but she felt the conversation needed to be finished. Maybe then the past would be laid to rest, or at least as much as it could be.

She stood in the doorway while he opened various cupboards, every movement taut with suppressed fury.

He took out a packet of dried pasta and tossed it onto the granite island. 'I'm afraid there's not much to eat.'

'I'm not hungry.'

'Don't be perverse. You probably haven't eaten anything all day. You should keep up your strength.'

The fact that he was right made Sierra stay silent. She was being perverse because she didn't want to spend any more time with him than necessary. Her stomach growled loudly and Marco gave her a mocking look.

Sierra forced a smile. 'Very well, then. Let me help.' He shrugged his indifferent assent and Sierra moved awkwardly through the kitchen, conscious how this cosy domestic scene was at odds with the tension and animosity that still tautened the air.

They worked in silence for a few minutes, concentrating on mundane things; Sierra found a large pot and filled it with water, plonking it on the huge state-of-the-art range as Marco retrieved a tin of crushed tomatoes and various herbs from the cupboards.

This was his home now, and yet it once had been hers. She glanced round the huge kitchen, the oak table in the dining nook where she'd eaten breakfast while her mother moped and drank espresso. Sierra had enjoyed a cautious happiness at the villa, but Violet had always been miserable away from Arturo.

Sierra shook her head at the memory, at the regret she still felt for her mother's life, her mother's choices.

Marco noticed the movement and stilled. 'What is it?'

She turned to him. 'What do you mean?'

'You're shaking your head. What are you thinking about?'

'Nothing.'

'Something, Sierra.'

'I was just thinking about my mother. How I missed her.'

His eyebrows rose in obvious disbelief. 'Why didn't you ever come back, then?'

The question hung in the air, taunting her. She could tell him the truth, but she resisted instinctively. Sierra didn't know if it was because she didn't want to be pitied, or because she suspected he wouldn't believe her. Or, worse, an innate loyalty to her father, a man who had shown her so much contempt and disgust.

She drew a deep breath. 'I couldn't.'

'Why not?'

'My father would not want me back, after…everything.'

'You're wrong.' She recoiled at the flatly spoken statement. He could be so sure? 'You judge people so quickly, Sierra. Me and your father both. He would have welcomed you back with open arms, I know it. He told me as much, many times.'

She leaned against the counter, absorbing his statement. So her father had been feeding him lies all along, just as she'd suspected. She could tell Marco believed what he said, deeply and utterly. And he would never believe her.

'I suppose I wasn't prepared to risk it.'

'You broke his heart,' Marco told her flatly. 'And your mother's. Neither of them were ever the same.'

Guilt curdled her stomach like sour milk. She'd always

known, even if she hadn't wanted to dwell on it, that her leaving would cost her mother. It hurt to hear it now. 'How do you know? Did you see my mother very much?'

'Often enough. Arturo invited me to dinner many times. Your mother became reclusive—'

'She was always reclusive,' Sierra cut in sharply. She could not let every statement pass as gospel. 'We lived here, at the villa, except when my father called us into action.'

'A country life is better for children.' He glanced round the huge kitchen, spreading one arm wide to encompass the luxurious villa and its endless gardens. 'This would be a wonderful place to raise children.' His voice had thickened, and with a jolt Sierra wondered if he was thinking about their children. The thought made her feel a strangely piquant sense of loss that she could not bear to consider too closely.

'So how was she more reclusive?'

'She didn't always join us for meals. She didn't come to as many social events. Her health began to fail…'

Tears stung Sierra's eyes and she blinked rapidly to dispel them. She didn't want Marco to see her cry. She could guess why her mother had retreated more. Her father must have been so angry with her leaving, and he would have taken it out on her mother. She'd have had no choice but to hide.

'The truth hurts, does it?' Marco said, his voice close to a sneer. He'd seen her tears and he wasn't impressed. 'I suppose it was easy to forget about them from afar.'

'None of it was easy,' Sierra choked out. She drew a deep breath and willed the grief back. Showing Marco how much she was affected would only make him more contemptuous. He'd judged her long ago and nothing she could do or say would change the way he felt about her.

And it shouldn't matter, because after today she would never see him again.

A prospect that caused her an absurd flash of pain; she forced herself to shrug it off.

'It seemed easy from where I stood,' Marco answered. His voice was sharp with bitterness.

'Maybe it did,' Sierra agreed. 'But what good can it do now, to go over these things? What do you want from me, Marco?'

What did he want from her? Why was he pushing her, demanding answers she obviously couldn't or didn't want to give? Did it even matter which? It was seven years ago. She'd had cold feet, changed her mind, whatever. She'd treated both him and her parents callously, and he was glad to have escaped a lifetime sentence with a woman as cold as she was. They'd both moved on.

Except when he'd seen her standing in the doorway of di Santis's office, when he'd remembered how she'd tasted and felt and even more, how he'd enjoyed being with her, seeing her shy smile, the way those blue-grey eyes had warmed with surprised laughter...when he'd been looking forward to the life they would build together... It didn't feel as if he'd moved on. At all. And that realisation infuriated him.

Marco swung away from her, bracing his hands against the counter. 'I don't want anything from you. Not any more.' He busied himself with opening the tin of tomatoes and pouring the contents into a pan. 'Seeing you again has made me ask some questions,' he answered, his voice thankfully cool. 'And want some answers. Since I never had any.'

'I can understand that.' She sounded sad.

'Can you?' *Then why...?* But he wouldn't ask her anything more. He wouldn't beg. Wordlessly, he turned back to their makeshift meal. Sierra watched him, saying nothing, but Marco felt the tension ease slightly. The anger that had been propelling him along had left in a defeated rush, leaving him feeling more sad than anything else. And he didn't want to feel sad. God help him, he was *over* Sierra. He'd never loved her, after all—he'd desired her, yes. He'd wanted her very much.

But love? No. He'd never felt that and he had no intention of feeling it for anyone.

He slid his gaze towards her, saw the way her chest rose and fell under the baggy T-shirt. He could see the peaks of her nipples through the thin fabric, and desire arced through him. He still wanted her.

And did she want him? The question intrigued him and, even though he knew nothing would happen between them now, he realised he wanted to know the answer—very much.

There was only one way to find out. He reached for the salt, letting his arm brush across her breasts for one tantalising second. He heard her draw her breath in sharply and step back. When he glanced at her, he saw the colour flare into her face, her eyes widen before she quickly looked away.

Marco only just suppressed his smile as satisfaction surged through him. She wanted him. Seducing her would be easy…and such sweet revenge. But was that all he wanted from Sierra now? A moment's pleasure? The proof that she'd missed out? It felt petty and small, and more exposing of him than her.

And yet it would be so satisfying.

'What will you do with the estate?' She cleared her throat, her gaze flicking away from his as she stirred the pasta. 'Will you live here? Or sell it?'

'I haven't decided.' His thoughts of revenge were replaced by an uncomfortable flicker of guilt for taking Sierra's inheritance from her. Not that he'd actually wanted to; Arturo had insisted, claiming Marco had been far more of a son to him than Sierra had ever been a daughter. And, in his self-righteous anger and hurt, Marco had relented. Sierra had walked away from the family that had embraced him. He'd believed she deserved what she'd got: nothing.

'Is there anything you want from the villa?' he asked. 'Or the *palazzo* in Palermo? Some heirlooms or pictures?'

She shook her head, her certainty shocking him even though he knew it shouldn't. She'd turned her back on all of it seven years ago. 'No. I don't want anything.'

'There's nothing?' he pressed. 'What about a photograph of your parents? There's a wedding picture in the front hall of the *palazzo*. It's lovely.' He watched her, searching for some sign of softness, some relenting towards her family, towards him.

'No,' she said, and her voice was firm. 'I don't want anything.'

They worked in silent tandem, preparing the simple meal, and it wasn't until they were seated at the table in the alcove with steaming plates of pasta that Sierra spoke again.

'I always liked this spot. I ate breakfast here. The cook was an old battleaxe who thought I should eat in the dining room but I couldn't bear it, with all the stuffy portraits staring down at me so disapprovingly. I much preferred it here.' She smiled, the gesture touched with sorrowful whimsy.

Marco imagined her as a child sitting at the table, her feet not even touching the floor. He imagined their daughter doing the same, and then abruptly banished the thought. Dreams he'd once had of a proper family, a real life, and now they were nothing but ashes and smoke. He'd never live here with Sierra or anyone.

'You can have the villa.' His voice came out abrupt, ungracious. Marco cleared his throat. 'I won't be using it. And it was your family home.'

She stared at him, her eyes wide. 'You're offering me the *villa*?'

He shrugged. 'Why shouldn't I? I didn't need any of your inheritance. The only thing I wanted was your father's shares in Rocci Enterprises.' Which gave him control of the empire he'd helped to build.

'Of course.' Her mouth curved in a mocking smile. 'That's why you wanted to marry me, after all.'

'What do you mean?' He stared at her in surprise, shocked by her assumption. 'Is that what you think? That I wanted to marry you only for personal gain?'

'Can you really deny it? What better way to move through the ranks than marry the boss's daughter?' She held his gaze and even though her voice was cool he saw pain in her eyes. Old, unforgotten pain, a remnant of long past emotion, and strangely it gratified him. So this was why she'd left—because she'd assumed he had been using her?

'I won't deny that there were some advantages to marrying you,' he began, and she let out a hard laugh.

'That's putting it mildly. You wouldn't have looked twice at me if my last name hadn't been Rocci.'

'That's not necessarily true. But I was introduced to you by your father. I always knew you were a Rocci.'

'And he stage-managed it all, didn't he? The whole reason he introduced you to me was to marry me off.'

Marco heard the bitterness in her voice and wondered at it. 'But surely you knew that.'

'Yes, I knew.' She shook her head, regret etched on her

fine-boned features. Marco laid down his knife and fork and stared at her hard.

'Then how can you object? Your father was concerned for your welfare. It made sense, assuming we got along, for him to encourage the match. He'd provide for his daughter and secure his business.'

'Which sounds positively medieval—'

'Not medieval,' Marco interjected. 'Sicilian, perhaps. He was an old-fashioned man, this is an old-fashioned country, with outdated ideas about some things. Trust me, I know.'

She looked up, the bitterness and regret sliding from her face, replaced by curiosity. 'Why do you say that? Why should you know better than another?'

He shouldn't have said that at all. He had no intention of telling Sierra about the shame of his parentage, the sorrow of his childhood. The past was best left forgotten, and he knew he could not stomach her pity. 'We've both encountered it, in different ways,' he answered with a shrug. 'But if you knew your father intended for us to marry, why do you fault me for it now?'

Sierra sighed and leaned back in her chair. 'I don't, not really.'

'But...' He shook his head, mystified and more than a little annoyed. 'I don't understand you, Sierra. Perhaps I never did.'

'I know.' She was quiet then, her face drawn in sorrowful lines. 'If it helps, I'm truly sorry for the way it all happened. If I'd had more courage, more clarity, I would have never let it get as far as it did. I would have never agreed to your proposal.'

And that was supposed to make him feel *better*? Marco's chest hurt with the pressure of holding back his anger and hurt. He was not going to show Sierra how her words wounded him. She saw their entire relationship as a mistake, an error of judgement. Until she hadn't come down the aisle, he'd been intending to spend the rest of his life with her. The difference in their experiences, their feelings, was too marked and painful for him to remark on it.

'I didn't intend to marry you simply because it was good business,' he finally managed, his voice level. He would not have her accuse him of being mercenary.

'I suppose it helped that I didn't have a face like an old boot,' Sierra returned before he could continue. 'And I was so biddable, wasn't I? So eager to please, practically fawning over you.' She shook her head in self-derision.

Marco cocked his head, surprise sweeping over him. 'Is that how you saw it?'

'That's how it was.'

He knew there was truth in what she said, but it hadn't been the whole truth. Yes, she'd been pretty and he'd been physically attracted to her. Overwhelmingly physically attracted to her, so his palms had itched to touch her softness, to feel her body yield to his. *And they still did.*

And yes, he'd liked how much she'd seemed to like him, how eager and admiring she'd been. What man wouldn't?

She'd been young and isolated, but so had he, even though he'd been almost thirty. Back then he hadn't had many, if any, people who looked up to him. He'd been a street rat from the dusty gutters of Palermo, a virtual orphan who had worked through half a dozen foster homes before he'd finally left at sixteen. No one had missed him.

Seeing Sierra Rocci look at him with stars in her eyes had felt *good.* Had made him feel part of something bigger than himself, and he'd craved that desperately. But Sierra made it sound as if he'd been calculating and cold, and it had never been like that for him.

'You are painting only part of the picture,' Marco finally said.

'Oh, I'm sure you felt an affection for me,' Sierra cut in. 'An amused tolerance, no doubt. But eventually you would have tired of me and I would have resented you. It would have been a disaster, like I said.'

He opened his mouth to object, to tell her what he'd hoped would have happened. That maybe they would have liked each other, grown closer. No, he hadn't loved her, hadn't wanted to love her. Hadn't wanted that much emotional risk. But he'd hoped for a good marriage. A real family.

She stared at him with challenge in her eyes and he closed his mouth. Why would he say all that now? Admit so much pathetic need? There was nothing between them now, no hope of any kind of future. Nothing but an intense physical awareness, and one he could use to his own ruthless advantage. Why shouldn't he? Why shouldn't he have Sierra Rocci in bed? Surely she wasn't the innocent she'd once been, and he could tell she desired him. Even if she didn't want to.

'Perhaps you're right,' he said tonelessly. 'In any case, you never gave us the opportunity to discover what might have happened. And, as you've said, it's all in the past.'

Sierra's breath left in a rush. 'Yes.' She sounded wary, as if she didn't trust his words, that he could be so forgiving.

'I'm glad you've realised that,' she said, her voice cool, and Marco inclined his head. 'I think I'll go to bed.' She rose gracefully and took her plate to the sink. Marco watched her go. 'It's been a long day and I have to get up early tomorrow for my flight.'

'Very well.'

She turned to him, uncertainty flashing in her eyes. 'Goodnight.'

Marco smiled fleetingly, letting his gaze rest on hers with intent, watching with satisfaction as her pupils flared and her breath hitched. 'Let me show you to your room.'

'It's not necessary—'

He rose from the table and strode towards her, his steps eating up the space in a few long strides. 'Oh,' he assured her with a smile that had become feral, predatory, 'but it is.'

CHAPTER FIVE

SHE COULDN'T SLEEP. Sierra lay in the double bed in the guest room Marco had shown her to a few hours ago and stared up at the ceiling. The rain drummed against the roof and the wind battered the shutters. And inside her a tangle of fear and desire left her feeling restless, uncertain.

She didn't think she'd been imagining the heightened sense of expectation as Marco had led her from the kitchen and up the sweeping marble staircase to the wing of guest bedrooms. She certainly hadn't been imagining the pulse of excitement she'd felt low in her belly when he'd taken her hand to guide her down the darkened corridor.

She hated how immediate and overwhelming her response to him was, and yet she told herself it was natural. Understandable. He was an attractive, virile man, and she'd responded to him before. She couldn't control the way he made her body feel, but she could certainly control her actions.

And so with effort she'd pulled her hand from his. The gesture seemed only to amuse him; he'd glanced back at her with a knowing smile, and Sierra had had the uncomfortable feeling that he knew exactly what she was thinking—and feeling.

But he hadn't acted on it. He'd shown her into the bedroom and she'd stood there, clearly *waiting*, while he'd turned on lights and checked that the shutters were bolted.

For an exquisite, excruciating second Sierra had thought he was going to do something. Kiss her. He'd stood in front of her, the lamplight creating a warm golden pool that bathed them both, and had looked at her. And she'd waited, ready, expectant...

If he'd kissed her then, she wouldn't have been able to resist. The realisation should have been shaming but she'd felt too much desire for that.

But Marco hadn't kissed her. His features had twisted in some emotion she couldn't discern, and then he'd simply said goodnight and left her alone. *Thank God.*

There was absolutely no reason whatsoever to feel disappointed about that.

Now Sierra rose from the bed, swinging her legs over so her bare feet hit the cold tiles. Music. Music was what she needed now. Music had always been both her solace and her inspiration. When she was playing the violin, she could soar far above all the petty worries and cruelties of her day-to-day life. But she didn't have her violin here; she'd left it in London.

Still, the villa had a music room with a piano. It was better than nothing. And she needed to escape from the din inside her own head, if only for a few minutes. Quietly, she crept from her bedroom and down the long darkened hallway. The house was silent save for the steady patter of rain, the distant rumble of thunder as the storm thankfully moved off.

Sierra tiptoed down the stairs, feeling her way through the dark, the moonless night not offering even a sliver of light. Finally, she found her way to the small music room with its French windows opening onto the terrace that was now awash in puddles.

She flicked on a single lamp, its warm glow creating a pool of light across the dusty ebony of grand piano. Gently she eased up the lid; the instrument was no doubt woefully out of tune. She quietly pressed a key and winced at the discordant sound.

Never mind. She sat at the piano and softly played the opening bars to Debussy's *Sarabande*, not wanting to wake Marco in one of the rooms above. Even with the piano out of tune, the music filled her, swept away her worries and regrets and left only light and sound in their wake. She closed her eyes, giving herself up to the piece, to the feeling. Forgetting, for a few needful moments, about her parents, her past, *Marco*.

She didn't know when she became aware that she wasn't alone. A prickling along her scalp, the nape of her neck. A shivery awareness that rippled through her and caused her to open her eyes.

Marco stood in the doorway of the music room, wearing only a pair of pyjama bottoms, his glorious chest bare, his gaze trained on her. Sierra's fingers stilled on the piano, plunging the room into an expectant silence.

'I didn't know you played piano.' His voice was low, husky with sleep, and it wove its sensual threads around her, ensnaring her.

'I don't, not really.' She put her hands in her lap, self-conscious and all too aware of Marco standing so near her, so bare and so beautiful. Every muscle of his chest was bronzed and perfectly sculpted; he looked like an ad for cologne or clothes or cars. Looking the way he did, she thought he could sell anyone anything. 'I had a few lessons,' Sierra continued stiltedly, 'but I'm mostly self-taught.'

'That's impressive.'

She shrugged, his surprising praise unnerving her. Having Marco standing here, wearing next to nothing, acting almost as if he admired her, sent her senses into hyperdrive and left her speechless.

'I never even knew you were musical.' He'd taken a step closer to her and she could feel the heat from his body. When she took a breath the musky male scent of him hit her nostrils and made her stomach clench. Hard.

'The violin is actually my chosen instrument, but it's not something I usually tell people. It's a private thing.' She forced herself to meet his sleepy, silvery gaze. She'd been a fool to come out of her bedroom tonight, and yet a distant part of her recognised she'd done it because she'd wanted this. Him. And even though desire was rushing through her in a torrent, both nerves and common sense made her back off. 'I'm sorry I disturbed you. I must have got carried away.' She half rose from the piano bench, halting inexplicably, pinned by his gaze.

'It sounded lovely.'

'The piano is out of tune.'

'Even so.'

He held her gaze, and inwardly Sierra quaked at how intent he looked. How utterly purposeful. So she wasn't even surprised when he reached a hand out and cupped her cheek, the pad of his thumb stroking the softness of her lower lip. Her breath caught in a gasp that lodged in her chest. Her heart started to pound. She'd been waiting for this, and even though she was afraid she knew she still wanted it.

'Almost,' he said softly, 'as lovely as you. Do you know how beautiful you are, Sierra? I've always thought that. You undid me, with your loveliness. I was caught from the moment I saw you, at your father's *palazzo*. Do you remember? You were standing in the drawing room, wearing a pink dress. You looked like a rose.'

She stared at him, shocked by how much he had admitted, how much he'd felt. 'I remember,' she whispered. Of course she remembered. She'd glimpsed him from the window, seen him gently stroke that silly cat, and felt her heart lift in both hope and desire. How quickly she'd fallen for him. How completely. Not in love, no, but in childish hope and longing. He'd overwhelmed her senses, even when she'd thought she'd been acting smart, playing safe.

'Do you remember when I kissed you?' Marco asked. His thumb pressed her lip gently, reminding her of how his lips had felt on hers. Hard, hot, soft, cool. Everything, all at once.

'Yes,' she managed in a shaky whisper. 'I remember.'

'You liked my kisses.' It was a statement, and he waited for her to refute it, confident that she couldn't. Sierra tried to look away but Marco held her gaze as if he were holding her face in place with his hands. He was that commanding, that forceful, and he hadn't even moved.

'You don't deny it.'

'No.' The word was drawn from her with helpless reluctance.

'You still like them, I think,' he said softly, and her silence condemned her. Slowly, inexorably, Marco drew her to him. She knew he was going to kiss her, and she knew she wanted him to. She also knew it was a bad idea, a *dangerous* idea, considering all that had—and hadn't—happened between them and yet she didn't resist.

His lips brushed hers once, twice. A shuddering sigh escaped her and she reached up to clutch his shoulders and steady herself. His skin felt hot and hard under her palms and she couldn't keep herself from smoothing her hands down his back, revelling in the feel of him. How could a man's skin feel so silky?

Marco's hands framed her face as he deepened the kiss,

his tongue sliding sweetly into her mouth as he tasted and explored her. He slid his hands from her face to her shoulders and then, wonderfully, to her breasts, cupping them as he had that day under the plane tree. She remembered how exciting it had felt, or at least she thought she had, but the reality of his touch now was so intense, so exquisite, she almost cried out as his thumbs brushed over her nipples. She hadn't remembered this, not enough.

'Marco.' His name came on a breath, and she didn't even know why she said it. Was she asking him to continue or telling him to stop?

He moved his mouth to her jaw, blazing kisses along her neck and collarbone as he slid his hand under her T-shirt and cupped her bare breast, the feel of his rough palm against her soft flesh, the gentle abrasion of it, making every nerve-ending blaze almost painfully to life. It was too much, and yet she wanted more.

'I want you.' He spoke hoarsely, firmly, declaring his intent. Sierra could only nod. He touched her chin with his fingers, forcing her to meet his blazing gaze. 'Say it. Say you want me, Sierra.'

'I want you,' she whispered, the words drawn from her, falling into the stillness, creating ripples.

Triumph blazed in his eyes as he pulled the T-shirt off her. She hadn't bothered with the tracksuit bottoms for pyjamas, so in one fluid movement she'd become naked. She sucked in a hard breath when he pulled her towards him, her breasts colliding and then crushed against his chest. The feel of their bare skin touching sent another tingling quiver of awareness shooting through her. Marco's hands were on her waist and then her hips as he fitted her against him. She could feel his arousal through the thin pyjama bottoms and it made her gasp. So many sensations all at once; she could barely acknowledge one before another came crashing over her.

Marco eased her back onto the piano bench, spreading her legs so he could stand between them. Her head fell back as he kissed his way from her collarbone to her breasts, and Sierra moaned as his tongue flicked across her sensitive flesh. She'd never realised you could feel this way, that a man could make you feel this way. He glanced up at her, his grey eyes blazing with triumph, and then he moved his head from her breasts to between her thighs and her breath came out in a shaky moan as he touched her centre.

'Oh.' She arched against his mouth, astonished at how sharp and intense the pleasure was, how consuming as his tongue found the very heart of her. *'Oh.'* She threaded her hands through his silky hair as her body arched helplessly against his mouth and his hands gripped her hips. It only took a few exquisite moments for her world to explode in glittering fragments around her and she cried out, one jagged note that echoed through the stillness of the villa.

She *really* had no idea.

She sagged against the piano as her body trembled with the aftershocks of her climax and Marco lifted his head to gaze at her with blatant—and smug—satisfaction. Realisation thudded sickly through her; his look said it all. He'd been trying to prove something, and he'd just proved it—in spades.

Shakily, colour rushing to her face, Sierra pushed her tangle of hair from her hot cheeks and closed her legs, pushing him away from her. The intensity of the moment had splintered, leaving her feeling raw and exposed. Wounded and ashamed. She'd been so wanton, so shameless, and Marco had been utterly in control. *As always.*

'Now at least you know a little of what you've missed,' he said and her mouth opened on a soundless gasp.

'You've proved your point, then, I suppose,' she managed and on shaking legs she grabbed her T-shirt and rushed from the room.

Marco stalked upstairs, his whole body throbbing with unfulfilled desire—and worse, regret. He'd behaved like a cad. A heartless, cruel cad. And he needed an icy-cold shower. Swearing under his breath, he strode into his bedroom and went straight to the en suite bathroom, turning the cold on full blast. He stepped beneath the needling spray, sucking in a hard breath as the icy water hit his skin and chilled him right through. And even then he couldn't quench the fire that raged in his veins, heated his blood, born of both shame and lust.

He'd wanted her so much, more than he'd ever wanted another woman. More than he'd ever thought possible. The sweetness of her response, the *innocence* of it... Marco braced his hands against the shower stall. He could almost believe she was still untouched. She'd seemed so surprised by everything, so enthralled. And when she'd fallen to pieces beneath his mouth...

Forcefully he pushed the memory away. The last thing he needed now was to remember how that had felt. Better to remember the sudden look of uncertainty on her face, of shame. The realisation that he'd been low enough to exact some kind of revenge, using her body against her. Forcing her to respond to him, even though she'd once rejected him.

He'd been tempted to seduce her, yes, and he could have had her earlier, when he'd shown her to her bedroom. He'd seen the uncertainty and desire in her eyes, how she had hesitated. But he'd resisted the temptation, had told himself he was better than that.

Apparently he wasn't.

His body numb with cold, his blood still hot, Marco

turned off the shower and wrapped a towel around his hips. Sleep would not come for him tonight, not when too many emotions still churned through him. He went to his laptop instead, powered it up and prepared to work.

By dawn his eyes were gritty, his body aching, but at least the rain had stopped. Marco stood at the window and gazed out at the rain-washed gardens. The once manicured lawns and groomed beds were a wild tangle of shrubs and trees; he hadn't looked after the estate in the last few years, when Arturo had been too ill to do so himself. He'd hire a gardener to clean it up before he sold it. He didn't want to have anything more to do with the place.

When he came downstairs Sierra was already in the kitchen, dressed in the silk blouse and pencil skirt she'd worn yesterday. Both were creased but dry; she'd put her hair back up in its sleek chignon and all of it felt like armour, a way to protect herself against him.

Marco hesitated in the doorway, wondering whether to mention last night. What would he even say? In any case Sierra looked as if she wanted to pretend it hadn't happened, and maybe that was best.

'We should get on the road if your flight is this afternoon.'

'We?' She shook her head firmly. 'I'll drive myself.'

'The mountain roads still aren't passable, and your rental car looks like little more than a tin can on wheels,' Marco dismissed. 'I'll drive you. My car can handle the flooding.'

'But what about my rental…?'

'I'll have someone pick it up and deliver it to the agency. It's not a problem.'

She licked her lips, her eyes wide, her expression more than a little panicked. 'But…'

'It makes sense, Sierra. And, trust me, you don't have

to worry about some kind of repeat of last night. I don't intend to touch you ever again.' He hadn't meant to sound quite so harsh, but he saw the surprised hurt flicker in her eyes before she looked away.

'And I have no intention of letting you touch me ever again.'

He was almost tempted to prove her wrong, but he resisted the impulse. The sooner Sierra was out of his life, the better. 'It seems we're agreed, then. Now, we should get ready to go.' Marco grabbed his keys and switched off the lights before ushering Sierra out of the kitchen. He followed her, locking the villa behind him, and then opened the passenger door to his SUV. As Sierra slid inside the car he breathed in her lemony scent, and his gut tightened. It was going to be a long three hours.

They drove in silence down the sweeping drive, the villa's gates closing silently behind them. Sierra let out a sigh of relief as Marco turned onto the mountain road.

'You're glad to leave?'

'Not glad, exactly,' she answered. 'But memories can be…difficult.'

He couldn't argue with that. He had a truckload of difficult memories, from his father's retreat from his life, to his mother leaving him at the door of an orphanage run by monks when he was ten years old, to the slew of foster homes he'd bounced through, to the endless moment when he'd stood at the front of the church, the smile slipping from his face as Arturo came down the aisle, his face set in extraordinarily grim lines.

Sierra was staring out of the window; it was as if she'd dismissed him entirely. As he would dismiss her. For better or worse, last night's episode would serve as a line drawn across the past. Perhaps he had evened the score between them. In any case, his tie to Sierra Rocci was cut—firmly and for ever.

Setting his jaw, Marco stared straight ahead as he drove in silence all the way to Palermo.

CHAPTER SIX

'You need Sierra Rocci.'

Marco swivelled around in his chair to gaze out of the window at Palermo's business district as everything in him resisted that flatly spoken statement. 'I've been Arturo's right-hand man for nearly ten years. I don't need her.'

Paolo Conti, his second-in-command and closest confidant, sighed. 'I'm afraid you do, Marco. The board isn't happy without a Rocci to front the business, at least at first. And with the hotel opening in New York in a few weeks...'

'What about it? Everything is going according to plan.' He'd overseen the work on Rocci Enterprises' first hotel in North America himself; it had been his idea to expand, and to take the exclusive chain of hotels in a new direction. His credibility as CEO rested on The Rocci New York succeeding.

'That's true,' Paolo replied, 'but in the seventy years of Rocci Enterprises, a Rocci has always headed the board.'

'Things change.'

'Yes,' Paolo agreed patiently, running his hand through his silver hair, 'but for the last seventy years a Rocci has opened each hotel. Palermo, Rome, Paris, Madrid, London, Berlin.' He ticked them off on his fingers. 'A Rocci at every one.'

'I know.' He'd seen a few of the grand openings himself. He'd started work for Rocci Enterprises when he was sixteen years old, as a bellboy at the hotel in Palermo. He'd seen Sierra walking with her parents up the pink marble steps to eat in the hotel's luxurious dining room. He'd watched her walk so daintily, her hands held by both her mother and father. The perfect family.

'Change is a part of life,' Marco dismissed, 'and Arturo Rocci willed his shares to me. The board—and the public—will simply have to adjust.' It had been nearly a month since he'd left Sierra at the Palermo airport. Four weeks since he'd watched her walk away from him and told himself he was glad, even as he felt the old injustice burn. She hadn't looked back.

He wasn't angry with her any more, but he didn't know what he felt. Whatever emotion raged through him didn't feel good.

'It's not that simple, Marco,' Paolo said. He'd been with Rocci Enterprises for decades, always quietly serving and guiding. As Arturo had become more and more ill, Marco had relied increasingly on Paolo's help and wisdom.

'It can be,' he insisted.

'If the board feels there is too much separation from the Rocci name and values, they might hold a vote of no confidence.'

Marco tensed. 'I've been with this company for over ten years. And I hold the controlling shares.'

'The board needs to see you in public, acting as CEO. They need to believe in you.'

'Fine. I'll appear at any number of events.'

'With a Rocci,' Paolo clarified. 'And, as you know, Sierra is the only Rocci left.' Arturo's brother, a bachelor, had died a dozen years ago, his parents before then. 'There needs to be a smooth transition,' Paolo insisted. 'For the

'Yes, of course you did,' Sierra murmured. 'Well done.' She leafed through the music she'd brought before selecting another piece. 'Why don't you try this one now that you've managed "Twinkle, Twinkle" so well?'

An hour later Sierra packed up her things and headed out of the school where she'd been running music lessons. It had taken a few years, but she'd managed to build up a regular business, offering lessons to schoolchildren across London's schools.

After her tumultuous and panicked flight from Sicily, she'd found her mother's friend Mary Bertram living in London; she'd moved house but, with the help of the internet, Sierra had managed to track her down. Mary had sheltered her, helped her find her feet along with her first job. She'd died three years ago, and Sierra had felt as if she'd lost another mother.

Outside the school, she started down the pavement towards the Tube station, the midsummer evening sultry and warm. People were spilling out of houses and offices, laughing as they slung bags over their shoulders and made plans for the pub.

Sierra regarded them with a slight pang of envy. She'd never been able to make friends easily; her isolated childhood and her innate quietness had made it difficult. Her job was isolated, too, although she'd become friendly with a few of the other extracurricular teachers at various schools. But in the seven years she'd lived in London, no one had got close. She'd never had a lover or even a boyfriend, nothing more than a handful of dates that had gone nowhere.

'Hello, Sierra.'

Sierra came to a shocked halt as Marco Ferranti stepped out in front of her. Her mouth opened soundlessly; she felt as if she'd conjured him from thin air, from her lonely thoughts. He quirked an eyebrow, his mouth curving in the gentle quirk of a smile she recognised from seven years ago.

'What…what are you doing here?' she finally managed.

'Looking for you.'

A thrill of illicit pleasure as well as of apprehension shivered through her. He'd come to London just for her? 'How did you know where I was?'

He shrugged, the movement assured, elegant. 'Information is always easy to find.'

And just like that she was unnerved again, realising once more how little she knew him, the real him. How powerful he was. 'I don't know why you'd want to talk to me, Marco.'

'Is there somewhere private we could go?'

She glanced around the busy city street and shrugged. 'Not really.'

'Then let me find a place.' Marco slid his phone from the pocket of his suit jacket and thumbed a few buttons. Within seconds he was issuing instructions and then he returned his phone to his pocket and put his hand on the small of Sierra's back, where it rested enticingly, his palm warm through the thin fabric of her summer blouse. 'I've found a place.'

'Just like that?' Sierra hadn't heard what he'd said into the phone; his Italian had been low and rapid, inaudible over the sounds of traffic.

'Just like that,' Marco answered with a smile and guided her down the street, his hand never leaving her back.

A few minutes later they were entering a wine bar with plush velvet sofas and tables of polished ebony and teak. Sierra gaped to see a sofa in a private alcove already prepared for them, a bottle of red wine opened and breathing next to two crystal wine glasses.

'Some service,' she remarked shakily.

'As a Rocci, you must be used to such service,' Marco replied. He gestured for her to sit down while he poured the wine.

'Perhaps, but it's been a while.' In the seven years since she'd come to London she'd lived on little more than a pittance. She rented a tiny flat in Clapham and she bought everything second-hand. The days of luxury and privilege as Arturo Rocci's daughter were long over.

As she sank into the velvet sofa and watched Marco pour her a glass of wine, Sierra couldn't help but enjoy the moment. Even if Marco's presence overwhelmed and unnerved her. She had no idea why he'd come to London to find her, or what he could possibly want.

'Here.' He pressed a glass of wine into her hand and she took a much-needed sip.

'What do you want from me?' she asked, and then steeled herself for his answer.

Whatever they were, Marco wasn't going to reveal his intentions so easily. 'I didn't realise you were a music teacher.'

So he'd done some digging. She took another sip of wine. 'I teach children in after-school clubs.'

'And you play the piano and violin yourself.'

'Only in private.' Her cheeks heated as Marco's knowing gaze locked with hers. She knew they were both remembering the last time she'd played, and just how private it had been.

'I'd like to hear you play the violin.' His gaze seemed to caress her, and she felt goosebumps rise on her arms as a familiar ache started in her centre. 'I'd like you to play it for me.' His voice was low, sensuous, his gaze never leaving hers, his words making images and ideas leap into her mind in a vivid and erotic montage.

Sierra shook her head slowly, forcing the feelings back. 'Why are you acting this way, Marco?'

He took a sip of wine, one eyebrow arched. 'What way?'

'Like…like a lover,' she blurted, and then blushed. 'The last time we saw each other you seemed glad to be shot of me.'

'And I must confess you seemed likewise.'

'Considering the circumstances, not to mention our history, yes.'

'I'm sorry for the way I acted,' Marco said abruptly. His gaze was still locked on hers, his expression intent. 'In the music room. When I made love to you. I was trying to prove you still desired me and it was a petty, stupid thing to do. I'm sorry.' His lips curved in a tiny smile. 'Even if it seemed you enjoyed it.'

His words were gently teasing, and they made her blush all the more. She had no idea how to respond.

'Thank you,' she finally muttered. 'For your apology. But I still don't know why you're here.'

Marco shifted in his seat, his powerful thigh brushing her leg. The contact sent sizzling arrows of remembered sensation firing through her, and Sierra only just resisted pulling away. She wouldn't show him how much he affected her. In any case, he undoubtedly already knew.

'I've been thinking about you, Sierra.' His voice flowed over like her melted chocolate, warm and liquid, enticing but also a way to drown. 'A lot.'

Her mouth had dried, her lungs emptying of air, and yet suspicion and doubt still took hold of her heart. She shook her head slowly. 'Marco…'

'I've been thinking that it's unfair you didn't receive anything from your father's will.'

The abrupt reality check felt like falling flat on her face. Left her breathless, smarting. Of course he wasn't thinking about her *that* way. She shouldn't even want to be thinking of him *that* way. Good grief, where was her backbone? Her resolve? She'd spent the last seven years telling herself she'd done the right thing in walking away from this man, and now she was panting and dreaming like some lovesick teenager.

'I don't care about my father's will.'

'You should. You had a birthright, Sierra.'

'Even though I walked away from my family? In di Santis's office you seemed to think I was getting exactly what I deserved. Almost nothing.' She hadn't cared about her father's inheritance, but Marco's smug triumph had rankled. More than rankled, if she was honest. It had hurt.

'I was angry,' Marco admitted quietly. 'I'm sorry.'

So many apologies. She didn't know what to do with them. She didn't entirely trust them—or him. And her own feelings were cartwheeling all over the place, which made sounding and feeling logical pretty difficult. 'It's all in the past, Marco. Let's leave it there.'

'I think you should have a part in Rocci Enterprises.'

She drew back, truly startled. If anything, she'd been expecting him to offer her the villa again, or perhaps some family heirlooms she had no need for. Not her father's business. 'I've never had a part in Rocci Enterprises.' Her father had been very much of the persuasion that women didn't need to be involved in business. She'd left school at sixteen at her father's behest.

'A new hotel is opening in New York City,' Marco continued as if she hadn't spoken. 'It will be the most luxurious Rocci hotel yet, and I think you should be there. You deserve to be there.'

'In New York?' She stared at him in disbelief.

'You opened four hotels before you were nineteen,'

Marco reminded her. 'People are used to seeing a Rocci cut the ribbon. You should be the one to do it.'

'I had nothing to do with that hotel, or any of them.' She was filled with sudden and utter revulsion at the thought of opening one of her father's hotels. Playing happy families, and this time from the grave. How many times had she smiled and curtsied for the crowds, how many times had her mother waved, wearing a long-sleeved dress to hide the bruises? She had no desire whatsoever to revisit those memories or play that part again. 'I appreciate your consideration,' she said stiffly, 'but I don't need to open the hotel. I have no wish to.' Some of her distaste must have shown on her face because Marco frowned.

'Why not?'

Sierra hesitated, stalling for time by taking a sip of wine. She was still hesitant to tell Marco the truth of her father, her family, because she didn't think he'd believe her and even if he did she didn't want his pity. It was shaming to admit she'd allow herself to be abused and used for so long, even if she'd only been a child. And if he didn't believe her? If he accused her of lying or exaggerating to sully her father's name? Or maybe he *would* believe her, and think her father had been justified. Maybe he countenanced a little rough handling. The truth was, she had no idea what his response would be and she had no intention of finding out.

'Sierra?' He leaned forward, covering her hand with his own. She realised she was trembling and she strove for control.

'Like I said, the past is in the past, Marco. I don't need to be part of Rocci Enterprises. I left it behind when I left Sicily.' She forced a smile, small and polite, definitely strained. 'But, as I said, thank you for thinking of me.'

His hand still rested on hers; it felt warm and strong.

Comforting, even if it shouldn't be. Even if she still didn't understand or trust this man. She didn't pull away.

Confused frustration surged through him as Marco gazed at Sierra, tried to figure out what she was thinking. His magnanimous approach had clearly failed. He'd hoped that Sierra would embrace his suggestion, that she'd be glad to have a chance to mend a few bridges, be a Rocci again. More fool him.

He sat back, letting go of her hand, noticing the loss even as his mind raced for another way forward. 'You don't seem to bear much good will for Rocci Enterprises,' he remarked, 'even though you were obviously close to your family at one time.'

Her mouth twisted. 'I don't feel anything for Rocci Enterprises,' she said flatly. 'I was never part of it.'

'You were at every hotel opening—'

'For show.' She turned away, her expression closing, her gaze downcast so he could see her blond lashes fanning her cheeks.

'For show?' He disliked the thought instinctively. 'It looked real to me.'

'It was meant to.'

'What are you saying? I know your parents loved you very much, Sierra. I saw how they reacted when you left. They were devastated, both of them. Your father couldn't speak of you without tears coming into his eyes. And you never even wrote them a letter to say you were safe.' His voice throbbed with intensity, with accusation, and Sierra noticed. Her gaze narrowed and her lips pursed.

'You don't think my father could have found me if he wanted?'

'Of course he could have. He was a very powerful man.'

'So why do you think he didn't?'

Marco hesitated, trying to assess Sierra's tone, her mood. 'Sierra,' he said finally, 'I am under no illusions about your father. He was a proud and sometimes ruthless man, but he was honourable. *Good.*' Sierra pressed her lips together and said nothing. 'You hurt him very much by leaving. Even if he'd never admit it.'

'Of course.' She shook her head. 'Why did you ask me to come to New York?' she said. 'Really?'

Unease spiked in his gut. 'What do you mean?'

'I mean you're not telling me the truth. Not the whole truth,' she amended when he opened his mouth to object. 'Just like always. This isn't some act of chivalry, is it, Marco? It isn't some benevolent impulse you've had out of the goodness of your heart.' She shook her head slowly. 'I almost bought it. I almost bought the whole act, because I was almost so stupid. Again.'

'Again?'

'I trusted you seven years ago—'

'I wasn't the one who betrayed a trust,' Marco snapped.

Sierra leaned forward, her eyes glittering icy-blue now, two slits of arctic rage. 'And you say you're not angry any more? Why are you here? Why am *I* here?' She folded her arms, levelling him with her glare. 'What do you really want from me?'

CHAPTER SEVEN

SHE COULDN'T BELIEVE how gullible she'd been—*again*. Wanting to believe the best of Marco Ferranti. Wanting, instinctively, to trust him. Hadn't she learned *anything*? No matter how kind he could seem, he'd been her father's apprentice for ten years. He'd wanted to marry her to further his business interests. And yet some part of her still wanted him to be kind.

'Well?' she demanded. 'Have I actually managed to render you speechless?'

'You're jumping to conclusions,' Marco said, an edge entering his voice. The charm was gone, dropped like the flimsy, false mask it was. She knew how it went. Fear spiked through her and she tamped it down. She would be no man's punching bag, emotional or physical, again.

'Then why don't you try being honest?'

'I was being honest. I do think you should have some part in Rocci Enterprises. In fact, if you'd given me a chance, I would have told you I'm prepared to give you most of your inheritance back.' He eyed her coolly, as if waiting for her to trip over herself with gratitude.

'That's very big of you,' she answered, sarcasm spiking her voice. 'You're *prepared* to give me *most*. That's so very, very noble.'

Marco's lip curled. 'You want more?'

'I don't want anything but the truth. Stop trying to manipulate me. Just tell me what you want.'

A muscle ticked in his jaw as their gazes clashed. Even with the anger simmering between them, Sierra felt an unwelcome kick of desire. A sudden sharp memory of the way he'd plundered her mouth, her body...and how good it had felt.

She saw an answering spark of awareness in Marco's eyes and knew he was remembering, too.

Good grief, what was *wrong* with her? How could she still want a man whom she couldn't trust, didn't like? Why did she have to have this intense physical reaction to him?

'I'm still waiting,' she snapped.

'Having you open the New York hotel is of some benefit to me, too,' Marco finally bit out. 'Fine, I'll admit it. The public would like to see a Rocci cut the damn ribbon.'

She sat back against the sofa, strangely deflated by his admission. 'So you were trying to make it seem like you were being nice. Thoughtful. When really you just wanted me to come for your sake.'

'For the company's sake. You might have no great interest in Rocci Enterprises, but do you want to see it fail? Seventy years of history, Sierra, and most of my life.'

'I don't care about Rocci Enterprises,' she said flatly. 'I don't care if it fails.'

'You don't care about your family's livelihood?'

'The only family left is me, and I make my own living,' she retorted. 'Stop trying to guilt me into this.'

'What about the livelihood of all the employees? Five hundred people are going to be employed by Rocci New York. If the hotel fails—'

'The hotel is not going to *fail* if I'm not there,' Sierra declared. 'My father has opened several hotels in the last seven years. I haven't been at any of them. I'm not needed, Marco.'

'As you pointed out yourself, you're the only Rocci left and people want to see you.' He paused. 'The board wants to see you.'

'Ah.' It was starting to make more sense now. 'Your job is in jeopardy.'

His mouth tightened. 'I have the controlling shares of the company.'

'But if you lose the confidence of the board as well as the public?' She shook her head. 'It won't look good.'

Fury flared in his eyes and Sierra felt an answering alarm. She was baiting him, and why? Because she was angry. She was furious and hurt that he'd been using her. Again. And she'd almost let him.

'I'm leaving.' She shoved her wine glass onto the coffee table with a clatter and rose from the sofa, grabbing her bag. 'Thanks for the drink,' she tossed over her shoulder, and then she strode from the wine bar.

She was halfway down the street, her heels clicking loudly on the pavement, when she heard his voice from behind.

'I need you, Sierra. I admit it.'

She slowed but didn't stop. Was this simply more manipulation?

'I don't want to need you, God knows.' There was a note in his voice that she hadn't heard before, a weary defeat that touched her even though she knew it shouldn't. 'I don't want to be at your mercy. I was once before and it didn't feel all that great.'

She turned around slowly, shocked when she saw him standing there, his expression unguarded and open in a way she'd never seen before.

'When were you at my mercy?'

'When I stood at the front of the church and waited for you to show up at our wedding.' He took a step towards her. People had been streaming past them but now a few slowed, curious about the drama that was being enacted on a London street. 'Why would you help me?' he asked. 'I didn't feel I could simply ask. I didn't want to simply ask, because I didn't want to be refused. Rejected.' His mouth twisted in a grimace and Sierra realised how hard this was for him. This—here, now—was real honesty. 'Again.'

'Marco…'

'I poured my life into Rocci Enterprises,' he said, his voice low and intense. 'Everything I had. I've worked for the company since I was sixteen. I started as a bellboy, which is something you probably didn't know.'

'A bellboy…' Sierra shook her head. She'd assumed Marco had come in on the executive level. She'd never asked, and he'd never spoken about his history, his background or his family. A painful reminder of how little she knew about him.

'Your father saw my potential and promoted me. He treated me like a son from the beginning. And I gave everything in return. Everything.'

'I know you did.' And Marco's unwavering loyalty was, Sierra surmised, why her father had chosen him in the first place, both as business associate and prospective son-in-law. Because her father had wanted someone who would forever be in his debt.

Marco closed his eyes briefly. 'The company is my family, my life. Losing it…' His voice choked and he ran a hand through his hair. 'I can't bear the thought of it. So I am sorry I tried to manipulate you. I apologise for not being honest. But you have my life in your hands, Sierra, whether you want to or not. I know you bear no love or even affection for me, and I accept that my behaviour recently hasn't deserved it. But all I have left, all I can do now, is to throw myself on your mercy.' His gaze met hers, bleak, even hopeless. 'Not a position I ever wanted to be in, and yet here I am.'

He hadn't meant to say all of that. He'd come into this meeting wanting to keep his pride intact, and instead he'd had everything stripped away. Revealed. He might as well be standing by the damned altar, waiting for his bride. If she refused him now...

He couldn't tell what she was thinking or feeling. She'd cloaked herself in that cool composure he'd once admired. He waited, breath held, having no idea what he could say or do if she told him *no*. If she walked away. Then she spoke.

'I'll go to New York,' she said. 'And I'll open the hotel.'

Relief poured through him, made him nearly sag with the force of it. 'Thank you.'

She nodded stiffly. 'When is it?'

'In two weeks.'

'You can forward me the details,' she said, and for a second her expression wobbled, almost as if she was going to cry. Then she nodded her farewell and turned and walked down the street, away from him.

Sierra peeked out of the window of her ground floor flat at the sleek black limo that had just pulled up to the kerb. Marco had said he would send a car, and she supposed she shouldn't be surprised that it was a limo.

But she was surprised when he stepped out, looking as devastatingly sexy as ever in a crisply tailored navy blue suit. She'd assumed she would meet him at the airport. Apparently Marco had other ideas.

Nervously, she straightened the pale grey sheath dress

she'd chosen for travel. She didn't have too many fancy clothes and after she'd agreed to Marco's suggestion, out on the street, she'd realised she didn't have anything to wear to the ball on the night of the hotel's opening. She'd used some of her paltry savings to buy a second-hand dress at a charity shop and hoped that in the dim lighting no one would notice the fraying along the hem.

Marco rapped on the front door and, taking a deep breath, Sierra willed her shoulders back and went to answer it.

'Hello, Sierra.' His voice felt like a fist plunging inside her soul. Ever since she'd seen him out on that street, admitting everything, being honest and open, she'd been plagued by doubts, filled with hope. *Here* finally was the man she could trust and like. The man she'd glimpsed seven years ago. And she didn't know whether to be glad or fearful of the fact. In some ways it had been easier, simpler, to hate Marco Ferranti.

'You're ready?' His gaze swept over her in one swift assessment as she nodded.

'Yes, I'll just fetch my case.'

'I'll get it.' He shouldered past her so she could breathe in the scent of his aftershave and hefted her single suitcase easily. 'This is all you're bringing?'

'I don't need much.'

He frowned, his straight eyebrows drawing together as his gaze moved around the tiny sitting room with its shabby sofa and rickety chairs. She'd tried to make it homely with some throws and framed posters, but it was a far cry from the luxury Marco was used to. 'What about a hanging case, for your evening clothes?'

She thought of the second-hand dress folded in her suitcase. 'It's fine.'

Marco didn't answer; he just took her suitcase and

walked out of the flat. Sierra expelled a shaky breath and then followed him, locking the door behind her.

In the two weeks since she'd agreed to accompany Marco to New York, she'd questioned her decision many times. Wondered why on earth she was entangling herself with Marco again, when things between them were complicated enough. Surely it would be better, or at least easier, to walk away for good. Draw a final line across the past.

But there on the street she'd seen Marco as she'd never seen him before. She'd seen him being open and honest, *vulnerable*, and she'd believed him. For once suspicion hadn't hardened her heart or doubt clouded her mind. She'd known Marco was speaking the truth even when he didn't want to, when it made him feel weak.

And so she'd said yes.

And not just because he'd been so honest, Sierra knew. It was more complicated than that. Because she felt she owed him something, after the way she'd walked away seven years ago. And, if she was as honest as he had been, because she wanted to see him again. And that was very dangerous thinking.

The driver of the limo took her suitcase from Marco and stowed it in the back as Marco opened the door and ushered her inside the car.

Sierra slid inside the limo, one hand smoothing across one of the sumptuous leather seats that faced each other. She scooted to the far side as Marco climbed inside, and suddenly the huge limo with its leather sofa-like seats and coffee table seemed very small.

It was going to be a long three days. An exciting three days. Maybe that was another reason she'd agreed; as much as she liked her life in London, it was quiet and unassuming. The thought of spending three days in luxury in New

York, three days with Marco, was a heady one. Even if it shouldn't be.

The door closed and Marco settled in the seat across from her, stretching his legs out so his knee nudged hers. Sierra didn't move, not wanting to be obvious about how much he affected her. Just that little nudge sent her pulse skyrocketing, although maybe it was everything all at once that was affecting her: the limo, the scent of his after-shave, the real and magnetic presence of the man opposite her, and the fact that she'd be spending the next three days with him.

She looked out of the window, afraid all her apprehension and excitement would be visible on her face.

'Are you all right?'

She turned back, startled and a little embarrassed. 'Yes, I'm fine.'

'Have some water.' He handed her a bottle of water and after a moment Sierra uncapped it and took a drink, conscious of Marco's eyes on her as she swallowed. 'I do appreciate you agreeing to do this,' he said quietly.

She lowered the bottle to look at him; his expression was shuttered, neutral, all the openness and honesty he'd shown two weeks ago tucked safely away. 'It's no hardship, spending a few days in New York,' she said.

'You seemed quite opposed to the idea initially.'

She sighed and screwed the cap back on the bottle of water. 'Revisiting everything in the past has been hard. I want to move on with my life.'

'After this you can, I promise. I won't bother you again, Sierra.'

Which should make her feel relieved rather than disappointed. Not trusting herself to speak, Sierra just nodded.

They kept the conversation light after that, speaking only of innocuous subjects: travel and food and films. By the time they reached the airport Sierra was starting to feel more relaxed, although her nerves jumped to alert when Marco took her arm as they left the limo.

He led her through the crowds, bypassing the queue at check-in for private VIP service.

'This is the life,' Sierra teased as they settled in the private lounge and a waiter brought a bottle of champagne and two flutes. 'Are we celebrating?'

'The opening of The Rocci New York,' Marco answered easily. 'Surely you've travelled VIP before?'

She shook her head. 'No, I've hardly travelled at all. Going to London was the first time I'd left the mainland of Europe.'

'Was it?' Marco frowned, clearly surprised by this information, and Sierra wondered just how rosy a view he had of her family life. Had he not realised how her father had tucked his family away, bringing them out only when necessary? But she didn't want to dwell on the past and neither, it seemed, did Marco, for after the waiter had popped the cork on the champagne and poured them both glasses, he asked, 'So how did you get into teaching in London?'

'I volunteered at first, and took some lessons myself. It started small—I took a slot at an after-school club and then word spread and more schools asked.' She shrugged. 'I'm not grooming too many world-class musicians, but I enjoy it and I think the children do, as well.'

'And you like London?'

'Yes. It's different, of course, and I could do without the rain, but...' She shrugged and took a sip of champagne, enjoying the way the bubbles zinged through her. 'It's become home.'

'You've made friends?' The innocuous lilt to his voice belied the sudden intensity she saw spark in his eyes. What was he really asking?

'I've made a few. Some teachers, a few neighbours.' She shrugged. 'I'm used to being solitary.'

'Are you? Why?'

'I spent most of my childhood in the mountains or at convent school. Company was scarce.'

'I suppose your father was strict and old-fashioned about that kind of thing.'

Her stomach tightened, memory clenching inside her. 'You could say that.'

'But he had a good heart. He always wanted the best for you.'

Sierra didn't reply. Couldn't. Marco sounded so sincere, so sure. How could she refute what he said? Now seemed neither the time nor the place. 'And for you,' she said after a moment, when she trusted her voice to sound measured and mild. 'He loved you like a son. More than I ever even realised.'

Marco nodded, his expression sombre, the corners of his mouth pulled down. 'He was like a father to me. Better than my own father.'

Curiosity sharpened inside her. 'Why? What was your own father like?'

He hesitated, his glass halfway to his lips, his mouth now a hard line. 'I don't really know. He was out of my life by the time I was seven years old.'

'He was? I'm sorry.' She paused, feeling her way through the sudden minefield of their conversation. It was obvious from his narrowed eyes and his tense shoulders, that Marco didn't like talking about his past. And yet Sierra wanted to know. 'I've realised how little I knew about you. Your childhood, your family.'

'That's because they're not worth knowing.'

'What happened to your father when you were seven?'

He was silent for a moment, marshalling his thoughts,

and Sierra waited. 'I'm illegitimate,' he finally stated flatly. 'My mother was a chambermaid at one of the hotels in Palermo—not The Rocci,' he clarified with a small, hard smile. 'My father was an executive at the hotel. Married, of course. They had an affair, and my mother became pregnant. That old story.' He shrugged dismissively, as if he wasn't going to say anything more.

'And then what happened?' Sierra asked after a moment.

'My mother had me, and my father set her up in a dingy flat in one of Palermo's slums. Gave her enough to live on—just. He'd visit us on occasion, a few times a year, perhaps. He'd bring some cheap trinkets, things guests left behind.' He shook his head, remembrance twisting his features. 'I don't think he was a truly bad man. But he was weak. He didn't like being with us. I could see that, even as a small child. He always looked guilty, miserable. He kept checking his watch, the whole time he was there.' Marco sighed and drained his flute of champagne. 'The visits became less frequent, as did the times he sent money. Eventually he stopped coming altogether.'

Sierra's mouth was dry, her heart pounding strangely. Marco had never told her any of this before. She'd had no idea he'd had such a childhood; he'd suffered loss and sorrow, just as she had, albeit in a different way. 'He never said goodbye?'

Marco shook his head. 'No, he just stopped coming. My mother struggled on as best as she could.' He shrugged. 'Sicily, especially back in those days, wasn't an easy place to be a single mother. But she did her best.' His mouth firmed as his gaze became distant. 'She did her best,' he repeated, and he almost sounded as if he were trying to convince himself.

'I'm sorry,' Sierra said quietly. 'That must have been incredibly difficult.'

He shrugged and shook his head. 'It was a long time ago. I left that life behind when I was sixteen and I never looked back.'

Just like she had, except he would never understand her reasons for leaving, for needing to escape. *Not unless she told him.*

Considering all he'd just told her, Sierra felt, for the first time, that she could tell Marco the truth of her childhood. She wanted to. She opened her mouth to begin, searching for the right words, but he spoke first.

'That's why I'm so grateful to your father for giving me a chance all those years ago. For believing in me when no one else did. For treating me more like a son than my own father did.' He shook his head, his expression shadowed with grief. 'I miss him,' he said quietly, his tone utterly heartfelt.

Bile churned in her stomach and she nodded mechanically. The memories Marco spoke of were so far from her own reality of a man who had only shown her kindness in public. He'd chuck her under the chin, heft her onto his shoulders, tell the world she was his little *bellissima*. And everyone had believed it. Marco had believed it. Why shouldn't he?

And in that moment she knew she could never tell him the truth. Not when his own family life had been so sadly lacking, not when her father had provided the love and support he'd needed. She'd had her own illusions ripped away once. She wouldn't do the same to him, to anyone, and for what purpose? In three days she'd be back in London, and she and Marco need never see each other again.

CHAPTER EIGHT

BY THE TIME they were settled in the first-class compartment on the flight to New York, Sierra had restored her equilibrium. Mostly. She felt as if she were discovering a whole new side to Marco, deeper and intriguing layers, now that they'd laid aside the resentment and hostility about the past.

She was remembering how kind and thoughtful he could be, how he saw to her small comforts discreetly, how he cocked his head, his mouth quirking in a smile as he listened to her, making her feel as if he really cared what she said.

She didn't think it was an act this time. She hoped it wasn't. The truth was she still didn't trust herself. Didn't trust anyone. But the more time she spent with Marco, the more her guard began to lower.

And she was enjoying simply chatting to him over an amazingly decadent three-course meal, complete with fine crystal and china and a bottle of very good wine. She liked feeling important and interesting to him, and she was curious about his life and ambitions and interests. More curious than she'd been seven years ago, when she'd seen him as little more than a means to an end—to escape. Now she saw him as a man.

'It was your idea to bring Rocci Hotels to North Amer-

ica?' she asked as she spooned the last of the dark chocolate mousse they'd been served for dessert.

He hadn't said as much, but she'd guessed it from the
way he'd been describing the New York project. He'd
clearly been leading the charge.

'The board wasn't interested in expansion,' Marco answered with a shrug. 'They've never liked risk.'

'So it's even more important that this succeeds.'

'It will. Especially since you've agreed.' His warm gaze
rested on her, and Sierra felt her insides tingle in response.
It would be so easy to fall under Marco's charm again, especially since this time it felt real. But where would any of
it lead? They had no future. She knew that. But she still
enjoyed talking to him, being with him. She even enjoyed
that tingle, dangerous as it was.

The steward dimmed the lights in the first-class cabin
and Marco leaned over her seat to let it recline. Sierra
sucked in a hard breath at the nearness of his body, the
intoxicating heat of him. His head was close to hers as he
murmured, 'You should get rest while you can. Tomorrow
will be a big day.'

She nodded wordlessly, her gaze fastened on his, and
gently Marco tucked a strand of hair behind her ear. It was
the merest of touches, it meant nothing, and yet still she
felt as if he'd given her an electric shock, her whole body
jolting with longing. Marco smiled and then settled back
in his own seat, stretching his long legs out in front of him
as his seat dipped back. 'Get some sleep if you can, Sierra.'

Marco shifted in his seat, trying to get comfortable. It was
damned difficult when desire was pulsing in his centre,
throbbing through his veins. It had been nearly impossible
to resist touching Sierra as they'd talked. And he'd enjoyed
the conversation, the sharing of ideas, the light banter. He'd

even been glad, in a surprising way, to have told her more about his past. He hadn't been planning to reveal the deprivations of his childhood and he'd kept some of it back, not wanting to invite her pity. But to see her face softened in sympathy...to know that she cared about him, even in that small way, affected him more than he was entirely comfortable with.

He'd been glad to move on to lighter topics, and Sierra had thankfully taken his cue. He'd enjoyed talking with her seven years ago, but she'd been a girl then, innocent and unsophisticated. The years had sharpened her, made her stronger and more interesting. And definitely more desirable.

In the end he hadn't been able to resist. A small caress, his fingers barely grazing her cheek as he'd tucked her hair behind her ear. He could tell Sierra was affected by it, though, and so was he. He longed to take her in his arms, even here in the semiprivacy of their seats, and plunder her mouth and body. Lose himself in her sweetness and feel her tremble and writhe with pleasure.

Stifling a groan, Marco shifted again. He needed to stop thinking like this. Stop remembering what Sierra's naked body had looked like as she'd been splayed across the piano bench, her skin golden and perfect in the lamplight. Stop remembering how silky she'd felt, how delicious she'd tasted, how overwhelming her response to him had been.

Marco clenched his eyes shut as a sheen of sweat broke out on his forehead. Next to him Sierra shifted and sighed, and the breathy sound made another spasm of longing stab through him. It was going to be a long flight. Hell, it was going to be a long three days. Because one thing he knew was he wouldn't take advantage of Sierra again.

He must have fallen into a doze eventually, because he woke to find her sitting up and smiling at him. Her hair was in delightful disarray about her face and she gave him a playful look as he straightened.

'You snore, you know.'

He drew back, caught between affront and amusement. 'I do not.'

'Hasn't anyone ever told you before?'

'No, because I don't snore.' And because he'd never had a woman stay the night to tell him so. Since Sierra, his love life—if he could even call it that—had been comprised of one-night stands and week-long flings. He'd had no intention of being caught again.

'Not very loudly,' Sierra informed him with an impish smile. 'And not all the time. But you do snore. Trust me.'

Trust me. The words seemed to reverberate through him before Marco shook them off. 'I suppose I'll have to take your word for it. And I might as well tell you that *you* drool when you sleep.'

'Oh!' Mortification brightened her cheeks as one hand clapped to her mouth. Marco instantly regretted his thoughtless quip. He'd been teasing and it wasn't true anyway; she'd looked adorable when she slept, her chin tucked towards her chest, her golden lashes fanning across her cheeks.

'Actually, you don't,' he said gruffly. 'But I couldn't say you snored, since you don't.'

'You cad.' Laughing, she dropped her hand to hit him lightly on the shoulder, and before he thought through what he was doing he wrapped her hand in his, savouring the feel of her slender fingers enclosed in his, the softness of her skin. Her eyes widened and her breath shortened.

Always it came back to this. The intense attraction that seemed only to grow stronger with every minute they spent in each other's company. Carefully, Marco released her hand. 'We'll be landing soon.'

Sierra nodded wordlessly, cradling her hand as if it was tender, almost as if he'd hurt her with his touch.

The next few hours were taken up with clearing Customs and then getting out of the airport. Marco had arranged for a limo to pick them up but nothing could be done about the bumper-to-bumper traffic they encountered all the way into Manhattan.

Finally the limo pulled up in front of The Rocci New York, a gleaming, needle-like skyscraper that overlooked Central Park West.

'It's gorgeous,' Sierra breathed as she stepped out of the limo and tilted her head up to the sky. 'I feel dizzy.'

'I hope you're not scared of heights.' He couldn't resist putting his hand on the small of her back as he guided her towards the marble steps that led up to the hotel's entrance. 'We're staying on the top floor.'

'Are we?' Her eyes rounded like a child's with excitement and Marco felt a deep primal satisfaction at making her happy. This was what he'd wanted seven years ago: to show the world to Sierra, to give it to her. To see her smile and know he'd been the one to put it there. No, he hadn't loved her, but damn it, he'd *liked* her. He still did.

'Come on,' he urged as they mounted the steps. He realised he was as excited as she was to see the hotel, to share it with her. 'Let me show The Rocci New York.'

Sierra followed Marco into the hotel's soaring foyer of marble and granite, everything sleek and modern, so unlike the faded old world elegance of the European Rocci hotels. This was something new and different, something created solely by Marco, and Sierra liked it all the more for that reason. There were no hard memories to face here, just anticipation for all that lay ahead.

Marco spoke to someone at the concierge desk while

Sierra strolled around the foyer, admiring the contemporary art that graced the walls, the sleek leather sofas and chairs and tables of polished wood. Everything felt clean and polished, sophisticated and streamlined. Empty, too, as the first guests would not arrive until tomorrow, after the official opening. Tomorrow night the hotel would have a gala in its ballroom to celebrate, and then the next day she'd fly back to London. But she'd enjoy every moment of being here.

Marco returned to her side, a key card resting in his palm. 'Ready?'

'Yes…' She eyed the key card uncertainly. 'Are we staying in the same room?'

The smile he gave her was teasingly wolfish. 'Don't worry, there's plenty of room for two.'

It didn't feel like there was plenty of room, Sierra thought as she stepped into the mirrored lift that soared straight towards the sky. The lift was enormous, their hotel suite undoubtedly far larger, and yet she felt the enclosed space keenly; Marco's sleeve brushed her arm as he stood next to her and Sierra's pulse jerked and leapt in response.

She needed to get a handle on her attraction. Either ignore it or act on it. And while the latter was a thrilling possibility, the former was the far wiser thing to do. She and Marco had way too much complicated history to think about getting involved now, even if just for a fling.

But what a fling it would be…

She could hardly credit she was thinking this way, and about *Marco*. What had happened to the man who had seemed so cold, so hostile? And what about the man she'd fled from seven years ago, whom she'd felt she couldn't trust? Had it all really changed, simply because he'd finally been honest? Or had *she* changed and let go of the past, at least a little? Enough to make her contemplate an affair.

Not, she reminded herself, that Marco was thinking along the same lines. But she didn't think she was imagining the tension that coiled and snapped between them. It wasn't merely one-sided. She hoped.

The lift doors opened into the centre of the suite and Marco stepped aside so she could walk out first.

'Welcome to the penthouse.'

Sierra didn't speak for a moment, just absorbed the impact of her surroundings. The penthouse suite was circular, with floor-to-ceiling windows surrounding her so she felt as if she were poised above the city, ready to fly.

Marco's footsteps clicked across the smooth floor of black marble as he switched on some lights. 'Do you like it?' he asked, and he almost sounded uncertain.

'Like it?' Sierra turned in a circle slowly, taking everything in: the luxurious but understated furnishings, nothing taking away from the spectacular panoramic view of the city. 'I love it. It's the most amazing room I've ever seen.' She turned to him, gratified and even touched to see the relief that flashed across his face before he schooled his features into a more neutral, composed expression. 'But surely this isn't the whole suite?' The circular room was a living area only. 'I don't see any beds. Or a bathroom, for that matter.'

'The rest of the suite is upstairs. But I wanted to show you this first.'

'It really is amazing. You must have a fantastic architect.'

'I do, but the idea for this suite was mine.' Sierra saw a slight blush colour Marco's high cheekbones and she felt an answering wave of something almost like tenderness. 'He didn't think it was possible, and I nagged him until he conceded it was.'

'Clearly you're tenacious.'

'When I have to be.'

His gaze held hers for a moment and she wondered at the subtext. Was he talking about them? If she'd confessed her fears to him all those years ago, would he have been tenacious in helping to assuage them, in making their marriage work? It was so dangerous to think that way, and yet impossible to keep herself from wondering. But she didn't want to imagine what life could have been; she wanted to think about what still could be.

'Let me show you the upstairs,' Marco said and took her hand as he led her to the spiral staircase in the centre of the room, next to the lift, that led to the rooms above.

Upstairs there were still the soaring views, although the space was divided into several rooms and the windows didn't go from ceiling to floor. Marco showed her the kitchen, the two sumptuous bedrooms with luxurious en suite bathrooms, and Sierra noted the small amount of hallway between them. There was room for two as Marco had assured her, but they would be sleeping right across from each other. The prospect filled her with excitement and even anticipation rather than alarm.

What was happening to her?

'You should refresh yourself,' Marco said when he'd shown her the guest room that she would use. 'Rest if you need to. It's been a long day.'

'Okay.'

'The ribbon-cutting and gala are tomorrow but if you feel up for it we could see a few sights today,' Marco suggested. 'If you're up for it?'

'Definitely. Let me just get changed.'

As she showered and dressed, Sierra gave herself a mental talking-to. She was playing a dangerous game, she knew, and one she hadn't intended to play. She was attracted to Marco and she was discovering all over again how much she liked him. She knew he was attracted to her; maybe he even liked her. They had plenty of reasons to have a nice time together, even to have a fling.

It didn't have to be for ever. They'd contemplated marriage once before, a marriage based on expediency rather than love, but they didn't have to this time. This time whatever was between them could be for pleasure. In her mind it sounded simple and yet Sierra knew the dangers. Trusting any man, even with just her body, was a big step, and one she hadn't taken before. Did she really want to with Marco?

And yet the three days that stretched so enticingly in front of her, the excitement of being with Marco... How could she resist?

But perhaps she wouldn't need to. Perhaps Marco had no intention of acting on the attraction between them. Perhaps he'd meant what he'd said back at the villa about never touching her again.

With her thoughts still in a hopeless snarl, Sierra left her bedroom in search of Marco. She found him downstairs in the circular salon, talking in clipped English on his phone. Sierra had become fluent in English since moving to London and she could tell he was checking on the hotel's readiness for tomorrow.

'Everything okay?' she asked as Marco slid the phone into his pocket.

'Yes. Just checking on a few last-minute details. I don't want anything to go wrong, not even the hors d'oeuvres.'

He smiled ruefully and Sierra laid a hand on his sleeve. 'This is really important to you.'

He gazed down at her, his wry smile replaced by a sombre look. 'I told you the truth before, Sierra. The whole truth. The hotel is everything to me.'

Everything. Sierra didn't know whether to feel rebuked or relieved. She decided to feel neither, to simply enjoy the possibilities of the day. 'So what sights are you going to show me? You must have been to New York loads of times, overseeing the hotel.'

'Do you have anything you want to see in particular?'

'Whatever your favourite thing is.' She wanted to get to know this man more.

A smile curled Marco's mouth, drawing Sierra's attention to his firm and yet lush lips. Lips she still remembered the taste of, and craved. 'All right, then. Let's go.'

It wasn't until they were out on Central Park West and Marco had hailed one of the city's trademark yellow cabs that Sierra asked where they were going.

He ushered her into the cab first, sliding in next to her so their thighs were pressed together. 'The Museum of Modern Art.'

'Art!' She shook her head slowly. 'I never knew you liked art.'

'Modern art. And there are a lot of things you don't know about me.'

'Yes,' Sierra answered as Marco held her gaze, a small smile curving his wonderful mouth. 'I'm coming to re-alise that.'

CHAPTER NINE

Marco could not remember a time when he'd enjoyed himself more. He and Sierra wandered around the airy galleries of the MoMA and, at some point while looking at the vast canvases and modern sculpture, he took her hand.

It felt so natural that he didn't even think about it first, just slid his hand into hers and let their fingers entwine. She didn't resist, and they spent the rest of the afternoon remarking on and joking about Klimt's use of colour and Picasso's intriguing angular forms.

'I'm not an expert, by any means,' Marco told her when they wandered out into the sunshine again. It was August and New York simmered under a summer sun, heat radiating from the pavement. 'I just like the possibility in modern art. That people dared to do things differently, to see the world another way.'

'Yes, I can understand that.' She slid him a look of smiling compassion. 'Especially considering your background.'

Marco tensed instinctively but Sierra was still holding his hand, and he forced himself to relax. She knew more about him than anyone else did, even Arturo, who had been as good as a father. Arturo had known about his background a little; he'd raised him up from being a bell-boy and, in any case, Marco knew his accent gave him away as a Sicilian street rat. But Arturo had never known about his father. He'd never asked.

'Where to now?' Sierra asked and Marco shrugged.

'Wherever you like. Are you getting tired?'

'No. I don't know how anyone can get tired here. There's so much energy and excitement. I'm not sure I'll ever get to sleep tonight.' Her innocent words held no innuendo but Marco felt the hard kick of desire anyway. She looked so lovely and fresh, wearing a floaty summery dress with her hair caught in a loose plait, her face flushed and her eyes bright. He wanted to draw her towards him and kiss her, but he resisted.

That wasn't the purpose of this trip…except now maybe it was. At least, why shouldn't it be? If they were both feeling it?

'I'd love to walk through Central Park,' Sierra said and Marco forced his thoughts back to the conversation at hand.

'Then let's do it.'

They walked uptown to the Grand Army Plaza, buying ice creams to cool off as they strolled along the esplanade. Sierra stopped in front of a young busker by the Central Park Zoo, playing a lovely rendition of a Mozart concerto. She fumbled in her pockets to give him some money and Marco stopped her, taking a bill from his wallet instead.

'Thank you,' she murmured as they continued walking.

'Why do you only play in private?' Marco asked. He was curious to know more about her, to understand the enigma she'd been to him for so long.

Sierra pursed her lips, reflecting. 'Because I did it for me. It was a way to…to escape, really. And I didn't want anyone to ruin it for me, to stop me.'

'Escape? What were you escaping from?'

Her gaze slid away from his and she licked a drip of ice cream from her thumb. 'Oh, you know. The usual.'

Marco could tell she didn't want to talk about it, and yet he found he wanted to know. Badly. He'd painted a rosy, perfect picture of her childhood; considering his own, how could he have not? She had two parents who adored her, a beautiful home, everything she could possibly want. He'd wanted to be part of that world, wanted to inhabit it with her. But now he wondered if his view of it had been a little too perfect.

'But now that you're an adult? You still play in private?'

She nodded. 'I've never wanted to be a performer. I like teaching, but I play the violin for me.' She spoke firmly and he wondered if she would ever play for him. He thought that if she did it would mean something—to both of them.

And did he want it to mean something? Did he want to become emotionally close to Sierra, never mind what happened between them physically?

It was a question he didn't feel like answering or examining, not on a beautiful summer's day with the park stretched out before them, and everything feeling like a promise about to be made. He took Sierra's hand again and they walked up towards the Fountain of Bethesda, the still waters of the lake beyond shimmering under the sun.

By early evening Marco could tell Sierra was starting to flag. He was, too, and although he wanted to spend the entire day with Sierra, he knew there was pressing business to attend to before tomorrow's opening. He took a call as they entered the hotel, flashing a quick apologetic smile at Sierra. She smiled back, understanding, and disappeared into her room in the penthouse suite while Marco stretched out on a sofa and dealt with a variety of issues related to the opening.

He loosened his collar and leaned his head back against the sofa as one of his staff droned on about the guest list for tomorrow night's gala. From upstairs he could hear Sierra moving around and then the sound of a shower being turned on. He pictured her in the luxurious glass cubicle, big enough for two, water streaming down her golden body, and his whole body tightened in desperate arousal.

'Mr Ferranti?' The woman on the other end of the line must have been speaking for a while and Marco hadn't heard a word.

'I'm sorry. Can you say that again?'

A short while later Sierra came downstairs, dressed in a T-shirt and snug yoga pants, her hair falling in damp tendrils around her face.

Marco took one look at her and ended his call. His mouth dried and his heart turned over in his chest. She was utterly delectable, and not just because of her beauty. He liked having her in his space, looking relaxed and comfortable, being part of his world. He liked it a lot.

'You've finished your calls?' she asked as she came towards him. She curled up on the other end of the long leather sofa, tucking her feet underneath her.

'For the moment. There are a lot of details to sort out but first I think I want to eat.' His eyes roved over her hungrily and a blush touched her cheeks. Marco smiled and gestured to the city lights sparkling in every direction. 'The world is our oyster. What would you like to eat? We can order takeaway. Whatever you want.'

'How about proper American food? Cheeseburgers and French fries?'

He laughed and pressed a few buttons on his phone. 'And here I thought you'd be asking for lobster and caviar and champagne. Consider it done.'

* * *

Sierra watched as Marco put in their order for food. She felt jet-lagged and sleepy and relaxed, and she laid her head back against the sofa as Marco tossed his phone on the table and rose in one fluid movement.

'I'm going to get changed. The food should be here in a few minutes.'

'Okay.' It felt incredibly pleasant, no, wonderful, to sit there and listen to him go upstairs. The snick of a door closing, and she could imagine his long, lean fingers unbuttoning his shirt, shrugging it off his broad shoulders. He was the most beautiful man she'd ever seen. She remembered the feel of his body against hers, her breasts crushed against his chest…

A smile curved Sierra's mouth and she closed her eyes, picturing the scene perfectly. Then she imagined going up those stairs herself, opening that door. What would she say? What would she do? Perhaps she wouldn't have to do or say anything. Perhaps Marco would see her and take control, draw her towards him and kiss her as she wanted him to.

'I think the food's here.'

Sierra's eyes flew open and she saw Marco standing in front of her, wearing jeans and a faded grey T-shirt that clung to his pecs. His hair was slightly mussed, his jaw shadowed with stubble, and she didn't think she'd ever seen anything as wonderful, as desirable.

'You look like you were about to drop off,' Marco remarked as he took the food from the attendant who stepped out of the lift.

'I think I was.' She wasn't about to admit what had been going through her head. The mouth-watering aroma of cheeseburgers and fries wafted through the room and Marco brought the tray of food to the coffee table in front of the sofa.

'We might as well eat here.'

He handed her a plate heaped with a huge burger and plenty of fries and Sierra bit in, closing her eyes as the flavours hit her. 'Oh, this is *good.*'

Marco made a choked sound and Sierra opened her eyes, her heart seeming to still as his hot gaze held hers. 'Look like that much longer and I'll have to forget about this meal,' he said, his voice a low growl, and awareness shivered through her.

'It's too delicious to do that,' she protested, her voice breathy, and Marco shrugged, his gaze never leaving hers. 'I can think of something more delicious.'

Colour flooded her face and heated her body. This was so dangerous, and yet…why shouldn't she? Why shouldn't *they*? They were in a glamorous hotel in one of the most amazing cities in the world. There was nothing, absolutely nothing, to keep them from acting on the desire Sierra knew they both felt.

Marco plucked one of her French fries from her plate. 'Your face is the colour of your ketchup.'

She laughed shakily and put her burger down, wiping her hands on the napkin provided. 'Marco…' She trailed off, not knowing what to say or how to say it.

Marco smiled and nodded towards her still full plate. 'Let's eat, Sierra. It's a big day tomorrow.'

That sounded and felt like a brush-off. Trying not to feel stung, Sierra started eating again. Had Marco changed his mind? Why did he say one thing and then do another? Maybe, Sierra reflected, he felt as conflicted as she did. Maybe a fling would be too complicated, considering their history.

Considering her lack of experience, she didn't even know if she could handle a fling. Would she be able to walk away after a couple of days, heart intact? The truth was, she had no idea.

Marco's phone rang before they'd finished their meal and he excused himself to take the call. Sierra ate the rest of her burger and then tidied up, leaving the tray of dirty dishes by the lift. She wandered around the living area for a bit, staring out at the glittering cityscape, before jet lag finally overcame her and she headed upstairs to bed. Marco was still closeted in his own bedroom and so, with a sigh of disappointment, Sierra went into hers. Despite her restlessness, sleep claimed her almost instantly.

When she woke the sun was bathing the city in gold and she could hear Marco moving around across the hall.

The ribbon-cutting ceremony was that afternoon, and it occurred to Sierra as she showered and dressed that she really didn't have the right clothes.

Back in London, her one smart day dress and second-hand ball gown had seemed sufficient but now that she'd been to the hotel, now that she cared about it—and Marco's success—she realised she didn't want to stand in front of the crowd looking dowdy or underdressed. She wanted to look her best, not just for Marco and the public but for herself.

She dressed in jeans and a simple summery top and headed downstairs in search of Marco. He was standing by the window, scrolling through messages on his phone and drinking coffee, but he looked up as she came down the stairs, a smile breaking across his face.

'Good morning.'

'Good morning.' Suddenly Sierra felt shy. Marco looked amazing, freshly showered, his crisp blue shirt set off by a darker blue suit and silver tie. His hair was slightly damp, curling around his ears, and his smoothly shaven jaw looked eminently touchable. Kissable.

'Did you sleep well?'

'Yes, amazingly. But I wondered if there was time to go out this morning, before the opening.'

'Go out? Where?'

'Shopping.' Sierra flushed. 'I don't think the clothes I brought are…well, nice enough, if I'm honest.' She let out an uncertain laugh. 'A second-hand ball gown from a charity shop doesn't seem appropriate, now that I'm here.'

Surprise flashed across Marco's face before it was replaced by composed determination. 'Of course. I'll arrange a car immediately.'

'I can walk…'

'Nonsense. It will be my great pleasure to buy clothes for you, Sierra.' His gaze rested on her, his silvery-grey eyes seeming to burn right through her.

'You don't have to buy them, Marco—'

'You would deny me such a pleasure?' He slid his phone into his pocket and strode towards her. 'The car will be waiting. You can have breakfast on the way.'

Within minutes Sierra was whisked from the penthouse suite to the limo waiting outside the hotel; a carafe of coffee, another of freshly squeezed orange juice and a basket of warm croissants were already set out for her.

'Good grief.' She shook her head, laughing, as Marco slid into the seat next to her. 'This is kind of crazy, you know.'

'Crazy? Why?'

'The luxury. I'm not used to it.'

'You should get used to it, then. This is the life you would have had, Sierra. The life you deserve.'

She paused, a croissant halfway to her mouth, and met his gaze. 'The life I would have had? You mean if I'd married you?' She spoke softly, hesitant to dredge up the past once again and yet needing to know. Did Marco wish things had been different? Did she?

'If you'd married anyone,' Marco said after a pause.

'Someone of your father's choosing, of your family's station.'

'You think I should have married someone of my father's choosing?'

'I think you should have married me.'

Her insides jolted so hard she felt as if she'd missed the last step in a staircase. 'Even now?' she whispered.

Marco glanced away. 'Who can say what would have happened, how things would have been? The reality is you chose not to, and we've both become different people as a result.'

But people who could find their way back to each other. The words hovered on her lips but Sierra didn't say them. What were they really talking about here? A fling, a relationship, or just what might have been? She didn't know what she felt or wanted

'Ah, here we are,' Marco said, and Sierra turned to see the limo pull up to an exclusive-looking boutique on Fifth Avenue. She stuffed the rest of her croissant into her mouth as he jumped out of the limo. She swallowed quickly and then took his hand as he led her out of the car and into the boutique.

Several assistants came towards them quickly and Sierra glanced around at the crystal chandeliers, the white velvet sofas, the marble floor. There seemed to be very few pieces of clothing on display. And she felt underdressed to go shopping, which seemed ridiculous, but she could not deny the svelte blonde assistants were making her feel dowdy.

But then Marco turned to her, his eyes lit up as his warm, approving gaze rested on her. 'And now,' he said, tugging her towards him, 'the fun begins.'

CHAPTER TEN

MARCO STRETCHED OUT on the sofa, handling business calls while Sierra tried on outfit after outfit, shyly pirouetting in front of him in each one. He couldn't think of a better way to spend his time than watch Sierra model clothes. Actually, he could. He'd like to spend his time taking the clothes off her.

She'd started with modest day outfits, but even tailored skirts and crisp blouses sent his heart rate skyrocketing. He wanted to slip those pearl buttons from their holes and part the silky fabric to see the even silkier skin beneath. He wanted to shimmy that pencil skirt off her slim hips.

Instead he issued a terse command to the fawning assistant. 'We'll take them all.'

Sierra was in the dressing room and didn't hear him; a few minutes later she came out, frowning uncertainly. 'I think maybe that blue shift dress might be the best choice…'

'You can decide later,' Marco answered indulgently. It amused him that Sierra thought he was going to be satisfied by simply buying her a single outfit. What kind of man did she think he was?

A man who was falling in love with her.

The words froze inside him, turned everything to ice. He couldn't be falling in love. He didn't *do* love. He'd seen what it had done to his mother. He'd felt what it had done to him. Waiting for someone who wasn't going to come back, who didn't feel the same way. His mother. *Sierra.* And he hadn't even loved Sierra, back then. Did he want to set himself up for an even harder fall?

No, he was not falling in love with her. He was just enjoying himself. And yes, he might be thinking about what might have been; it was damned hard not to. Seeing Sierra in her element, where she belonged, every inch the Rocci heiress, her desire shining in her eyes…how could he not think about it?

'What do you think about this one?' Sierra emerged from the dressing room in an evening gown, a blush touching her cheeks. Marco stared at her, his whole body going rigid. The dress was a long, elegant column of grey-blue silk that matched her eyes perfectly. A diamanté belt encircled her narrow waist, and her hair was loose and tousled about her shoulders.

Marco couldn't even think when he saw her in that dress. 'We'll take it.' He bit the words out gruffly, and Sierra's eyes widened.

'But if you don't like it…'

'I like it.' From the corner of his eye Marco saw an assistant smile behind her hand. 'Please go wrap up the other outfits,' he barked and she melted back into the boutique, leaving them alone.

'The other outfits?' Sierra frowned. 'But I thought you were just buying the blue dress.'

'You thought wrong.' He stalked towards her and to his satisfaction he could see a pulse begin to hammer in her throat. 'I'm buying them all, Sierra. I want to see you in them all.'

She pressed a hand to her fluttering pulse as she swallowed convulsively. 'There are a few more evening gowns to try on…'

'And I want you to try them on. But I think I'd better help you with the zipper on that dress.'

Her eyes had gone huge, as blue and glassy as twin mountain lakes. Her pink lips parted, and when her tongue darted out to moisten them, Marco groaned.

'The assistant…' she murmured and he shook his head, everything in him demanding that he touch her. Now.

'Is gone. I'll do it.' Gently but purposefully, he pushed her back into the dressing room, drawing the thick brocade curtain closed behind them. The space was private, the silence hushed and expectant. After a second when she just stared at him, Sierra turned and offered him her back.

Marco moved the heavy, honeyed mass of her hair, revelling in the softness of it as it slipped through his fingers. With the nape of her neck bare he couldn't keep from kissing her. He brushed his lips against the tender skin and felt her whole body shudder in response.

She swayed against him silently and he put his hands on her shoulders to steady her. Desire raged through him, a fierce and overwhelming need that obliterated all rational thought. He'd take her right in this dressing room if she'd let him, but he didn't want their first time together to be urgent and rushed. No, he'd take his time, prolong the exquisite agony.

Slowly Marco drew the zip down the dress, the snick of the fabric parting one of the most erotic sounds he'd ever heard.

The strapless dress slipped from her body, leaving her bare, her skin golden and perfect. He slid his hands around her waist, spanning it easily, and then, because he couldn't keep himself from it, he slid them up to cup her breasts, his thumbs flicking over her nipples, his hands full of her lush softness.

Sierra sagged against him, her breath coming out in a shudder. Marco pushed into her, and she gasped again at the feel of his arousal against her bottom.

When she pushed back gently, her hips nudging him with intent, he almost abandoned his resolution to take his time. It would be so easy, so overwhelmingly satisfying, to pull her dress up and bury himself inside her right then and there.

He slid his hands back down to her hips, anchoring her against him, pushing into her and having her push back, their bodies moving in an ancient rhythm. Sierra's breath caught on a gasp and her whole body went tense. Marco knew she was close to climaxing, just from this. Hell, so was he.

'Mr Ferranti?' The musical trill of the assistant's voice caused reality to rush in. Sierra stiffened and reluctantly Marco eased back.

'We're not finished here,' he told her in a low voice.

Sierra let out a laugh that sounded close to a sob. 'Dear heaven, I hope not.'

He smiled as he kissed the nape of her neck once more and then slipped from the dressing room to deal with the ill-timed assistant.

As soon as Marco had gone Sierra sank onto one of the padded benches, the dress pooling around her waist, her head in her hands. Her whole body trembled with the aftershocks of his touch. She'd been so close to losing control, and simply by the feel of his body pressing into hers. And as amazed and mortified as she felt that she'd been so shameless in a public dressing room, the overwhelming feeling she had now was a desire to rush out of this shop, jump in a limo and race back to the hotel where Marco could make good on his promise.

We're not finished.

Not, Sierra hoped, by a long shot.

'Sierra?' Marco called, his voice sounding crisply professional and not as if he were remotely affected by what had just happened between them. 'We should be getting on. You'll need to leave some time to get ready and I have a few things to finish before the opening.'

'Of course.' Hurriedly, she slithered out of the evening gown. 'Let me just get dressed.' She yanked on her jeans and pulled her T-shirt over her head, finger-combing her tousled hair as she slipped from the dressing room, her body still weak and trembling from their encounter. Marco, of course, looked completely unruffled. Maybe this was a normal experience for him. 'What about the evening gown...?' she asked, glad her voice came out sounding even.

'We're taking them all,' Marco informed her blithely. 'The assistant will have them wrapped and sent to the hotel. It's all taken care of.'

'Taking *all* of the evening gowns? But I didn't even try them on.'

'I'm sure you'll look fabulous in them. And if you don't like any of them, I'll arrange for them to be returned.' Marco took her elbow. 'Now, the limo is waiting.'

Sierra let herself be ushered out of the store, amazed by the whole experience, from the sheer number of clothes Marco had bought her to the exciting interlude in the dressing room.

'You make everything seem so easy,' she commented as she slid into the limo. 'Like the world is at your fingertips, or even your feet.'

Marco gave her a quick smile as he checked his phone. 'I've worked hard to have it be so.'

'I know you have. But do you ever…do you ever feel like pinching yourself, that this is your reality?'

For a second Marco's gaze became distant, shuttered. Then he turned back to his phone. 'Money doesn't buy everything,' he said, his voice clipped. 'No matter how many people think so, it can't make you happy.'

The honest statement, delivered as it was so matter-of-factly, both surprised and moved her. 'Are you happy, Marco?'

He glanced up with a wolfish grin. 'I was very happy with you in the dressing room. And I intend to be even happier before the day is done.'

She felt a flush spread across her body as her insides tingled. She knew Marco was deliberately avoiding a serious conversation, but she wanted him too much to care. 'I hope you do mean that.'

He paused, lowering his phone. 'I do mean it, Sierra. I want you very badly. So badly I almost lost control in a dressing room, which is something I've never done before.'

'You haven't?' she teased, trying to ignore the jealousy that spiked through her. 'I imagine you've got quite a lot of experience under your belt.'

'Not as much as you probably think, but I know my way around.' Her face heated even more and she looked away. Yes, he most certainly did. 'What about you?' he asked abruptly. 'You must have had lovers over the last seven years.' She opened her mouth to admit the truth but before she could he held up a hand. 'Never mind. I don't want to know.' His face had hardened into implacable lines, and his eyes blazed. 'But make no mistake, Sierra. I want you. Tonight.'

'I want you, too,' she whispered.

His gaze swept over her, searching, assessing. 'We're not who we were seven years ago. Things are different now.'

'I know.' She lifted her chin and met his gaze directly. 'I know what this is, Marco. We're in an amazing city for a short period of time and we happen to be attracted to each other. *Very* attracted. So why shouldn't we act on it?' She smiled, raising her eyebrows, making it sound so simple. As if she had had this kind of experience before. 'It's a fling.'

'Yes,' Marco said slowly. 'That's exactly what it is.'

Back in the hotel, Marco disappeared into the office to deal with some business before the opening while Sierra headed upstairs to the penthouse. The elegant lobby was bustling with staff as they prepared for the champagne and chocolate reception that would immediately follow the opening. And then, tonight, the ball…

Staff hurried and worked around her as she walked towards the private penthouse lift. One middle-aged man caught her eye and executed a stiff bow. 'Good afternoon, Miss Rocci. I hope you find everything to your satisfaction.'

'Yes, yes, of course,' Sierra nearly stammered. She was shaken by the way the man knew her, knew she was a Rocci. She hadn't truly been a Rocci in seven years. She'd turned her back on it all, and in that moment the memories came back in a sickening rush—the hotel openings so different from the modern elegance of The Rocci New York and yet so frighteningly familiar.

'Miss Rocci? Are you all right?' The man who had spoken to her before touched her elbow cautiously and Sierra realised she must have looked unwell. She felt sick and faint, and she reached out a hand to the lift door to steady herself.

'I'm fine. Thank you. I just haven't eaten today.'

'I'll have something sent up to your room.'

'Thank you,' Sierra murmured. 'I appreciate it.'

The lift doors opened and she stepped inside, grateful for the privacy. For a few seconds she'd heard her father's voice, felt his hand pinch her in warning as they mounted the steps of one hotel or another.

Be a good girl, Sierra. Smile for everyone.

She could hear the implied threat in his voice, the promise of punishment if she didn't behave, all against the background of a crowd's expectant murmurings, the clink of crystal...

The lift doors opened and Sierra stumbled out into the penthouse's living area, the city stretching all around her, one hand clamped to her mouth. She swallowed down the bile and then hurried upstairs to the freestanding kitchen units and poured herself a glass of water. Dear heaven, she couldn't fall apart now. Not when the opening was about to start, everyone was waiting for her. Marco was depending on her.

Sierra closed her eyes, memory and regret and fear coursing through her in unrelenting waves. She didn't want to let Marco down. How much had changed in such a short time—six weeks ago she'd been hoping never to see him again.

And now...now she was hoping he'd make love to her tonight. She wanted to stand by his side at the opening and make him proud. *She was halfway to falling in love with him.*

Sierra's eyes snapped open. *What?* How could she be? She'd always avoided and disdained love, seen how her mother had prostrated herself at its altar and lost her soul. And now she was poised to fall in love with a man she still didn't entirely trust? Or maybe it was herself she didn't trust. She didn't trust herself to keep her head straight and her heart safe.

She was inexperienced when it came to romance or sex, and here she was, contemplating a fling? For a second Sierra wondered what on earth she was doing. And then she remembered the feel of Marco's hands on her, his body behind her, and a shiver of sheer longing went through her. She knew what she was doing—and she needed to do it.

And as for the opening... She glanced at the clock above the sink and saw with a lurch of alarm that the opening was in less than an hour. An hour until she had to face Marco and the crowds of people who would be watching her, knowing she was a Rocci who had fallen from grace. Her stomach clenched and she half wished she could cry off, even as she acknowledged that she would never leave Marco in the lurch, publicly humiliated and alone. It would be almost as bad as leaving him at the altar.

She took a deep breath and willed her nerves back. Lifted her chin and straightened her shoulders. *Show no fear.* She could do this.

Marco paced the foyer of the hotel as the reporters, celebrities and guests attending the opening of The Rocci New York waited outside the frosted glass doors. It was three minutes past two o'clock and Sierra was meant to be down here. He'd already sent a staff member upstairs to check on her; she'd promised to be down shortly. He'd thought of going up himself, but some sense, or perhaps just an innate sense of caution, had stopped him. What if she didn't want to see him now?

'We should start...' Antony, the head of the hotel, looked nervously at the waiting crowds.

'We can't start without a Rocci,' Marco snapped. He felt his 'less than' status as the non-Rocci CEO keenly then,

but worse, he felt it as a man. Sierra's lateness was too powerful a reminder of another time he'd been kept waiting.

Another time he'd felt the blood drain from his head and
the hope from his heart as he'd realised once again someone wasn't coming back. Wasn't coming at all.

He blinked back the memories, willed back the hurt
and fear. This was different. He and Sierra were both different now.

Then the lift doors opened and she stepped out, looking ethereally lovely in a mint-green shift dress—and very
pale. Her gaze darted round the empty foyer and then to
the front doors where the crowd gathered, waiting; she
took a deep breath and threw her shoulders back. Marco
frowned and started forward.

Sierra saw his frown and faltered and Marco caught her
hands in his; they were icy.

'Sierra, are you all right?'

'Yes…'

'You look ill.'

'Jet lag.' She didn't quite meet his gaze. 'Everything
has been such a whirlwind.'

But he knew it couldn't just be jet lag. As beautiful as
she was and always would be to him, she looked awful.
'Sierra, if you're not up for it…' he began, only to stop. She
had to be up for it. The security of the company and his
place at its head rested on having a Rocci at this opening.

And yet in that moment he knew if she said she wasn't,
he would accept her word.

'I'm fine, Marco.' She squeezed his hands lightly and
gave him what he suspected was meant to be a smile. 'Really, I am. Let's do this.'

Sierra watched as Marco scanned her face like a doctor
looking for broken bones. She knew she must look truly

awful for him to seem so worried and she tried to dredge
up some confidence and composure. It was just the memories. So many of them, crowding her in like jeering ghosts.
She wanted to drown out the babble of their voices but it
was hard. She hadn't been at an opening like this since
she was a teenager, her father's hand hard on her elbow,
his voice in her ear.

Be good, Sierra. With the awful implied *or else.*

Finally Marco nodded and let go of her hands. 'All right.
The crowd is waiting.'

'I'm sorry I'm late.' She'd been trying not to be sick.

'It's fine.' He strode towards the front doors and resolutely, holding her head high, Sierra followed.

A staff member opened the doors and Sierra stepped
out into the shimmering heat and the snap and flash of
dozens of cameras. She recoiled instinctively before she
forced herself to stop and straighten. Foolishly, perhaps,
she hadn't realised quite how big a deal the hotel opening would be, bigger than any of the ones her father
had arranged, but then she hadn't considered Marco's
ambition and drive.

Marco had stepped up to a microphone and was welcoming the guests and media, his voice smooth and ur-
bane, his English flawless. Sierra stood stiffly, trying to
smile, until Marco's words began to penetrate.

'I know Arturo Rocci, my mentor and greatest friend,
would be so proud to be here with us, and to see his daughter cutting the ribbon today. Arturo believed passionately
in the values that gird every Rocci hotel. He valued hard
work, excellent service and, of course, family ties.' He
glanced at Sierra, who stood frozen, her stomach churning. She hadn't expected Marco to mention her father. She
couldn't keep his words from washing over her like an acid
rain, corroding everything.

The crowd clapped and someone pressed an overlarge pair of gilded scissors into her hand. The silver satin ribbon that stretched across the steps glinted in the sunlight.

'Sierra?' Marco asked, his voice low.

Somehow she moved forward and snipped the ribbon. As it fell away the crowd cheered and then Marco took her elbow and led her inside to the cool sanctuary of the foyer.

'You don't look well.'

'I'm sorry, it must be the heat. And the jet lag.' *And the memories.* And her father's ghost, hurting her from the grave. Marco still believing the best of him, and she could hardly fault him. She hadn't said anything, hadn't thought it was necessary. And when she'd been planning never to see Marco again, it hadn't been. But now? Now, when she was thinking of something actually happening between them?

'Do you want to sit down?' Marco asked. 'Catch your breath?'

Sierra shook her head. 'I'm fine, Marco. I came here for this, and I'll see it through.' She plucked a flute of champagne from a waiter's tray. She definitely needed some liquid courage. Guests were starting to stream into the foyer, chatting and taking pictures. 'Let the party begin,' she said, and raised her glass in a determined toast.

CHAPTER ELEVEN

A FEW HOURS into the reception Sierra finally started to relax. The memories that had mocked her were starting to recede; her father's grip not, thankfully, as tight as she'd feared it was. She avoided reporters with their difficult, probing questions and chatted with various guests and staff about innocuous things: New York, London, the latest films. She was actually having a good time.

The three glasses of champagne helped, too.

'This is the most amazing thing I've ever seen,' she told a waiter as she studied the chocolate fountain with floating strawberries. He smiled politely and a firm hand touched her elbow. Even though Sierra couldn't see who it was, she felt it through her marrow. Marco.

'You're not drunk, are you?'

'Drunk? Thanks very much.' She turned around, misjudging the distance, and nearly poured her half-full flute of champagne onto his front. Marco caught her hand and liberated her glass. 'Slightly tipsy only,' she amended at his wry look. 'But this is a fun party.'

Marco drew her aside, away from the waiter and guests. 'You seemed tense earlier. Even upset. Was it something I said?' Concern drew his straight dark eyebrows together, his wonderful mouth drawn into a frowning line.

'No,' Sierra answered. 'It wasn't something you said.'

'Are you sure?'

She nodded, knowing she couldn't explain it to him here, and maybe not ever. The deeper things got with Marco, the harder it became to come clean about her past. She didn't want to hurt him, and yet if they were to have any future at all she knew she needed to explain. He needed to understand.

But why was she even thinking about a future? They were just having a fling. And they hadn't even had it yet.

'When is the ball tonight?'

'Not for a few hours. But if you'd like to retire upstairs and get ready, you can. You've shown your face here. You've done enough.' He paused, and then rested a hand on her arm. 'Thank you, Sierra.'

Marco watched Sierra head towards the lift, a frown on his face. She'd looked so pale and shaky when she'd first come to the opening, almost ill. Something was wrong and he had no idea what it was.

At least she'd rallied, smiling and talking with guests, her natural charm and friendliness coming to the fore. She'd maybe rallied a little too much, judging by the amount of champagne she'd imbibed. The thought made him smile.

He was looking forward to seeing Sierra tonight at the ball, and then after. Most definitely after.

'Mr Ferranti, do you have anything to say about Sierra Rocci's presence at the opening today?'

Marco turned to see one of the tabloid reporters smirking at him.

'No, I do not.'

'You were engaged to Sierra Rocci seven years ago, were you not?' the weedy young man pressed. 'And she broke off the engagement at the last moment? Left you standing at the altar?' He smirked again and Marco stiffened, longing to wipe that smug look off the man's face.

He hadn't considered the press resurrecting that old story. His engagement to Sierra had been kept quiet back then; Arturo had wanted a quiet ceremony, not wanting to expose Sierra to media scrutiny. Marco had been glad to agree.

'Well?' The reporter smirked, eyebrows raised.

'No comment,' Marco bit out tersely, and stalked off.

'You can look in the mirror now.'

'Thank you.' Sierra smiled at the stylist, Diana, whom Marco had arranged to do her hair and make-up for the ball. It had been a nice surprise to emerge from an hour-long soak in the sunken marble tub to find a woman ready to be her fairy godmother.

Now Sierra turned around and gazed at her reflection in the full-length mirror, catching her breath on a gasp of surprise.

'Oh, my goodness…'

'My sentiments exactly,' Diana agreed cheerfully.

Sierra raised one hand to touch the curls that were piled on top of her head, a few trailing down to rest beguilingly on her shoulder. Diamond clips sparkled from the honeyed mass and when she turned her head they caught the light. Her make-up was understated and yet somehow transformed her face; she had smoky eyes, endless lashes, sculpted cheekbones and lush pink lips.

'I had no idea make-up could do so much,' she exclaimed and leaned forward to peer at herself more closely.

Diana laughed. 'I didn't use that much make-up. Just enough to enhance what was already there.'

'Even so.' Sierra shook her head, marvelling. She had never worn make-up as a teenager, and she hadn't changed much during her years in London. Now, however, she could see the advantages.

Her gaze dropped from her face to her dress. She'd chosen the dress Marco had seen her in, the silvery-blue column of silk with the diamanté belt around her waist. Looking at herself in the dress made her face warm and her blood heat as she remembered how Marco had unzipped it. How he'd put his hands on her hips and pulled her towards him and she'd gone, craving the feel of him, desperately wanting more.

'I wonder if I put a bit too much blusher on,' Diana mused and, with a suppressed laugh, Sierra turned away from the mirror.

'I'm sure it's fine.'

Marco was getting ready just across the hall, and she couldn't wait to see him. She couldn't wait for him to see her, and for this wonderful, enchanted evening to begin. No matter what had happened before or might lie ahead, she wanted to truly be Cinderella and enjoy this one magical night. The clock wasn't going to strike just yet.

Marco knocked softly on her bedroom door and, with a conspiratorial grin, Diana went to answer it. 'I'll tell him you're coming in a moment. You're going to knock his socks off, you know.'

Sierra smiled back, one hand pressed to her middle to soothe the seething nerves that had started in her stomach. She didn't want anything to ruin this night.

Diana told Marco with surprising bossiness to wait for Sierra downstairs and, after taking the filmy matching wrap and beaded bag, Sierra opened the door and headed out.

She walked down the spiral staircase carefully; the last thing she wanted was to go flying down the stairs and fall flat on her face.

She saw Marco before he saw her; he was standing by the windows, staring out at the city where the sky was lit up with streaks of vivid orange and umber, a spectacular summer sunset.

Her heels clicked on the wrought iron and he turned around, going completely still as he caught sight of her. Sierra couldn't tell anything from his face; his perfect features were completely blank as his silvery-grey gaze swept over her.

She came to the bottom of the staircase, her heart starting to beat hard. 'Do I...? Is everything all right?'

Suddenly she wondered if she had lipstick on her teeth or she'd experienced some unknown wardrobe malfunction.

Then Marco's face cleared and he stepped forward, taking her hands in his. 'You have stolen my breath along with my words. You are magnificent, Sierra.'

A smile spread across her face as he squeezed her hands. 'You look pretty good yourself.'

Actually he looked amazing. The crisp white tuxedo shirt was the perfect foil for his olive skin, and the tailored midnight-dark tuxedo emphasised the perfect, powerful musculature of his body. Marco wasn't the only one who was breathless.

He touched her cheek with his fingertips, and the small touch seemed to Sierra like a promise of things to come. *Wonderful* things to come. 'We should go, if you're ready.'

'I am.'

The gala was in the hotel's ballroom, several floors below the penthouse yet with the same spectacular view from every side. Sierra stepped into the huge room with a soft gasp of appreciation. The room was as sleekly spare and elegant as the hotel foyer, letting the view be its main decoration. Tuxedo-clad waiters circulated with trays of champagne and hors d'oeuvres and a string quartet played softly from a dais in one corner of the room. Sierra turned to Marco, her eyes shining.

'Did you have some say in this room, too?'

'Maybe a little.' He smiled, taking her by the hand to draw her into the ball. 'Let me introduce you.'

Sierra had never particularly liked social occasions, thanks to her father's silent, menacing pressure. Even in London she'd preferred quiet gatherings to parties or bars, and yet tonight those old inhibitions fell away. It felt different now, when she was at Marco's side. When she felt safe and confident and valued.

But not loved. Never loved.

She pushed that niggling reminder to the back of her mind as Marco introduced her to various guests—stars, socialites, business types and the odd more ordinary people, and Sierra chatted with them all. Laughed and drank champagne and felt dizzy with a new, surprising elation.

After a few hours Marco pulled her away from a crowd of women she'd been chatting with, plucking the half-drunk glass of champagne from her fingertips and thrusting it at a waiter, who whisked it away.

'What is it…?' Sierra began, only to have her words fall away as Marco drew her onto the dance floor.

His gaze was hooded and intent, the colour of his eyes like molten silver as his hands slid down to her hips and he anchored her against him.

'Dance with me.'

Sierra felt as if the breath had been vacuumed from her lungs as she wordlessly nodded, placing her hands on his broad shoulders, the fabric of his tuxedo jacket crisp underneath her fingers.

The string quartet was playing a lovely, lazy melody, something you could sway to as you lost your soul. And

Sierra knew she was in danger of losing hers, of losing everything to this man. Tonight she wasn't going to worry, wasn't even going to care. She'd let herself fall and in the morning she'd think about picking up the broken pieces.

'It seems like the ball is going well,' Sierra said as they swayed to the music. 'Are you pleased?'

'Very pleased. The hotel is booked solid for the next three months. That's in part because of you.'

'A very small part,' Sierra answered. 'You're the one who put in all the hard work. I'm proud of you, Marco.' She smiled shyly. 'I know you told me how much your job meant to you, but I realised why tonight. You're good at this. You were meant for this.'

Marco didn't speak for a few seconds; a muscle flickered in his jaw and he seemed to struggle with some emotion. 'Thank you,' he said finally. 'That means a great to deal to me.'

The song ended and another one began, and neither Marco nor Sierra moved from the dance floor. She felt as if she could stay here for ever, or at least until Marco finally, thankfully took her upstairs.

'You are the most beautiful woman in the world tonight.' Marco's voice was low, his tone too sincere for her to argue with.

'As long as you think so,' Sierra murmured.

His eyes blazed for a second, thrilling her, and he pulled her even closer to him. 'Do you mean that?'

'Yes,' she said simply. After everything that had happened, everything he'd made her feel, she knew there could be no dissembling.

Marco drew a shuddering, steadying breath and eased her a little bit away from him as he smiled wryly. 'I don't want to disgrace myself here.'

She smiled, the curve of her lips coy. 'Then disgrace yourself upstairs.'

Regret flashed across his features like a streak of pain. 'We can't leave the ball yet.'

'Do you have to stay to the end?' Some of the socialites and celebrities seemed ready to party until dawn.

'No,' Marco answered firmly. 'And even if I needed to, I wouldn't. I can't last that long without touching you, Sierra. Without being inside you.'

The huskily spoken words sent a spear of pure pleasure knifing through her. 'Good.'

Marco shook his head. 'Keep looking at me like that and I really won't last.'

'How am I looking?' Sierra asked with deliberate innocence.

'Like that.' He pulled her closer again. 'Like you want to eat me.'

'Maybe I do.' A blush pinkened her cheeks but she held his heated gaze. She could hardly believe the audacity of her words, and yet she meant them. Utterly.

Marco groaned softly. 'Do you enjoy torturing me?'

'Yes,' she answered with a shameless smile. 'It's payback for the way you tortured me this morning.'

His gaze swept over her body. 'That was torture for me, as well. Sweet, sweet torture.'

She felt as if she could melt beneath the heat of his gaze. Or maybe combust. She'd felt an intense excitement spiralling up inside her from the moment Marco had taken her onto the dance floor, and it was overwhelming now. The need for him was a physical craving, so fierce and wonderful she was helpless to its demand.

Her tongue shot out and dampened her lips as she gave him a look of complete yearning. 'Marco…'

'We're going,' Marco bit out. 'Now.' His long, lean fingers encircled her wrist as he led her purposefully from the dance floor.

In any other circumstance Sierra would have baulked at being led from the ballroom like a sulky schoolgirl or a flagrant harlot. Now the need was too much to feel even a twinge of embarrassment or anger. She just wanted to get upstairs fast.

Marco muttered a few words to one of his staff standing by the door, and then they were out in the hall, the air cool on Sierra's heated cheeks. A few guests loitering there shot them speculative looks, but Marco ignored them all. He stabbed the button for the penthouse lift and Sierra held her breath until the doors opened and Marco pulled her inside.

CHAPTER TWELVE

THE LIFT DOORS had barely closed before Marco pulled Sierra to him, her breasts colliding with his chest as his mouth came down hard on hers. He couldn't have waited another moment, not even one second, to touch her, and the feel of her lips on his wasn't the water in the desert he'd thought it would be; it was a match to the flame, igniting his need all the more.

He backed her up against the wall of the lift, his mouth plundering hers as his hands fisted in her hair. Diamond-tipped pins scattered across the floor of the lift with a tinkling sound. Marco couldn't get enough of her. He moved his hands from her hair to her hips, yanking up a satiny fistful of her dress, needing to touch her skin.

He found the curve of her neck with his mouth and sucked gently, his desire knifing inside him as Sierra groaned aloud.

'You'll ruin the dress...' she gasped.

'I'll buy you another. I'll buy you a dozen, a hundred others.'

The doors pinged open and Marco stumbled backwards into the penthouse, pulling Sierra with him. She came with him, laughing and breathless, clutching his shirt as she tried to pull it away from his cummerbund.

'I need to see you,' Marco said. He tugged at the zip at

the back of her dress. 'Now.' He tugged harder at the zip and the dress slithered off her, leaving her in nothing but a scrap of lace pants. Marco inhaled sharply at the sight of her pale golden perfection, the lights from the city gleaming on her smooth skin.

She stepped out of the dress, chin lifted, smile shy, wearing nothing but lace and stiletto heels. Marco had never seen a more magnificent sight.

'This feels a bit unequal,' she said with a little uncertain laugh. 'I'm in my birthday suit and you're completely dressed.'

He spread his arms wide. 'Then maybe you should do something about it.'

'Maybe I should.' She stepped closer to him so he could breathe in the lemon scent of her hair; it had come undone from the pins he'd pulled out in the lift and lay in twists and curls about her shoulders. She pursed her lips slightly as she fumbled with the studs on his shirt; her breasts grazed his chest every time she moved.

Finally she'd managed to release the studs; she tossed them aside with a breathless laugh and then tugged his shirt out from his cummerbund and parted it, smoothing her hands along his chest. Marco closed his eyes, his breath hissing between his teeth. It amazed him how profoundly her touch affected him. He'd been with plenty of women over the years, gorgeous women with experience and expertise and plenty of confidence, but Sierra's hesitant touch reduced all those women to a pale memory.

'You're very beautiful,' she whispered, and tugged his shirt off his body before undoing the laces of his cummerbund. He wore only his trousers now, and he saw the hesitation in Sierra's face and wondered what she'd do about it. Sometimes she seemed so innocent and inexperienced he wondered how many lovers she'd actually had. But it wasn't a train of thought he enjoyed dwelling on, and so he made himself stop thinking about it. It didn't matter. The only thing that mattered was that she was with him now.

'Well?' He arched an eyebrow, his mouth curving in a salacious smile. 'I'm not naked yet.'

'I know.' She laughed again, a soft, breathy sound, and then tugged his trousers down. Marco kicked them off his feet, and followed with his shoes and socks. Now all he wore was a pair of navy silk boxers and his arousal was all too evident.

Sierra's gaze darted up to him and she licked her lips. Marco groaned. Then she reached out a hand and touched his shaft through his boxers, her fingers questing uncertainly and then wrapping more firmly around him.

Marco clenched his jaw against the almost painful wave of pleasure that crashed over him. 'Sierra...'

'Is this okay?' She jerked her hand back as if she'd hurt him and he laughed, albeit shakily.

'More than okay. What you do to me... But I need to do some things to you.' He reached for her then, because he needed her next to him. The feel of their naked bodies colliding made them both gasp aloud, her breasts against his chest, their legs tangled.

Marco kissed her deeply and she responded with all of her clumsy ardour, tangling her hands in his hair as he fitted her body more closely to his. Marco backed her towards the wall, pressing her against the sheet of glass as Sierra let out a soft laugh.

'Half the world now has a glimpse of my backside.'

'No one can see you from up here,' he promised her, 'but, if they could, it would be the most splendid view. Not,' he added in a growl as his mouth moved down her body, 'that I want anyone to see you but me.' *Ever*, he silently added, and then pushed the thought away as he turned his attention to her breasts. Her skin was pale and gleaming in the moonlight; she looked like a statue of Athena or Artemis, naked and proud.

Sierra's head came back against the glass, her hair tumbling about her shoulders, and her legs buckled as Marco lavished his attention on each breast in turn and then moved lower.

She gasped, a ragged pant, as he parted her thighs. 'Marco...'

'I want to taste you.' Was she thinking of before, in the villa, when he'd touched her like this? Then it had been confused, born of both need and anger, a twisted revenge he hadn't wanted to articulate even to himself. Now he felt nothing but this deep physical and emotional connection he needed to act on. To show her how important she was to him. 'I want to feel you come apart beneath me,' he muttered against her. 'I want you to give me everything, Sierra.' *For ever.*

Sierra sagged against the window, Marco supporting her with one arm, as he plundered her centre. She didn't know how she could have, but she'd forgotten how intense and exquisite and *intimate* this was. Marco's hands were cupping her bottom as pleasure spiralled inside her, up and up, tighter and tighter until she felt as if she were apart from her body even as she dwelt so intensely in it. When she came, she cried out, Marco holding her to him as she slid into boneless pleasure.

A few moments passed while he cradled her and her breathing slowed and then he scooped her up in his arms and took her up the spiral staircase to his bed.

He deposited her on the navy silk sheets tenderly, like a treasure, and Sierra lay there, gazing up at him with pleasure-dazed eyes as he stripped the boxers from his body and then stretched out next to her.

Completely naked, he was magnificent, every muscle perfectly sculpted, the hard ridge of his abdomen begging for her touch. She slid her hand down his toned stomach, a thrill of wonder and pleasure shooting through her at Marco's ragged gasp. It amazed her that she affected him so much. That she had that much power. It was a heady feeling but a serious one, too, because she knew all about the abuse of power.

'You're amazing,' she whispered, and wrapped her fingers around his shaft. His skin was smooth and hot, and it thrilled her.

'*You're* amazing,' he muttered and pulled her to him, sliding a hand between her thighs, where she was still damp from his touch. 'I want you now, Sierra. I want to be inside you.'

'I want you inside me.'

He rolled on top of her, poised at her entrance as a frown furrowed his forehead. 'Birth control...'

She blushed even as she opened herself to him. 'I don't... That is, I'm not on anything.'

In one swift movement Marco rolled off her. Sierra felt the loss of him keenly. 'Marco...'

'I'm sorry. I should have thought of it sooner. I was so wrapped up in you...'

Disappointment made her feel as if she'd swallowed a stone. 'But don't you have anything?'

He arched an eyebrow, a wry smile twisting his lips. 'I wasn't expecting to need *anything* on this trip.'

'You didn't think you'd get lucky?' she teased and his expression turned serious.

'I didn't dare hope, Sierra.'

'Even so...'

'I'm not quite,' he said, 'the super stud you seem to think I am. But thanks, anyway.'

She laughed softly. 'But you must have had plenty of women…' Even if she felt like scratching their eyes out just then.

Marco's expression closed and he shook his head. 'Let's not talk about that. The past is in the past, for both of us.'

She nodded and Marco left the room. He came back seconds later, condom in hand. 'Fortunately, the penthouse is admirably stocked. Now, where were we?'

She arched her body against the sheets, eyebrows raised as a provocative smile curved her mouth. 'Right about here?'

His gaze darkened with desire as he watched her move. 'Yes, I think so. But I'd better check.'

He rolled on the condom and Sierra watched, transfixed by the sight, by the sheer beauty of him. Now would probably be a good time to tell him that she hadn't actually done any of this before. The feel of him in her hand had caused her a twinge of alarm, wondering how he was going to fit inside her. Wondering how the mechanics of this actually worked.

But she didn't want to break the moment, and she knew any explanation she gave would be clumsy and awkward. Marco had said the past was in the past. Better to leave it there.

He lay down next to her again, stirring up the embers of need into roaring flame with just a few touches, his mouth on hers, his hand between her thighs. She arched against him, a sound like a kitten's mewl emerging from her lips.

He laughed softly and then rolled on top of her, braced on his forearms as he nudged at her entrance. 'Are you ready…?'

'Yes,' she panted. *'Yes.'*

He moved inside her and Sierra stiffened instinctively at the entirely unexpected feeling. Her gaze widened and her mouth parted on a soundless gasp. She felt so…full. Invaded, yet in an exciting way. He moved again and she let out a little gasp as the first twinge of discomfort assaulted her.

Marco froze, his face twisted in a grimace of shock and restraint. 'Sierra…'

'I'm all right,' she assured him. 'Just…give me a moment.'

He stared at her in disbelief as she adjusted to the feel of him, her body expanding naturally to accommodate his. The twinges of discomfort receded and she arched upwards to take him more fully into herself. 'You can move,' she whispered. 'Slowly.'

He slid deeper inside and she gasped again, the sensation acute and overwhelming. He froze, and she let out a shaky laugh. 'This isn't quite…'

He touched his forehead to hers, his biceps bulging with the effort of holding himself back. 'Why didn't you tell me?'

'I don't know,' she confessed. 'I didn't want to ruin anything. It seemed so…' She laughed again, softly. 'I don't know.' Maybe part of her had liked the idea of Marco thinking she was experienced, worldly. Maybe part of her had wanted to match him for sophistication and expertise, even though she knew she never could. In some unvoiced corner of her heart she'd wanted to make their positions more equal.

'Are you okay?' he whispered, and she nodded. It hurt more than she'd expected, but within the hurt were flickers of pleasure, and her body arced towards those, seeking them out of instinct. Marco moved again, sliding deeper inside and then out again and Sierra tried to relax. He was

so big, and he filled her so completely. It was overwhelming, both emotionally and physically, to be completely *con-
quered* by another person. She felt him in every nerve,
every cell of her body. There was no part of her that he did
not possess, and it was a complex and frightening feeling.

'Okay?' he asked again and she laughed, a hiss of
sound, as she clutched his shoulders.

'Stop asking me that.'

'I don't want to hurt you.'

'You're not.' Except he was, and in a way she hadn't
expected. The physical pain was nothing compared to the
emotional onslaught, the sense that Marco Ferranti was
battering every defence she had, leaving her completely
bare. Exposed and vulnerable and *wanting.*

And even as these feelings crashed over her, pleasure
came, too. Tiny at first, little whispers that promised something greater, and her body responded instinctively, arch-
ing up towards his as she wrapped her legs around his waist
and drew him completely into herself. She could feel him
everywhere, and it made tears start in her eyes.

Marco was moving faster now and Sierra found his
rhythm and matched it, awkwardly at first and then with
more grace as the sensations whirling inside her coalesced
and drove her body onwards. The pain had receded and
pleasure took its place, so she clutched him and threw her
head back, letting out a ragged cry as she climaxed, the
feeling more intense than anything she had ever experienced. Marco shuddered on top of her, his body sagging
against hers even as he bore his weight on his arms.

He kissed her temple, his lips lingering against her skin.
'That was incredible.'

'Was it?' she asked, her voice trembling a little with
everything she felt.

'You have to ask?' He smiled tenderly and smoothed the hair away from her flushed face.

'Well, I don't have much experience of this kind of thing. As you know.' She let out a shaky laugh and averted her face. She was, quite suddenly and inexplicably, near tears and she didn't want Marco to see.

'Sierra…' He trailed his fingers down her cheek, the gesture so tender it brought a lump to her throat. In a few seconds she'd be bawling. 'You should have told me.'

'It didn't feel like the right moment.'

'I'm not sure when a better moment would have been,' he said wryly, and then pulled out of her, rolling away to dispose of the condom. Sierra took the reprieve from his scrutiny to tidy her hair and wipe quickly at her eyes, wrapping the duvet around herself.

Marco glanced back at her, eyes narrowed. Was she so obvious? Could he see the torment and confusion in her eyes, her face? 'Are you sure you're okay?' he asked, and she nodded. 'You don't…you don't regret this?'

'No,' she whispered, because that much was true. Mostly.

He stretched out next to her, unabashedly naked, and tucked a few stray tendrils of hair behind her ear as he studied her face. 'Then why do you look like you're about to cry?'

'Because it's so *much*.' The words burst from her and a few rogue tears trickled down her cheeks. She batted at them impatiently. 'I wasn't expecting to feel so much. And I don't mean physically,' she clarified quickly. 'I'm not talking about the pleasure.'

'I hope you felt that, too.'

'You know I did,' she said, and she sounded almost cross.

Marco frowned, shaking his head. 'Then what?'

Did he not get it? But then maybe Marco hadn't felt the

emotional tidal wave that had pulled her under. Maybe she was the only one who felt so exposed, so vulnerable and needy. She felt as if Marco had stripped away everything she'd had to protect herself and left her reeling, wondering how to recover. Wondering how she would ever live without him even as terror clutched her at the thought of living with him. At being this vulnerable again, ever.

'I need to use the bathroom,' she muttered and wriggled away from him, the duvet snagging about her body.

Marco reached for her arm. 'Sierra—'

'Please, Marco.' She finally freed herself from the bedcovers and hurried towards the en suite bathroom. 'Please just let me be.'

Marco watched Sierra barricade herself in the bathroom, a frown deepening on his face. What the hell had happened? He'd had the most incredible sexual experience of his life, and he'd reduced his lover almost to tears. It didn't make sense. He knew, despite the initial pain, she'd enjoyed herself. He'd felt her climax reverberate through his own body. And he knew she'd been touched emotionally, too, but then so had he. Sex had never felt so important as it did right then.

But Sierra seemed to think that was a bad thing. She'd been tearful, cross, even angry—and why? Because she didn't want to feel those things? She didn't want to have that kind of connection with him?

The answer seemed all too obvious. Swearing under his breath, Marco rose from the bed and reached for his boxers. The intimacy they'd wrapped themselves in moments before was already unspooling, loose threads they might never knit back together, which was just as well. This was a fling, nothing more. No matter what he'd felt moments before.

And yet it still stung that Sierra was withdrawing from him. The possibility that she might regret what had happened filled him with a bitter fury he remembered too well. This time he'd be the one to walk away first. He'd make sure of it.

CHAPTER THIRTEEN

BY THE TIME Sierra emerged from the bathroom twenty minutes later she'd managed to restore her composure. Cloak herself in numbness, just like she used to during her father's rages. Strange that she was using the same coping mechanisms now, after the most intimate and frankly wonderful experience of her life, as she had then.

She unlocked the door to the bathroom and stepped out, thankfully swathed in an enormous terry-cloth dressing gown. Marco was sitting in bed, his back propped against the pillows, his legs stretched out in front of him, his arms folded. His face was unsmiling.

'Better?'

'Yes.' She tucked her hair behind her ears and came gingerly towards the bed. What was the fling protocol now? Should she thank him for a lovely time and beat it to her own bedroom? That was what she wanted to do. She wanted an out, even if the prospect filled her with an almost unbearable loneliness.

Marco arched an eyebrow. 'You're not actually thinking of leaving my bed, are you?'

It disconcerted her that he could guess her thought processes so easily. 'I thought… I thought maybe it was best.'

'Best? How so?' There was a dangerous silky tone to Marco's voice that she remembered from when she'd first seen him at the lawyer's office, and then at the villa. It made alarm prickle along her spine and she took an instinctive step backwards.

'You no doubt want your space, as do I. We know what this is, Marco.'

'What is it?'

'A fling.' She forced herself to say the words, to state it plainly. 'We're agreed on that. Nothing's changed.' Even if she felt as if her whole world had shattered when Marco had made love to her.

Love... How had she not realised how dangerous this would be? How had she not seen how much a so-called fling would affect her?

'And does having a fling mean we can't sleep together?' Marco bit out. 'Does it mean you've got to hightail it from my bed as if you've been scalded?'

Sierra stared at him in surprise, understanding trickling through her. He was *hurt*. He'd taken her sprint to the bathroom as a personal slight. The realisation softened her, evened out the balance of power she'd felt so keenly had been in his favour.

'Maybe you ought to tell me what the rules are. Since I've obviously never been in this situation before.'

'I haven't either, Sierra.' Marco rubbed a hand across his jaw as he gazed at her starkly. 'No other woman has made me feel the way you do.'

Sierra swallowed hard, a thousand feelings swarming her stomach like butterflies. Disbelief. Fear. Hope. Joy. 'Marco...'

'Don't,' he said roughly. 'Like you said, we both know what this is. But you can still stay the night.'

'Is that what you want?'

He hesitated, his jaw tight. 'Yes,' he finally bit out. 'It is.'

'It's what I want, too,' Sierra said softly.

'Good.' Marco held out his arms and she went to him easily. Suddenly it seemed like the simplest thing in the world to accept Marco's embrace. Moments ago she'd wanted to escape, but now she felt there was no other place to be.

Sierra closed her eyes and snuggled against him, wondering how a supposed fling could be so confusing and make her feel so much.

Marco woke slowly, blinking in the sunlight that streamed through the huge windows. Sierra lay curled up in his arms, her cheek resting against his bare chest. They'd slept in each other's arms all night, and Marco had marvelled at how good it had felt, how much he didn't want to move. Even if he should. No matter what he'd said last night, this felt like more than a fling...to him.

Now he eased slowly from Sierra's sleepy embrace and stole downstairs to the living area; dawn was streaking across the city sky and the first rays of sunlight were touching the skyscrapers of midtown in gold.

He gazed out of the window at the beautiful summer morning, but his thoughts were with the woman he'd left upstairs in bed. Sierra was supposed to fly back to England this afternoon. He'd booked her ticket himself. A few weeks ago it hadn't seemed an issue. He'd convinced himself that he wanted her only to open the hotel, not in his bed. In his life. *Maybe even in his heart.*

Marco let out a shuddering breath and pressed his fists to his eyes. He couldn't be in love with Sierra. He'd written off that useless emotion. He'd seen how people who supposedly loved you were able to walk away. His father. His mother. And even Sierra, seven years ago, although at least no love had been involved then. No, then it had only been a lifetime commitment. And if Sierra had been able to walk away from him then, how much more easily could she do it now?

He should let her go. Kiss her goodbye, thank her for the memories and watch her walk onto the plane and out of his life. That would be the sensible thing. It also made him recoil with instinctive, overwhelming revulsion. He didn't want to do that. He wasn't going to do that.

So what was he going to do?

Marco turned away from the window and reached for his laptop. He'd leave the question of Sierra for a little while, at least until she woke up and he got a read on what she was feeling.

He clicked on his home news page, freezing when he saw one of the celebrity headlines: *A Rocci Reunion?*

Quickly, he scanned the article, which covered the hotel opening yesterday. Very little was about the hotel; the journalist was far more interested in lurid speculation about the relationship between him and Sierra. There was even a blurry photo of him and Sierra slow-dancing last night, which infuriated him because no paparazzi had been invited to the private ball. It looked, he decided, like a snap someone had taken on their phone and then no doubt sold to the press.

Marco swore aloud.

'Marco?'

He turned to see Sierra standing in the doorway, an uncertain look on her face. She was wearing that ridiculously huge dressing gown, her hair about her shoulders in tousled golden-brown waves. She looked delectable and yet also nervous.

'Is something wrong?' she asked, and she took a step towards him.

Marco glanced back at his laptop. 'Not exactly,' he hedged. He realised he had no idea what Sierra's reaction to the news article would be. He didn't even know what *his* was. Irritation that someone had so invaded his—their— privacy. And anger that someone was plundering their shared past for a sordid news story. And, underneath all that, Marco realised, he felt fear. Shameful, hateful fear, that Sierra would see this article and be the one to walk away first.

'What does "not exactly" mean, Marco?' Sierra's gaze flicked to his laptop and then back to his face. He'd closed the browser window, thankfully, so she hadn't seen the article. But he knew he couldn't, in all good conscience, keep it from her.

'We've made the news,' he said after a pause. 'Someone must have snapped a photo of us on their phone.'

'On their phone? But why?'

'To sell to a celebrity tabloid.'

'A celebrity tabloid...' She shook her head, bewilderment creasing her forehead. 'But why would a celebrity tabloid want photos of us? I mean...I know I opened the hotel, but it's not as if I'm actually famous.' Her gaze widened. 'Are *you* famous? I mean, that famous?'

'We're famous,' Marco stated flatly. 'Together. Because of our past.'

'You mean...'

'Yes. That's exactly what I mean.' He bit out each word, realising he was sounding angry, but he couldn't keep himself from it. This was the last thing he wanted to have happen now.

'What does it say?'

After a moment's hesitation, Marco clicked to enlarge the browser window. 'See for yourself.'

Sierra stepped forward, her mouth downturned into a frown as the gist of the article dawned on her. '"Will these star-crossed lovers find happiness off the dance floor?"'

she quoted, and then shook her head. 'Goodness,' she murmured faintly.

'I'm sorry. Press were forbidden from coming to the
ball. I had no idea something like this would happen.'

'I had no idea our engagement seven years ago was so
well known,' Sierra said slowly. 'I thought it had been a
quiet affair.'

'Not that quiet. Your father made a public announcement at a board meeting. It was in the papers.'

'Of course. It was business to him. And to you.' She
spoke without rancour, and Marco let the comment pass.

The last thing he wanted to talk about now was what
had happened all those years ago. He wanted to take Sierra back to bed and he wanted, he knew, for her to stay
past this afternoon.

Sierra took a deep breath and turned to face him directly. 'Do you mind? About the article?'

'It's an annoyance. I value my privacy, and yours, as
well.'

'Yes, but...' She hesitated, fiddling with the sash of
her robe. 'Having it all in the papers? The fact that I...
that I left you?'

Tension knotted between his shoulder blades. 'It's not
something I particularly relish having bandied about,' he
answered, keeping his voice mild with effort. 'But I'm not
heartbroken, Sierra.' He'd refused to be.

'Of course not,' she murmured and then nodded slowly.
'I should get ready for my flight.'

'Don't.' The word came out abruptly, a command he
hadn't intended to give.

She gazed at him, her eyebrows raised. 'Don't?'

'Don't get ready for your flight. Don't go on your flight.'
He held her gaze, willing her to agree.

'But the opening is over, Marco. I'm not needed here any more.'

'Not needed, maybe.' He paused, trying to find the right words. 'We're having fun, though, aren't we?'

Her gaze widened. 'Fun…'

'Why should we end it so soon?' Smiling, he reached for the sash of her robe and tugged on it gently, pulling her towards him. She went, a small smile curving her lips, and triumph roared through him. 'Stay with me,' he said when she'd come close enough for him to slide his hands under her robe, around her waist. Her skin was warm and silky soft. She let out a breathy little gasp of pleasure. 'Stay with me a little while longer.'

'I have a job, you know,' she reminded him, but she didn't sound as if it mattered much.

'Teaching a few after-school lessons? Can't you re-schedule?'

She frowned slightly but didn't move away. 'Maybe.'

'Then reschedule.' He pulled her close enough so their hips collided and she could feel how much he wanted her. 'Reschedule, and come with me to LA.' A few more days with her, nights with her, and then perhaps he'd have had enough. Perhaps then he'd be willing to let her go.

It was amazing how tempted she was, and yet not amazing at all because what woman on earth could resist Marco Ferranti when his hands were on her skin and his smile was so seductive?

And yet…to leave her job, her obligations, her life back in London and go with him wherever he beckoned?

'Sierra?' Marco brushed her neck with his lips in a kiss that promised so much more. 'You will come?' He nibbled lightly on her neck and Sierra let out a helpless gasp of pleasure as she reached up to clutch his shoulders so she could steady herself.

'Yes,' she managed, knowing there had never really been any doubt. 'Yes, I'll come with you.'

Later, lying amidst the tangled sheets while she admired the view of Marco's bare and perfect chest, Sierra finally summoned the mental energy to ask, 'Why are you going to LA?'

'I'm hoping to open the next North American Rocci hotel there.'

'Hoping?' Lazily, she ran her hand down the sculpted muscles of his chest, her fingers tracing the ridge of his abdomen before daring to dip lower.

Marco trapped her hand. 'Minx. Wait a few minutes, at least.'

'A few minutes?' Sierra teased. 'And here I thought you were some super stallion with superhero capabilities in the bedroom.'

'I've just proved my capabilities in the bedroom,' Marco growled as he rolled her over so he was on top of her, trapping her with his body. 'But I'll gladly prove it again.'

She smiled up at him, feeling sated and relaxed and happy. Happier than she'd been in a long time, perhaps ever. 'So have you started plans for a hotel in LA?'

'Preliminary plans.' Marco released her, rolling onto his back, but he kept one hand lying on her stomach and Sierra found she liked it. She'd had so few loving touches in her life. Her mother had hugged her on occasion, and her father only in public, but to be caressed and petted and stroked. She felt like a cat. She could almost start purring.

'What's got you looking like the cat who's just eaten the cream?' Marco asked as he shot her an amused look and Sierra laughed.

'I was just comparing myself to a cat, as it happens.'

'Comparing yourself to a cat? Why?'

'Because I like being touched. I feel like I could start purring.'

'And I like touching you.' Marco moved his hand from her stomach to her breasts and then Sierra almost did start purring. 'Very much.'

They spent the day in bed. Although not technically in bed; some time around noon Marco ordered food in and they ate it downstairs in the living area, in their dressing gowns. And some time in the late afternoon Marco ran a deep bath full of scented bubbles and just as Sierra was about to sink into all that bliss he actually joined her.

Water sloshed out of the tub as Sierra scooted to one side and Marco settled himself comfortably, seeming undaunted by the bubbles that clung to his chest.

'I didn't realise you were going to get in with me,' Sierra exclaimed, her voice coming out in a near squeak, and Marco arched an eyebrow.

'Is that a problem?'

'No, but...' How could she explain how it felt even more intimate to share a bath with this man than what they'd done in the privacy of the bedroom? And the things they'd done...

Quickly, Sierra realised she was being ridiculous. 'No, of course not,' she said and slid over so she was next to Marco, their legs tangling under the water. 'Actually, I can think of some interesting ways to wash.'

His gaze became hooded and sleepy as he watched her reach for the soap. 'Can you?'

'Oh, yes.' Her embarrassment and uncertainty, after a day's worth of thorough lovemaking, had fallen away. She felt confident, powerful in her knowledge of how much Marco desired her. 'Yes, indeed,' she murmured and she slid her soapy hands down his chest to his hips. After everything they'd done together that day she was amazed that Marco still desired her. But how could she be amazed, when she still desired him?

'Sierra…' His voice came out on a groan as she stroked his shaft. She loved giving him pleasure, loved knowing that she made him this way.

'You're going to kill me,' he muttered and stayed her hand.

She arched an eyebrow. 'But wouldn't it be a good way to go?'

'Yes indeed, but I have a lot more life in me yet,' he answered, and then showed her just how much.

Twilight was falling over the city several hours later as Sierra lay in bed and watched Marco get dressed. 'Are we going somewhere?' she asked as he pulled on a crisply ironed dress shirt.

'I have a business meeting,' he said with one swift, apologetic look towards her. 'It's been wonderful playing hookey today, but I've got to make back sometime.'

'Oh.' Sierra pulled the rumpled duvet over her naked body. 'Of course. So you're going out?'

'You can order whatever you like from room service,' Marco said as he selected a cobalt-blue tie.

Sierra watched him slide his tie in his collar and knot it with crisp, precise movements. She felt uneasy, almost hurt, and she wasn't quite sure why. Of course Marco had business meetings. Of course she couldn't tag along with him, nor would she want to.

'So.' He turned back to her with a quick smile that didn't reach his eyes. 'I'll see you later tonight. And tomorrow we'll go to LA.'

'I haven't even dealt with my plane ticket…'

'I cancelled it.'

She jerked back a little. 'You did?'

Marco was sliding on his jacket and checking his watch. 'Why should you worry about it?'

'But I need to book an alternative return flight...'

He gave her a wolfish smile. 'We don't need to think about that now.' Then he was dropping a distracted kiss on her forehead and hurrying out of the suite, all while she lay curled up in a crumpled duvet and wondered what she'd got herself into.

'A fling,' she said aloud. Her voice sounded small in the huge empty suite. 'You know very well what this is. A fling. You're here for sex.' What had seemed simple and safe now only felt sordid.

She got out of bed, trying to shake off her uncertain and grey mood, and dressed. She didn't feel like ordering takeaway and eating it alone upstairs; she'd go out, explore the city on her own for a bit.

Twenty minutes later Sierra headed downstairs and out of the modern glass doors of the hotel. The foyer was buzzing with guests; clearly the opening had been a success. A few people clearly recognised her, but Sierra ignored their speculative looks. She wasn't going to care about the tabloid article that had come out this morning. It would be forgotten by tomorrow, no doubt.

She strolled down Central Park West towards Columbus Circle, enjoying the way twilight settled on the city and the traffic started to die down. She found a little French bistro tucked onto a side street and went inside. As she sat down and glanced at the menu she realised she was ravenous. She supposed that was what making love all day did to you, and the thought made her smile. She ordered a steak and chips and ate it all and was just heading back outside, feeling replete and happy, when a reporter accosted her.

'Excuse me... Sierra Rocci?'

'Yes?' she answered automatically, before the flashbulb

popped in her face, making her momentarily blind, and the reporter started firing questions.

'Why are you out alone? Have you and Marco Ferranti had a lovers' tiff? Is it true you're staying in the same suite? Why did you jilt him seven years ago—'

'No comment,' Sierra gasped out and hurried away. The reporter kept yelling his awful questions at her, each one sounding like a horrible taunt.

'Did Ferranti cheat on you? Did you cheat on him? Are you together now merely as a business arrangement?'

Finally Sierra rounded the corner and the reporter's questions died away. She kept up a brisk pace all the way to the hotel, only slowing when she came to the front steps. Her heart was thudding and she felt clammy with sweat. She'd thought she could handle the press, but she hadn't been prepared for that.

She'd managed to restore her composure by the time she got into the penthouse lift, and she felt almost normal when the doors opened.

That was until she stepped out and Marco loomed in front of her, his face thunderous, his voice a harsh demand.

'Where the *hell* have you been?'

CHAPTER FOURTEEN

MARCO COULDN'T REMEMBER the last time he'd felt so furious—and so afraid. He'd come up to the penthouse suite expecting to see Sierra still lounging in bed, waiting for him. Instead, the place had been echoing and empty, and when he'd called downstairs the concierge had said she'd left hours ago.

He'd paced the penthouse for a quarter of an hour, trying to stifle his panic and anger, but rational thought was hard when so many memories kept crowding in. He told himself she hadn't taken her clothes and that she wouldn't just leave.

But she'd taken hardly anything when she'd left the night before his wedding. And the possibility that she might have skipped out on him again made everything in him clench. Damn it, he would be the one to say when they were done. And it wasn't yet.

'Well?' he demanded while she simply stared at him. 'Do you have an answer?'

'No,' Sierra stated clearly, her voice so very cold, and she stalked past him.

Marco whirled around, disbelieving. '*No?* You're gone for hours and you can't even tell me where you went?'

'I don't have to tell you anything, Marco,' Sierra tossed over her shoulder. 'I don't owe you anything.'

'How about an explanation?'

She walked up the spiral stairs, one hand on the railing, her head held high. 'Not even that.'

Marco followed her up the stairs and into the bedroom and then watched in disbelief as she took out her suitcase and started putting clothes into it.

'You're packing?'

She gave him a grim smile. 'It looks like it, doesn't it?'

'For LA?'

She stilled and then raised her head, her gaze clear and direct. 'No. For London.'

Fury and hurt coursed through him, choking him so he could barely speak. He didn't want to feel hurt; anger was stronger. 'Damn it, Sierra,' he exclaimed. He raised his hand to do what, he didn't know—touch her shoulder, beseech her somehow—but he stilled when she instinctively flinched as if she'd expected him to strike her.

'Sierra?' His voice was low, her name a question.

She straightened, her expression erased of the cringing fear he'd seen for one alarming second. 'I'm going.'

Marco watched her for a few moments, forcing himself to be calm. He'd overreacted; he could see that now. 'Were you planning on returning to London before you got back to the penthouse?' he asked quietly.

She gave him another one of those direct looks that cut right to his heart. 'No, I wasn't.'

He took a deep breath and then let it out slowly. 'I'm sorry I was so angry.'

She made a tiny shrugging gesture, as if it was of no importance, and yet Marco knew instinctively that it was. 'You flinched just then, almost as if…' He didn't want to voice the suspicion lurking in the dark corners of his mind. And maybe that flinch had been a moment's instinctive reaction, and yet...she'd had such a look on her face, one of terrible fear.

'Almost as if what?' Sierra asked, and it sounded like a challenge.

'Almost as if you expected me to...' He swallowed hard. 'Hit you.'

'I wasn't,' she said after a moment. She took a deep breath and let it out slowly. 'But old habits die hard, I suppose.'

'What do you mean?'

She sighed and shook her head. 'There's no point having this conversation.'

'How can you say that? This might be the most important conversation we've ever had.'

'Oh, Marco.' She looked up at him, and everything in him jolted at the look of weary sorrow in her eyes. 'I wish it could be, but...' She trailed off, biting her lip.

'What do you mean? What aren't you telling me?' She didn't answer and he forced himself not to take a step towards her, not to raise his voice or seem threatening in any way. 'Sierra, did a man...did a man ever hit you?'

The silence following his question seemed endless. Marco felt as if he could scarcely breathe.

Finally Sierra looked up, resignation in every weary line of her lovely face. 'Yes,' she said and then Marco felt a fury like none he'd known before—this time at this unknown man who had dared to hurt and abuse her. He'd *kill* the bastard.

'Who?' he demanded. 'A boyfriend...?'

'No,' she said flatly. 'My father.'

Sierra watched Marco blink, his jaw slackening, as he stared at her in obvious disbelief. She kept packing. Having him yell at her like that had been the wake-up call she needed, and in that moment she'd realised why she'd felt so uneasy earlier, when Marco had left her alone in the suite. She was turning into her mother. Dropping her own life at a man's request, living for his pleasure. There was no way she was walking even one step down that road, and when Marco had shouted at her, looking so angry, Sierra had realised the trap she'd been just about to step into. Thank God she'd realised before it was too late... even if the thought of leaving Marco made her insides twist with grief.

'Your father?' Marco repeated hoarsely. 'Arturo? No.'

'I knew you wouldn't believe me.'

He was shaking his head slowly, looking utterly winded. Sierra almost felt sorry for him.

'But...' he began, and then stopped. She reached for the dress she'd worn to the opening yesterday. 'Sierra, wait.' He grabbed her wrist, gently but firmly, and she went completely still.

He stared at her for a moment, his face white, and then he let her go and backed away, his hands raised like a man about to be arrested. 'You know I would never, ever hurt you.'

'I know that,' she said quietly. She believed it but even with that head knowledge she couldn't keep from fearing. Trust was a hard, hard thing.

Slowly, Marco dropped his hands. Sierra resumed packing. He watched her for several moments and his scrutiny made her hands tremble as she tried to fold her clothes. 'Do you mind?' she finally asked, and to her irritation her voice shook.

'What did you mean—that he hit you?' Marco asked.

'Does it really need explaining?'

'Sierra, your father was as good as my father. I loved him. I trusted him. Yes, it needs explaining.' His voice came out harsh, grating, and she forced herself not to flinch.

'Then let me explain it for you,' she said coolly. She was surprised at how much a relief it was to tell him the truth. She'd been keeping this secret for far too long, first out of fear that he wouldn't believe her, and then because she hadn't wanted to hurt him. Both reasons seemed like pathetic excuses now. 'My father hit me,' Sierra stated clearly. 'Often. He hit my mother, too. He played the doting father and adoring husband for the public, but in private he heaped physical and emotional abuse on us. Slaps, pinches, punches, the lot. And the words…the insults, the sneers, the mockery.' She shook her head, tears stinging her eyes as a lump formed in her throat. 'My mother loved him anyway. I've never been able to understand that. She loved him and wouldn't hear a word against him, although she always tried to protect me from his anger.'

Marco was shaking his head, his body language refuting every word she'd said. 'No…'

'I don't care if you believe me or not,' Sierra said, even though she knew that for a lie. She did care. Far too much. 'But at least now I've said it. Now you know, even if you don't want to.'

She closed her suitcase, struggling with the zip. Marco placed a hand on top of the case. 'Please, Sierra, don't go like this.'

'Why should I stay?'

'Because I want you to stay. Because we've been having a fantastic time.' He took a deep breath. 'Look, this is a tremendous shock to me. It's not that I don't believe you, but give me a few moments to absorb it. Please.'

Slowly Sierra nodded. She could see the sense in what he was staying, even if her instinct was to run. And in truth there was a part of her, a large part, that didn't want to leave. 'Okay,' she said, and then waited.

A full minute passed in silence. Finally Marco said hesitantly, 'Why…why didn't you tell me?'

'Would you have believed me? You hated me, Marco.' It hurt to remind him of that.

'I mean before.' The look he gave her was full of confusion and pain, and it made guilt flash through her like a streak of lightning. 'When we were engaged.'

'Even then you were his right-hand man.'

'But you were going to marry me. How could we have had a marriage, with such a secret between us?'

'I realised we couldn't.'

'Your *father* is why you left?' Marco stared at her in disbelief, his jaw tight.

'In a manner of speaking, I suppose.'

'I don't understand, Sierra.' He raked his hands through his hair and even now, in the midst of all this confusion and misery, Sierra watched him with longing. Those muscled arms had held her so tenderly. She'd nestled against that chiselled chest, had kissed his salty skin. She averted her gaze from him. 'Please help me to understand,' Marco said, and underneath the sadness Sierra heard a note of frustration, even anger, and she tensed.

'I don't know what you want me to say.'

'Anything. Something. Why did you agree to marry me?' The question rang out, echoing through the suite.

Sierra took a deep breath and met his gaze. 'To get away from my father.'

Marco's face paled as his jaw bunched. Sierra kept herself from flinching even though she could tell he was angry. She didn't completely understand why, but she felt it emanating from his taut body. 'That's the only reason?' he asked in a low voice.

Wordlessly she nodded, and then she watched as Marco turned and strode from the bedroom. Alone, she sank onto the bed, her legs suddenly feeling weak. Everything feeling weak. She felt nearer to tears now than she had a few moments ago, and why? Because she'd lost Marco? It was better this way, and in any case she'd never really had him. Not like that.

But it still felt like a loss, a gaping wound that was bleeding out. Another deep breath and Sierra turned to her suitcase. She struggled with the zip, but she finally got it closed. And then she sat there, having no idea what to do. Where to go, if anywhere.

After a few moments she worked up the nerve to lug her suitcase down the spiral staircase. Marco stood in the living room, his back to her as he stared out at the darkened city. She hesitated on the bottom step because now that she was here, she didn't really want to go. Walk out like she did once before, into a dark night, an unknown future.

Yet how could she stay?

The step creaked beneath her and Marco turned around, his dark eyebrows snapping together as he saw her clutching the handle of her suitcase. 'You're still planning to go?' he asked, his voice harsh.

'I don't know what to do, Marco.' She hated the wobble in her voice and she blinked rapidly. Marco swore under his breath and strode towards her.

'Sierra, *cara*, I've been an utter ass. Please forgive me.'

It was the last thing she'd expected him to say. He took the suitcase from her and put it on the floor. Then he stretched out his hands beseechingly, his face a plea. 'Don't go, Sierra. Please. Not yet. Not till I understand. Not till we've made this right.'

'How can we? I know what my father meant to you, and I hate him, *hate* him—' She broke off, weeping, half amazed at the emotion that suddenly burst from her, tears trickling down her cheeks. 'I always have,' she continued, but then her voice was lost to sobs, her shoulders shaking, and Marco had enfolded her in his arms.

She pressed her face into his hard chest as he stroked his hand down her back and murmured nonsense endearments. She hadn't realised she had so many tears left in her and, more than just tears, a deep welling of grief and sorrow, not just for the father she'd had, but for the father she'd never had. For the years of loneliness and fear and frustration. For the fact that even now, seven years on, she was afraid to trust someone. To love someone, and the result was this brokenness, this feeling that she might never be whole.

'I'm sorry,' she finally managed, pulling away from him a bit to swipe at her damp cheeks. Now that the first storm of crying had passed, she felt embarrassed by her emotional display. 'I didn't mean to fall apart...'

'Nonsense. You needed to cry. You have suffered, Sierra, more than I could ever imagine. More than I ever knew.' Sierra heard the sharp note of self-recrimination in Marco's voice and wondered at it. 'Come, let us sit down.'

He guided her to one of the leather sofas and pulled her down next to him, his arm around her shoulders so she was still nestled against him, safe in his arms. Neither of them spoke for a long moment.

'Will you tell me?' Marco finally asked.

Sierra drew a shuddering breath. 'What do you want to know?'

'Everything.'

'I don't know where to begin.'

He nestled her closer to him, settling them both more comfortably. 'Begin wherever you want to, Sierra,' he said quietly.

After a moment she started talking, searching for each word, finding her way slowly. She told him how the first time her father hit her she was four years old, a slap across the face, and she hadn't understood what she'd done wrong. It had taken her decades to realise the answer to that question: nothing.

She told him about how kind and jovial he could be, throwing her up in the air, calling her his princess, showering her and her mother with gifts. 'It wasn't until I was much older that I realised he only treated us that way when someone was watching.'

'And when you were alone?' Marco asked in a low voice. 'Always...?'

'Often enough so that I tried to hide from him, but that angered him, too. No monster likes to see his reflection.'

'And when you were older?'

'I knew I needed to get away. My mother would never leave him. I begged her to, but she refused. She'd get quite angry with me because she loved him.' Sierra shook her head slowly. 'I've never understood that. I know he could be charming and he was handsome, but the way he treated her...' Her voice choked and she sniffed loudly.

'So why didn't you run away? When you were older?'

She let out an abrupt yet weary laugh. 'You make it sound so simple.'

'I don't mean to,' Marco answered. 'I just want to understand. It all seems so difficult to believe.'

How difficult? Sierra wondered. *Did* he believe her? Or even now did he doubt? The possibility was enough to make her fall silent. Marco touched her chin with his finger, turning her face so she had to look at him.

'I didn't mean it like that, Sierra.'

'Do you believe me?' she blurted. The question felt far

too revealing, and even worse was Marco's silence after she'd asked it.

'Yes,' he said finally. 'Of course I do. But I don't want to.'

'Because you loved him.'

Marco nodded, his expression shuttered, his jaw tight. 'You know how I told you my own father left? He was hardly around to begin with, and then one day he just never came back. And my mother…' He paused, and curiosity flared within the misery that had swamped her.

'Your mother?'

'It doesn't matter. What I meant to say is that Arturo was the closest thing to a father that I ever had. I told you how I was working as a bellboy when he noticed me… I would have spent my life heaving suitcases if not for him. He took me out for a drink, told me he could tell I had ambition and drive. Then he gave me a job as an office junior when I was seventeen. Within a few years he'd promoted me, and you know the rest.' He sighed, his arm still around her. 'And all the while he'd encourage me, listen to me… accept me in a way my father never did. To now realise this man I held in such high esteem was…was what you say he was…' Marco's voice turned hoarse. 'It hurts to believe it. But I do.'

'Thank you,' she whispered.

'You don't need to thank me, Sierra.' He paused, and Sierra could tell he was searching for words. 'So you wanted to escape. Why did you choose me?'

'My father chose you,' Sierra returned. 'I was under no illusion about that, although I flattered myself to think I had a bit more discernment and control than I actually did.' She let out a sad, soft laugh. 'Do you know what convinced me, Marco? I saw you stroking a cat, the day I met you. You were in the courtyard, waiting to come in, and one of the street cats wound its way between your legs. You bent down and stroked it. My father would have kicked it away. In that moment I believed you were a gentle man.'

'You sound,' Marco said after a moment, 'as if you now think you were wrong.'

'No, I...' She stopped, biting her lip. It was so difficult to separate what she'd felt then and what she felt now. 'I was going to marry you for the wrong reasons, Marco, back then. I realised that the night before our wedding. No matter what is between us now—and I know it's just a fling—it would have never worked back then. I needed to find my own way, become my own person.'

'So what happened that night?' Marco asked. 'Really?' He sounded as if he were struggling with some emotion, perhaps anger. Sierra could feel how tense his body was.

'Just what I told you. I overheard you talking with my father. I realised just how close you were. I...I hadn't quite realised it before. And then I heard my father give you that awful advice.'

'"I know how to handle her",' Marco repeated flatly. 'I see now why that would have alarmed you, but...couldn't you have asked me, Sierra?'

'And what would I ask, exactly?' The first note of temper entered her voice. '"Will you ever hit me, Marco?" That's not exactly a question someone will answer honestly.'

'I would have.'

'I wouldn't have believed you. That's what I realised that night, Marco. I was taking too great a risk. It was about me as much as it was about you.'

'So you ran away, just as you could have done before we'd ever become engaged.'

'Not exactly. My mother helped me. When I told her I didn't love you...' Sierra trailed off uncertainly. Of course

Marco knew she hadn't loved him then. He hadn't loved her. And yet it sounded so cold now.

'Yes? When you told her that, what did she do?'

'She gave me some money,' Sierra whispered. 'And the name of a friend in England I could go to.'

'And you just walked out into the night? Into Palermo?'

'Yes. I was terrified.' She swallowed hard, the memories swarming her. 'Utterly terrified. I'd never been out alone in the city—any city—before. But I hailed a taxi and went to the docks. I waited the rest of the night in the ferry office, and then I took the first boat to the mainland.'

'And then to England? That must have been quite a journey.' Marco didn't sound impressed so much as incredulous.

'Yes, it was. I took endless trains, and then I was spat out in London with barely enough English to make myself understood. I got lost on the Tube and someone tried to pickpocket me. And when I went to find my mother's friend, she'd moved house. I spent a night at a women's shelter and then used a computer in a library to locate the new address of my mother's friend, and she finally took me in.'

'So much effort to get away from me,' Marco remarked tonelessly and Sierra jerked away from him.

'No, to get away from my father. It wasn't about you, Marco. I keep telling you that.'

He gazed at her with eyes the colour of steel, his mouth a hard line. 'How can you say that, Sierra? It most certainly was about me. Yes, it was about your father, as well, I understand that. But if you'd known me at all, if you'd trusted me at all, you would never have had to go to London.'

She recognised the truth of his words even if she didn't want to. 'Understandably,' she answered stiffly, 'I have had difficulties with trusting people, especially men.'

Marco sighed, the sound one of defeat, his shoulders slumping. 'Understandably,' he agreed quietly. 'Yes.'

Sierra stood up, pacing the room, her arms wrapped around her body. Suddenly she felt cold. She had no idea if what she'd told Marco changed things. Then she realised that of course it changed things; she had no idea how much.

'What now?' she finally asked, and she turned to face him. He was still sitting on the sofa, watching her, his expression bland. 'Should I leave?' she forced herself to ask. 'I can go back to London tonight.'

Marco didn't look away; he didn't so much as blink. 'Is that what you want?'

Was it? Her heart hammered and her mouth went dry. Here was a moment when she could try to trust. When she could leap out and see if he caught her. If he wanted to. 'No,' she whispered. 'It isn't.'

Marco looked startled, and then a look of such naked relief passed over his face that Sierra sagged with a deep relief of her own.

He rose from the sofa and crossed the room, pulling her into his arms. 'Good,' he said, and kissed her.

CHAPTER FIFTEEN

MARCO GAZED OUT at the azure sky, his eyes starting to water from staring at its hard brightness for so long. The plane was minutes away from touching down in LA and he'd barely spoken to Sierra for the six hours of the flight.

He'd wanted to. He'd formed a dozen different conversation openers in his mind, but everything sounded wrong in his head. He had a feeling it would sound worse out loud. The trouble was, since her revelation last night he hadn't known how to approach her. *How to handle her.*

Guilt churned in his stomach as he replayed in his mind all that Sierra had told him. It was a form of self-torture he couldn't keep himself from indulging in. A thousand conflicting thoughts and feelings tormented him: sadness for what Sierra had endured, guilt for his part in it, confusion and grief for what he'd felt for Arturo, a man he'd loved but who had been a monster beyond his worst imaginings.

In the end, beyond a few basic pleasantries about the trip and their destination, he'd stayed silent, and so had Sierra. It seemed easier, even if it made him an emotional coward.

'Please fasten your seat belts as we prepare for landing.'

Marco glanced at Sierra, trying for a reassuring smile. She smiled back but he could see that it didn't reach her eyes, which were the colour of the Atlantic on a cold day.

Wintry grey-blue, no thaw in sight. Was she angry at him? Did she blame him somehow for what had happened before? How on earth were they going to get past this?

Which begged another question—one he was reluctant to answer, even to himself. Why did they need to get past this? What kind of future was he envisioning with Sierra?

A few days ago he'd wanted to be the one to walk away first. But a realisation was emerging amidst all his confusion and regret—he didn't want to walk away at all.

But how could they build a relationship on such shaky, crumbling foundations of mistrust and betrayal? And how could he even want to, when he had no idea what Sierra wanted? When he'd been so sure he'd never love someone, never want to love someone?

'Are you looking forward to seeing Los Angeles?' he asked abruptly, wanting to break the glacial silence as well as keep from the endless circling of his own thoughts.

'Yes, thank you,' Sierra replied, and her tone was just as carefully polite. They were acting like strangers, yet maybe, after all they hadn't known about each other, they *were* strangers.

The next hour was taken up with deplaning and then retrieving their luggage; Marco had arranged for a limo to be waiting outside.

Once they'd slid inside its luxurious leather depths, the soundproof glass cocooning them in privacy, the silence felt worse. More damning.

And still neither of them spoke.

'Where are we staying?' Sierra finally asked as the limo headed down I-405. 'Since there isn't a Rocci hotel here yet?'

'The Beverly Wilshire.' He managed a small smile. 'I need to check out my competition.'

'Of course.' She turned back to the window, her gaze

on the palm trees and billboards lining the highway. The silence stretched on.

Sierra admired the impressive Art Deco foyer of the hotel, and when a bellboy escorted them to the private floor that housed the penthouse suite, Marco experienced a little dart of satisfaction at how awed she looked. It might not be a Rocci hotel, but he could still give her the best. He wanted to give her the best.

And the penthouse suite *was* the best: three bedrooms, four marble bathrooms, a media room, plus the usual dining room, living room and kitchen. But best of all was the spacious terrace with its panoramic views of the city.

Sierra stepped out onto the terrace, breathed in the hot, dry air of the desert. She glanced up at the scrubby hills that bordered Los Angeles to the north. 'It almost looks like Sicily.'

'Almost,' Marco agreed.

'I don't know if we need such a big suite,' she said with a small teasing smile. 'Three bedrooms?'

'We can sleep in a different one each night.'

Her smile faltered. 'How long are you planning on staying here?'

Marco noted the 'you' and deliberately kept his voice even and mild. 'I'm not sure. I want to complete the preliminary negotiations for The Rocci Los Angeles, and I don't need to be back in Palermo until next week.' He shrugged. 'We might as well stay and enjoy California.' *Enjoy each other.* He only just kept himself from saying it.

'I have a job to get back to,' Sierra reminded him. 'A life.'

And she was telling him this why? 'You have a freelance job,' Marco pointed out. 'What is that if not flexible?'

Her eyebrows drew together and she looked away. So he'd said the wrong thing. He'd known he would all along.

Sierra walked back into the suite and after a moment Marco followed. When he came into the living area he saw how lost she looked, how forlorn.

'I think I might take a bath,' she said without looking at him. 'Wash away the travel grime.'

'All right,' Marco answered, and in frustration he watched her walk out of the room.

Could things get more awkward and horrible? With a grimace Sierra turned the taps of the huge sunken marble tub on full blast. She didn't know what she regretted more: telling Marco the truth about her father or coming with him to LA. The trouble was, she still wanted to be with him. She just didn't know how they were going to get past this seeming roadblock in their relationship.

Whoa. You don't have a relationship.

She might be halfway to falling in love with him, but that didn't mean Marco felt the same. He'd made it abundantly clear that they were only having a fling and, in any case, she didn't even *want* him to feel the same. She didn't want to be in love herself. Not when she'd seen what it had done to her mother. Not when she'd felt what it could do to herself.

Since meeting Marco again her whole world had been tangled up in knots. Since making love with him she'd felt happier and yet more frightened than she ever had in the last seven years. Happiness could be so fleeting, so fragile, and yet, once discovered, so unbearably necessary. How much was it going to hurt when Marco was gone from her life?

Better to make a quick, clean cut. She'd told herself that yesterday and yet here she was. She was more like her mother than she'd ever wanted to be. Filled with regret and uncertainty, Sierra closed her eyes.

She almost didn't hear the gentle tapping at the bathroom door. She opened her eyes, alert, and then heard Marco call softly, 'Sierra? May I come in?'

She glanced down at her naked body, covered by bubbles. Everything in her seemed to both hesitate and yearn.

'All right,' she said.

Slowly the door opened. Marco stepped inside the steamy bathroom; he'd changed his business suit for faded jeans and a black T-shirt that clung to his chest. His hair was rumpled, his jaw shadowed with stubble, his eyes dark and serious.

'I haven't known what to say to you.'

Sierra gazed at him with wide eyes. She felt intensely vulnerable lying naked in the bath, and yet she recognised that Marco had come in here for a reason. An important reason. 'I haven't known what to say, either.'

'I wish I had the right words.'

'So do I,' she whispered.

Slowly Marco came towards her. Sierra watched him, her breath held, her heart beating hard. 'May I help you wash?' he asked and she stared at him, paralysed by indecision and longing. Finally, wordlessly, she nodded.

She watched as Marco reached for the bar of expensive soap the hotel provided and lathered his hands. He motioned for her to lean forward and after a moment she did and he began to soap her back. His touch was gentle, almost hesitant, and it felt loving. It also felt incredibly intimate, even more so than the things they'd done together in bed. Yet there was nothing overtly sexual about his touch as he slid his hands up and down her back. It felt almost as if he were offering some kind of penance, asking for absolution. Almost as if this act was as intimate and revealing for him as it was for her.

She let out a shuddering breath as he pressed a kiss

to the back of her neck. Desire, like liquid fire, spread through her as he kissed his way down the knobs of her spine.

'Marco...'

'Let me make love to you, Sierra.'

She nodded her assent and in one easy movement he scooped her up from the tub and, cradling her in his arms, he brought her back to the master bedroom. Sierra gazed up at him with huge eyes as he laid her down on the bed and then stripped his clothes from his body.

She held her arms out and he went to her, covering her body with his own, kissing her with a raw urgency she hadn't felt from him before. And she responded in kind, kiss for kiss, touch for touch, both of them rushed and desperate for each other, until Marco finally sank inside her, buried deep, her name a sob in his throat as they climaxed together.

Afterwards they lay quietly as their heart rates returned to normal and honeyed sunlight filtered through the curtains.

She would miss this, Sierra thought, when it was over. And despite the tenderness Marco had just shown her, despite the fierce pleasure of their lovemaking, she knew it would be over soon. She felt it in the way Marco had already withdrawn back into the shuttered privacy of his thoughts, his eyebrows drawn together as he stared up at the ceiling. She had no idea what he was thinking or feeling. Moments ago he'd been the most loving, gentle man she could have imagined, and now?

She sighed and stirred from the bed. 'I should dress.'

He barely glanced at her as he reached for his clothes. 'We can order room service if you like.'

'I'd rather go out.' She wanted to escape the oppressive silence that had plagued them both since last night.

'Very well,' Marco answered, and he didn't look at her as he started to dress.

An hour later they were seated at an upmarket seafood restaurant off Rodeo Drive. Sierra perused the extensive and exotic menu while Marco frowned down at the wine list.

'So what business do you have to do here exactly?' she asked after they'd both ordered.

'I'm meeting with the real estate developers to agree on the site for the new hotel.'

'Where is it?'

'Not far from here. A vacant lot off Wilshire Boulevard.' He drummed his fingers on the table, seeming almost impatient, and Sierra couldn't help but feel nettled.

'Sorry, am I wasting your time?' she asked tartly and Marco turned to her, startled.

'No, of course not.'

'It's just you seem like you can't wait to get away.'

'*I* seem…?' Now he looked truly flummoxed. 'No, of course not.'

Sierra didn't answer. Maybe the problem was with her, not with Marco. She could feel how his changing moods affected her, made her both worry and want to please him. Had her mother been like this, wondering if her husband would come home smiling or screaming? Bracing herself for a kiss or a kick?

She couldn't stand the see-sawing of emotions in herself, in Marco. The endless uncertainty. It had been better before, when she hadn't cared so much. That was the problem, Sierra realised. She really was starting to love him. Maybe she already did.

Cold fear clawed at her. *So much for a fling.* How had she let this happen? How had he slipped under her defences and reached her heart, despite everything? She'd never wanted love, never looked for it, and yet it had found her anyway.

'Is something wrong?'

Sierra jerked her gaze up to Marco's narrowed one. 'No...'

'It's just that you're frowning.'

'Sorry.' She shook her head, managed a rather sick smile. 'I'm just tired, I suppose.'

Marco regarded her quietly, clearly unconvinced by her lie. 'My business should only take a few days,' he said. 'I'll be done by the day after tomorrow. Maybe then we could go somewhere. Palm Desert...'

For a second Sierra imagined it: staying in a luxurious resort, days of being pampered and nights spent in Marco's arms. And then, after a few days, what would happen? Maybe he would ask her to go with him to Palermo. Maybe there would be more shopping trips and fancy restaurants and gala events. But eventually he would tire of her tagging along with him, leaving her own life far behind, just as her mother had. And even if he didn't tire of her, what would she be but a plaything, a pawn?

And yet still she was tempted. *This was what love did to you.* It wrecked you completely, emotionally, physically— everything. It took and took and took and gave nothing back.

Marco frowned as he noted her lack of response. 'Sierra?'

'How long would we go to Palm Desert for?'

Marco shrugged. 'I don't know—a few days? I told you, I have to be back in Palermo next week.'

'Right.' And never mind what she had to do. Of course. Sierra took a deep breath. This felt like the hardest thing she'd ever said, and yet she knew it had to be done. 'I don't think so, Marco.'

His mouth tightened and his eyes flashed. She knew he'd taken her meaning completely. Before he could respond the waiter came with their wine, a bottle of champagne that now seemed like a mockery, the loud sound of the cork popping a taunt.

The waiter poured two flutes with a flourish, the fizz going right to the top. Marco took one of the flutes and raised it sardonically.

'So what shall we toast?'

Sierra could only shake her head. She felt swamped with misery, overwhelmed by it. She didn't want things with Marco to end like this, and yet she didn't know how else they could end. Any ending was bound to be brutal.

'To nothing, then,' Marco said, his voice hard and bitter, and drank.

CHAPTER SIXTEEN

HE WAS LOSING HER, and he couldn't even say he was surprised. This was what happened when you loved someone. They left.

And he loved Sierra. Had loved her for a long time. And even though he'd been telling himself he would walk away, Marco knew he didn't want to. Ever. He wanted to love Sierra, to go to sleep with her at night and wake up with her in the morning. To hold her in his arms, hold their child in his arms. To experience everything life had to offer, good and bad, with her.

Marco put down his empty champagne flute, his insides churning with the realisation. He loved Sierra and she was slipping away from him every second.

'I think perhaps I'm not hungry after all,' she said quietly. Her face was pale, her fingers trembling as she placed the napkin on the table and rose from her seat.

She was leaving him, in a public restaurant? The papers would have a field day. Quickly, Marco rose, taking her elbow as he steered her out of the restaurant.

She jerked away from him the moment they were out on the street. '*Don't* manhandle me.'

'Manhandle?' he repeated incredulously. 'There were bound to be reporters in there, Sierra. Paparazzi. I was just trying to get us out of there without a scene.'

She shook her head, rubbing her elbow as if he'd hurt her. He suddenly felt sick.

'You think I'd hurt you? After everything?'

'No,' she said, but she didn't sound convinced. She'd never trust him, Marco realised. Never mind love him. Not after everything that had happened with Arturo, and not with how close he'd been to the man. The memories ran too deep. No matter what either of them felt, they had no chance.

'Let's go back to the hotel,' he said tersely and hailed a cab.

Back at the penthouse suite, Sierra turned to face him. 'I think I should leave,' she said, voice wobbling and chin held high.

'At least you had the decency to tell me this time,' Marco answered before he could keep himself from it. He felt too emotionally raw to be measured or calm.

Her face paled but she simply nodded and turned away. He sank onto a sofa, his head in his hands, as he listened to her start to pack.

He told himself it was better this way. The past held too much power for them to ever have a real relationship, if that was even what Sierra wanted.

But it was what he wanted. What he needed. Was he really going to let Sierra walk out of his life a second time?

The force of his feelings felt like a hammer blow to his heart, leaving him breathless. He *loved* this woman, loved her too much to let her walk away. Again.

But that was what people did. His father, his mother, Sierra. They'd all left him, slipped out without saying goodbye, leaving him with nothing to do but wait and grieve.

But this time he had a choice. He had a chance to talk to Sierra honestly, to ask or even beg her to stay. He wouldn't be proud. He loved her too much for that. The realisation sent adrenaline coursing through him and he rose from the sofa, pacing the room as panic roared through him. What if she said no? What if she still left?

Sierra emerged from the bedroom, her face still pale, her suitcase clutched in one hand. 'I can call for a taxi...'

'Don't.' The word came out like a command, and far too aggressive. Sierra blinked, then set her jaw. She didn't like him ordering her around, and he could understand that. He respected it, liked her—no, *loved* her—more for it.

'Please,' he burst out. 'Sierra, I don't want you to walk out of my life again.'

She hesitated and he took the opportunity to walk towards her, take the suitcase from her unresisting hand. 'Please listen to me for just a few minutes. And if you still want to leave after I'm done, I won't stop you, I promise.' His voice was hoarse, his heart beating painfully hard.

Sierra nibbled her lip, her wide eyes searching his face, and then finally she nodded. 'All right,' she whispered.

He led her over to the sofa and she sat down but he found he couldn't. He had too much raw energy coursing through him for that. 'I don't want you to go,' he said as he paced in front of her. 'I don't want you to go today or tomorrow or the day after that.' The words burst from him, a confession that hurt even though he knew he needed to make it. For once in his life he was fighting for what he wanted, who he loved, and even in this moment of intense vulnerability it made him feel powerful. Strong. *Love* made him strong. 'I don't want you to go ever, Sierra.'

'It hasn't been working, Marco.' Her voice was soft and sad. 'There's too much history...'

'I know there is, but we're giving the past too much power.' He dropped to his knees in front of her and took her cold hands in his. 'I love you, Sierra. I only realised how much when you were about to walk out that door. I've been a fool and an ass and whatever other name you want to throw at me. I deserve it. When you told me about your father, I didn't know how to handle it. I felt guilty and hurt and betrayed all at once, and I was afraid you'd always associate me with him, you'd never be able to trust or love me. And maybe you won't but I want to try. I want to try with you. Not just a fling, but something real. A relationship. Marriage, children—the fairy tale if we can both believe in it.'

Tears sparkled in her eyes and she clung to his hands. 'I don't know if I can. My mother loved my father and look what it did to her. It killed her in the end, maybe not literally, but she was never the person she could have been. She was like a shadow, a ghost—'

'That wasn't love. Love builds up, not breaks down. I have to believe that. I want the best for you, Sierra—'

'To follow you around from one Rocci hotel to another?' she burst out. 'I don't want to live in your shadow, Marco.'

'And you don't have to. We can make this work. I realise your life in London is important. I won't ask you to drop it to follow me around. I want you to be happy, Sierra, but I want you to be happy with me. If you think you can.' He held his breath, waiting for her answer.

'I want to be,' she finally said, her voice hesitant.

'I know I've made a lot of mistakes. I've let the past affect me more than I wanted it to. Not just your leaving, but my father's. And…' He paused because this was something he'd never told another person '…my mother.'

Sierra frowned. 'Your mother?'

'She left when I was ten,' Marco admitted quietly. 'After my father walked out she tried to hold things together, but it was tough as a single mother in a conservative country. She ended up taking me to an orphanage in Palermo, run by monks. She said she'd come back for me, but she never did.'

Tears filled Sierra's eyes. 'Oh, Marco...'

'I stayed until I was sixteen, and then I got the job at The Rocci. I tried never to look back, but I've realised I was looking back all the time, letting the past affect me. Control me. That's why I took your leaving before so badly. Why I've been afraid to love anyone.'

She bit her lip, a single tear sliding down her cheek, devastating him. 'I've been afraid, too.'

Gently, Marco wiped the tear from her cheek. 'Then let's be afraid together. I know it might be hard and there will be arguments and fears and all the rest of it. But we can find the fairy tale, Sierra. Together. I believe that. I have to believe that.'

Sierra gazed at him, her eyes filled with tears and yet also a dawning wonder, a fragile hope. 'Yes,' she said. 'I believe that, too.' And then, as Marco's heart trembled with joy, she leaned forward and kissed him.

EPILOGUE

Three years later

SIERRA STOOD AT the window of their London townhouse and watched as Marco came inside, whistling under his breath. A smile softened her features as she watched him, loving how light and happy he looked. There had been so much happiness over the last three years.

Not, of course, that it had been easy or simple. She and Marco had both had so many fears and hurts to conquer. So many mountains to climb. And yet they'd climbed them, hand in hand, struggling and searching, together.

They'd married in a quiet ceremony two years ago, and then decided to split their time between Palermo and London; Sierra continued with her music teaching, using holiday time to travel with Marco to various hotels all over the world. The Rocci Los Angeles had opened last year and Marco already had plans to open another hotel in Montreal, although he'd promised to reduce his work schedule in the next few months.

'Sierra?' His voice floated up the stairs and Sierra called back.

'I'm in the nursery.'

Grinning, Marco appeared in the doorway, his warm glance resting on the gentle swell of Sierra's bump. They were expecting a baby girl in just over three months—a new generation, a wonderful way to redeem the past and forge a future together.

'You're feeling all right?' he asked as he came towards her.

Laughing, she shook her head. 'You don't have to coddle me, Marco.'

'I want to coddle you.' He slid his arms around her, resting his hands over her bump. She laced her fingers with his, savouring his gentle touch.

That had been another mountain to climb: forcing her fears back and trusting in Marco's love and goodness. And he'd been so good, so gentle and patient with her in so many ways. It had taken her a few years before she felt brave enough to start a family, to trust Marco not only with her own heart but the heart of their child's.

The reality of their baby, their joined flesh, had made their marriage all the stronger. Sierra had never looked back.

As if agreeing with her, their baby kicked beneath their joined hands. Marco laughed softly. 'I felt that one.'

'She's a strong one,' Sierra answered with a little laugh and leaned her head back against Marco's shoulder.

'Just like her mother, then,' Marco said, and kissed her.

* * * * *

MILLS & BOON®

Why shop at millsandboon.co.uk?

Each year, thousands of romance readers find their perfect read at millsandboon.co.uk. That's because we're passionate about bringing you the very best romantic fiction. Here are some of the advantages of shopping at www.millsandboon.co.uk:

* **Get new books first**—you'll be able to buy your favourite books one month before they hit the shops

* **Get exclusive discounts**—you'll also be able to buy our specially created monthly collections, with up to 50% off the RRP

* **Find your favourite authors**—latest news, interviews and new releases for all your favourite authors and series on our website, plus ideas for what to try next

* **Join in**—once you've bought your favourite books, don't forget to register with us to rate, review and join in the discussions

Visit **www.millsandboon.co.uk**
for all this and more today!

MILLS & BOON®

Why not subscribe?
Never miss a title and save money too!

Here's what's available to you if you join the
exclusive **Mills & Boon® Book Club** today:

✦ *Titles up to a month ahead of the shops*
✦ *Amazing discounts*
✦ *Free P&P*
✦ *Earn Bonus Book points that can be redeemed
  against other titles and gifts*
✦ *Choose from monthly or pre-paid plans*

Still want more?
Well, if you join today, we'll even give you
50% OFF your first parcel!

So visit **www.millsandboon.co.uk/subs**
to be a part of this exclusive Book Club!